"SIMULTANEOUSLY A PAGE-TURNER AND AN ECHOING
CHAMBER ... LIKE NO NOVEL YOU'VE READ."
— **LAURA KASISCHKE**

THE
FINAL
APPEARANCE

OF AMERICA'S FAVORITE
GIRL NEXT DOOR

STEPHEN
STARK

GEEKVOODOO
BOOKS

PRAISE FOR STEPHEN STARK

The Final Appearance of America's Favorite Girl Next Door

"This blurb can't capture my admiration, or how entertaining, thought-provoking, and beautiful I found The Final Appearance of America's Favorite Girl Next Door. It is like no novel you've read. At the same time it is an extended and leisurely meditation on all things related to the human condition, it is a roller-coaster of psychological suspense. Ellen Gregory and her fellow-characters are so alive as to seem uncanny, and yet larger than life. This novel is full of realism and archetypal resonance. The writing, in its precision, is poetic and casual at once. "It's a flashy business compiling algorithms." Stephen Stark has as much in common, as a writer, with Cormac McCarthy as he does with James Ellroy. The result is a novel that is at once a page-turner and an echoing chamber."
—**Laura Kasischke**, award-winning poet and author of *The Life Before Her Eyes*, *Be Mine*, and *Suspicious River*.

"A celebrity tries to find herself with help from her dead lover's reality-bending invention.

"Somewhere between her early days scraping by doing stand-up in New York clubs while wearing an assless tutu and her current multimillionaire, Hollywood lifestyle as the star of a popular sitcom, Ellen Gregory stopped recognizing herself. Her 17-year-old self that carried a dream and ran away from home no longer exists. Neither does she know Ellen from the wildly popular TV show Girlfriends, who now makes a home on tabloid covers. So Ellen runs away again, except this time, back to her childhood home. While hiding from the world in Iowa, she meets Michael Webster, a man she falls in love with; only weeks later, though, he dies in a shark attack while the two are on vacation. Michael, a Ph.D. student, had invented the Black Box, a piece of unintentional brilliance that intertwines the human brain with a computer interface in a way that opens new windows into reality. The novel starts with the shark attack, thrillingly throwing the reader into the depths before the narrative slowly pieces together the psychological puzzle of Ellen's world. In starting so dramatically, Stark (Second Son, 2011, etc.) sets the stage for his wild style of storytelling, in which he marvelously toys with point of view, the timeline and the novel's internal reality to envelop the reader in alternating layers of acuity and confusion—the exact feelings Ellen and Michael experience in the Black Box. That seemingly impossible technological masterpiece is central to Stark's dig into Ellen's head; the contraption allows Ellen to enter an unknown world that even Michael, its creator, isn't sure is real.

"An intense, unexpected mind-meld in a captivating blend of technology and romance."
—*Kirkus Reviews*

"A shark attack, a starlet in hiding, a mysterious black box. The opening pages of Stephen Stark's The Final Appearance of America's Favorite Girl Next Door have all the makings of a Hollywood page turner, but the novel's style places the author in a far more literary league.... Complex, ambitious, and genre-bending, The Final Appearance of America's Favorite Girl Next Door is a philosophical page-turner that dares to ask what it means to really know someone."
—*Small Press Reviews*

Praise for Second Son

"Second Son is a marvelous kaleidoscope of a book. It reminded me of Larry Woiwode's *Beyond the Bedroom Wall*—it has that much power and beauty and pain; that much clear-eyed insight into what it's like to be a boy who's lost a beloved mother and been raised by a muddled but decent-souled father. It's lyrical, it's brilliant, and the best thing I have read in years."
—**Andrea Barrett**, author of the National Book Award-winning *Ship Fever, Servants of the Map*, and *The Voyage of the Narwhal*

"Second Son is a brutal and beautiful portrait of a father and son trembling on the terrible brink of betrayal and reconciliation. Stephen Stark shows us love's power to restore and to ruin, and he shows us as well the need for both to occur before we can see who we are. A harrowing and wonderful book."
—**Bret Lott**, author of *Jewel*, an Oprah Book Club selection

"I love the way Stephen Stark writes-fearlessly, and with uncommon wisdom and heart. This is a scary and beautiful book."
—**Hilma Wolitzer,** author of *Summer Reading*, and other novels

"This is strong stuff and it kept me up until I turned the last page at 4 A.M. Stephen Stark writes with plenty of power and grace. I love all his people, even the bad guys, simply because he makes them real."
—**Larry Brown**, author of *Joe, Big Bad Love*, and *Dirty Work*

"Second Son has all the intensity one could hope for in a novel about the searing responsibilities of a father-son relationship. Stephen Stark is a born storyteller, and his novel not only took me by surprise: it took my head off. There is enough material here for a lifetime of dreaming."
— **Jay Parini**, author of *The Last Station* and many other books

"Stark's characters are so well realized, and his vision of their lives probed so deeply, that their slightest motion can set off a powerful resonance.... One of the most gripping reads of the year."
—*Houston Press*

"... Stark angrily explodes stereotypes of men as violent or unfeeling or inconstant. His women, too, come perfectly alive. Stark is passionate, lyrical, even funny."
– *Kirkus Reviews*

"... The sustained elegaic tone is a powerful magnet that holds the reader to the page."
— *Publishers Weekly*

"'Second Son' is a loving, beautiful, melancholy novel about growing up in death's shadow, with no reasonable hope of happiness, and how, with luck, happiness may surprise us by its unreasonable and unexpected appearance."
—**Carolyn See**

"It is hard to forget Stephen Stark's family portrait – what's left of a family – because it is drawn with such emotional honesty."
—*The Richmond Times-Dispatch*

"…At times, the book is so correct, it's scary. Stark manipulates his double narrative and its complex time scheme with a craftsman's touch, creating a supple text that never hampers the story's momentum…. Second Son is quality work, done with skill and imagination, a credit to the laborer."
—*The Houston Chronicle*

Praise for The Outskirts

"Stephen Stark is a brave, brave and beautiful, writer, not shy to handle primitive tension, dangerous desire. The Outskirts is, at last, a brutally honest book about modern alienation, casting aside the non-values of the Brat Pack for the abiding myths of youth —because the adult world is a world the young must truly resist."
—**Bob Shacochis**, author of *Easy in the Islands*

"Stephen Stark handles the elements of his story with great economy and skill, and whie he explores these matters of innocence and experience, he breathes a suspenseful, edgy into the prose, a hint of violence, of disaster, and he keeps us reading on."
—**Richard Bausch**, *The Philadelphia Inquirer*

"Stark writes with genuine internal rhythm. The tempo is hurried and hungry…. And in the end, most readers will be filled with approval like that from a good meal. Not too sated. Ready for more from Stark, somewhere, sometime soon."
—*Grand Rapids Press*

ACKNOWLEDGEMENTS

The fictional television show in which Ellen Gregory appears, and the characters in it, are based on the novel *Girlfriends*, by Patrick Sanchez, and used with Patrick's gracious permission.

A portion of this novel appeared, in slightly different form, in *The Arts & Letters Journal*.

Cover design by Rachel Walling
rachelwalling.design@gmail.com

Geekvoodoo Books logo designed by Rophillar Loch
roph.loch@gmail.com

GEEKVOODOO BOOKS
Falls Church, Virginia
www.geekvoodoo.com

ISBN: 978-0-9847376-1-1

PART ONE: LAST DAY

According to Plato, the physical world is a mere representation of a deeper reality, which is composed of abstract forms. Theatrical imitation is therefore dangerous because it distances us even further from the essences of things; it's like a copy of a copy.

— Tim Blake Nelson, in *The New York Times*, November 12, 2006

MÖBIUS STRIP

Sunlight, the scent of saltwater on human skin. Sunscreen. Her own sweat. Michael laughing, his green eyes flashing. Blood red blood. Disinfectant. Hospital people in loose clothing whooshing past in clattering hallways. A perfect cup of hot coffee in her hands. Her own sweat. His voice calling out to her in the still June morning. The scent of disposable plastic gloves. Disinfectant. Sunlight again, Michael saying, *Last day*. The wooden stairs of the beach rental.

There was a moment of clarity on the beach, her leg screaming with pain as they bandaged it. She couldn't see. Wouldn't look.

The clarity was in the pain, an actual revelation of clarity that came from the pain. A dream you wake from, convinced you can know and see the meaning of everything, but which waking steals.

The guy in the blue emergency uniform had leaned over her with a syringe and pricked her arm and suddenly there was a flood of not-pain. The pain was a long way away. Her leg throbbed and the throbbing was in some kind of irrelevant distance and when the man spoke to her again, One to Ten, he said, perhaps, she just smiled and turned her head.

She was looking for Michael, but there was too much noise. There was a helicopter and as its rotors beat the air she could feel each discrete concussion of air. There was sand in the air and the air was cold. She was shivering.

Where's...? she started, but could not make her mouth work adequately. The man put a blanket over her and then suddenly she was inside a box, a metal box, and then she was coming out again, and Soraya was next to the gurney and she was talking to her, Ellen to Soraya, Soraya to Ellen, but Ellen could not make sense of it.

Call Marty, she said. He's got to know.

Although she knew she was in a hospital, for Ellen Gregory, the last ten or twelve hours had the odd sensation of having telescoped into a single, elongated moment, wrapped like a Möbius strip.

Now she was returning from her early morning run along the beach. Now she was here in this hospital corridor.

Now she was making love with Michael.

Now they were on the sand, eating the lunch that Hanna had made.

Now they were in the water, and Michael was laughing, splashing.

Now he was coming up out of the water, that instant before she knew that something was horribly wrong.

Now her head was woozy with morphine and Hanna and Soraya were next to this mobile metal hospital bed and her foot, her left foot, throbbed distantly, sending out tiny insistent messages of profound pain.

Now Michael was coming and she had one arm wrapped around his neck and her legs locked around him as his body shuddered.

Now there was the helicopter in the air, a monstrous dragonfly.

Now Michael stopped on the sand and put down the things he was carrying and the words *I love you* were escaping from his mouth.

All of it, every last thing that had happened, now seemed to be happening simultaneously. A chaos of echo and elation and despair. There was sand on her fingers, in her hair. Hanna and Soraya were here, next to the mobile hospital bed where she lay, waiting, the corridor far too bright and loud.

Hanna still wore her bikini, and her tanned, slight frame looked drawn and pale—a stark change from how she had looked on the beach after lunch. Soraya's normally wild hair was tied up tight, and her face gave away nothing. Ellen knew this look—it was Doctor Ouellette mode, her official persona, tight-lipped, no bullshit. And that Soraya and Hanna were both here with her, now, together, and had been—as far as she knew—from the moment she had arrived, did not seem to bode good news about Michael.

She, Ellen, tried to ask the question, Where's Michael? but the words would not come out. She was floating from bliss to the brief spasm of unspeakable violence.

Making love with him, clutching him, had almost been a decision in itself. A statement of unalloyed want. A choice. You. Here.

But they were waiting for some kind of doctor to evaluate her leg.

Marty, her manager, had been called. He was on his way.

Her parents had been called. They were on their way. Marty had booked them a private jet. The media had no doubt been alerted.

No one would say anything about Michael. Where is Michael? she thought she said, but he was here, his face with a couple of days growth of beard, grazing her cheek like sandpaper. What was that? I love you? Say again? I love you.

But when she tried to concentrate, the essence of now—here, this moment here, with Hanna Dory and Soraya Ouellette standing next to her, unknown hospital people emerging out of the clamor into her field of vision and then dissolving again—she could not. She found herself elsewhere.

Reality itself was channel surfing.

Hanna, she started to say, to ask—Michael?—but now she was on the beach after lunch and there he was, waking and brushing sand from his shoulder.

Now she was coming back from her morning run and Michael called out to her as she slowed up near the house, Hey, black-haired girl running on the side of the road.

If I can hear his voice he can't be dead.

Drenched with sweat in the creeping heat of the summer morning, a breeze coming, she started to stretch and he offered her a cup of coffee.

Where was he? *How* was he? She did not see how he could've survived.

She had been starting to stretch and cool down from her run, and had looked at him quizzically. It was, of course, the last day, and in every way it had a hugeness to it. The facts were simple: She was going back to LA to placate the TV studio, the cast members she had deserted in desperation, the humorless lawyers; she was going to do morning shows and late shows and who knew what the fuck else in order to soothe the savage beast; he was going back to Iowa to finish his research and his Ph.D. These were the facts. She knew them. She had simply been denying them.

This newly found ability to dance around within the pieces of the moment allowed her to see more than she had actually seen at the time. Even now, here, only hours later but what seemed a lifetime from the actual event, she could feel the attraction she had for this man, how just seeing his sinewy arms, the vast, green sparkle of his eyes, his dark mop of too-long hair and the casual way he held such shockingly sexy, angular shoulders, she could feel the electric snap of attraction, like neon lighting, a hum and buzz and explosion of color that she could feel somewhere in the area behind her solar plexus, rising up behind her ribs, a tightness, a sweet sort of tension that gripped her whenever she thought of him. She was not even going to entertain the possibility that he was gone.

From running, she was sweating furiously, something she had always hated about herself. He sat on the weathered wooden step gazing at her, holding two cups of coffee, offering her one. His hair was wild from bed, his face in all its wiry beauty was relaxed and rested. (She loved the way the muscles in his jaw flexed when he moved his mouth, the vague dimples when he smiled. The wicked way he laughed sometimes, a rusted *he, he, he.*) She took a cup, but then set it on the step.

She could see—now, later, in the hospital, when it didn't matter—that he also had been denying. She had not seen it during the actual moment because she was too busy navigating her own denial, trying to work out the kinks of her return, juggle the possibilities, the savage reality that she had deserted the beast and the beast was furious. She had been denying that it—LA—was a weird sick screaming animal that wanted to be fed. And she had denied it its food.

Soraya reached down and brushed her hand across Ellen's forehead. There was still sunscreen on her skin, still bits of sand in her hair.

Far away, someone said, Media are already starting to arrive, the words ballooning up from the distance and bursting gently like a child's bubbles. Ellen's hands were abraded and sore and wrapped in gauze. There was sand in the gauze and she wanted to tear it apart.

She remembered how thick and tough and unbelievably real the animal had felt when she struck it.

Last *day, Michael said, Let's have your confession. What did you not do on your vacation that you wish you had done?*

She laughed. It had been eight weeks and six days since she'd abruptly and secretly deserted the shooting of her sitcom. Her escape was just that, an escape—it was not any sort of vacation—it was the alternative to being found in the bathtub with a bottle of pills in her stomach, slit wrists and a plastic bag tied over her head. It was an attempt to find the self she had mislaid, the Ellen that had been beamed out into the stars and whom she could not—at least not in LA—reclaim.

But it had almost turned into a vacation when she met Michael. And then it had turned into something weird and profound. She found the self she was looking for and it was in him.

This—the week at the beach before they went their separate ways—was a *vacation*, but it was also something more, though she could not have said what. A swan dive.

She stretched her hamstrings, one leg at a time, counting in her head to 30 seconds on each. She was dripping and wiped her face with the towel.

Let's have it, he said.

Let's have what?

He looked at her with a what-planet-are-you-from sort of look.

Your confession, he said. He pushed curly hair out of his face.

My confession?

Yeah, he said. The last day of vacation is for the cleansing of the soul. You can't leave paradise with regrets.

She wiped her face and nodded uncertainly, the towel growing damper by the moment. (Did she notice, then, exactly how he was looking at her, undressing her with his eyes even as her skin dribbled perspiration on the sand?)

He said, What did you leave undone that you wanted to do? You know, the stuff you *intended*.... The dress you packed but didn't get to wear. That kind of thing. Before you go back, before the last day ends, you have to try to do at least one of them. Or cast your regret onto the waves and make a resolution for next year's vacation.

She thought of this: *Next year's vacation.* The thought butterflied in her with unrealistic hope. She said, puffing, I can't think of anything.

He shook his head in disbelief. Nothing?

Except I wish we'd made love about 10,000 more times.

Well, we can't quite manage that in one day, he said, But we could try valiantly. He went silent for a moment and gazed at her, eyebrows going wiggly, leering sweetly and simultaneously trying to work out the logistics.

A few years ago, he said, I had an epiphany. The scales fell from my eyes. We—I— we've been doing it ever since.

We?

Me, Soraya, Hanna, Jake, and last year, Adam, too. Others, over the years. We should do this now, go walk down to the water and cast our sins upon the waves.

She nodded, picked up and then put down the coffee cup. She moved to the step, next to him, to stretch her calves. She rested the ball of her left foot on the wooden tread and gently relaxed her weight onto that leg. (That was what her left leg needed right now, a good stretch.)

We should do this, right now. Go down to the water. When he looked at her, she would have sworn his eyes were wet with tears.

She smiled, then started with the other leg. Go right now, she said.

He reached out and put a hand on her thigh. Trust me, you'll feel way more relaxed after you confess your vacation sins—

She laughed at this. Vacation sins. It'll be a real vacation sin, she said, If I don't get in the shower.

Screw that for now, he said, Let's go.

His hand came up the inside of her thigh.

Come on, he said, rising, his hand rising up her thigh, too, but then falling away.

Michael, she said, Let me get into the shower and then we can get started catching up with all that lovemaking.

Then, as an afterthought, she said, And what about the others?

He shook his head. Softly, so softly that she was scarcely sure she heard it, he said, You're the only one I'm thinking about.

Had she been thinking about him? Had she heard—really heard—what he said, or had she been thinking ahead, creating some kind of narrative for her reappearance, of her life—inevitably—without him? She was thinking about Marty, she was thinking about going back to LA. She was thinking about how Michael (dreading this, actually), who had never seen her on TV before, would react to seeing her for the first time on the morning talk shows, *after*, spinning a whole alternate narrative about where she had been and what she had done, talking not about him, about the incredible, once-in-a-lifetime thing that had happened between them—was happening—but about a fictional sojourn in an exclusive South African rehab clinic—a narrative that as yet had no actual narrative.

Now he put both hands on her thighs, and she felt herself melting toward him, felt the terror of her desire for him.

She could've gone down to the water with him—a short walk over the dunes—but she did not. She went past him into the house, casting him the best, most calculated come-hither look she could manage while lathered in sweat, and he smiled. She had not seen it then, but there was a rueful quality to his smile, perhaps genuine sorrow.

She had not then seen how he was opening a door for her, giving her the chance to rewind. Trying to give them both the chance and the space to say what had not been said.

WHOLE

Ellen was here and she was there, here in Los Angeles in the summer of 2001, in her fortress of a house, the headset wrapping her, her retinae constantly being scanned, the EEG sensors pressed against her skull, reading her brainwaves—all of this that Michael had designed and built—carrying her back there, back then.

Whole again. The whole world whole. Ellen Gregory walked in sunlight, outside the Hy-Vee in Iowa City, next to Michael. She was on her own two feet. This ordinary thing of walking felt nearly like dancing. She said something and Michael laughed, and it was maybe—she wasn't sure—that same first time she had ever seen him laugh, the way the exhausted flesh at the corners of his eyes crinkled, the way his eyes sparkled. Here it all was again, the flood of memory that was not memory at all, but real. More real than real.

It was warm now, not yet the oppressive heat of summer, but the pleasant heat of a warm Iowa spring day, and the night that followed, as the night that had preceded it, would be chill, the sky black and deep and sparkling.

The light in the new growth of leaves on the trees that surrounded the grocery store parking lot was white and clear and made shine his black, curly, tousled hair. (Even in this darkened room in her fortress of a house, she could feel the heat of it, the sun.)

She helped him load the groceries into the trunk of his car, watched his wiry movements—slender, strong, but apparently (she now knew) unconscious of his sexy-beyond-belief appearance.

She could have interrupted the moment. She could have said, I will love you. You must believe me. She could have told him how things would unfold, that if this day continued as it would, if things between them continued as she knew they would, the probability was that it would kill him, and maim her.

But she would have been a mad woman, he would have seen that. And maybe that would have been the good thing, for him to look up, aghast, before she could follow him to the house he rented and make him fall in love with her.

Made whole. The dimensionality of the multiverse reuniting him with her.

She could have grabbed him, said, There isn't much time. There is so little time. Make love to me.

But she didn't. She couldn't spoil that April day. What happened happened, and would continue to happen, he told her later.

Please. How do you say goodbye to the one man to die for who does?

It was Larry who took the headset off her, and she blinked, his gleaming eyes and Kojak pate looming over her—no, not looming, just there. Nonjudgmental as always.

She looked at the Black Box and then at Larry.

It's like a drug, she said.

Arguably worse, he said.

How do I say goodbye?

LAST DAY

It was early, the morning of the last day, and Ellen Gregory slipped out of bed and went to the window in the bedroom of the rented beach house and pulled back the curtains to look. It was June 11, 2001. She was 32, at the apogee of her career. It was a new century, it was a gorgeous day with a cloudless sky, the kind of weather you expect in June, but somehow more perfect.

Everything should have been happy, happy, happy, but there were electric clouds of anxiety.

Ellen, naked, stood next to the window and turned back toward the bed, and in the act of turning, she felt something akin to the disembodied sensation she got when she made love with Michael, except this wasn't so much pleasant as it was vertiginous, as though the simple act of turning had loosened her grip on this present moment. He had tried to explain to her his idea about time, a notion that she wasn't sure that she even began to grasp. Yes, she was present in this present moment, the warm air on her skin, bed scars beginning to fade, the constant sound of surf outside. But also it was as though this present moment was merely one slice of time (she imagined it as some sort of glass blade that could be held in a brightly lit box next to other glass blades that were other moments) — one slice of time that coexisted simultaneously with countless other slices of time.

Perhaps his Black Box had knocked something loose in her mind, but right now, as real as this moment, she was in the bathroom at LAX, cutting her blonde hair short and dying it with the bottle of black dye that she'd been carrying in her purse for months the way, she had read, that Sylvia Plath had carried razor blades. That was eight weeks ago, a world away. Her surreptitious departure from LA and her smash hit sitcom, *Girlfriends*.

It was here, that moment, in the quiet of the bedroom. She could see inside it. There were other moments. Many weeks earlier, she had hid in a closet, clutching a 9mm pistol, when the crazy stalker had broken into her house and, baseball bat in hand, found her the way a bloodhound might have. She could taste the gypsum dust in her mouth when he had smashed through the wall, the tip of the bat blunt and huge. And even though she was standing here, naked, she could feel the tight spot opening up, smell and feel the gun in her hands, and then she could see the look on Wayne Townsend's face — blank as always — when the noise from the explosion had stopped and there was a bullet in his chest.

And also there was Michael, in the shower with her yesterday, the absolute hunger of his desire as they made love.

She could see him, Michael Webster, the first time she'd ever seen him, that day in the grocery store. And here he was, now, still sleeping, most unlikely of lovers, sexy, yes, but also an entirely geeky Ph.D. candidate at the University of Iowa — right around the putative corner from the place of her birth and idyllic childhood. Perhaps the sensation was just astonishment that she could be here at all, having fallen in stupid, wake-up-with-drool-on-your-pillow love.

The electric clouds of anxiety were as much about him as they were about her. Because of her disappearance, there were, she knew, cadres of black-suited lawyers and angry producers who wanted to eat her heart, carpaccio-style, in the best restaurants of LA. There would be, in her return, the implicit loss of this moment, and perhaps the explicit loss of this man. It seemed hard to imagine that LA would be anything more than a black hole into which she would be sucked without Michael. It was hard to imagine anything good coming from their imminent separation.

And so she stood here, savoring this moment of partial understanding, hoping that somehow this time out of time could be endless, immortal. She wished that the last several weeks could be an infinite loop of a love story, a slice of time that could live in an imaginary glass blade that could play over and over again.

And wasn't that what he had said about time? That the idea of beginnings and endings was a human construct to understand the incomprehensible? Didn't he say that what exists will always exist? That anything that can happen will happen, and will continue to happen?

She had always prided herself on not examining her own personal narrative too closely. Whenever she got into introspection, it made her self-conscious, and it was much better to just say fuck it all and let all that submerged crap seethe like a cauldron of boiling snakes. Being self-consciously un-self-conscious made for much better comedy.

And so even despite the slobber on her pillow, despite now and again choking up and crying in private at the thought of separating from him, there was a part of her that looked forward to going back. To seeing her friends, talking on the phone with Jon Stewart or Edie Hyde or Kevin James and laughing about it all.

She was still naked and so was careful—ever watchful of enterprising paparazzi—to shield herself with the curtains. It was early but the sky was clear and there was no sign of yesterday's torrential rain.

Michael, still in bed, woke and said, Hey, and propped his head on his hand and watched her. She started to cover herself but then didn't.

Hey, your own self, she said, and then stood watching him watch her. Even still mostly asleep, his eyes gave off enormous heat. His dark, curly hair was an unruly mess. He said, Come over here so I can get a better look at your birthday suit.

She planted her hands on her hips and said, Well, I do declare.

Don't make me chase you around the room.

That sounds like fun.

But you'd win. Unless of course you let me win.

Anxiety Alert: *In two days, she would wake up at home, without him.*

This was a thought that she could barely wrap her mind around. She had picked the date for her return after heavy pressure from Marty, her manager—he was getting hideous vibes from very powerful people, whose own people were leaping against their leashes, gnashing bared teeth. There was money at stake. (*How long does goddamned rehab take, anyway? As long as it needs to, asshole. Ellen, we both know... What, Marty? We both know what? Nothing. Listen, just get your gorgeous peach-blossom-ass back here, please. Save me from this inquisition.*)

She came next to the bed and his hand reached out. She watched his eyes, the way they studied her. No other lover she'd had had looked at her the way he did. No one in LA had ever seemed to look at her at all, except in a sort of photographic way (*click*: got that); she was interchangeable with any other A-List blonde. He looked at her with longing and with love, and the latter was, frankly, freakily unfamiliar.

She got back in bed and straddled him. He wrestled her onto her back and got to his knees.

She had a good sensation of being out of control, of her whole being focused on this single moment. His chest was taut and when he moved his arms, you could see the cords and fibers move beneath his uncharacteristically and freshly tanned skin.

She was overcome with a sensation of longing, which was strange because her longing was for this particular moment. It made her heart feel weak and frail and human to think it. To desire to have one thing so completely.

There was so much of her life that was caught on film, on tape, but none of it was her, and this was so real and so delicious that it hurt to think it would end.

She said, Do you think the machine—the Black Box—could record this? He said, Actually, I tried.

You did?

He held himself above her, and she watched his shoulders, his chest. She put two fingers on his sternum. She watched his eyes hopefully.

I dumped the memory from trips we took onto a couple of disks. It turns out you can't really control it. I still have a lot of figuring out to do. Some of it sort of works.

He got a distant look, and she wanted to hold him, envelope him. She could feel the heat of him, and wriggled her hips a little. He started moving again.

You can do it, Geek Boy.

He lowered himself to his elbows and moved his hands over her breasts, closed his eyes. Ellen, he said.

She reached up and took his head in her hands gently.

When it was over, she got out of bed and said, I'm going to go for a run. Go back to sleep.

Ellen was, herself, not big on sleep—she was one of those people who just didn't need much: she always woke early and went to bed late. And even though they had only spent the night together for a little while, they had done so long enough to establish a routine of her waking before him, then going running, coming home to the coffee he made (which he made very well).

Right now, she needed to run. A cloud of anxiety hung over her, and she could think of no other way of assuaging it. And so she got dressed in her running clothes, put on a baseball cap and sunglasses, and went outside to stretch. In New York, she would have run with at least one bodyguard, though sometimes you could get away with it. Once she passed Madonna running in Central Park and hadn't even recognized her until long after they had passed one another. In LA, it would have been in a gym. Here, she was probably taking a chance going alone, but the hat and the baggy shorts and sunglasses were good enough unless someone was actually looking for her, tracking her, and, anyway, even if that happened to be the case, there wasn't much she could do without a security detail.

The landscape was sere and mostly without shade. What did grow on the dunes did not grow to great height, and there was a quality to all of it of caprice—a narrow spit of sand that edged the North Carolina coast but could, seemingly, be wiped away in a single strong storm. She started slow and had the sensation she often did that she would much rather turn around and quit. But she needed this. She needed to think.

Over the last three evenings she had been on the phone with Marty—the cell phone that Michael had rejiggered to make it appear that she was far, far away, on the other side of the planet. She had agreed to do the morning shows, but she wanted to do Letterman first, because Dave was a friend, a mentor, and anyway it would be advantageous to do it once on late night TV, and then look at the reaction from the critics and bullshit peddlers before going in front of the much larger, and possibly less forgiving, daytime audience.

It took her a mile or so to warm up, even though the day was shaping up to be blazing, if not so humid as it had been before yesterday's thunderstorms and torrential rain. She and Michael would both get on separate planes tomorrow. As much a done deal as if they had signed contracts. But it was hard to know—precisely—how or why she was sticking to a deadline that had no real meaning except that she had to do it sometime.

Running was good. When she got into a rhythm, the anxiety lifted somewhat. She was addicted to running. She had been known, now and then, to run pretty much ridiculous distances—marathon training distances—just because it helped to exhaust her, made the anxiety easier to live with.

A therapist told her that she might be running away from something. Sure, fame. She had done an hour of stand-up on HBO that had become her second CD, and the money was good, but she could still walk down the street. When she did the pilot for *Girlfriends*, suddenly she was besieged. Even people who had never seen the show knew who she was, thanks to 24-hour news feeds, gossip magazines, the Internet. And then she had actually seen the show—of course she had seen it, but had actually seen it in an airport, on an airport bar TV, and it was strange to see herself. Not strange in a happy way but strange in a that-girl-is-not-me way. And when the network executives saw what she could do and started giving her more and more of the A-story, started emphasizing her abilities at physical comedy, it had gotten worse.

It—the pathological running—had started when she first saw the show and it had sent her into a weird downward spiral. She went from her usual four or six miles to 10 or eleven, half marathons. Sometimes at night, restless, sleep escaping her, she ran the perimeter of the house she rented then, and like a dog wore a path next to the fence. She lost weight. People murmured about an eating disorder. But it was the running. She actually ate more. Let people see her, let herself be photographed eating happily, food spilling out of her mouth.

She liked the way when she got into a rhythm she could at least feel that she could think more clearly. And what she wanted to do now was think what to do.

She kept thinking that she should call Marty. Call him up and say. What?

Last night when she was fretting about this, when it was raining and the dinner was over and they were in bed after making love, Michael had said, Why not the truth?

She had got up in the dark and paced. She didn't say it but she had no idea what the truth was or how to speak it if she knew it. There was likely no use for it, anyway.

Although she knew that she knew why she left, it was not something she could have put into words. The closest she could come was that it was better than suicide, and while she didn't want to kill herself in the least, she also didn't want to live the way she had been living. The constant feeling of watching her whole life like it was an out of body experience.

Why she left was still largely an unconscious, or subconscious, morass. It wasn't the burnout thing, it wasn't the psycho stalker thing, it wasn't the midlife actress thing. She had told Marty before and she told him again that she felt like she'd had her soul stolen, that when she saw herself on a TV, she had no idea who that person was—not the person on the screen, but the person she was now, this minute. The person on screen had more substance. And that's the way she had felt, even when she first came home. Even when she first met Michael. But then something had shifted. Something had melted or something had annealed, and that separation seemed to have gone away.

This time with Michael, being away from LA, was the first time in ages she had felt like her soul had reentered her body—somehow.

She said to him last night, I can explain this to you and you nod and get it, but I can't explain it to Marty. It would be so much easier if I did have a drug problem.

I guess just because a person doesn't have a drug problem doesn't mean that a person doesn't need rehab.

She said, I feel like doing the opposite of calling in sick. You know, Hi, I feel too good to come into work today.

He laughed.

When she finished her run, she was sweating like a boxer after fifteen rounds.

Michael shouted, Hey, black-haired girl running on the side of the road.

She had been gone more than an hour, and he was awake—just—sitting on the wooden step, a mug of coffee in his hands, and another on the stair beside him.

This brought her to a halt, and she looked up—she was so deep in thought that she had not noticed him. Her feet skidded on the pavement and sent splashes of sand up.

You're beautiful, he said.

This was what she wanted. To come home and have him waiting there with a cup of coffee.

Michael, she said, shaking her head, You're the one who's beautiful.

He said, I brought a towel for you. He raised a white towel and waved it at her.

She looked at him long and hard—this was what she wanted. This. This moment to be stuck in amber: to have made love with him an hour ago, to have got in a good run and been ignored, to come back and have him waiting, happy to see her because—and only because—he was happy to see her.

He said, You think you'd like to fuck? I haven't been laid in ages. You're beautiful.

She laughed and came to where he was.

You think I could shower first?

I don't care. I like it when you're slippery.

While she stretched and cooled down, he said, *Last day*. And when he said it, the words shivered her to her bones.

ELLEN GREGORY CLINGS TO LIFE

TALENT:

As the convicted terrorist Timothy McVeigh volunteered for his own death, one of television's crown jewels is fighting to live.

Today, Ellen Gregory, beloved star of TV's *Girlfriends*, clings to life in a North Carolina hospital.

As America turned its attention toward Terre Haute, Indiana, today, for the first federal execution in half a century, a brutal shark attack off the shore of North Carolina, near Cape Hatteras, left the woman who has been called America's Favorite Girl Next Door fighting for life.

The star of *Girlfriends* was swimming with a friend off the small vacation hamlet of Avon in the Outer Banks when tragedy struck.

Just two months after shooting to death a stalker in a bizarre home invasion incident, television's Ellen Gregory - thought to be out of the country in rehab - clings to life.

She and a male companion, who has not been identified yet — a possible tragic love interest for America's Sweetheart of the Airwaves — were savagely attacked by what authorities say was a 17-foot tiger shark. Her companion, said by friends to be a computer scientist, has not been identified. He did not survive.

From Virginia to Texas, this is the fourth report of a shark attack in as many weeks, the second death by shark attack since 10-year-old David Schaffer died after being attacked in shallow water off Virginia Beach, Virginia, about 100 miles to the north. But this is the first incident in which two people have been attacked, apparently by the same shark.

Reporter George Rice, with affiliate WWMD, is standing by on the scene at Avon Hospital with Dare County sheriff's deputy Ron Houser. George?

GEORGE:
It was a breathtakingly gorgeous afternoon when beautiful comedian and sitcom star Ellen Gregory and the man friends have said was the love of her life were enjoying their final day of vacation. And then friends said things went drastically wrong.

Ron Houser of the Dare County Sheriff's Department, what can you tell us?

DEPUTY:
Well, George. It was – We responded to a radio call from shore patrol with a report of a shark attack just after six PM local time. The rescue chopper from Avon Memorial was dispatched to the scene. When I arrived on the beach, the two Caucasian adults, a male and a female, were in the sand, wrapped in bloody towels. The adult male had been quite badly mauled and he showed no pulse upon our arrival. Witnesses said that he was still talking when he came ashore, but he was gone by the time we arrived. One witness had performed CPR on the male and used her shirt to apply a tourniquet to his leg, but he did not respond. The female was also mauled but she was still breathing and conscious. However she was by this time

delirious. Medevac removed the male to Avon
Memorial immediately. The female was brought
here by ambulance.

GEORGE:

Did you know that it was Ellen Gregory?

DEPUTY:

No sir, I did not.

GEORGE:

What were your feelings when you discovered
who'd been attacked?

DEPUTY:

Shock. You know, my wife and me, we're big
fans of *Girlfriends* and, well, it was a
shock. We haven't had a shark attack here
in a very very long time and, well, it don't
matter—I mean we're all flesh and blood, no
matter what we do for a living. I will say
that when I saw her, she didn't look like
herself. [*Brushes at eyes.*]

As I understand it, they will move her today
to Norfolk, where they can treat her better.

GEORGE:

Thank you, deputy.

[*Transition from medium close-up to
establishing shot to show the area around
where the reporter is standing. Several
people mill around, cameramen dressed in
shorts and T-shirts, reporters in dresses
and slacks and ties. Onlookers beyond a
police tape.*]

As you can see, Rene, quite a number of
reporters from newspapers and television
stations all over the world have descended
on this tiny town in an all-night and all-
day vigil.

RENE:

What else do we know, George?

GEORGE:

At a brief news conference earlier this morning, Ellen's doctors said that she is in serious but stable condition. Her life is not in danger. Doctors so far have refused to say what the extent of her injuries are, but sources have told us that she lost a foot in the attack. As Deputy Houser told us, she is to be moved to Sentara Hospital in Norfolk, which is better equipped to handle her trauma, but right now, they say, she is doing as well as can be expected.

The Coast Guard this morning has been overflying the area in helicopters and has been out in boats. Tiger, blue, and hammerhead sharks are common in this area. One very large tiger shark was spotted, but attempts to hunt it down have yet proved fruitless.

This is a very international crowd here, Rene. From Europe to South Asia to Moscow, there are reporters from television and radio stations around the world here. You could say she wasn't just America's Favorite Girl Next Door, but the world's.

It appears that Ellen and her companion made a crucial mistake, Rene. They were in waters that sharks frequent — and they were there at supper time.

RENE:

I know we're all praying for the recovery of Ellen Gregory.

What do we know about the man who was killed?

GEORGE:

Not very much. He has not been formally identified to the media, but we do know that he was identified by friends who were with the couple and that the rest of his family is here. We have unconfirmed reports that he was a doctoral student in computer science at the University of Iowa and that Ellen only met him a few weeks ago.

RENE:

Thanks, George.

(Cut away from George and back to René. As she speaks, the camera pulls back from her to reveal her guest.)

We have in the studio with us Jayson Grainge, a network publicist who has worked with Ellen Gregory since the inception of *Girlfriends*.

JAYSON:

Actually, I've worked with her since before *Girlfriends* went on the air. I saw her perform in New York and I went straight to the network – we had to have this young woman. She was simply irresistible, the sort of talent you see only once or twice in a generation.

RENE:

And you know her well. Will you tell us what you knew about her disappearance?

JAYSON:

I wish I could, Rene. I think those of us who were close to her did not see the warning signs, the absolute terrorizing trauma of the events with Wayne Townsend. I was there at her house shortly after she shot him to death, and I thought she was a hero, or heroic, and told her so. I thought she should have seen it as empowering. This hulking former soldier brought down by this pretty little comedian. But I don't think you can underestimate how traumatizing it can be for someone to have their home, their property violated like that.

RENE:

And so you think she disappeared out of fear?

21

JAYSON:

I think it more likely that it was a combination of factors. The terror, yes. The terror.

RENE:

I think there are a lot of people wondering why you didn't find her.

JAYSON:

People disappear because they don't want to be found. She was in fact in contact with her manager, he knew she was fine, but he also knew she needed some time. He respected that. I respected that. We can all second guess ourselves, but I don't think that there's anything that could have been done to prevent what happened, as horrible as it was.

RENE:

What do you know about the man who died?

JAYSON:

My understanding, based on conversations with her manager, is that he was - at long last - the love of her life. Beyond that, I don't know very much about him, but I think it's safe to say that before long, we will know everything about him.

RENE:

Thank you, Jayson Grainge.

(Camera pulls in on René.)

Stay with us for continuing coverage of the shark attack.

THE L WORD

It was early afternoon and Ellen sat on the sand, watching Michael as he dozed on the blanket. He was on his side, his knees pulled up slightly in a sort of extended fetal position, and his elbows were bent and his hands folded together. Hanna lay on a towel nearby, her skin glistening with sun block. Ellen slid her pocket camera out of her bag and framed Michael's face in the display and pressed the shutter release. Hanna looked up at the sound and pushed hair out of her face. She smiled at Ellen, noticing the way she gazed at Michael. She said, Beautiful, isn't he?

Ellen nodded. It was either nod or swoon. He was beautiful. She pushed her floppy hat back a little and used the brim to shade the display so that she could look at the photo. It was a delicious moment of idleness, and she wanted to enjoy it. This, here, on the beach, the hot sand, the blue sky, the having nowhere to go and nothing to do. She wanted to enjoy it, but she could not escape her own restlessness, the inertia she felt at the murderous, forward rush of time. She looked at the photo: Michael's hair gleaming in sunlight; the sand bleached white; the shadows where his head rested against the blanket. That moment of light frozen in the display was gone.

Some day she would look at this photo and remember this day, long ago.

She said to Hanna, Wouldn't it be cool if he could figure out a way to use the Black Box to actually grab moments. The good ones. The way you can just take a picture.

Hanna sat up and pushed her hair behind her ears, hugged her knees. Her bikini bottom had a white background printed with perfect little bunches of bananas, the top was Chiquita blue. (This was something of a gag, a sweet response to Michael's calling her Hanna banana.) Maybe we will, she said.

Ellen cocked her head, put her camera on her leg, then pushed her hand beneath her silly, floppy hat and ran her fingers through her damp, salty hair.

I just can't believe it's going to end, she said.

Are you thinking about tomorrow? Hanna said. She wore sunglasses, but the sun was so bright you could still see her eyes. At that moment Ellen was envious of her. Deeply. To have a life as comparatively uncomplicated.

23

No. I'm completely in denial. I find that if I don't think, I'm much better off. Hanna laughed.

It's the American Way.

Hanna, giggling, pretended to throw sand at her.

Ellen had only known Hanna for a few weeks—had only known all of them, Hanna, Soraya, Adam, Jake, and Michael, for no more than two months, or roughly a week less than it had been since she had fled LA and the shooting of the new season of her smash hit sit-com—but the two of them had hit it off in a way she hadn't hit it off with anyone since kindergarten. One of those instant and unquestioning sorts of friendships. Something, she was convinced, that was impossible in LA. Or impossible for her in LA.

It's a good day, anyway, Hanna said. Isn't it? She had an adorable way of putting her head to the side when she asked a question.

Ellen nodded. Yes. It's a good day, Ellen said. I just wish it weren't. Last, I mean.

Ellen thought of making love with Michael in the morning, before she had gone for her run. She thought of how she had clung to him, like a drowning woman to a shard of flotsam. She thought of him standing in the sand, saying, I love you. You're beautiful. And now all that too was over. She was sitting here and time was moving mercilessly forward.

You know what? Ellen whispered.

Hanna's eyes widened. What?

He said it. (She felt like a school girl.)

It? Hanna's pale eyes gleamed. The L-word?

It, Ellen said.

Did *you*?

No. (She had, actually, said it once. It had slipped out in an unguarded moment back in Iowa City. But then she had pretended that she hadn't.)

Why *not*, you goof? You said you do. You *do*, don't you?

Yes. *Yes.*

Ellen looked at her camera, away from Hanna's sensible, sensitive eyes.

I don't know why not. I just never really said it before. I mean said it and meant it.

Hanna looked at her, wide-eyed. No way.

Okay, I did. A long time ago, like forever. But it didn't work out so well. I just didn't want to mess it up.

You are such a total goof.

How do I say it now?

Just say it.

Adam and Soraya were gone, walking on the beach. Jake was not far off, chasing a seagull, squatting when it landed, then, like a seven-year-old, trying to pounce. Hanna followed Ellen's gaze to Jake. She shook her head and said wearily, What an idiot.

Are the two of you…? Ellen started, but let it trail off. For a long time, she'd had the suspicion that Hanna had more of a thing for Michael, a thing Michael didn't share. And that Jake had been more of a consolation prize.

Hanna said, You couldn't tell?

What? Ellen said.

Nothing. Just, you know. There was a long pause, and Ellen looked away from her friend to Jake, Hanna's boyfriend, Michael's childhood friend, best friend.

Hanna said, Weariness. You know.

Ellen shook her head. She only knew too well. She said, I thought there might have been something. But I didn't, you know, want to say anything.

No, Hanna said. I don't know. It's like our narratives have diverged.

Ellen thought about the word. Narrative. She hadn't heard anyone quite use it the way that Michael used it, the way the people around him used it.

Hanna was a trim and petite woman, 30, with limp, slightly reddish corn silk hair that she wore cut short and usually pulled back or pushed behind her ears. She had the slender but shapely, athletic body of a committed distance runner, and pale blue, almost gray eyes. She rarely if ever wore any noticeable makeup, and had an almost studied air of plainness. She was not textbook pretty. Someone snarky might have said she was mousy, that her ears were too big and her nose was too pointy. And compared to Soraya with her boobs and her cascading sheaves of curls and her Victorian butt, she looked almost scrawny. But Ellen thought she was striking. She had a sort of intellectual air mixed with a personal radiance that gave her a directness, an elegant simplicity. Ellen liked her electric intensity—she always seemed to be leaning slightly toward you, peering, as though trying to read you (she was, after all, a psychologist), making sure she never missed anything you said.

Hanna looked at Michael for a long time, and Ellen watched her as she mouthed, *Is he asleep?*

Ellen raised her eyebrows, shrugged her shoulders.

Hanna said, Do you know when the last time we made love was?

Ellen grinned, pushed her hat back a little more, shook her head.

Neither do I. And I keep track. You know.

I know. Yeah. Well.

Ellen thought again of making love with Michael, and a jangle of sexual excitement went through her.

25

Sex isn't everything.

The hell it isn't, Hanna said, and they both laughed. It was one of those kind of laugh moments when you're trying to be quiet and can't be.

God, Hanna giggled. I don't even know if he'd notice if I broke up with him. He'd look up from his computer, and go, like, huh? and that would be it.

Sweetie, Ellen said.

Now there was silence between them. There was the constant thunder of the waves, the call of seagulls.

Will you come to visit me? Ellen said. In LA? You and Soraya?

I'd love to. But you have to introduce me to Bradley Whitford.

I think he's spoken for.

I don't care. He's, like, *oh*. Oh.

He's nice.

There was silence again. Hanna broke it, I don't think I'd actually want to. Meet him, I mean.

Why?

I don't know. It's nice to have illusions or delusions, or whatever.

I guess so, Ellen said, sad, suddenly.

Hanna said, I'm sorry. I didn't mean... I mean, that guy was delusional, wasn't he. Townsend?

Ellen smiled vaguely. Wayne Townsend. Delusions.

But will you come? You and Soraya? It'd be fun.

I'd love to, sweetie. I know Soraya would, too.

She was inviting Hanna to LA and she had not invited Michael. What did that mean? She didn't want to think of it. She saw Soraya and Adam and waved. Soraya wore a bikini, her old-fashioned voluptuousness spilling over, and a sarong. Adam looked much less like an English professor than a body builder in his cut-off board shorts.

It's not an end, Hanna said. Do you feel like it's an end? Tomorrow?

Ellen said nothing, but watched Soraya, her fabulous, wild hair. She thought of being back in LA. It, tomorrow, did feel like an end. There was so much that she and Michael had not talked about, had avoided assiduously. This was just a game they were playing. Michael would go back to his research and she would go back to the life that she wasn't ready to return to.

Adam grabbed Soraya and lifted her, grabbed her by her hips and spun her around and then held her, one meaty forearm mashing her buttocks and pressing her against him.

Ellen thought of what Hanna had said about narratives. Her own narrative seemed like a nasty river current she'd been caught up in. The act of leaving LA, her escape and this moment out of time, felt—right now—like clinging to a rock before being swept off in the same current. Her reappearance would be something in which she was merely a participant.

But so how did you square that, an improbable romance between the wacky comic who already felt like life was a simulation, and the computer geek bent on turning the world into a simulation of itself?

When Michael woke, he sat up and said, God, I feel like a king. Hanna, that was the best lunch I've ever had that didn't include pizza.

It was a tuna sandwich, Hanna said, and even beneath her tan, Hanna turned red.

Yes, but it was a singular tuna sandwich. It was a sublime tuna sandwich. It was the best tuna sandwich in the history of tuna sandwiches.

Then he crawled over to where Ellen sat and threw his arms around her. She toppled onto the sand and met his mouth with hers when he kissed her. She held him a long time, only letting go when he pushed himself up on the balls of his hands. He said, Did I snore?

No, dollink, you did not snore. You don't snore.

He jumped up.

Hanna said, I'm surprised you could sleep after drinking those little blue caffeine bombs.

Michael laughed and he shook and swept at himself to clear away the sand. He crouched in front of Ellen and growled, Ready for a swim? then threw his sandy arms around her and lifted her up.

She giggled. Yeah, she said. Let's rock, surfer geek.

Last day. Last day. Last day.

He put her down and kissed her long and hard. His lips were dry but his mouth was wet, and it was another moment she wished she could freeze in time. It was strange how deeply and clearly she could see him—the black nubs of his whiskers, the creamy tan of his skin, the almost pouty plump of his mouth, his long eyelashes—and yet see beyond him, beyond herself.

It had started in LA, this sensation of being almost entirely disassociated from herself, her feelings, a spectator to her own life, a helpless bystander to an unceasing series of moments that fell like petals that dried and blew away, out of her grasp. There was a terror to it, an endless sense of loss. Perhaps this was what Hanna had meant when they had talked about why she had deserted the show, why she had disappeared—grief for her younger self. Perhaps even an unconscious attempt to stem the flow of time. The maddening part was the constant, raw awareness of things falling away.

Michael took her face in his hands and said, What is it?

She looked away, then back. I don't know, she said. I guess I was just thinking about tomorrow.

She could have said it then. Three words. The L word in the middle.

Tomorrow, and tomorrow, and tomorrow, Michael said with a histrionic flourish, Creeps in this petty pace from day to day, to the last syllable of recorded time; and all our yesterdays have lighted fools the way to dusty death.

It would have been infuriating if it hadn't been so charming.

Geek Boy knows Shakespeare. I'm impressed, she said, but she was more saddened that he would evade the word *tomorrow*. She scowled at him, but then he swept her up in his arms, saying, Come brief candle, into the water with you. She whooped in surprise and then he kissed her, swung her around.

Yesterday, in the rain, during an unguarded moment after shopping for dinner, she had almost said it for real, again.

At that moment, it would have been right. Easy. It was nothing, really, just an appreciation of who he was. It would have tripped off her tongue.

Later, in the rental car, she was trying to say it but then, out of nowhere, two dogs ran into the road. Michael slammed on the brakes, but hit one of them. The dog—suddenly vivid in the headlights, white spots, splotchy brindle, heavy head and blunt snout—slammed against the front of the car and sprawled out on the sandy road, stunned. She stared at it bleached in the headlights. Michael started to get out of the car, but she held his arm. The door was open when the dog dragged itself up.

What should I do? he said.

Clearly it was injured. She said nothing, but waited to see if it magically repaired itself.

Maybe it's okay, she said.

He shook his head, but said nothing. He had one leg out of the vehicle and stood, uncertain, gazing at the massive dog, its pained eyes.

The dog took a tentative step, then another, then limped, dragging a hind leg, over the limits of the headlights and disappeared in darkness.

It was a female, he said.

She nodded. She had seen the nipples, too. It would die, and the puppies would die. But it was probably for the best. Feral dogs.

They had talked so much and yet they had not talked at all. At first, the possibility that the relationship would endure had seemed almost ludicrous—at least to her. It wasn't, could not be, anything more than a fling. Both of them had the lives they'd had before they'd met; each had tangles and failures that required confrontation, reconciliation—and, in her case, perhaps very expensive legal counsel.

Except as time had gone on, she had begun to think of his presence as something completely necessary.

How was this going to work, after? She had been going over it in her head endlessly. Bottom line, she didn't want to go back. But, bottom line, she could do nothing else. At least in the short term. On the phone with Marty, he had spoken of snarling lawyers, cauldrons of network executives, ready to boil over.

And she, Ellen, had not felt more human, more herself in years than she had with Michael. Yet if she somehow stayed with him—*Ellen Gregory Leaves Multimillion Dollar TV Show Contract Over Unknown Nerd!!*—what would it look like? What would it *be* like? All she knew was that she had left LA for a reason, and nothing surrounding that had changed. She still hated the show, she still hated her LA self. No, she was not thinking of trashing her career—at least not completely. She had little real idea how much damage she had done, but she suspected that at this point, there was little—really—that could not be mostly undone. If she just called up Marty and said… What? I want off the show. Out of the contract. Then what?

He lifted her again and started down the beach with her in his arms, toward the water.

Michael, she said, My hat! But he spun her around and she laughed, her hat flew off and her words choked in her own laughter, the sky a blur, and when he hit the surf the water splashed up around them, cold against her sun-warmed skin. He stopped and she clung to his neck, kissed him. When she slid out of his arms and into the knee deep surf, she hesitated, took one of his hands and held it tightly, said, Michael?

Ellen.

Tomorrow, she said.

Tomorrow is tomorrow, he said. Neither of us can stop the planet from turning and get off.

She stared at him. She wanted to say, You can't? Why can't you? but she said nothing.

He gave her an almost blank look, his green eyes sparkling—it was the look of a boy wanting to be told what to do.

She tugged at his hand. She said, Let's…, and then stopped. She was going to say, Let's go back to the house, make love again, talk about this. Why she didn't, she didn't know. There was still time. She loosened her grip on his hand and he turned and took off running into the waves. She chased him, the waves knocking her back, until he had swum a few yards out, beyond the place where the waves broke. She swam though a wave, toward him where he floated in the gentle swells. His hair gleamed black with wet and she was in love. Ridiculous, tongue-lolling love. Gulls squawked overhead. He took a couple of powerful strokes and was next to her. He kissed her again, and she held him, wrapped her legs around him and held him as though she'd never hold him again.

She had no way of knowing that she would not.

Hey, he said, you're going to drown me.

ELLEN GREGORY IN LOVE

The water was warmish, at least for North Carolina in June, and you could feel the warmth of the water at the surface, with an icy bite from the depths, almost as though the water were swimming within itself. You could see the beach. The taste of salt water was in her mouth and she looked at Michael, his curly, dark hair matted from the wet, his face full of joy. He was just beyond her and he was laughing, rising and falling in the swells—he had that Midwesterner's delight in the ocean. Now he was floating on his back and pointing at the gulls, which were everywhere now.

The water caught a thousand mirrors of sunlight, and for a moment, she lost sight of Michael. The gulls were everywhere, wheeling in the sky, dipping into the water, floating. There was a strange moment of panic as she scanned the water for him—and suddenly he was next to her, his mouth right next to her ear.

Hi, he said.

Hi, yourself, she said.

You're beautiful, he said and kissed her.

Are you cold? he said.

No, she said, It's wonderful.

He kissed her again, and when he moved away, she went to him and kissed him again. This is what it could be like, she thought, as he dove under again and resurfaced a few yards from her. He splashed at her and she ducked, and then he went underwater again.

And then she was floating in the swells, watching the gulls and other sea birds dipping into the water, watching the man she loved, his dark hair gleaming wet.

ELLEN GREGORY IN LOVE!!!

Michael had completely flunked whatever litmus tests she'd had. He was a nerd, a geek—good-looking—but still. A scientist. A video-game-playing, ABD Ph.D. professor-to-be, with geeky friends, who argued passionately about things she'd never heard of. And who had never heard of her because while he did own a TV, it was kept safely in a closet, just in case something important actually happened.

Love: Well, here it was, the strangled breath when she was near him, this waking up in the morning next to him feeling like every day was Christmas.

They were not terribly far out—ten or fifteen yards from shore. Not far from here the bottom would fall off and sweep deeper and deeper into the cold darkness of the Atlantic, where it would give way to shipping lanes and container ships and vast unseen storms and would not rise again except to the sweet calls of some child across the world, the endless thunder of surf. She floated on her back, looked at the blue, blue sky. Here she could watch the irregular vortices of gull-flight, the perpetual motion of the waves. Here she could see her friends—blurs on the sand, stripes of color. She thought of Michael and wondered at the bizarre way that life happens. You get to a place and look at what surrounds you—sun, water, sky—and marvel at the circumstances that brought you here.

But where was she? On the precipice between today and tomorrow, between with him and without. She thought she felt a cold current come up from the deep and a chill of fear rode through her.

Michael was beyond her, his skin darker than she had ever seen it, his hair catching sunlight, blackly metallic. He had been next to her a moment ago, the warmth of him, the brush of his legs, the cup of his hand on the back of her head, treading water and kissing her, and then he had drifted away, and she knew he would swim back to her, and that was the way she was thinking of it, the future, or near-future. They would drift away and come together. Lather. Rinse. Repeat.

Until.

It was nauseating to think of it.

When the fish bashed scraping against her leg, almost dragging her under with its mass and speed, she thought for a moment it was Michael, being uncharacteristically rough. This pissed her off—the scrape burned in the saltwater and she could feel herself going hot with anger she had never felt with him. She shouted, but he could not hear, and then suddenly that thought dissolved into confusion. Just a few yards away from her, he burst through the surface, way too high speed, jetting like a water skier almost, sideways, his head rising up out of the water and leaving a gorgeous arc of shimmering water droplets, one arm flailing down toward his hips, his legs, the other grappling somehow to right himself. His face had a broken, aghast look. Inhaled water gagged his scream of *Get out now*.

And in that hill of water, that wake-like wave that thrust him sideways, she could see the fish, could see how enormous it was, bigger around than a barrel and long enough that she couldn't even see where it ended. Just the fin itself was enormous. At least as tall as her arm. And she felt the way she felt when Wayne Townsend had kidnapped her, with absolutely no control over anything.

The fish thrust him out of the water as high as his waist and drove him toward shore, then sideways, and she froze utterly, the reality of it just too bizarre and monstrous to believe. And then the adrenaline came and she willed herself to swim.

ANESTHESIA

She looked over and now Michael was thrashing, gulping and shouting, *Swim, swim*. And she did. There was screaming on the shore. Every time she glanced at him, the fish seemed to be coming back at him from a different direction and he seemed to be battling with it, fighting it off, perhaps even winning. But she did not stop moving, she swam and swam—deserted him in her own panic—and she did not know how far she had gotten when the thing hit her in the foot, but it still seemed miles from shore. The contact felt like smashing into rocks and then more rocks smashing in on top. It stopped her dead in the water and she could see its rounded, gray snout, and she could not panic, there wasn't time. In fact, everything in the moment slowed to super slow-motion and became so clear that she could think in astonishing detail what to do.

She banged at it, gulping at the air—the air suddenly taking on a sweet taste like anesthesia—and it released, but when she looked up again as she started to swim, Michael had started toward her and she waved at him, pointed to shore. Oddly, there was no pain, just an incredible, single-minded notion to get to shore, and so she swam. There were screams from shore—God, she hoped Soraya had her cell phone.

SALT

*O*ur father, who art in heaven. She was swimming, salt in her mouth, the picture of the blunt snout in her head, her lungs burning.

Michael was next to her and she would not later remember this, how mangled he was, most of him invisible in the gory water. It had let go of her and it had him and she reeled over and punched it to try to make it release him and it held on, its whole huge body thrashing, but also pushing them into shallower water *Give us this day our daily broad*, and then Michael *hallowed be thy name* was smashing, punching, an astonishing, inhuman effort *thy kingdom come* rising up in his own death and rescuing her and *thy will be done* it was gone.

Swim, he said, gulping at the air, gurgling, his beautiful sun-darkened skin gone ghostly, Swim. She did and then she kicked sand and pushed herself up and rose up on a wave and was slapped down into sand as hard as concrete, scraping her face, shoulder, gagging on saltwater. Sand in her teeth. Soraya was there—*Dr. Ouellette. Oh my God, Soraya is a doctor. Look at him. Michael. I'm okay.* But shock was setting in, and Hanna was pulling her up. A wad of towels. Hanna working rapidly. Wrapping her. Her teeth were chattering. Her whole body froze. The cold was setting in.

She did not see Michael slide into shore beside her, but felt him, and they were back in Iowa, walking next to the river, talking. He was telling her about his concept of the afterlife, if there was one. It was conceivable that there was one, and it wasn't necessarily about God. It was about dimensionality. About the crossing from one strand of time to another, because time is far more. Time is far more than the ticks of the clock.

It was a fabulous spring day and she was in love. The word had not been spoken, yet, and the word made every difference. She'd had no idea that love was even possible, but it had crept up on her. It was going. It was the day they first made love, which was later, and she had known then that she was in love, and she wanted him in a way she had never wanted anyone before. Body, soul. She wanted to steal him from himself and absorb him. They walked along the river and she knew she would make love to him and that it would be a little clumsy at first, then better. It was going. There was gurgling and it was the waves it was her throat and there was a hard, unpleasant rhythmic sound but. But. The spring was beautiful, as it always was in Iowa after the long winters, after the final thaw. Ducks waddled along the bank, straight lines of ducklings following. It was the happiest she ever was.

PART TWO:
THE ICARUS COMPLEX

CAFFEINE LIFE

The old adage that workplace romances are fraught with difficulty was especially true if your workplace was Hollywood—or more specifically, the soundstage of *Girlfriends*, the sitcom heading into its highly anticipated fourth season—and the 'romance' in question was with your incredibly vapid and self-involved (if genuinely hot) costar, Masters Wood, whom Ellen Gregory was now watching as he watched himself in the mirror.

Ellen Gregory understood exactly why she had decided to have an affair—affair being not really the word that she would have preferred—with Masters Wood. It was simple and it was ugly: He was attractive and he was available, and she had insisted that he get tested for STDs and he was clean. That she found him spiritually, morally, and intellectually vacuous—even if he was totally hot—and more or less personally repugnant went with what Dr. Ling, her therapist, described as her self-loathing.

The thing was that when you're working on a sitcom it's pretty much a 24/7 sort of thing, and there's really very little time for an actual relationship. In a sense, the choice to sleep with Masters was about two things, a) relieving her sexual tension through purely animalistic sex, and b) a perhaps semi-subconscious desire/need to punish herself for her complete inability to have a (real) romantic relationship by having sex with someone she found more or less personally repugnant. And, okay, perhaps there was also a c), which c) she would likely not have admitted to herself but had to do with a deep and persistent and really annoying desire to be close to someone.

She wasn't sure exactly how long she had been sleeping with Masters — not because she didn't know, but because she didn't want to know. Every time she saw him, she wanted to break it off. And every time she did not.

And so when he suggested to her that they make a sex tape, because that's what everyone was doing, she wasn't really surprised. And there was a truly repugnant part of her that sort of fit in with b) (see above), and her desire for moral and emotional self-flagellation.

We should do a sex tape, he said.

Why on earth would I want to do that?

Career move. Think about it, Masters said. A sex tape would be, like, totally inspired as a career move. For both of us. I mean think of all the people who've done sex tapes, and all of them have just gotten more famous. You know...? Masters was looking at himself in one of the many mirrors in his bedroom, trying different angles, watching where the shadows fell on his chest (he was in love with his pecs) and now and then glancing back at her.

She said: First of all, you have to be a certified loser for that to be any sort of positive career move at all. And while that may be true of you, Masters, I do not include myself in that category.

But someday everyone's a loser.

Speak for yourself.

Ellen sat up in his bed.

If you ever so much as *mention* it again—not to mention if you've stuck a video camera around somewhere around here that I can't see—I will make sure your contract is cancelled. I will make sure that you are off the show. I will however see to it that your character has a beautiful death. Better than your own. I will personally pay for gangsters to come and deface you. Literally. And you will not die but live out your life as the miserable, ugly person you are.

Masters Wood played Peter on *Girlfriends*. Peter was a handsome, chest-waxing hypochondriac who had once dated her character, Gina, but was now Gina's best friend. Masters was perfect for the part because he was essentially a handsome, chest-waxing hypochondriac, and since he was a marginal-at-best actor, with a bit part in a lucky sitcom, it didn't require a lot of work. He was gorgeous in a *prima facie* sort of way, tall and slim and athletic, with washboard abs, and a gym-defined chest that was picture perfect. But his kind of beauty—common in LA as sunshine—was a thing that did not wear well. The longer you knew him, the less attractive he was. His character, Peter, was slightly more tolerable, if only because you only had to spend 22 minutes with him at a time.

You couldn't do that, he said.

It was more a question than a statement. He had a look that inspired nothing but distrust. She searched his face, and it was a look she had seen before—like a dog caught getting into the dog food bag.

Ellen said: Where is it, you slimy shit.

What? he said, but he was such an unconvincing actor, it was almost impossible for him to lie effectively, even though he did it habitually. He just stood there, looking dull and vacant.

I'm going to make a few phone calls, Ellen said. We do a quick little Masters-ec-tomy, and then you'll be free to wait tables again. I mean once your face and kneecaps heal. She got out of bed. She was still naked.

She wanted nothing more than to humiliate him and, if possible, grind out whatever self-esteem he had like a cigarette butt. She went to her purse, took out her phone, and clicked it on.

I just signed a new contract. You can't do anything.

Masters, sweetie, you are so totally dumb, she said, her voice going from tough old broad to syrupy coquette. I am so like completely kidding. I think it would be a really super idea.

You do? He blinked.

Sure. It'd be fun. But how would we do it? Would we hire a crew to shoot us to make it look good, or would we shoot it ourselves for that sort of *cinema verité* look?

Masters got a smug, incredibly pleased-with-himself look. No need, he said. He went to one of the mirrors and it opened almost like a medicine cabinet. His bed-room, it turned out, was essentially all false walls. Inside, there was a camera mount-ed on a tripod. The walls inside were painted black so you couldn't see through the mirrors.

She laughed: What is this, the Gene Simmons setup?

Still completely naked, she went toward it, so that he would think he was getting the best footage of his life, and stood looking at it. This was footage—or boobage—that he would most definitely *not* be seeing again.

So this has been on for how long?

Since we came in. There are motion detectors.

He was beaming with pride. He simply had no idea how much of an asshole he was.

She turned and got her clothing and started to put it on. So where'd you get this? she said casually.

Came with the house. That was half the reason I bought it.

He was in the bathroom now. A key turned in a lock and he came through into the other side where the camera was. As she followed him, she buttoned her blouse. Behind the mirrors were several more cameras, each strategically placed. Tying them all together was a computer. No doubt there were others in the ceiling.

Dude who owned the house before me, Masters said, He was some kind of bas-ketball player or something. He had, like, *thousands* of women on tape. Masters was so proud of his setup that he seemed utterly clueless that another person might find it completely disgusting and perverted to be videotaped during sex without their knowledge or consent. Like a twisted frat boy real estate agent, he gave her the complete tour.

The cameras were connected to the computer wirelessly and transmitted their video feeds back to it. You could fit about 200 years worth of video on the computer, and then each session—this was the word he used, *session*, like he was a fucking portrait photographer at Sears—could be filed and saved and edited professionally if you wanted it to be.

So we could just use the footage you've already got?

Sure, he said. Easy. I didn't have any of ours edited, but, you know....

She cut him off: Show me what you have.

No doubt this town was full of women who would be delighted to be in Masters's complete home porn collection. She was not one of them. Every time she was with him, she had wanted nothing more than to go home and take a shower and rid herself of any trace of him. Which was more or less how she felt about all the affairs and/or liaisons she'd had since she'd been in LA. And maybe even since back in New York.

Each of which of course had been strategic. In a business that aims to mimic life, it was hard for life not to mimic business. And in a business that relied on suspension of disbelief, it was not uncommon for otherwise perfectly intelligent people to convince themselves of nearly anything.

But of course nothing ever exactly seemed this way at the time. You always found a way to convince yourself that you were so wild about this producer or that actor not because of the money or the house or the show, but *because he was such a great guy*. But just because you woke up in someone else's bed didn't mean there was a relationship. Or love, which she was growing increasingly certain did not exist—or existed only for fools.

Once at dinner with Marty, she had mentioned it, the death of love, and he had said something that for her encapsulated it pretty well: Out here you either have ice water running in your veins or you don't have a career.

She watched Masters and was overcome with a feeling of deadness. Or perhaps it was that she was overcome with a feeling of being *aware* of her deadness. Masters pushed some buttons and looked up at her eagerly. He said, Look, a surprise, and hit a button.

On the enormous plasma display in his bedroom, up popped a rather too familiar face, framed by naked shoulders and dangling hair. It wore a heavy-lidded, weirdly sneering, nostril-flared look of someone chewing on a hangnail, but both hands grasped at the sheets as it bobbed toward and away from the camera. The face was blurry and bouncing, but it was impossible not to recognize it as belonging to her best friend.

You screwed Patti *Gelfman,* my best friend, my publicist? When did you shoot this?

Couple of days ago. You don't mind that Patti and I, you know. Do you?

No, no, she said. I was just going to say that the color is really good. You did a great job of lighting it.

I knew you'd be cool about it.

Patti Gelfman had been Ellen's best friend for at least a decade, and to find out that Masters had fucked her—actually, that *Patti* had fucked *him*—was a bit like a punch in the gut. Not that Ellen had any sort of exclusivity with Masters. And not that she herself *wanted* any exclusivity. But what kind of asshole had she been to Patti that Patti would want—as soon as Ellen had let it slip that she was screwing Masters—to run over and screw him too? (As if she didn't know.)

Was this a kind of payback for her so-called best friend?

Long ago and far away in New York, Patti had, like Ellen, been a wannabe comic/actress, but while Ellen kept at it, Patti quit and started taking marketing and public relations classes at NYU. She was something of a trust fund baby—a kid whose daddy-the-colorectal-surgeon made it possible, through his good will and generosity, for her to be an endless sort of dilettante. Which was, in its way, fine with Ellen. She'd had more than one dinner on the Gelfmans. She had sat with them, felt jealous at their familial bond but at the same time had felt grateful to her own parents for their reserved aloofness, their insistence that she separate herself from them (although perhaps not quite to the extent she had). For Patti, the skids had been greased. She did not have the ever-present sense of incipient failure that Ellen did, the sense of desperation. At first she had talked about going to law school, being an entertainment lawyer, but she liked sitting around talking, on the phone or in cafes or bars, a lot better than she liked studying—which was also just fine with Ellen.

They had walked through New York streets at dawn more than once after Ellen's gigs, drunk and laughing, and Patti had always been a person Ellen could rely on as a friend as much as a conceptual best friend. The thought was ugly, and Ellen had always realized it but Ellen's ultimate, if unstated and maybe unconscious goal had been to buy Patti away from the doting and loving daddy. Sick avarice. Yes. When she started to make money, she hired Patti as her publicist and, while she was good at it, mainly Ellen just wanted to have her around, like a homie or something, to pay her more and more, to make her hang up on mom or dad. Just to prove that she could. Okay, so it was twisted, except that she never actually knew that she was doing it until a therapist brought it to her attention. And then it was sort of hard to deny.

Then somewhere along the line, Patti came to have a kind of power over her as her best friend, because the more recognition she got, the harder it became just to have girlfriends, to sit in a café and have a cup of coffee and rely on some sense that this was a person who had no designs on you, who could be trusted. The people you tended to feel most comfortable around were people you had known forever, and Patti was the only person she trusted, or the only girlfriend type. And now—she was smart enough to realize the obvious—she knew that she had been scammed as much as she had scammed, and there was an emptiness. Who knew if all those late nights on the telephone, chatting, being catty, were not on tape somewhere in a safe deposit box, just waiting for the day.

It had been said—more than once—that Hollywood is like high school, but worse, and it was a trope that you couldn't deny but only add to, like but the drugs are better, but the kids are more vicious, but the clothes are better, etc etc blah blah blah blah.

So Patti had fucked Masters, whom she knew Ellen was fucking, and from all those late night chats knew just about as much about Masters as it was possible to know.

This was Hollywood-style naked resentment, pardon the choice of words. There was no way Patti could have thought it wouldn't piss her off. And yet it didn't exactly. Somehow it was just business.

Masters said, Look, here *we* are.

How about that? You have cameras in the ceiling, too?

The feeling of deadness grew and it had the effect of elongating time, making each moment insufferably long. Everything unfolded like a slow motion replay.

So where's the video stored? Ellen said.

There's a bunch of really big hard drives in the computer, Masters said. I could take it off and transfer it to beta tapes.

Hey, listen, I'm, like, feeling so parched. Could you get me a Coke or something?

Masters got up. You want diet or regular.

Regular, she said.

When he came back, he handed her an ice cold can and she took it.

Such a gentleman, she said.

Did you want me to open it for you? he said.

Glass would have been nice, but never mind. I'm not going to drink it anyway.

Why not?

Masters, you're a stud, but can you really be so, like, dim? She was shaking the can.

Why are you shaking it? he said before reality started to dawn.

He tried to grab her, but when her stalker had started following her, she had taken classes, and now she kicked him as hard as she could in the nuts and he went down, fast.

She cracked open the Coke can and sprayed it all over the computer until the screen fritzed out. Then she took one of the cameras and, while Masters retched on the floor, she folded up the tripod and swung it, smashing the nearest hinged mirror.

She kept swinging until she had broken everything she could break, including the computer monitor and the camera.

Sandy, the director, yelled, *Cut*, cut. But there was a great release in all this break-age, even if the glass was theater glass.

Ellen, Sandy said. *Ellen*! You're fucking up the set. Stop.

Sandy was bald and not very old and completely neurotic, but a good director. Right this second she hated him. She kept going, swinging and breaking mirrors and prop cameras until her arms were numb. There was so much glass. When at last she did stop, it was when she fucking felt like it. Her arms felt like jelly. A lot of people in the crew looked genuinely freaked. Masters was cowering.

The whole sex tape concept had been her idea. The fifteen or more minutes they'd just shot would be whittled down in the edit to a couple of decent but sugges-tive thirty- and sixty-second teaser spots. She would produce and supervise the edit.

She didn't usually do conceptual comedy, but everyone thought it was inspired. It was win-win-win. She got to make some indirect comments on the world within a world within a world that television was—not that anyone would get it. She got to put some edge into their usually-really-dull shooting, the network got a scandalous but topical series of promos for the show, and Masters got to look like a stud. And Patti got to look like the slut she was. Except in this town, it would probably only promote her career.

Later, at home, Ellen fell into bed and the deadness came over her. She wanted to be done with it all.

She had been on a manic jag for something like five or six unbroken years, a personal record, and a fact that was, she was certain, in no small way responsible for her pretty incredible success. She was a poster girl for what America could do for you if you were lucky (which included not just being drop-dead gorgeous, but also having a *look*, some indefinable quality that made people remember you). She was a poster girl for what could happen if you stood at or near the front door when oppor-tunity knocked, opened the door, then worked your highly desirable type A ass to the bone—and slept with the right people. There was also the little issue of a possibly self-induced, bi-polar-ish situation that you wouldn't so much call a *disorder* as you would a lifestyle. And the last several years had been all up, not so much a manic jag as a totally prolonged bender.

It was Caffeine Life, totally jabbered personal talk radio 24/7—gallons of Starbucks and Diet Cokes, ma-huang and kola capsules, then nicotine patches (even though she'd never smoked), a couple of unhappy experiments with X and other amphetamines and mind-blowing amounts of serotonin-pumping exercise (dozen mile runs in the mornings, step-aerobics in the afternoon, six days a week). But she had been working, working, and happy happy happy happy all the time, able to walk into a room and win it, no matter how big, win it in a matter of a few seconds because she had the stuff, she was the *woman*, she was Ellen, or *ELLEN!*™, America's Favorite Girl Next Door (certified, bona fide A-List Pussy, or so she had been informed by the Hollywood council that kept track of pussy listings).

And now. A few years ago, even a year ago, the chance to do this kind of comedy would have been totally inspiring and uplifting, but a few years ago, it would have been *fiction*. She *had* fucked Masters, and he had surreptitiously videotaped it. He had fucked Patti and videotaped that, too. And she had kicked him in the nuts and destroyed his computer.

Her life had been a sort of jujitsu act, from the moment she had been nicknamed Runt in high school. She had learned—painfully—to take up the part of herself that was most vulnerable and naked and terrified—learned to take it away from other people, that is—and make it funny.

Now, she almost dreaded sitting down at the Avid with the editor and looking at it again. It was just a reminder that she was no longer particularly real. That she had the multiple personality disorder of TV. That somewhere along the way she had gone from a wide-eyed and naïve and ambitious kid to some sort of reptilian Hollywood creature. That leather-skinned, hardened Hollywood broad with ice water juicing through her veins. She did—had done—things she knew were ugly, and somehow all of it was supposed to have been justifiable. But none of it was.

THE BLACK BOX

Michael Webster had not slept in something like two or three days, and while this would have been nothing ten years ago when he was twenty, these days, he was nearing his limit.

Old man, he said out loud, but there was no one but his computer array to hear him.

He had also only had one real meal in the last couple of days, but he was used to working through meals, and had the vaguely gaunt, incredibly pasty appearance to show for it.

Right now, he wasn't exactly sure what day it was, or time. This wasn't an unusual state of affairs, either. His office at the university was in the basement of a 1950s-era building that had been repurposed with a lot of very expensive processing power for very serious number-crunching by physicists and mathematicians who took number-crunching very seriously. The office had no windows, but it was aggressively air conditioned pretty much year round (despite the cold Iowa winters) because of the heat that the servers generated. This had become his favorite place on earth, largely because he had, in the last few years, been nowhere else, except for the annual beach trip he took with friends at the beginning of each summer. That one-week trip represented about 80 percent of his social life. It had been more than a year since Soraya had broken up with him, and he had not had a lover since. This wasn't because he and Soraya still worked together closely, it was just because he didn't have the time.

He was almost there, almost to the virtual grail that he had been seeking as soon as he had realized that it was possible.

He rebooted the computer and picked up the headset and put it on again, then reset the Black Box.

The headset consisted of a custom-made and -built goggle display that fit tightly over your eyes and blacked out everything else, headphones that did essentially the same thing for your ears, and a sort of modular headband that fit tightly against the temples and other key brain areas so that its sensor-stimulators could interact with the head of the user. Right now he was almost literally goggle-eyed from weariness and wearing the headset (but also from frustration and anxiety).

A few hours ago, it had seemed that he was perilously close to a breakthrough, that it was at last going to work. He had actually dropped in—he had been inside the sweet blue sphere that he had designed—but then it had crashed. It had taken hours to find the bug in the astonishingly complex operating system code, and now he was giving it a final try before he would give up and go back home and go to sleep for a day or two.

When he plugged in again, he had the sense he got sometimes when he'd spent too long coding. His field of vision was no larger than the frame of his monitor.

He hit the safe switch, which shut the system down after a pre-determined time just in case you happened to induce some grisly neurological horror (another Soraya precaution).

He saw flashing lights, and there was a hum that was actually binaural tone code that was in the same frequency range as beta brainwaves, and suddenly there were colors—what would have looked like a pixellated screen if this were a screen and not a retina-painting goggle display. And then he dropped in.

What he expected to see was what he had designed, and what he had seen hours ago: a three-dimensional correlative of a common computer desktop, a virtual space where a user could operate using nothing but thought and almost-unconscious eye gestures. His operating system had leapfrogged the tools that others in the field used to manipulate icons and data. That was what his collaboration with Soraya had done for him.

It turned out that the whole brain-hand-keyboard interface was totally unnatural, no matter how completely second nature it seemed to someone like Michael who had spent so many hundreds of thousands of hours at it. But that was Soraya's point, it shouldn't be *second* nature, it should just be natural.

That old interface involved several different neurological processes in completely different areas of the brain (something that he did not know until he met Soraya). His interface tapped directly into the areas of the brain where things happened. No middleman. You didn't have one neurological process handing off to another to another. It was intuitive in the purest sense.

Ultimately, it wasn't about laptops or desktops, but about computers that didn't exist yet, computers that would simply be a part of you, worn or carried or even implanted and connected to the cloud—servers that existed somewhere—through ubiquitous bandwidth at the same time you were connected to the real world, and you could be on a treadmill, or on the john, and you'd get an idea and you'd just open up that file, mentally, and make your notes, fire off a message—not dictating but think-tating. There would be the prosthetic reality of the computer right next to real reality, and the prosthetic reality would augment the real reality, and it would be like what people like Michael's heroes Doug Englebart and Ted Nelson had been predicting for thirty-plus years.

And it wouldn't be some kind of *Matrix*-like horror show, it would be a thing that came close to approaching—if not actually achieving—the singularity, and whatever knowledge you had would be augmented by knowledge that was out there, in the cloud, but instantly attainable with nothing more than the flick of an eyelash.

You'd sort of be able to just think your way through a task. Productivity would leap exponentially, by an order of magnitude similar to the it had leapt when in the 1990s and businesses had migrated en masse from paper to computers. And then it would grow even more as people locked onto the idea and built things around the concept. It would no longer be point and click to open a document or application, it would be point and think. It was to be a 360 x 360 environment (he would have to remember that, *point and think*). The implications were well understood. But this was—when it worked—still very primitive, very much a proof of concept.

Michael had begun his research on this transparent man-machine interface during his master's days. It was largely viewed to be an impossible, or at least not-yet possible, artificial intelligence sort of endeavor. But that was what appealed to Michael about it. And Michael viewed it as within reach, a natural step in the evolution of the graphical user interface, and as far as he was concerned, there was nothing in computing that had not seemed impossible before it had been done.

The way he viewed the Black Box (so far a name for it had not come to him) was that it should be simple. A proof of concept first. And so he had begun with the simplest possible version of an open source operating system, and then had built onto and around it with a combination of brain research and the help of the university's gridded computer system (a reasonable facsimile of a super computer), and a tool he had spent almost two years helping to develop, the EvoCoder, a genetic coding development environment that enabled something akin to coding on steroids. You could go from concept to application at very high speed because now you could pull strings of open source code in seconds that otherwise you might have had to hand code. And, of course, you had to be smart about what you were doing—you had to have the right kind of heuristic model.

And you had to have just the right combination of arrogance and stupidity and naiveté to think that you were the guy who could pull it off. The code was now so good, so elegant, that it didn't take up enormous amounts of storage or draw vast amounts of memory or energy—it could fit easily on a modified laptop.

It had yet to work in any sustained sort of way, but that was merely a speed bump. Over the last few months, Michael had had glimpses, moments that had said, *Dude, you are the Man.* But these were mostly punctuation in the midst of long strings of nothing, of coding and research and theorizing, and the EvoCoder's bots nosing tirelessly around the Internet, crawling and capturing and adapting strings of code, like an alien virus with the very simple but complex instruction to build a brain.

His life during this time had been like crossing an ocean but becoming increasingly uncertain that there was another side. Until today.

The pixelation made him dizzy—a feeling like motion sickness—and then, as the image resolved, the sensation went away. Another one took its place. Mostly it was confusion. The virtual space he thought he had created—and which he had glimpsed—had disappeared completely. What was in its place was confusing not so much for what it was but for what it wasn't.

Suddenly, when the pixelation had gone, he was not in a mid-winter computer lab in Iowa, but on a beach.

He reeled a little. Too little sleep, too much caffeine. He tried to reach for his desk, something to give him poise. But the beach was so *real*. Almost more real than real.

It was the same stretch of beach where he had been each summer for the last seven or eight years, and it was as real—the constant sound of the waves, the heat of the sun, the shimmering water—as if he were there.

In video games and computer animation, people talk about the physics of the environment, meaning essentially Newtonian physics, so, like, if your car bumps up against a wall, does the wall react like a wall and does the car react like a car? Do sparks fly? Do metal and paint get scraped off? Do you careen from the force? Even the best games had physics limitations. Unless you programmed it that way, you couldn't break down a wall, or dig into the earth. This all took enormous processing power.

Like a dreamer not sure if he was awake, Michael put his feet hard into the sand and could feel every last grain against his bare feet, the soft and shifting sift of it—no matter that he was [really] wearing thick socks and hiking boots. He stood up—in actual fact, he was still sitting—and walked across a stretch of sand and climbed up a sun-faded wooden stairway and sat down again. He couldn't guess the season except to say it was summer, and he was wearing shorts, a T-shirt, and he had a view to the road.

It was the fragrance of the environment that was the most remarkable—the salt air, the vague scent of fish rotting—that made him think that the physics were beyond impeccable; they were remarkable, like nothing he'd ever seen.

On the stair, he could feel the heat of the sun-soaked, pressure-treated timbers against his feet, could feel the solid heft of them beneath him. Despite it being a virtual environment, he couldn't help but wonder if he should have put on sun screen. A woman ran down the road toward him. This was no virtual woman, but a real, 3-D, flesh and blood woman. Her running shoes dug spectacularly into the sand at the side of the road; the muscles visible in her calves, above her shoes (the little white balls of footie socks), were perfectly rendered. Everything about her—her short, spiky black hair, the pale skin of her face, reddened slightly from exertion and damp—was perfect. There was no pixelation. There was none of the blur that you would expect from motion in any kind of display. None of that weird seasickness that came in video pans.

He decided to call out, just to see what would happen. Hey, he said, but she did not respond.

Since this world was not real in any conventional sense, and because he was exhausted and weirdly giddy, it didn't matter if he made a fool of himself. And it had been so long since he had been with a woman. He shouted, Hey, black-haired girl running on the side of the road.

This brought her to a halt, and the way her feet hit the sand, it sent splashes of sand up.

You're beautiful, he said because she was, and since she was not real there was no reason not to.

The way she looked at him was peculiar—she clearly knew him. But since this was no more real than a dream, he said, I haven't been laid in ages. You're beautiful.

She laughed. She had a grin that could kill you, he thought. There was something in it that was almost magical. She had a brilliant aura of femaleness that left him almost dumbfounded (it really had been too long since he'd got laid).

Michael, she said, shaking her head knowingly, You're the one who's beautiful.

Okay, *this* was good. Not only did she know him—which, from a certain angle, could be interpreted as this just being *his* dream, his own erotic fantasy—but concomitantly he had the most intense sense of déjà vu he'd ever had. Both here and there: Here in his lab where he wore boots and socks. And there next to the ocean, with his feet in the sun-warmed sand. A sort of double déjà vu.

She came to where he was.

You think I could shower first?

He tossed her the towel he suddenly realized he was holding. Sure, he said. Or not. I don't care.

This was a place where he had been and this was a situation—he knew this with absolute certainty—he had been in. But of course this was not possible. There was something going on here that was completely beyond him, beyond his machine, beyond his code— and not something that the Black Box should have been able to do. It was a failure, but one of a spectacular sort. But the girl. He knew what she smelled like if you came close and pressed your nose against her neck, kissed the downy hair at its nape. He knew the taste of her sweat.

Michael wasn't sure what to feel. Should he feel good that he'd created his own strange erotic paradise—but it was too soon to know about that—or good that at least something had happened without crashing, horrible because the environment he had been trying to create seemed to have completely disappeared, or totally and completely insane because this was just so spectacularly nuts that it defied every law of sanity he thought he knew.

Then, just as he started to follow her inside, the machine's safety kicked on. Everything began to pixelate and now he was in his office again.

She, the girl, however, was still in his head. A glimpse of the curve of her neck, the spiky black hair, and the very pale down along the skin that rose from her shoulder to her hairline.

What the fuck was this?

SLEEP WOULD BE GOOD

Michael picked up the telephone in his office and dialed Soraya's number across campus. She wasn't in her office, so he called her house.

It was Adam who picked up.

What day is it, dude?

Sunday, Adam said.

Soraya there?

When she got on, she sounded sleepy. He said, Come here, Watson, I want you.

Michael, Soraya said, What is it?

It's working. Or it's sort of working. He said: I've tried it three times, and it works. It's not doing what it's supposed to do but it fucking *works*.

No way, she almost screamed.

Well, I mean, I'm kind of a little, like, dazed at the moment, so.... But it's not doing—it's doing something—I mean..., he said, and stopped. He wanted to share it, but he also wanted to cry with something like grief.

But it's fucked up. I have no idea what it's doing. I think..., he started, but in his exhaustion, he wasn't sure what he thought. At last, he said, It's Sunday?

Yes, darling, it's Sunday.

Is it too early?

Adam and I were in bed, talking about getting brunch.

Don't let me get in the way.

It's okay. Do you want me to come over or not?

Yeah. No. I mean.... Fuck.

When did you last sleep? Never mind. I'll be there as soon as I can.

Okay, he said, and hung up as quickly as he could. He could not have explained to her why he was crying and was glad he did not have to. Exhaustion, the incredibly sweet lost moment with the black-haired girl, whose face he now could not even see, or some other thing he could not name.

After the first time, he had gone in again, and she was gone. He was at the beach again, but this time it was last year, after he and Soraya had broken up, and he was sitting on the beach with Hanna, and he was talking about the Black Box, talking about how close he was—this was *almost a year* ago—and here he was, no further along, it seemed. It was winter and he had been running in place since summer. And then he had gone in again and now he was driving, and it was a strange and terrifying experience, just to drop in behind the wheel of his car. There was a snow storm, and he was driving back to Iowa City on I-80, and the driving was sheer madness, a near complete whiteout, the wipers and heater going furiously, a car in front of him just losing it and drifting from lane to lane before ending up in the ditch between the east and westbound lanes.

He was confused as hell. He was so fucking tired and so fucking wired, and there was a part of him that said, Dude, you have stumbled on something awesome here, but there was another part that said, You're fucked.

But it was doing something. Years of programming, thousands of pounds of pizza and several million gallons of coffee and hyper-caffeinated soda and it was starting to come together. Except it wasn't. The thing that had just happened was not what he had expected. But it wasn't one of those 10 seconds in the blue sphere moments, it finally worked in a sustained and repeated way. Didn't it? This was close to proof of concept, except, a concept of what? He wanted to jump up and scream, but instead he said, It can work, to himself, to the room, to the racks of servers that had helped him build the code. I'm not saying it doesn't have bugs, but it works.

The real test, though, was to see if it worked with someone else. To see if it wasn't just some kind of fucking hallucination.

It was almost an hour before Soraya came, and when she burst in the door—her attire absolutely typical of Soraya Ouellette, MD, his business partner and former lover, a flamboyant low-cut blouse or shirt or whatever it was with maximum cleavage, beneath a red leather jacket, her long, curly hair tied up in back, but billowing out reddish gold. A skin-tight short skirt that was only a skirt in the technical sense (more like a tube of black fabric she had snugged her butt into).

Michael was in a chair by now, chewing on a stirrer from his coffee.

Well, Dr. Ouellette, want to come give it a try?

She was breathing like she had run the last 50 yards to his office. It works?

The good news is that it works, he said. The bad news is that I have no idea what the fuck it's doing.

You said that, but what do you mean?

I mean I have no idea what it's doing. I don't know whether to crack the champagne or put a bullet through my head.

She sighed. Michael, Michael. I find that generally life falls somewhere in between such extremes. By the way, you look like shit. You look like a literal lab rat. Have you eaten recently? She came close.

You have coffee breath, Michael, which is masking fasting breath.

I had some pizza a while ago.

How long is a while?

I don't know. Michael shrugged. I lose track of time. You have to try it, he said.

When he had first met her, he had expected someone quite different, some stereotype of a brain researcher, like maybe someone with a cranium the size of a basketball and a lightning bolt in her hair. Or someone kind of invisible, more white lab coat than anything else. Soraya had confounded nearly every expectation he'd had. His first impression of her was a gum-snapping white hot bimbo (even though she wasn't chewing gum). When you got over the rush of pheromones and Barbie curves and generous displays of flesh, what you found was a really sharp mind at the top of her game.

When he had understood that he was going to need to know a lot more about how the brain processed information in order to make a seamless connection with a computer, he put up an ad. Soraya had answered it, and she had blown him away with her looks, her knowledge, and her frank acknowledgement that what he was doing was probably impossible but also amazingly cool.

They had become lovers soon after—this was nearly three years ago—but it seemed like a long time ago. She got her MD with a specialty in neurology and then she went the research/Ph.D. route rather than the intern/residency/practice route. And now it seemed like she was closer to her Ph.D. than he was to his. He was not jealous of her; it was just another indication that he was falling behind, that he had to work harder.

Michael, she said. You're falling apart. I'm guessing you don't even remember what sleep is.

I do too.

Come on. I'll come back later with you after you've had some sleep. I need a living business partner, Michael, if we're going to make anything of it.

Outside, the sunlight felt alien, and the chill air disoriented him. She opened the door on the passenger side of her Volvo and waited until he folded his lanky frame inside, then shut the door and went around to the driver's side and got in. He took a deep breath and lounged against the door, his head lolling against the window.

Can you explain to me what it's doing that it's not supposed to be doing?, she asked when she got inside.

I mean—I don't know what I mean. I mean you're supposed to go into a space, just like you were logging onto a desktop, right?

Right.

She put the car into gear and backed out of the spot to head back across the river. She insisted on driving a stick, but she was terrible at it, and so rides with her were mostly clunky, hesitant starts, or even stalls, followed by mad acceleration.

Well, over the last few sessions, I saw it. You know, folders you could reach out and touch. But it kept crashing. And so I tinkered for a while to try to find the bugs, and when I tried it, it was like. Man, it's fucking unreal. Maybe it was just an hallucination or something.

It's certainly possible. But *what* was an hallucination?

I was in a virtual world, but it was as real as this one. I was on the beach, you know. North Carolina. And I saw this woman running. I could hear and—this is weirder—*smell* the ocean. I could smell it. I could feel every last grain of sand on my toes—and I was wearing shoes and socks. I could feel the sunlight on my arms. I did this not once, but three times. They weren't all at the beach. Once I was in a snow storm.

Was the girl pretty? Were there *pina coladas*? Little umbrellas?

Soraya, come on. It was real. Matter of fact, it was realer than real. You could stop and take time to notice. I can still see the grain patterns in the wood deck. I could see the woman. I *talked* to her and she talked to me.

Maybe it was an hallucination, Michael. Maybe it was God telling you to get yourself a life—or at least some sleep.

Yeah, I don't know. Yeah. But the weird part is she seemed to *know* me.

I think it's time for boy genius to get some rest. Then maybe get laid.

She pulled up outside his house. The landscape was typical for mid-March in Iowa, ancient snow in piles next to cleared walks. A chilly but clear blue sky. She said: Go inside, get in bed. Sleep.

He climbed out of the car.

Soraya called after him: Go to sleep and when you wake up, call me. We'll have breakfast and then we'll go check out your masterwork.

LUCKY CHARMS

When Michael awoke, he had no idea where he was or what day it was, only that it was light outside. His bladder was swollen painfully, but he did not move. He stared at the window across the room and listened to the traffic outside. He closed his eyes again and saw the beach. He saw the girl, though he could no longer see her face. She had a kind of sexual brilliance to her, a physical charisma. That was the thing he remembered.

Even in—or perhaps especially in—the baggy athletic clothing she wore, it seemed to disguise that sexual brilliance. Yet he could remember almost nothing of her except that. Which was merely proof—Soraya would likely say—that he needed to get a life.

He lay there thinking of her, but that just gave him an erection, which just made his need to pee worse, so he got up and went to the bathroom. He looked at himself in the mirror. He had not had a haircut in perhaps two or three months; he had several days growth of beard. He said to his reflection: *You're a cat lady. You're getting to be a cat lady.*

He took a shower, and in the white noise of water, he wondered if the thing that the machine did was some sort of desperate hallucination. He wondered if any of what he remembered was real. Now, as he shaved, what he really wanted was to get back to the lab.

He went downstairs. The house was empty. Jake had roomed with him for a while, and he thought he ought to get another roommate, but he never seemed to get around to it. He liked having the place to himself, even if he wasn't here most of the time.

He had a bowl of Lucky Charms, because that was the only thing in the house. And the milk was, surprisingly, not sour. Then he called Soraya at her office. Her research assistant (whom she merited because she had an MD) got her, and when she came on, he said, Hey.

She said: You awake?

Not sure. I had a nightmare that I forgot where my office was, and then when I remembered, it was gone.

I've had those.

What time is it? How long was I asleep?

When did you wake up?

An hour or so ago.

I'd say a day and a half. It's Tuesday.

Wow, he said, but there was no surprise in his voice. Is it morning or afternoon?

Morning.

You said you'd buy me breakfast.

I will. You want me to pick you up or do you want to meet me somewhere. No, wait a minute. Your car is probably still at the lab. I'll come get you.

Good, he said.

When he hung up, he put his head in his hands and rubbed his face. There was a part of him that hated the necessity to sleep, the necessity to eat, the whole rigmarole of being animal. For Michael, this was the ugliness of being human—you could think godlike thoughts, but you still had to acknowledge your own death, you still had to pack yourself full of food and then excrete its depleted remains. You still needed to sleep, you still needed to mate, and you needed not to be lonely. As an animal, you needed so much upkeep, so much crap that got in the way of getting things done. What he wanted was just to work, to be a brain without all the fetters. He liked a good meal and a glass of wine as much as anyone. He liked to get laid as much as anyone. But he found it almost completely astonishing that people spent so much time conceptualizing and fetishizing food and drink and sex.

When he had gone to sleep, he had done so with a sense of having accomplished something, even if he wasn't sure what it was. At least it worked. At last. This morning he understood that in his exhaustion and desperation he had taken a wrong turn, had screwed something up. Who knew how many more hours in the lab it would take before he could figure out where he had gone wrong, where his lovingly designed interface, his 3-D tactile portal, had gone.

Sure, the beach stuff was cool, and the physics were impeccable, but it was useless. This whole thing was to be about productivity, about finding a way to dissolve the human-computer barrier. The last time he was in the lab, at least for a few minutes, he'd landed in a blue sphere, and touched a folder that had sprung open to pour out its contents. He had touched a document and started to make notes on it just by thinking—and he had done it all without moving anything, without a mouse or a keyboard.

That, that right there, that was proof of concept. That—if he had been able to demonstrate it (which he would have to in order to be able to defend his dissertation)—would have been enough for his elusive doctorate. But then the crash, after which he had obviously done something wrong.

He got up and found his home laptop and woke it, then sat at the sticky kitchen table and checked his email. He hadn't been online for days—in the lab, he was never online; too many distractions—and when he opened mail, there were too many to look at. He scrolled though to make sure there was nothing important he was missing. And there it was, the one he was expecting and dreading. He clicked on it: Dr. Sprague, his advisor, ever cheerful, wanted to see him at his earliest for a status update. He deleted it, then undeleted it, then closed the computer and got up, put his jacket on and went out onto the porch. It was sunny but cold. Soraya was nowhere in sight, and so he went back inside and got his portable CD player and put on *OK Computer*. He clicked through the songs and found 'No Surprises.' The song played like a tinkling music box dirge, which was perhaps how it was intended.

There was an old couch on the porch, musty and cold, and he sat on it, put his feet up on the rail, closed his eyes.

He had been through this before: building something so beautiful and perfect that you had to have been in total awe to behold it, but then there was a glitch, a bug, a crash, and no backup, and it was gone, the electrons evaporated like a life snuffed out. This time there was a backup of a sort. But what good was it? His perfect dome of effectiveness and productivity had been punctured by something that looked like a fucking beach vacation.

He opened his eyes when Soraya honked.

He took the CD out and put the player back in the house, locked it, then shambled to the car. Soraya looked gorgeous, as always, and he realized that he hadn't held anyone for what seemed a lifetime. For Michael, this was as much an annoyance as it was anything.

Hey, she said before putting the car in gear. Where's the joy boy from Sunday?

He held up the CD and said, Can I put this on?

What is it?

Radiohead.

He pressed the eject button on her dash to make sure that she didn't have a disk in it, then put the CD in. He skipped forward to 'No Surprises.'

The music played a little and she said, Well, this is fucking cheery. What's with you? The last time I saw you, you were over the moon, at least in the ragged-street-person sense of the phrase.

I'm fucked, Soraya. I have to brief Sprague soon. I don't know what I'm going to do.

Let's get some food in you, she said.

I ate *something*.

What?

Ucky Charms.

So why am I taking you to breakfast?

That's not food. And I didn't say I wasn't hungry.

Why do you eat that crap?

Because it's magically delicious.

Where do you want to go?

The Hamburg.

The music played while Soraya navigated.

At the Hamburg, they found a booth against the wall. It was late morning—early enough that there was no lunch crowd and late enough that there wasn't any breakfast crowd. The menu was vaguely greasy and Michael paged through it without seeing anything. There was the beach. There was the way the girl who was running—the woman—the way when her feet hit the ground as she stopped, they tossed up little shimmering coronas of sand. At least in his memory.

So what are you going to have? she said.

Southwestern omelet. You?

Eggs.

The waiter, who had been a student of Michael's but appeared not to remember him—or to not want to remember him—took their order and there was silence. He felt like he had fallen into this world from another parallel universe, suddenly come into real, flesh-and-blood being from some dry mathematical simulacrum. He wished he could have explained this to her.

So what's with the glum mood? You're finally rested, you've had at least some success with the interface....

He cut her off. It's fucked. Somehow I fucked it up.

I love how positive you can be.

Shut up. I was working, and a couple of times, I had it. I could see it exactly the way I designed it, and then it crashed. It crashed.

Things crash. There are always bugs.

Except when I debugged it, then rebooted into it, it was like, I don't know. Everything I had done was *gone*. It was a whole other thing entirely. It was something, but it wasn't *it*. It was like someone else's work.

So you go back, you tweak. You tweak some more. You've been tweaking forever. It'll work.

He rolled his eyes. No, no. No. You don't get it. It was something completely different. Somehow something else was there in place of my work, and it was good. It was *really* fucking good. (He growled the word 'really.') I have no idea what happened, but it was not what I wanted to happen.

There was silence for a long time. Michael, one of the most charming, driven men she had ever met, looked like he was at the end of his rope. But she didn't mention it. She wasn't sure what she would or could say.

The food came quickly and Soraya buttered her toast. There was a kind of perfection to the restaurant toast—the bread perfectly machine-browned, the butter melting and the knife's edge scraping across its surface.

Michael said: Can you stop that?

Stop what?

That. The scraping. It's driving me nuts. (Soraya made a mental note to wonder about situational perception.)

He watched as her hand reached out across the table and rested on his. He was aware that she was looking at him, studying him, but he did not look at her because he didn't want to know whether it was as a friend or as a concerned healthcare professional. He wanted to jerk his hand away but felt powerless.

Michael, she said, and she wished she could hide the pleading tone of her voice. Don't say it.

Don't say what?

Whatever it is you're going to say with that toast-scraping tone of voice.

Suddenly she was angry. You know, fuck you, she said, just a little above a whisper. I love you, Michael, and I admire you, but this is the reason I left you.

What? He nearly spat the word.

You get so fucking absorbed with this stuff that you just disappear. She gave a little wave. Hello in there. Hello? You *need* to get a life.

That's original, Michael said glumly, and stabbed his omelet, then stopped, poured ketchup and Tabasco sauce on it.

Okay, listen.

She hadn't touched her eggs. Listen, she said. You need to add some life to your work. Get some....

No, listen. The funding is essentially gone. My grants are gone. I have—oh fuck. Oh fuck. I have an appointment with Dr. Sprague and I have to report progress....

So report progress.

And I have to report progress. I have to. Soraya. I can defend my thesis this summer or wait until the fall. If I have to wait until the fall. Fuck.

He groaned the last word, stretching the syllable out to an almost unbearable length.

She wasn't hungry but started to eat anyway, just to give the conversation some breathing room. At last, she said, Ten years from now, Michael, you'll look back on this and laugh.

No. I fucking won't. I will look back on this as the worst fucking period of my life.

Michael, darling, it'll work. Just give yourself a break. Breathe, darling. Give yourself a chance to breathe.

She watched him eat his food. At least he was hungry. More likely, starved. She wanted to say something more, but she couldn't think of anything.

It seemed like forever before he spoke again. Soraya, he said, his voice a whisper. Why did you break up with me?

Because it didn't work. I've told you that.

But why didn't it work?

Because it was always about you, Michael, about you and your work—

It's *your* work too.

You don't need to be defensive. It's just that that's not all there is to life.

I never said it was.

She laughed. You never had to.

Well, then, what?

It was always all about you, Michael. Mind you, I think you're the most brilliant man I've met. But that isn't enough. A girl sometimes wants it to be about her.

Just sometimes? he said and laughed weakly.

Well, maybe more often than sometimes.

His plate was empty, which was good because he almost dropped his face into it.

I can't help if it's just for me. I can't help that I do what I do.

And that's what I love about you. But I can't be *in* love with you, Michael. I couldn't. It's too hard.

Oh, he said, I'm a fucking basket case. What am I going to tell Sprague?

Start with the truth.

THE MIRACLE OF THE MOBILE PHONE

Ellen was halfway to the car when she became aware of the man, and almost upon it when it became clear that he was following her. This was in the studio parking lot, late afternoon. There should have been people, security, but it was as if everyone had vanished. She had glanced at him—he was an ordinary-looking man, middle-aged, perhaps, but unremarkable, and so she did not think twice until he had closed the distance between them—long, silent, unhurried strides—and suddenly he was next to her, a strong smell of fast food hamburgers on his breath, and he was looking down on her, and everything was suddenly shadow, except it was vivid, too, the rumpled gray work jacket with food stains, his translucent, colorless eyes, the blackness of the pistol—all incredibly vivid, even though it, and he, seemed to block out the sunlight completely. He gestured toward her car with the gun, but did it in a way such that only the two of them could see the gun.

Give me your keys, he said. He was bigger than he had looked from a distance—close to a foot taller than she, and had grayish translucent stubble on his chin, with a pasty, flushed complexion, as if he had lived in the dark for years.

Go to the other side, he said.

Even though she had seen something like a hundred pictures of Wayne Townsend, he was so unremarkable that she did not recognize him until he peered down at her, the hand with the gun steady, the other hand beckoning for the keys. At first the letters had seemed innocuous, the product of loneliness, and the fallacy of confusing the character with the actor. Not terribly different from those of a hundred other lonely souls except that his had an odd, creepy poetry to them. And, oddest part of all, his fixation wasn't apparently or overtly romantic. When the letters started to turn weird and dark, Marty had hired a private investigator to look into their author. He had tracked Townsend down in a small semi-rural Pennsylvania town—he was single and lived alone, no pets, a military veteran on unspecified medical disability. No significant community ties. No family.

Once Townsend had the keys, he escorted her briskly to the passenger side of the car, opened the door and ushered her in. As soon as the door was shut, he clicked the automatic door locks and went briskly around to the driver's side. Her heart raced, but she did not panic. Not yet. She dug into her purse and found her phone, then pressed a sequence of keys that would—should—speed-dial Marty. By the time Townsend had climbed in, her hand was back in her lap.

He was such a completely unremarkable looking person, completely bland, standard, off the shelf, that she would've had to do more than glance at him to recognize him.

She had no idea how he got in the studio lot—perhaps it was just this almost invisibly ordinary look.

Why are you doing this? she said, almost shouting. Why are you kidnapping me?

She wanted Marty to hear this, she wanted them to use the phone to find her, rescue her.

He said nothing, but started the car. When the radio came on, he turned it off. He laid the gun on his lap and backed her Acura out of her parking space, then drove with his right hand while the left held the gun on his lap, the barrel pointed in her direction. They drove off the lot, through the gate, all the time he was holding the gun in one hand.

He pulled out onto West Alameda.

Where are we going? she said, fear rising.

Again he said nothing.

I know who you are, she said, But why don't you tell me?

He stopped at the light at West Olive. Instead of going toward the freeway, he headed the opposite direction.

Who *are you*? he said.

It was probably only seconds, but it seemed like forever that he had stayed silent. Her head felt noisy, her mind racing. This was the man who was going to kill her. You never think something is going to happen and then it does happen. She looked at him—really looked at him. He had wire-rimmed glasses, smudged. His hair was graying, thinning. He had skinny legs but his torso was thick, his midsection soft looking and pudgy. Still, she had no doubt that he was vastly more powerful than she.

She tried to think about the letters. What had he said? The Secret Society. That she was an Enemy of God, an Instrument of something she had no idea she was a part of. An Industry of Hell.

For a moment she had the crystalline realization that she was not a person to him, she was a caricature of a character who played a character on TV, but filtered through tawdry gossip and innuendo. She was some sort of electronic extrusion, and so killing her would make no difference, the magnetic particles of her soulless being would be erased.

She tried to think of something to say to him that would make him speak. Her head was doing a strange Rolodex kind of thing, ideas, strategy, little flashes of memory, dreamlike in their clarity, but incredibly fast.

I do think, she said, her voice loud, edging toward hysteria, That when you point a gun at someone, when you steal their car and kidnap them, I really think you owe them some kind of explanation.

There was a lock release button on her side of the car, and she glanced at it, thought about hitting it, tumbling out of the car.

He turned onto a residential street and stopped the car.

Get out of my car! Her own scream surprised her.

He put the gun inside his jacket and swung his right arm, backhand, and struck her across the face. It was a powerful blow that snapped her head back into the headrest, stunned her. Some part of his wrist had hit her mouth and there was a strange taste now, and her lips burned.

In New York she had been mugged at least three times. But the person just wanted money. What were you supposed to do when the thing was something you couldn't just hand over?

When he spoke, it was in a weird, calm voice, the kind of voice you maybe heard in a classroom. He said: Let's start all over again, shall we? My name is Wayne Townsend.

She could say nothing. She rubbed the place on her mouth where he had struck her, and there was a kind of ghastly simplicity to it, a larger creature batting down a smaller one.

You find this perplexing, and I have some appreciation for your confusion.

She gaped.

Did you read my letters?

Yes.

Then you understand that we are each instruments of our own allegiances.

I didn't say I understood your letters.

She stared out at the houses along the street. Again, everything was empty, as if they were on the set of the movie about a post-apocalyptic world.

A forensic psychologist who had read his letters and the private investigator's report commented that the invention of a secret society was an enabler of 'moral displacement.' If he can convince himself, the psychologist said, that he is working for some larger cause that has power over him, like an army, a religion, or a secret society with rules and norms that supersede his own moral authority, then he can displace any sense of moral responsibility he may have. That would enable him to do something that he himself might consider evil or immoral. He can shift moral responsibility to the secret society.

At the moment, these were not exactly comforting words.

The psychologist said that Townsend may feel that his disability—whatever it was— had emasculated him; the pretense of the secret society also gave him power where he was otherwise powerless.

She said to Townsend: Would you mind telling me why you're doing this? As she said this, she looked at the dashboard clock. No more than six minutes had passed.

She said: I have a right to know.

He slid the gun out of his jacket again and held it in his hand.

What you fail to understand, Miss Gregory, he said, his voice actually an oddly high, taut, tenor, Is the part you play in the larger social dynamic. The mothers milk of your industry is debasement.

I'm an entertainer, she said. She prayed that her cell phone was on, that someone was coming.

Entertainment is a fascinating concept, Miss Gregory, he said, and seemed to muse a moment. But, he said, you fail to see the larger picture. You may have the notion that your forward motion, the successes of your excesses, are your own doing. But they are not. They are your undoing. Just as I am an instrument, so are you. I am aware of my place in the scheme of the inevitable dream real. You are unaware. For either of us, we are just rolling against the shape of time. No matter how much we will, no matter how much we want, no matter how much we may believe that we control our lives, we are like pebbles in the surf of time. I see this. You do not. You do not.

I do, she said, surprising herself. I feel that way all the time. He was not amused.

The car was still running, and with his free hand, he adjusted his glasses, looked straight ahead. He did not seem nervous.

It was better to be angry than scared and so she said: Then since I'm so completely clueless about my place in all of this, can you please teach me up a little bit, Mr. Townsend? Can you do that for me? And maybe skip the bad poetry?

All right, Miss Gregory. Let me spell it out for you. You teach young girls what it is not okay to teach them. You teach them to be obscene. You tell them that obscenity can be good and pretty and funny and this is the wrong thing to teach them. And you teach them these things not because you want to teach them these things, but because you are an instrument. You don't even know what you're doing. *That* you're doing.

His face had reddened as he spoke, and he moved the gun, laid it on his lap. You are who you are because it was a mathematical uncertainty in this string of time.

It made no fucking sense whatsoever, but suddenly they were surrounded. Everywhere were black-suited, helmeted police who looked like storm troopers, and without thinking she hit the unlock button and fell out of the car and immediately she was pulled away, while others slammed back the driver's side door and jerked him roughly from the car, and he flopped out, surrounded by helmeted men in black, and they slammed him to the pavement, helpless as a big fish, his hands in the air, rapidly handcuffed behind his back.

And Marty was there, and it was okay.

She looked at Townsend; she couldn't help it. He gazed at her, his gaze steady and weirdly neutral.

God, you were fucking spectacular, Marty said.

When they had put him in the police cruiser, she crouched on the sidewalk and vomited.

KIDNAPPER OF "GIRLFRIENDS" STAR GREGORY VANISHES FROM CUSTODY

Police at a Loss to Explain Escape
Associated Press

BURBANK, Calif., APRIL 19 – The man police suspect of kidnapping comedy star Ellen Gregory, of television's *Girlfriends*, disappeared from police custody today.

The bizarre incident began early yesterday afternoon, when police allege that Wayne Townsend held comedian and actress Gregory prisoner in her own car at gunpoint. Police spokesman Mark Shaver said.,"We're as baffled as we can be."

As Gregory made to leave her studio for an appointment, Townsend accosted her at gunpoint and forced her into the passenger seat of her car.

Gregory's agent, Marty Klein, said he was furious over what he called "police mishandling" of the prisoner, and said it was Gregory's own quick thinking that led to the arrest in the first place. "Somehow she called me on her cell phone without him knowing," Klein said. "I could hear the entire incident."

Police found the vehicle with Gregory and Townsend in it. As Gregory tumbled out of the car, a special police team captured Townsend and subdued him.

"That part of it was great police work," Klein said. "And then somehow, they just [expletive] lose him? It's just [expletive] idiotic."

At some point during police transport of Townsend he slipped away.

Police spokesman Mark Shaver said that so far, the police have no explanation for the disappearance, but they are investigating. He added that police have stepped up their protection of Gregory, but declined to elaborate on how they were protecting her.

According to Klein, Townsend has been stalking Gregory for more than a year, beginning with

a string of bizarre letters received over the last 14
months.

"Here is a guy who's a complete nutcase, is on
record as wanting to kill Ellen Gregory," the exasperated Klein said, "He kidnaps her at gunpoint,
threatens to kill her, and now he's out there wandering around."

Townsend, a disabled Vietnam veteran, should
be considered armed and dangerous, police said.

RAINY DAY IN LA

It was one of those rainy late-winter, early-spring LA days when you worry about mudslides, about apocalyptic fires in the summer. Ellen had spent the morning working out, swimming at the gym, then doing weights. A steady drizzle had started while she was in the gym, and when she left, it was dreary and chilly and she kept her wipers on interval because she hated the squeak they made on only-slightly-wet glass. Then, on Wilshire, sitting at a traffic light, the rain suddenly the kind of downpour where you can hardly see for more than a second each time the wiper crosses in front of your eyes, she saw him standing across the street.

Wayne Townsend.

No doubt about it, and the certainty just froze her. She remembered him sitting in the very seat she sat in now, and the thought glued her there. He was like a nightmare image that just floated out of your subconscious.

He was even more ordinary looking at a distance than close up. And there he stood in the rain, and each time the wiper sluiced across the windshield, there was an almost photographically clear picture of him just standing there, that colorless jacket, wet now, his hair plastered to him. He gave a vague smile when they made eye contact.

Someone honked behind her and she pulled away from the light—now green— and hurried to meet Marty for lunch. She used the valet and hurried inside.

You look like you've seen a ghost, Marty said as she sat down and pulled her hair out of her face.

Worse, she said. Wayne Townsend.

Marty got his puffed up, Mighty-Mouse look and pulled out his phone. I can't believe those fuckers, he said, fingering the keypad of his phone. Now, into the phone, he said, Detective Anderson, please—hello? Detective Anderson, this is Marty Klein, Ellen Gregory's manager....

She watched him as he talked. She loved Marty. He had, since she left home, been the closest thing to family she had, someone she could come to and count on no matter what. When she met him in New York, he was a bartender at a club where she

69

was trying to get work. He was six or seven years older and seemed like a man of the world. Even though she was underage, he gave her a beer after he was off, and they sat together in the empty bar and he gave her pointers on the owner. She didn't much care for beer, but sipped it, and when he said, Well, show me some of your stuff, she shot out of the chair and started into one of her earliest bits. Called 'Five Hundred Dollar Car,' it was about her trip east from Iowa in a demonically possessed Subaru that she'd bought for five hundred bucks with babysitting money, and it was full of asides, like, *I had this idea that I would baby-sit my way across country. It was not a good plan.* But, *Want to know how to really freak people out? Just, like, pick a random house, go knock on the door and say, Hi, I'm the babysitter. I have tried this.*

She was a couple of weeks shy of her 18th birthday, but looked more like a 14-year-old when she made her way east. Sure, there were the total pervs who tried to take advantage of her, but more often the guys she met—and they were legion in comedy—felt some sort of protective thing. Marty had swooped in first, and she shed the nickname Runt for Marty's Jailbait, which—now and then—he still called her.

Marty laughed and then proceeded to tear the whole thing apart and tell her what not to do, told her how to streamline it. So much of it is about confidence. Confidence and precision. You can do the same bit the same way in front of the same audience, but if you don't come out with the attitude that you own the space, he said, You're dead. You're fucked. Good comics, he said, get into a rhythm with an audience. It's almost mystical, really. You learn how to read an audience, you learn watching other people, and you learn by doing your own stuff. And it's really really fast. You get about two seconds to establish yourself because an audience can smell fear like a pack of dogs.

He talked fast in a lancing, acerbic New York sort of way, and he was funny and charming. He told her later that he was just winging it himself—he saw something in her that he liked, that he believed in—but in truth, he didn't know any more about comedy than she did. But he actually had a good feel for it. It was her energy. And that was the thing. The energy, he said. Some people had it and some didn't.

He was tending bar at night and during the daytime, he worked at a huge Manhattan talent agency as an underpaid assistant while he tried to get his own clientele together. He had a fourth floor walk-up in the Village with very little but a futon on the floor, a TV and a VCR. He told her to take acting classes, elocution classes, and she did theatre, small productions. Learned how to be in front of people. Learned confidence. Marty was small and frumpy and pushy and endlessly charming. You could have put a wig on him and he would have looked like somebody's grandmother. He liked to say he looked like Bob Dylan, which was sort of true if you really stretched it. She became his third client—the first two eventually gave up and disappeared into the mists.

Marty clicked off his phone, and slipped it back into his pocket and reached across the table and put a hand on hers. Okay, he said, Anderson is sending an unmarked car by and we'll see if we can't get this creep. I bet they've got him before we finish lunch.

If Marty's head had had a crest, it would have been standing straight up.

She said: He was just standing there.

This is good, he said, rubbing his hands together, They'll get him.

She could not get Townsend out of her head. He's probably evaporated again. I don't see how a guy can be so invisible.

BLUE SPHERE

Soraya came to Michael's office with him after breakfast. It was early afternoon and no one else was there. He sighed deeply as he sat down in his chair and unpacked the headset. Soraya had helped design the thing, both the visual part and the sensor-stimulator part. The visor, as she called it (everyone else said headset) scanned your retina and eye movements, including the minimal movements of your eyelids. It scanned for slight vascular changes and fed those data back into the computer to tell it where you were looking, what you were focusing on, and how you were reacting to what you were looking at. Simultaneously, there were special sensors that picked up localized brainwaves and brain activity that were task- and mood-related.

One of the things that Soraya had brought to the project was the notion that the old saying of the eye being the window on the human soul was only half right. As it turned out—she maintained—the retina was also a pretty good window on the body's general status, and therefore the brain. So you not only used it to download images as directly as possible to the brain, but you could use it simultaneously to monitor how the brain was reacting to the images. And then the code triangulated between the activity of the eyes and the brain to determine the user's intent.

The Black Box used low-powered diffused lasers to project a stream of images right onto your retina, which gave you a quality of resolution necessary for virtual reality applications, but which you could not get with any sort of standard retina-painting display. But the lasers also worked a bit like barcode scanners, keeping a constant read on the vasculature of the eye, the orientation of the eye—how it was orbiting, where it was looking and how you were reacting.

The visor display worked like a movie theater with your retinae themselves as the screen, so the image was easier and faster for your brain to process.

Where Soraya's work really came into play was in the sensor-stimulators. Her own dissertation work was in functional neurology. She was a sort of geographer of the functionality of the brain. But it wasn't just about vision being here and sound being there, it was much deeper than that. It was about how the various areas of the brain worked together in particular kinds of tasks, and how different brains handled the same sorts of tasks or thoughts. And it was the thought part that was interesting—how the brain created a sort of narrative of its activities—a neurological narrative—that you could read. And if you could read the narrative, then you could also write the narrative.

You could use a magnetic resonance imaging setup—those big, scary, loud magnetic tubes used to analyze certain kinds of injuries—to do a functional MRI, or fMRI, which you did by giving your subject a task to do while you imaged the parts of the brain stimulated by the task. (There were other functional mapping tools coming online, too.) You could show a person a porn movie, for example, and certain parts of a man's brain would light up in particular ways, and certain parts of a woman's brain would light up in particular ways. You did this with a lot of different subjects and then analyzed and skewed the results. You set up a million different kinds of tasks and did this with as many subjects as you could find, and you got a pretty good idea of which parts of the brain were stimulated and how by different activities—taste, smell, reading, writing, sex, sports, anger, bliss—you name it, you could assign a particular area of the brain to that sort of stimulation. And you used other kinds of imaging techniques to triangulate the kind of stimulation that was happening, what kind of neural activity, what kind of brainwaves.

It was her idea that through light and sound, you could modulate brainwaves and get pretty exciting results, if you knew what to stimulate. The code was designed to leverage this.

She had spent so much time in the MRI room that Michael joked that she gave off a magnetic glow.

This was the thing that Michael had been looking for when he put up the ad and found Soraya. He had had a vague idea of creating a way to stimulate the brain in particular task- or work-related areas, but he had no idea how to do it. At least until he met Soraya.

Her idea was through all this brain mapping, you could start to artificially stimulate the brain to provoke a certain kind of mental task state. And then you could write the neurological narrative of the task pretty much by reversing it all so that in a VR interface, you could make accomplishing a task exponentially faster. And the interface he designed was elegant—the way a typical computer interface was a desktop, his 3-D VR interface was not an office in any conventional sense (just as a desktop was not). It was a blue sphere that you could walk around in. Blue was an arbitrary choice on his part.

Soraya sat down in an office chair and Michael looked at her. It seemed astounding to him that they had once been lovers. They were great as business partners, assuming that there would one day be a product to go into business with. Whatever romantic thing there had been was completely gone. They were friends now, and the thing about Soraya was that she believed in him. That much he knew. And it was one of the things that kept him going.

He put on the headset, but before his eyes were obscured, he looked at her and said, You might want to observe what I'm doing while this is happening, just to see.

As if I wouldn't, she said, and smiled warmly. The smile depressed him: it was clinical; she was humoring him.

Michael finished putting on the headset and sat back and found the boot switch by touch.

The same thing that had happened on Sunday happened again, the vague sense of motion sickness with the color shock, and then there was cold winter sunlight and there were snow and trees and ice. He was on ice, on ice skates, and he knew this place and did not want to be here, but since he was—and knew, simultaneously, that he was not—he went with it.

This was the day he almost drowned, more than 20 years ago. The day he fell through the ice.

ELLEN GREGORY UN-PLUGGED

Entertainment Now!, March, 2001

"America's favorite girl next door" talks with Entertainment Now! *about life, comedy, and the stunning kidnapping that almost took her life.*

The first thing you notice about Ellen Gregory when you meet her in person is how little she resembles the ditzy, conniving, clumsy character she plays on her hit sitcom, *Girlfriends*. Neither does she bear much resemblance to the character—or characters—she impersonates in her stand-up routines. Yes, she is the same fetchingly pretty, shapely, intensely focused young blond. She really does have that ineffable "girl next door" quality. It should also be said that she has two laughs, one that she does on stage, that conspiratorial *he, he* giggle, and her own raucous, delicious at-home laugh. The latter has a clear, bell-like peal, and reinforces her overall sense of warmth and loveliness. But at home, greeting you in khakis and a pressed, white blouse and bare feet, repeatedly offering you a drink or a snack, she comes across more as an eager-to-please, slightly nervous, young Midwestern professional, than as a long-time New York (and occasionally profoundly foul-mouthed) stand-up comic and hot, sought-after actress.

We had scheduled her interview a few weeks before her brief but harrowing kidnapping, and she met with us at home just a little more than a week after it happened. At her request, we will not describe any of the security precautions she is taking. Except she did show us a recently acquired handgun, which she clearly has been trained to use. She also made clear that she did not want to focus on the kidnapping, but on her comedy.

ENow!: David Letterman dubbed you "America's Favorite Girl Next Door." Is that the way you see yourself?

EG: I think actually that Dave was being ironic when he said that. And I might argue that he "dubbed" me. It was on one of my earlier appearances, and I had just finished my set, and we were joking around during the commercial break. Dave said something sort of snarky about Dr. Phil that I don't even remember, and I said something kind of blue about his anatomy, Dr. Phil's, and Dave sort of looked shocked. The funny thing is that he really is this kind of shockable Midwestern boy. That isn't just an act. I said, It's my peach blossom ass and girl-next-door looks that let me get away with that kind of crap, and I said this while he was getting the countdown to air, and so when he got the nod, Dave said something like, We're back with our guest, Ellen Gregory, a very funny comic, and frankly, America's favorite girl next door. It was a gibe. It made me laugh. And it stuck.

ENow!: Though it would seem that it stuck because, ironic or no, it has some core element of truth to it.

EG: If that's true, then I would suggest to everyone that they get up right now and go next door and ask for the girl, and see if she looks or acts anything like me. I think it's probably like this entirely American idea. And it probably comes from the movies. I don't see that, I mean that isn't my own narrative. Maybe there's some kind of meta truth to it, but that would be too intellectual for me.

ENow!: So it's nothing that…

EG: [interrupts] One of the most interesting things about life, it seems to me, is that some of the best ideas are mistakes. Or at least mine are. A lot of the best jokes I've come up with happen because I mis-hear what someone says. Or I could. Dave was just riffing, and out it came. I'm not saying this is Dave, but think about malapropisms, you know? Think about all of the mistakes that have been made in science that led to great inventions. The different ways that people read the same string of words. Or hear.

ENow!: Hard to explain comedy.

EG: I'll say.

ENow!: The signature in your stand-up act, and one of the things that drew huge attention to you early on, was your tutu. That was a very provocative statement. What made you decide on the tutu?

EG: It was cute.

ENow!: You're kidding.

EG: I'm a professional. You're in good hands. It *was* cute.

ENow!: But there was more to it.

EG: There always is more to it. Isn't there? At least that's what my therapist keeps telling me. [Laughs.] This was in the early nineties, and there was a whole lot of stuff going on in the comedy scene in New York. You had the success of *Seinfeld* and Paul Reiser had his show and I think a lot of people thought that, Hey, if I do stand-up, I'll get a sitcom. Which is kind of like the brass ring of stand-up—that or a long-term gig on *Saturday Night Live*. Which, pardon me if I slam on the brakes and veer over to the shoulder [she actually mimes this perfectly, complete with sound effects that would make a 10-year-old boy proud] because stand-up is a very strange art. A lot of people I know from those days are completely unknown outside the world of comedy. A lot of them gave up. The ones who hung on and kept with it are now writers on sitcoms and comedy shows. But the thing is, I could probably drop a dozen names, people who are incredible, stellar, side-splittingly funny comics, and you, the average American, would never have heard of them. Why? I don't know. Because comedy is a strange art, is the only answer I have. You have a sort of underground economy of comedy, and those people who are part of that economy would know exactly who I was talking about. But whoever heard of Seinfeld before his show? You know? So I'm not sure that it's the prime aspiration of comics to be on sitcoms, but it's one of the few ways you have to increase your audience. And make a living. I mean, I did an HBO special that became my second CD, and no one recognized me on the street. I did the pilot of *Girlfriends*, and I couldn't walk down the street anymore. So they're kind of like two different economies, two different worlds. Sometimes they intersect, but most of the time they don't.

ENow!: Back to the tutu?

EG: You are savage, merciless [giggles]. The tutu. Someday it will be the first thong in the Smithsonian. [Giggles again.] That will be the highlight of my career. Right next to Archie Bunker's chair, you know?

ENow!: The tutu—do you see that as a cultural artifact like Archie's chair?

EG: I wish I had the time to think about that sort of thing. I envy, like, professors and philosophers and people who are smart enough to sit around and unpack all this stuff. Cultural significance and everything. I'm just not that smart. And I don't have that much time.

ENow!: The tutu.

EG: The tutu. It was, actually a mistake. I was sitting back stage somewhere and I thought I heard someone say the words, G-string tutu. Seriously. So it was the early nineties, and backstage at the clubs on open-mic nights it was kind of like the subway at rush hour. It's a tough and weird business, and there were people who were *really* good. And the people who got called, the people who got noticed, were most often people who could be identified in, like, ten words or less, you know? That guy that screams like a banshee. The girl who looks like a weasel. You needed some way to stand out. I don't know where I got the idea, but I was a very desperate person, a very hungry and cold person, freezing like a kitten in a blizzard, and one

Millions of years of buttocks and the world was not ready for my magnificent peach blossom ass.

night I'm waiting to do five minutes at some crappy club in, like, Oklahoma or Arkansas, and I hear this, and I think, *That could work!*, and I just started sketching it, and I knew some theater people, and so when I got back to New York, I found someone who could sew, and spent, like, my whole bankroll having it made. It was a make-or-break moment. If I couldn't make it work, if I couldn't be funny and be "that chick in the tutu," then I pretty much felt like I was going to be dead. And when it was made, I just loved it. It was totally cute, but suddenly I was like Spiderman in his Spidey suit. I could finally use my secret powers. There was an unleashing of forces beyond human comprehension. [Giggles] It was empowering, somehow.

ENow!: Speaking of empowering, I've read different things about it—even a couple of scholarly pieces on its significance. The outfit itself—tutu, boots, fishnet stockings—as a sort of post-feminist statement. The frilly tutu and leotard as a signifier of innocence. The fishnet stockings and garters as a symbolic tease. The, um, thing—

EG: The G-string, thong thingie.

ENow!: The thong. The G-string back. Yes. That as an icon, so to speak, of sexual animality. Feminine embodiment. The boots a symbol of can-do certainty. What do you think about those kinds of interpretations?

EG: They might just be bullshit. [laughs] I don't really know.

ENow!: You can't be that much of a naïf.

EG: A what?

ENow!: Was the tutu a calculated statement?

EG: [Laughs hysterically, almost falling out of her chair.]

ENow!: I'll let you recover.

EG: You're very thoughtful. No, really. I never thought of it like that. I was looking for a signature, something that would say *Ellen!*, you know? I wasn't thinking about post-feminist symbolism or whatever.

ENow!: Was there a sexual element to it? Were you—?

EG: If I can butt in here, so to speak, and cut you off at the pass [giggles her signature giggle], and say yes. This was the early nineties, 1989, 1990, even. I was a kid. I was becoming aware of a lot of things. Female genital mutilation. I had heard about religions, lots of them, frankly, that made women dress so-called modestly because of the sinful thoughts they caused in men, and I thought, *Fuck* that. *Men* caused those thoughts in men. I mean, I felt at the time that I should be able to walk down the street naked if I wanted to, not that I did—I mean want to—but if men had indecent or sinful thoughts, then *I* was *not* responsible for that. My response was, Are gay men having these thoughts? Because if they aren't then don't bother me with your fucked up ideas about decency. Let the indecent assholes wear blind-

77

folds. Not to climb onto the high horse here [whinnies, which is actually very funny] I mean, I've been told that people have all kinds of sinful thoughts about me *anyway*, regardless of what I happen to be wearing, so I felt like, I don't know, the indecency was not *my* problem, it was *theirs*, you know? If there is any sort of feminist thing in my act, post or not, then it's that idea. Women get all this male shit shoveled onto them, and then we—because I'm no different—just, like, take it. The tutu was just a way of, like, legitimately, sticking my ass in the face of all that.

ENow!: So there was a statement.

EG: I don't know if you'd call it a statement. I was, like, 19 or 20 or something. Twenty-one, maybe. Can you make any kind of real, true statement when you're that age? I had *no idea* what I was doing, at least consciously. I have no idea what I was thinking at the time. If you could see into my subconscious, which thank God you can't, it'd probably look like some dank cauldron of weird snakes and horrors, and I have no desire to unpack any of that.

ENow!: But you never wore it on Letterman.

EG: No.

ENow!: Why?

EG: The network wouldn't let me, without revising it. They were happy to pay for it. They just didn't think America was ready for my ass. Millions of years of buttocks and the world was not ready for my magnificent peach blossom ass. Imagine that. Seriously, though, Dave and I talked about it and decided that the best thing to do was just be funny. And I never did anything that I thought was gratuitously sexual, which in my view would have marginalized my act. I did the 'does this tutu make my ass look fat?' thing in clubs, but that was clubs. There were far weirder things happening in the bathrooms. And Dave is really a very shy guy, which is actually true of a lot of people in show business. I mean you saw how he reacted to Drew Barrymore, right? He would have died if I'd done, like, a *Basic Instinct* kind of thing on the show. But that's not my act. And let me emphasize act.

ENow!: You have a bit that you do about religion, about going to church. Are you against religion? Or do you go to church? How do you feel about religion?

EG: A joke is a joke is a joke. [giggles] I don't mean religion. That bit is not based on religion, actually. It's really about…, well, I'd prefer not to talk about *who* it's about. But let's just say that it's about cultural traps. We set up these, like, rules for how we're going to live, and then we don't like the rules and make up new ones to get around the old ones. It's not just religion.

ENow!: Are you evading the question?

EG: I don't think so. I found a way to get a laugh that almost killed people. Which I think is the only legitimate way to kill, by the way.

ENow!: Do you go to church?

EG: Sometimes. But I don't think of myself as part of any organized religion. I participate in religion. I just think that organized religion gets too political, and Christ himself said that's a no-no. So, you know, I read my Bible, and I watch Pat Robertson—just kidding. Do you know he has horns? Really. I've seen them. They're retractable. No. I never met Pat Robertson. I'm I guess what you would call an ambivalent Christian, which is to say that I'm not ambivalent about Christ. Let me tell you a story.

ENow!: Sure.

EG: I went through a period after *Girlfriends* went on the air when I did not go out. I just shut myself in my house and watched TV. And ran. I ran a lot. I had been working my butt off for what seemed like forever and then it was just, bang, you know? And so there I was, just completely freaked out, and then of course watching TV all day long can make you even weirder, so I did a lot of reading. I grew up in the Lutheran church—confirmation and the whole schmear—and as I was freaking out about my new celebrity, it came to me that I never really read the Bible. And I was really looking to get centered, you know? So I read the New Testament, and I kept thinking, *This is what I believe.* Whether you think of it as philosophy or religion or whatever. So there you have it. I'm an ambivalent Christian because I have no idea whether the Bible is the word of God. So.

ENow!: Can we talk about your personal life?

EG: No.

ENow!: You don't want to talk about it?

EG: I don't have one. I work. That's what I do.

ENow!: No men in your life? No relationships?

EG: I pick up good looking waiters and then toss them out like old tissue.

ENow!: I can't help but feel that you're evading this question.

EG: I do, actually. It's my revenge for bad service. Or my reward for good service. It puts an entirely different light on tipping. You tend to get really good service if the waiter has the idea that there might be something in it [winks] for him.

ENow!: You're evading.

EG: Yeah. This is kind of a painful subject, okay? But I really would like it if you got that story out there about the waiters. That'd be good. I will get the *best* service in town. I do keep a couple of great apes and a jar of Vaseline in the basement.

ENow!: Another topic: Can we talk about the incident with your stalker? The kidnapping?

EG: My stalker? I prefer to think of him as the mother and grandmother of all bad blind dates.

ENow!: You'd been receiving letters from this individual for quite some time. Your people were aware of him, but couldn't do anything.

EG: I didn't read any of the letters. A psychologist who examined them said they were kind of psychotically poetic, but that the essence of them was that this guy had created a secret society in his head to, what was the word?, *displace* his feelings. Like, I'm in the army, it's my job to kill people. So he could turn me into an object that he needed to eradicate.

ENow!: You're being very intellectual about what must have been a very emotional experience.

EG: [At this point, Gregory produced a semi-automatic pistol and pointed it at the interviewer. She did it remarkably fast, and her face went stone cold with an astounding and violent intensity] Call me an intellectual again, *asshole*, and I will fucking *splatter* your brains against the wall.

ENow!: [Stuttering sounds]

EG: [Almost as instantly, Gregory's face went back to normal, and she put the gun away.] So, was that emotional?

ENow!: It is, um, pretty startling to find yourself looking at the muzzle of a pistol.

EG: My thinking *exactly*. Can I get you a glass of water or something?

ENow!: That was a very strange moment.

EG: You didn't pee your pants.

ENow!: [laughs] You seem to be very aware of what you're doing—even if you claim not to have any sort of theoretical framework for it. Would you....

EG: [interrupts] What does that mean? Theoretical framework?

ENow!: You seem to be very, um, calculating in what you do. You seem to have a very considered opinion of the effect what you do will have on other people.

EG: That's what comedy is. I think Jerry Seinfeld put it really well when he said that what a comic does is kind of lead an audience over a cliff. You pretty much have to be calculating.

ENow!: Which brings me back to something that you said earlier about comedy being a strange art.

EG: Stand-up, is what I was talking about.

ENow!: Can you elaborate on that?

EG: If you think about it, it's one-person theater, and when it works well, it can be completely sublime, you know? I mean you think of some of Robin Williams's shows and Steve Martin's early albums [does a perfect Steve Martin] "rat feces are some of my favorite things," and sure, there's a calculation there. George Carlin. Bob Hope or Phyllis Diller standing there firing off jokes with incredible precision. With some comics, you can hear the clock tick, their timing is so good. I mean, at it's best, it's like jazz, a framework that allows some improvisation, which comes out even better than you could have imagined, And when it's bad, you cringe hideously with embarrassment.

ENow!: What's it like to bomb?

EG: You want to slit your wrists even more than usual.

ENow!: Was that a joke?

EG: What I mean is that you know it's on you. Really great bits are not just funny on their own. They're funny because you, the comic, make them funny. You know? And that's a weird interaction of you and your sense of an audience and your material and almost a gambler's sense of when to stay in a hand and when to get out of it. But in comedy, in stand-up, you can't just fold. Over the years you develop a bag of tricks. I'm kind of in the wacky, Robin Williams school of off-the-wall impersonation and improvisation. I can't do what he does—no one can; there is no one in the world who's in his class, or a classier person—but I'm not your sort of suave Steve Allen or Bob Hope type. If one of those guys ever did wacky, it'd be ghastly. Or if you had Bobcat Goldthwaite doing Steven Wright kind of aphoristic one-liners. Which I think is part of what I'm talking about. It's on you. Funny isn't just funny. You, the comic, have to make it funny.

ENow!: We haven't talked at all about *Girlfriends*. You are currently shooting the fourth season. The show is a great success. You've done a few movies.

EG: Small parts in small movies.

ENow!: But the show has broken you out. You're a star. What can you tell us about the show?

EG: Nothing without lawyers present. [*Giggles*.]

ENow!: There have been rumors, I should say persistent rumors, that you're unhappy with the show. That you've thought of leaving.

EG: I have a job. It's a very good job.

ENow!: That hardly sounds like a ringing endorsement.

EG: If you want me to disrespect my show, I won't. *Girlfriends* has been very good to me. I've made a lot of friends. It's got great writers and great people. But a sitcom is a sitcom. You know? And unless it's a show like *Seinfeld*, where he's actually playing a version of himself, the stand-up comedian, and gets to do stand-up, then I think any comic would tell you that the show reins her in, which can be a good thing. I mean, even a show that supposedly highlights what a comic does best can be really bad. Like *Mork and Mindy*. I mean, Jesus. But I will tell you this, after years of starving, of not having medical coverage and driving around the country in a beat up van, doing what Bill Hicks called the flying saucer tour of America, you know, landing in the weirdest, godforsaken parts of America, you are not going to bite the hand that feeds you.

GYPSUM DUST

The morning that Wayne Townsend broke into Ellen's house and tried to kill her was less than two weeks after the kidnapping. It was April now, and the editing on the sex-tape commercials was almost done; all the nude stuff was gone, although she didn't really care if something showed up somewhere. It wasn't as though it would be a bad career move.

She was alone in the house. It was the housekeeper's day off, and she was doing her normal routine, stoking on her second or third pot of coffee, looking for that just right blend of insanity that was caffeine and her personality. She was in the kitchen, a room she liked to joke about because its opulence was as remarkable as its lack of use (like lots of those within a 20 or so mile radius). (She was, actually, a super good cook, but did it only rarely these days.)

Everything was restaurant quality or better, from the mind-blowingly great cooktop with its burners that got as hot as the sun in three to five seconds to the super-energy-efficient refrigerator that no one who actually needed to save money on energy could actually afford, to the beyond razor-sharp set of Kershaw knives, to the rubber mats on the marble floor that prevented leg fatigue. All of this opulence for two or three bananas, some cottage cheese, a couple of cups of yogurt, some odd vegetables and two or three bottles of Italian sparkling water, a couple of bottles of white wine and not much else at all in the refrigerator.

Compared to some of my neighbors, I'm stocked like an army mess hall. Isn't America great?

She was—as an homage to Jerry Seinfeld—something of a cereal fanatic and had boxes and boxes of the stuff, most of which had never been opened.

The house she had bought in LA was a modernist masterpiece with a swimming pool and a pool house on an acre in a gated community. From every window you could see one or another gorgeous aspect of the gorgeous California landscape. There wasn't another house in sight, although there were plenty. Close to the house, there was a shaded, grassy area she called the grotto, a sliver on her parcel of land that was green and lush and cosseted from the rest of the area.

She also kept three smallish but expensive thin-panel screen televisions arrayed around the room so that she could watch all the morning shows, and then surf an assortment of popular programs. It was her experience that this combination of caffeine and inanity (Matt Lauer interviewing a celebrity about a book that the interviewer hadn't read and the 'author' obviously hadn't written) was fertile ground for comedy. But you had to be choosy. You had to be in the right caffeinated sort of state, just this side of hysteria, to be able to react to it, to get your freak on, so to speak, and really freak out over the utterly insane simulacrum of the world that was television.

She wrote in the morning and would keep her PowerBook on the table and talk to the mirror on the fridge, and watch television, looking for cultural nuggets she could turn into comedy. Sometimes it was easy, but other times you waited forever for something that was not going to be completely over by midnight. It went something like this—you saw something, and then you started riffing on it, and then, if the riff looked promising, you got up off your Thos. Moser stool and stood in front of the mirror and did the riffing again. This was to model it, to try it out on her most difficult audience. If it seemed to have some sort of integrity, then she drifted around the kitchen, talking it out, sometimes using a tape recorder, sometimes not, and finally sat down at her PowerBook and hammered it out and saved it for later. Nine times out of 10, it was garbage and she archived it. But that 10 percent of the time, there was good stuff. And that morning, sitting at the custom-made granite counter, drinking strong black coffee, she was trying to work on a bit about Timothy McVeigh, who struck her as a patently absurd character, a guy with this sort of classic boy-next-door look who was proud of murdering babies and mommies. But it was almost impossible to come up with anything funny on him.

He looks good in orange.

Nothing. A dry hole. It wasn't that death itself wasn't funny. There was comedy in death. That was easy, like, Isn't it romantic? My grandpa wanted to be buried with my grandma… so as long as she's buried alive.

What it was, was that she could remember the day when she'd heard about the explosion in Oklahoma City. She could remember the little walk-up apartment where she was living in the Village in New York. It wasn't long after someone had tried to bomb the World Trade Centers.

She got up to get another cup of coffee and she noticed movement in her yard. Movement in her yard—a high-walled perpetual garden with virtually nothing of the conventional yard except the grotto—and movement in her yard was not a normal thing. She had just poured the coffee, and in her peripheral vision she had seen something, and now, the cup of hot black $25-a-pound boutique coffee almost spilling on her hand, she went to the window next to the back door, next to the garage, and there was a man in coveralls. He saw her as instantly as she saw him and she recognized him as instantly.

Almost immediately after the kidnapping attempt, Marty hired a security firm to come into her house and 'harden' it. There were new windows and doors, there were new locks. There was a wireless phone hookup, there was backup power. And there were the panic buttons in the kitchen, in her bedroom, in her media room, in her bathroom, and in the 'hardened' closet in the guest room. There was so much stuff installed, it seemed like overkill. Marty ignored her while he talked with the security consultant, a skin-headed man with an impossibly narrow waist (compared to his impossibly broad shoulders) who moved—there was no other way to put it—like a dancing cat. Later, over lunch, while the guys were still working on her house, Marty extolled the virtues of this consultant. Former special ops commando. Bodyguard to heavyweight government VIPs and selected celebrities.

Townsend wore a ball cap, walked with a purposeful stride—not fast, not slow, but deliberate—and carried a (she was later informed) 34-inch Hillerich & Bradsby Louisville Slugger baseball bat. When he saw her, when he saw her see him, he did not change his stride, but lifted the bat and took a test swing, like a Dodger on deck, doing dry swings before he got up to the plate and did the real dirty work. All while staring at her.

An electric jolt of panic went through her. But it was followed almost immediately by a weird, almost out of body sense of calm.

She hurried to the phone and picked it up, but it was dead. She went to the door and bolted it, but as she backed away, the tip of the bat, the business end, smashed against the thick Plexiglas window. She watched, almost curiously, as it hit again and bounced with a thud. Next he smashed at the door, and though it looked like a beautiful quartersawn oak door, it was steel reinforced and as solid—the consultant had said—as a bank vault. Another hit, and then another. She was frozen, the unreality of the situation steeping in her bones. The bat hit the window again, then hit the door, and then it stopped. Now his face was in the window. He was sweating and when he saw her, he grinned.

ICE IN SUMMER

The cold whistled and the skates Michael had were new. His old ones were figure skates, which he had liked, but his father, concerned that he did not share his own interest in sports, that perhaps with all his reading and his dreamy disconnection with the masculine world, he needed a push toward manliness, had bought him hockey skates with a hard plastic toe and no teeth, hoping against hope that his son's love of skating would morph into a love of hockey—while of course having no idea that skating was the one sport Michael liked because it was a thing you could do alone. He had loved his old skates with the kind of passion that he could only muster for books, for formations of objects. He had been so excited to get the new skates for Christmas that he had ripped the box open—and there they were, this ugly pair of long skates. His father's hope had been electric and his disappointment (thinking, like a kid, that they would be just a new incarnation of the old ones) had pressed up behind his eyes and squeezed out tears, and then his father's face had gone to such uncertainty (*Is my son a girl?*) that he had hugged him, as if in love, so he could hide his disappointment from the man who mattered most. Perhaps his father would think he was crying for joy.

He could not recall, now, how it was he could have loved ice-skating so much.

It had been a relatively late-onset winter, and even though it was mid-January, it had the feel of November, the first ice, the first cold spell. No snow yet and the ice sweetly glassy slick, and his ears hurt and his throat hurt and there was a burning and he was not thinking at all about anything but the insult when he glided close to the edge of the lake, where the trees hung over and where in summer his father and Uncle Ben, who was nobody's uncle but 'Uncle Ben' because his last name was Rice, sat in Ben's boat and tried to catch fish. The skates weren't so bad, but you couldn't catch them on a reverse and jump.

In skating here, he had hoped that the denuded trees would offer shelter from the wind, which was wicked, but there was no shelter and everything was just gray, the sky and trees and their skeletal branches. When he hit the thin patch and heard the crack he did not realize how far he was from everyone else, how far he had traveled in not wanting to skate into the wind. The lake was enormous. Acres and acres and you could scarcely see the other side.

It was not like falling through a trap door but like the plates and dishes must feel when someone pulls the tablecloth out from under them, a slow thing, with clattering and breaking and he was sliding, going sideways now, a great lip of ice opening. He knew what everyone said about being caught in the water, the ice overhead—he was only 10 years old but he had dreamt of how you had to find the air bubbles that collected under the ice, how there wasn't much time because of hypo something and had dreamt it waking and shuddering with fear before, the cold, your lungs screaming for air while your hands froze and you shed your coat, your skates, trying to lighten yourself enough to get to the rough underbelly of ice, find the hole. There was a moment when his skates were in the water but not wet, but then a flood, and he was turning, going down, millimeter by millimeter, seeing the others, the whole skating party of Mother and Father and Jamey and the Sorensens (why were the minister's kids the nastiest kids in town?) and others he knew who had come in other cars, and the cold slammed into you, the pain of it worse than the blowing wind because the wind was merely annoying and this would maybe kill you in a horrible, lonely death. They said in the books that he read that, with drowning, once you breathed in the water, it was almost pleasurable, but how anyone knew—

And then his skates knifed the shallow, rocky bottom and there he was, chest deep in water, the cold hitting him like a baseball bat on a backswing, and the strike of his skates against the rocky bottom jerking him against the shelf of ice left at the hole, the implacable ice knocking the breath out of him so he could not even choke out a single breath, the rocky bottom jolting his ankles, his legs, the wind running along the ice like a slap shot and suddenly he screamed, a long, thin, hollow girl-sounding thing that did not come from him, but from someone else—Michael, the sound of his name become a song, become a thing long and drawn out and merged into a monosyllable of hysteria.

DAY OF DAYS

Smashing at the door with the baseball bat was all for show, evidently, because even as Ellen stood and gawked at the insane bastard outside, her feet glued to the same spot, came the sound of a key scratching in the lock, and the panic returned. She leapt over to the counter and reached under and hit the panic button that Marty's people had installed, grabbed her purse, and raced upstairs. She shut herself in the guest bedroom and, distantly, thought she could hear the deadbolt clicked back, then there was scratching. He was using picks. She heard the door open—oh, fucking Christ—and then closing.

She darted into the closet of her guest room (this was something she had practiced with Marty and the consultant), locked and propped the solid oak door behind her, and then, as quietly as she could, searched in the dark for the pistol that Marty had bought her.

Townsend was in the house now; she knew that. But suddenly everything had gone silent. All she could hear was the gale rush of blood in her ears.

The pistol—which the consultant had simply referred to as 'the nine'—was a Beretta 9mm semi-automatic 92F, with a magazine capacity of 15 rounds. It was easy to find, and she pushed the safety to free the trigger—except even though she had practiced with the gun, at this moment she had no idea if the safety was on or off. The only way she would find out would be to pull the trigger.

She forced herself against the back wall of the closet and tried to think how long it had been since she pushed the panic button. How long had the consultant said it would take? She dug into her purse and got out her cell phone, flicked it open and speed-dialed Marty's office. She had the gun—a slick and heavy thing like a hard black fish—in one hand and the phone in the other and prayed for someone to answer. She tried to see the gun in the light from her phone.

Now she could hear him climbing the staircase, and she closed her eyes and tried to even out her breathing. Tried to remain as motionless as stone. The sound of footsteps stopped. She was nearly certain that she could hear Townsend breathe. Finally

Marty's assistant came on the line. Ellen spoke before she could say anything, He's here, she hissed into the phone.

The moment the words were out of her mouth—or more like simultaneous to their uttering—the bat came through the wall beside and above her, sending light flooding in and a spray of crushed drywall over her head before the bat got hung up in wiring and he took it out and took another swing. He wrenched it out and there was a moment of silence before the bat came through the wall again. She held the gun in her hand and dropped the cell phone, still on, and clasped the pistol with both hands as she tried to scramble out of the range of the blows. She tried to make herself small, to set herself up to take a shot at him if she could.

But now the bat came down low, breaking the stud in the wall and she jerked herself backwards and her foot slipped on the dust and slid sideways into the open as she scrabbled to conceal herself. Now his hand flashed down and locked around her left ankle. With one arm, he pulled at her through the bashed-in opening like she was nothing more than a Barbie doll. There was gypsum dust in the air, in her eyes, in her mouth, but she had the gun and pointed it at him, both hands locked around it.

He just looked down on her and smiled. He had released her and had the bat in both hands now and was raising it above her. She had the gun pointed at him, and blinked away the dust.

When she pulled the trigger, it would not budge, and Townsend could see this, and laughed—or at least that's the way she would remember it.

Suddenly, though, he turned. She thought she heard another male voice. Townsend said, What the…, and paused a moment, looked away, toward the stairs. *Had the cops come?* But now he turned back, and she fumbled a moment and now the safety was off, and the bat over his head and she squeezed the trigger and it was not one explosion but several and suddenly Townsend got a surprised look on his face, and there were black spots on his coveralls and the bat came down, but fell harmlessly beside her and he just stood there, looking stunned.

This seemed to last forever. His arms were still in the air, and his face just relaxed, and there was a gurgling noise that came not from his mouth but somewhere else. There were siren sounds now and the air was filled with dust and smoke, and there were holes in the wall—she had no idea how many times she had pulled the trigger. All she knew was that it was more than once.

It may not have been true, but it seemed like he came down very slowly, his expression frozen from a few moments ago, and he came down and down, and now he was on his knees, and he looked at her, a strangely pleased look on his face, and as soon as he got to his knees, he flopped forward, landing on the bat and the floor, his head smashing against the wall, and gypsum dust flying up.

She shouted, Is someone there? Hello? She choked, and crawled through the wall, scrambled to her feet. She held the gun, both hands clasped together, and went down the stairs slowly—someone had been there, distracted him, but who? What if he'd had someone with him? Is someone there? she shouted. I'm armed.

She went slowly around corners the way she had seen people do it in the movies, and worked her way to the front door. She had a horrible feeling in her bones that she could not name. Cool spring air came through the open door, and when the police cars pulled up, she dropped the gun and screamed one of those screams you hear and cannot believe came from yourself.

THE WORLD LINE

Soraya, when she saw Michael shuddering and convulsing, rose out of the chair and came close, killed the computer, and peeled the headset quickly but deliberately off his head. And when it was off, his body relaxed. She stood over him, waiting. It took a moment, but he blinked and opened his eyes.

What happened? she said.

Can you turn off the air conditioning, I'm freezing. And he appeared to be. He was shaking, and his teeth were chattering, and she got up—Is there a switch? she said.

He said, I don't... No. There's, in the hall, a... He was gasping, as though he had been knocked in the chest.

Dr. Ouellette, for once, had the appearance of being freaked out and this gave him a certain amount of satisfaction, even though he could not keep his teeth from chattering.

He stood and his legs were cold, his whole body felt as though it had been immersed in ice water. Which it both had and hadn't.

Michael? She almost screamed his name. What happened?

He shook his legs, jogged a little, tried to get feeling back, and it came quickly.

What the fuck happened?

See, he started, then hesitated. This is the problem. What I designed, he said. It isn't there. What did I look like?

You looked comatose, and then like an epileptic.

He rubbed his chin and thought about it, tried to make sense of it, but there was no sense in it. He had to go back into the code, figure it out.

Weird, he said.

He was warming again now, but it was strange how something so far away could come back so immediately. Father Sorensen had been the one who pulled him out. The minister's daughters—this was perhaps why he had blacked it out—had stripped him almost immediately and wrapped him in their own clothing. There was one of the three Sorensen sisters, Monica, he thought her name was, that he had been attracted to, and he could now, suddenly see her unzipping his wet jeans and yanking them off with a professional quality that Soraya might have admired.

So what happened?

He took a deep breath, then sighed. Fuck....

What? He shook his head. This was so not what he had intended. This was so... something.

It starts out with a sort of queasy feeling, and then you feel like you're crossing some sort of threshold, into some other world. And then you're there. The other day—Sunday—I was at the beach. This time was the opposite. This time I knew exactly where I was, it was like a piece of my life replayed and it was so real. It was like—I can't. No. It was like living it again.

Living what again?

When I was about twelve, I was ice skating. I fell through the ice. I was lucky. I was in a place where the water was shallow enough that I could stand.

And so you were freezing.

Yes.

But it was entirely in your head.

Soraya was into this now. She had that gleam in her eye as though she were onto something. It made him happy to see this. He had not seen her so excited in ages.

Sure. And in the Black Box.

Michael, what I saw was a person getting hypothermia. And it's hot in here. She laughed. Do you have...? She was pacing now, running her hands through her hair, thinking. No. No. This... This is—I have to try it. Hook me up, big boy.

THE DOCTOR IS SHOPPING

Soraya tied her hair up tightly and sat in the chair where Michael had been. Michael put the headset on her and explained as best he could what he had experienced, the sensation of breaking through, the awareness of being in two places at the same time. She said: Just keep an eye on me.

What makes you think I wouldn't?

The way she looked at him before he closed the headset over her eyes was sweet—there was admiration in them again, not just concern.

He started the Black Box and then stood over her and watched. Here in the quiet of his office—the quiet not so much quiet but white noise—he looked at her hair, her hands. Her hands were moving. Not a lot, but moving. They were slender and pale and it looked like she was touching something in the middle of the air. Her legs were pressed together at the knees, and except for her hands she was still. He looked at the clock—only two minutes had gone by. He said her name to see if she would hear him, but the headphones blocked the sound.

She had a nice smell to her, an admixture of perfume and girl. He tried to remember what it had been like to be with her, to be with someone. A woman was such a strange and spectacular thing—not in the object sense of the word, *thing*, but in the sense of a force, an effect. Being around women changed the whole warp of the universe. She was right. He needed to breathe. He needed to get a life. Except all he wanted to do was get back to work.

When the time they had agreed upon had passed, he turned off the machine. Soraya sat up, said, Help me out of this thing.

As Michael did so, he said, So? What did you see?

After the headset was off, she didn't say anything for a long time.

She was smiling but she was not talking.

What? he said.

At last she said, I was shopping.

You were shopping.

Yeah. I was shopping. She laughed.

You're dangerous when you shop. Good to see you didn't get anything.

She got up out of the chair and hugged him. She kissed his cheek and said, You've got something, Michael. This is something.

We've got something, he corrected. But the question is what?

You don't see it, do you? she said. This is better. I don't know what it's doing, either, but if we can figure that out, then we have something really—she grabbed his face. We have something *really* spectacular.

SPIN

E llen was still shaking and the detective said, You want a Xanax or something? She looked at him—did he carry Xanax or did he just assume she had a stash?

He was youngish and lanky, with a really good haircut and a slightly effeminate face, a vague, almost apologetic stoop to his shoulders, and very large brown eyes against skin that could only be called mocha latte. His name—which was on the ID he wore in his shirt pocket, just like on TV—was Clancy Johnson. He had joked earlier about being black Irish.

She was still covered in gypsum dust: it was in her clothing and her hair and made her totally look her absolute best. She couldn't get the smell of the gun out of her nostrils.

She had walked the detective through what had happened at least twice now, first on foot, showing where Townsend was standing outside and where he had been, where she had been. She told him how Townsend had been distracted, somehow, as if someone else was in the house. They had searched the house again and found no one. But, she said, if it hadn't been for that, I might…. I might not have had the time.

Then she went through it all again sitting at the table, shaking.

There were police everywhere, in the yard, upstairs—suddenly her life, her privacy, had been opened up in an ugly and very personal way, first by Townsend, and now again by the cops. She had no doubt that because of who she was, they were doing an extra-thorough job, just in case the *Sun* or the *Inquirer* happened to call.

She said, No, no, I'm fine. It's just not every day I shoot someone.

Is there anyone you want to talk to? Detective Johnson said.

You mean like my therapist or something?

He didn't answer because there was suddenly a commotion outside. One of the network publicists, a greasy bastard called Jayson Grainge—who, in all honesty, she did not hate—and Masters Wood (the sleazy opportunist) had come through the police boundary and, with a photographer and a small gaggle of other people, which may have included a video crew, were barging toward her front door. Detective Johnson's hackles went up and he got up and went for the door. Ellen looked around for Marty but couldn't find him anywhere. So the story was all over town now. The detective stopped them at the door, but Jayson slipped past and headed straight for her. Johnson was now telling Masters how much he liked his work. There was the theory that all jobs in LA were temp jobs—until you got your big break in movies or TV. Detective Johnson seemed to prove the theory, right this minute.

Jayson hugged her and came away smudged with gypsum. He was one of those people who had the most astonishing ability to connive people into doing whatever he wanted. He could convince you—in moments, *moments*—that cutting off your left hand was, frankly, the best thing in the world you could do for yourself but, clearly, humanity as a whole.

My *God*, he said, You just saved your own life and you look *fabulous*.

Jayson....

No, darling, you must take me seriously. You look, you look *fucking radiant*, Ellen.

He held her shoulders and leaned back from her and looked down on her, into her eyes—would not let her escape his gaze. You look, he said, Like…

Jayson, you have to leave. There's a police investigation…, she said and tried to push him away. Did she? Did she look radiant? That was how good Jayson Grainge was.

Listen, this is going to be win-win. I talked to *People* and I talked to *Us* and I talked to half a dozen newspapers, and we have a scoop, here, Ellen. You have to let the studio handle this. We are going to make lemonade. You had a psycho come into your home and you justly defended yourself. You were totally empowered. We do not want anyone casting ugly glances in your direction. Ellen Gregory is not a killer. (*What the fuck was he talking about?*) Ellen Gregory is a hero. A hero. Do you know how *empowering* this is? Think of the girl in the trailer park, Ellen, think of that kid who's got two kids at 20 and an abusive husband—no, we don't want her to whack him, but we want her to know she's empowered to act. We want him to know that she can act. Let me handle this, Ellen, let me be your friend, here. We can frame this. We have to frame this. We have to be the ones who set the terms for this discussion. We want lily white. You are lily white. Are you with me? We can get you on Oprah. It will be fabulous. Are you with me?

I'm with you, Jayson, she said. She was weary. She wanted to sleep—she wanted to sleep somewhere far away where none of this could bother her.

We've got a great story here, Ellen. We've got the story of a lifetime. America's Favorite Girl Next Door is nearly beaten to death by a stalker, but saves her own life. It's fucking riveting.

He threw his hands up and did a little dance. It's empowering. It's the bomb of bombs. And we've got people who are willing to pay for it. We *have* to do this. We have to frame the story before anyone else can frame it.

Lights came on and she turned and the video crew, which turned out to be bigger—way bigger—than she had first imagined—this was Jayson Grainge sleight of hand—was all over the place, and a producer was directing Detective Johnson as they brought the bagged body downstairs.

And then she noticed that there was a camera on her.

THE SUN FROM UNDER WATER

For most of the next two weeks Ellen holed up in Marty's pool house, an architectural dreamscape of glass and steel with views of the garden and pool, a full bath for each of its two spacious bedrooms, a fully equipped and stocked high-end kitchen with stone counters and a restaurant grade cooktop, and a fully equipped gym with a studio quality sound and video system. (It was always nice to see what people could buy with the money they made off you.) Two burly bodyguards in suits (lightweight, expensive, form-fitting, un-constructed Hollywood suits that showed off their muscles and concealed their armaments—they both had body builders' asses, and she suspected they were wearing thongs, or no underwear at all, because you did not get that kind of gluteal definition in boxers) drove her to the studio in a black limo and limited their conversation to greetings. Good morning, Miss Gregory. Goodbye, Miss Gregory.

She swam laps. She ran on the treadmill. She talked on the phone with Patti and Felicity, both of whom were sympathetic, but just didn't get it. She talked to Dave, and he got it. But then he had had his own psycho stalker. She talked to Robin, and he got it. Maybe you had to be out there, in the public eye.

She talked on the phone with Dr. Ling.

She had several lunches with Marty's wife, a slender, quiet, blonde woman who, despite Ellen's long relationship with Marty, she barely knew. Patti said she was an Ellen stand-in, but that didn't really do her justice.

She ran on the treadmill and watched old movies while she trotted in place, sweating and sweating. She swam more laps.

There was a thing she liked to do in the pool—after running and sweating—and that was to exhale as much air as she could stand, then hold her nose and sink to the bottom and just look up at the surface of the water, the way the sun hit it, the way the liquid moved, and more than once Marty's wife had jumped in, thinking she had drowned or was trying to drown herself. No.

It was just the most peaceful place she could find, and learning to hold your breath for long periods of time was an old singer's trick, a way of building up your breathing. So she modified it and made sure she kept moving even though what she wanted to do was hold completely still.

She slept little, and after sobbing for extended periods of time, sat in the mornings in his garden, sipping coffee and listening to the sprinklers doing their *pffffft-chocka-chocka-chocka* thing. In the garden, she was the picture of self-contained peaceful Zen perfection.

Workmen were at her house, patching the walls and erasing all traces of Townsend. Her home was not her home, she told Dr. Ling, the only person who seemed to have any idea of how her soul had been torn from her and crumpled and ground up.

The police were trying (insofar as the police actually *tried* to do anything) to find out how the slippery Townsend had slipped away from them, where he was staying, where he learned to pick locks. (According to what she'd read on the Internet, locks were no more secure than butterfly wings. They just provided the illusion of security. A third grader with a little prepping could pick the toughest lock.) And they and she—and the rest of TV-viewing America, for that matter, were trying to figure out why it was that Townsend had chosen this bizarre way of doing what he did—almost as though he knew she would shoot him. He could have come at any time. He could have come in the middle of the night. It didn't have to be so theatrical.

But Townsend was a short book, no footnotes. No study guide. There were only his letters, which the police had.

This was a classic rewind moment, one of those places in your head where you just want to go backwards and make things that happened unhappen, then stop and do something different. But in this case, what did you rewind? How did you get someone out of your life when you had no idea when they ever got into it? But of course the thing she kept rewinding was the moment itself—rewind, play, rewind—the jaunty look on his ghastly pale face as he handled the baseball bat. Was he going to beat her with it? *Oh, Jesus, that had to hurt.* (She laughed.) *No, seriously, getting beat to death with a baseball bat has got to hurt like a motherfucker.*

She had a dogging, endless feeling of loss, anxiety, a thing close to panic. Dr. Ling said it was a perfectly reasonable grief reaction, a perfectly normal train of thought for a victim to have—*how could I have stopped it?*—when of course, it was not your doing. There was essentially nothing you could do to stop it.

It all made her want to scream, to tear out her hair. That something so irrational could just rear its ugly head and take control of your life. It was one thing to be aware of that in some intellectual way—like some sort of 12-step bromide—but to suddenly understand it viscerally and fundamentally was excruciating. No one seemed to get just how violated she felt. No one seemed to get that it could happen to them, some irrational idiotic thing that could suddenly steal your soul—or take it and mutilate it. There were moments when she was fine, just fine, and then there were others that swam up out of her subconscious and suddenly she was back in her bedroom closet, balled up and trying to get her hands around the gun. She could hear him on the stairs, see the baseball bat come through the wall, the explosion of gypsum powder and dust, could see every minute particle of it; she could taste it in her mouth. She could feel the sensation of his hand, pulling her through the broken wall.

(But that wasn't it entirely. For a year or more, she had been having weird, sort of nervous out-of-body experiences. She had been having the sense that her soul had somehow slipped from her body, and the Ellen who was on TV had more of a soul than the quote unquote real Ellen ever did.)

The weird thing was that her flashback moments were perhaps more real and more horrifying than the original moment had been. It was almost as though her head had collected much more of the moments than she knew at the time, and she could see each of them, the moments from first seeing him in her yard to actually shooting him, as discrete scenes. Like if you had them on the Avid and could scroll through each in minute detail. (Well, yes, Dr. Ling said. These are classic symptoms of post-traumatic stress. The thing you have to do is to learn to control the memories.)

This was not something you could explain, the complete helplessness of having to revisit these things. The lock clanking open, (Marty: *We'll get to the bottom of this*), the way your trust, your trust in anything was in a moment transformed. It was the kind of thing that made you think about the whole tenuous chain of trust that made up life. Get on an airplane, entrust your life to people whom you've never met. Rent a car from people you've never seen before and will never see again. How fucking weird that a person would break down—and then systematically break down that chain just to exploit it.

It didn't matter if they got to the bottom of it. She would still remember the hand on her ankle, the gun in her hand.

After a few days, she began to see it as a pattern. Townsend was just as much an oblivious force as nature. He could have been a tornado. She thought about what he had said the day he had kidnapped her, about the shape of time, about having no real volition. And in a way, he was right—she did not see things the way he did, but perhaps that was changing.

She thought of all the parties she'd been to, the places where someone could have stabbed her, shot her; she thought of all the places where the hand of fate could have dragged her—and had perhaps dragged her already (with her volition?) into this particular life, pulling her into the life that (now) seemed surely to lead to her death.

To which Dr. Ling said, Of course. Where else does life, stripped of everything else, lead?

It was as if the moon had suddenly decided to crash into the earth—and what could you do about it?

Exactly nothing.

One blousey nameless LA evening, Marty came home from the office and while they were having drinks—Marty, his wife, Ellen—said, Why don't you go to New York for a few days? I have a client who's in LA for a few months and his apartment is available. It's in the eighties, on the Upper West Side. Off Broadway. Pre-war.

Which war? Ellen said, or choked. She looked at him. She had just taken a sip of her chardonnay when he said it, and she held the glass in front of her mouth, the idea sinking in and leaving her mouth dry and her heart doing some insane flip job.

She had left New York almost the way she had left Iowa—a sudden departure that was never supposed to be permanent, but which had over time become something like that. She saw herself on Broadway, shop windows going past. She saw herself getting on the subway and rattling down to the Village. She saw herself maybe trying to get a little work at one of the clubs she had abandoned for television.

I could talk to a booker—maybe you could do Dave. Talk about the incident.

She shook her head. I don't want to talk about the incident. Jayson had all sorts of shit lined up and I won't do it.

Then just get away.

Are you trying to get rid of me?

Ellen, sweetheart—Marty did a really bad Humphrey Bogart—I'm not trying to get rid of you. I just hate to see you—you know.

I'm sorry, she said. It's just….

I could get you a plane. Private. Just go and chill.

She took the suggestion under consideration and the conversation went onto something else. A young actor called Adrian or Adam or something who had got some early success, too early, and had blown through so much money he could have fed a couple of third world nations for a couple of years. Ellen had never heard of him. It was his plane. Some sort of aeronautical timeshare.

Ellen had never done that—the new-Hollywood-money thing. Sure, she had spent her share, but she had done without for so long, and her parents' penny-pinching Midwestern caution was so ingrained in her that even buying her house—for which she'd paid cash—seemed like the apogee of frivolity. At restaurants, she still felt nervous, after all this, that her credit card was going to be declined.

When could I go? she said.

IT ALL COMES TO THIS

There was a time when Ellen and Marty had been inseparable. A single organism. Marty, as penniless back then as she, was rich now. He had a shitload of clients. It was a long time since she'd thought of how desperate and dangerous and just totally mind-blowingly exhilarating those days were, their trips around the country, Marty booking her anywhere he could, the two of them sharking it out together, Ellen in love with him then, confusing ambition and increments of success and affirmation with love. She would have married him then because he saw in her what she wanted everyone to see, the real her, the secret identity. It was—and remained— one of those kinds of professional marriages, a thing not about romance but about work, a symbiotic relationship, the two of them working as one. Even when they called quits to whatever minimal romance they'd had, they stayed married in that way. She wanting to do every stage she could, wanting to hone and hone her comic's killer instinct, and him always on the phone, then agent and publicist and manager, booking her wherever he could, whenever he could—and there was sort of a comic boomlet then, clubs all over. There had been years when she was pretty sure that she had worked every night.

She could not remember how many times the two of them had sat up in his apartment, in his van, or in crappy motel rooms, with his tiny portable VCR-TV combo, watching other comics on videotape—not just contemporaries he had filmed in clubs, or gotten tapes of, but Phyllis Diller, W.C. Fields, Mae West, Buster Keaton, Allen Sherman, Johnny Carson, Jack Benny, Bob Hope, Rodney Dangerfield, Woody Allen, Steven Wright, Robin Williams, Cheech and Chong and more Bob Hope—anyone who had ever made anyone laugh. There was a huge collection of audio cassettes in the van, and they played them over and over as he drove, checked maps, stopped for gas: Bill Cosby, Richard Pryor, Jack Benny, Andy Griffith (yes, he of Mayberry fame), and thousands more. Literally boxes—and not, mind you, any sort of orderly system, just cardboard boxes, from shoeboxes to moving crates. You listen to the rhythms. You listen to the way the joke's set-up worked.

From one perspective, stand-up comedy was the most insane sort of theater she could imagine. A single person gets on a stage and it's entirely up to you to create the narrative, get the audience to buy into the narrative, and there was something about it—now, after years of comfort in the sitcom—she found terrifying. She could not, now, remember exactly how she'd had the courage to do it.

But she had done it, or some other, earlier version of Ellen had done it, and done it well. *How* was the current mystery. And a depressing one.

The shitty living, the sleeping against the passenger seat window in Marty's van as they went from town to town, gig to gig, the total rush of performing, then nodding off, exhausted, in the backs of clubs with your mouth tasting like someone else's beer and cigarettes, getting paid in an envelope full of cash and then sitting in your cheap rental—at some point it began to change. At some point—when a fresh donut was an unbelievable luxury, waking to dry cereal and cheap black coffee and trying to decide what to pay, how to eat something other than lentils and macaroni, the desperation on some days so desolate when you thought about getting a real job and stopping it all, surrendering, but then performing again and wondering if your ambition was burning you up—at some point, or over some slow accretion of skill and success, there was suddenly money.

Her ambition was on a par with her desperation, not just desperation to succeed, but to eat. It was also exploration, discovery. She left home a dewy-eyed kid with a vivid and histrionic imagination, a knack for impersonation that she always—according to her mother—carried too far. She crammed in more in two or three years, more human transformation, than most people cram into a lifetime. People at home, her mother and father told her, couldn't believe what a success she was, how funny people were saying she was, how proud they were—except it was always sort of backhanded, people just don't know where all this came from. And the reality was that she had no idea where it came from, either. It was like channeling on good days, like some effortless thing that just happened. It was as inexplicable as some sort of superpower. Spiderman may have known how it happened—becoming Spiderman—but where it came from was something else entirely.

It wasn't as if she had transformed; she *was* transformed. She had become, part out of curiosity, part out of necessity, a student of comedy, and now she was mastering the masters. But to what end? Money? It was—she could say this conclusively—not about money. It was who she was.

She'd always had the desire, some sort of weird churning located behind her solar plexus, like wheels spinning on pavement. And Marty had seen it, had smelled the burning rubber. But the blistering ambition was something she hadn't really understood until Marty put it to her:

What are you talking about? You're the single most ambitious person I've ever met.

Me? Ambitious? I'm just doing what I want to do even if it kills me.

That's what I mean.

She'd always had some kind of inchoate desire (okay, the truth was that she wanted to eat the soul of every single comic she admired, particularly Robin Williams; when she told him about this later, backstage before a gig, he laughed about it, and he knew exactly what she was talking about. He did a vampire voice: Perhaps you did, he said).

When she really started working, really started to see what she could do, when she was a year or so into the Greyhound bus tour, that was when it multiplied, when she really learned how to be a comic, how to steal, how to imitate. And then suddenly she realized after about 50,000 gigs that she knew how to make people laugh. That she knew how to manipulate an audience, how to veer out of a dying routine into what she hoped would be a killer, then come back to the dead one and bring it to life—these kinds of things that can be understood only by doing, by failing, by nursing a sense of competition that could sometimes seem like a vicious troll that lived on your shoulder, an ugly beast that would gnaw at you if you did not keep moving, if it ever sensed someone or something would pass you by. Then she could just be herself.

For years her life felt like a high wire act. No net. And there was nothing better. Maybe there was an arrogance to it. Maybe there was a vicious ambition. But it was better than sex, and for the longest time it was the only substitute she had.

And then suddenly (of course, it wasn't suddenly, but so these things always seem) she was on top. An early-ish shot on Letterman, who became a friend, a couple of guest spots on now-defunct sitcoms, a Japanese commercial for Scotch, Marty pitching her as the next Seinfeld to executive after executive, most of whom balked at how raw and unpredictable she could be. (She'd be in the middle of one of her routines, then sense something in the audience—this was also sort of inexplicable, that channeling thing—and bang, she'd veer off into something harrowingly purple, talking like a sailor on 24-hour shore leave, freaking her own self out at what was coming out of her mouth, but people just going nuts and hurting themselves with laughter. This was not something you could plan, only hope for. But it made the suits soil their silk boxers.) Then a couple of small roles in straight-to-DVD movies, then a funny and personal bit as the sister of a lesbian AIDS patient in the indie film, *Side Door*. (Real acting, which required real restraint.) Marty taking more meetings with TV suits who assured him that they were wholly and completely head-over-heels in love with Ellen except there was that whole edge deal with her (as though she was an unstable isotope that could cause a meltdown instantly) that pretty much gave them night sweats, jock itch, and other assorted discomforts. Marty turned on the charm and restated the obvious—there were scripts, the audience may be live but the show certainly wasn't. And in there somewhere, in the dot com zoom in the mid-90s, was the breakthrough, a commercial for which she was actually hired to be herself, in her trademark psycho G-string tutu and stockings and shitkicker boots (she never turned around) for a dot com that died a few months later, after burning through millions—but the commercial, which just featured her standing on what appeared to be a street corner, with stuff dropping all around her, and Ellen doing a short, bleeped monologue at lightning speed (it had wrapped on the first take). Despite the quick death of the company by unstanchable cash hemorrhage, the commercial became something of an underground smash, an early piece of Internet viral marketing. But with the company dead, it was only Ellen that was being marketed. And suddenly a whole new audience of consumers was saying, Have you *seen* that insane blonde chick? And, Who *is* she?

Because the reality was, even the best known comic is about as well known to the average American as a discontinued Starbucks roast. Until they're on TV.

The studio that had been considering her for *Girlfriends* suddenly was on the phone with Marty nonstop, and because her price, concomitant with her cachet, had gone through the roof, there it was, the brass ring. Champagne dinner with Marty. Marty rolled his eyes and deadpanned: They don't know from talent. When they can have you for free, do they want you? No, they do not want you. It's when they're scared that they won't be able to afford you, that's when they've got to have you.

Insane whoops and hollering, and, at least for Ellen, a weird sense of vertigo mingled with regret. They had pulled the rabbit out of the hat and she sat with her second or third glass of champagne, woozy and utterly uncertain of how to feel, or what indeed she felt.

Suddenly, as if waking after winning the lottery, the bills were paid. She had enough that she could not only buy a house, but buy a big concrete and iron motherfucker of a house with a pool and pool house, with a maid and a gardener and a driver (if she wanted one), a gated community that still felt like it was in the middle of nowhere, not a neighbor in sight. Cash money.

She tried to buy her parents a new house but they had no desire to move or upgrade—Why on earth would we want a bigger house when this one is perfectly fine? her father said, and there was no way she could refute that any more than she could have convinced him that sushi might be better than a burger. But she could not deny the sting of it, the perhaps unintended rebuke.

It didn't take long for it all to seem very, very old. *Girlfriends* was largely unchallenging. *No*—unchallenging didn't even come close to how boring and soul-sucking it was, even if it was occasionally engaging and even fun. The set was as clean as a hospital and as distant from the smoky, sticky-floored joints she had grown up in as LA was from New York. And so her ambition sat on the sidelines, sulking, not at all sure what to do.

But the show had that ineffable chemistry—as a group, the cast had a spark that existed in one or two shows a decade. Somehow it just—in television terms—clicked. It took on a life of its own. To Marty, it was proof of the Barnum Theorem that 'no one ever went broke underestimating the intelligence of the American people.' (Didn't matter to Marty that it was H.L. Mencken who had said it.) And in a couple of years she began to feel that some elemental part of her was being sucked away by the show, by other people's fantasies. Once, during a fight with Marty about staying with the show, he said to her that she had no idea who she was. There was another her that people loved, and that while she might rather be doing stand-up in bars again and getting her paycheck in a greasy paper bag, there were people out there who would be heartbroken—literally fucking heartbroken—if she quit. I mean what if Johnny Carson had quit?

He did quit.

That's not what I mean. What if he had just up and walked away back in the day when you were a teenager at home and lonely? I mean what the fuck would you have thought? People have these mean little lives scrubbing floors or putting meat in cans or scrubbing toilets, and appointment television means something to them. It means that they can escape their little lot for a moment or two. It means that there is something stable and solid in the world. For now, that's you.

Now, thinking about it, wondering what the hell was going to happen next, she saw that he was right. There was something bone-chilling about that, something that made you want to vomit as much as it made you want to walk away and do something else, something with edge. There was another Ellen that Ellen herself had lost control of—she, this other Ellen, was taking over, and Ellen had lost control of her real actual self.

The thing about Marty was that he'd missed the other part of the equation—a fundamental part of the equation—and when he said, This is what you wanted, she wanted to say no, except it was, in some perverted way. But the part Marty missed was that he no longer knew who she was. She was financially and professionally set and he was busy with other clients, none of whom excited her very much, but she understood the weird paranoia of wealth, how nothing was ever enough. And she could see Marty—who had no particular talent of his own beyond maniacal industriousness and charm—trying to build his own castle, trying to outdo anyone who was above him in the food chain. And so while they still talked often, his attention was no longer 100 percent on her. It was now maybe 10 percent. Which in itself was not such a big deal for her, except that the person who had been her best friend now hardly knew her.

And so she stayed. Signed the new contract, went on to the morning shows, and listened to America cheer. And then she looked at what younger comics were doing, looked at badly lit old videotapes of her own act from 10 years ago and was appalled at her own brash energy, how good she had once been, her own inventiveness and rapacity. She would stare with a kind of bafflement that she had ever done it so well, that she had ever done it at all.

After Marty (her first real romance if you didn't count her teenaged delusion with Joshua, whom she had totally envisioned marrying), there were a few years of semi-celibacy with work getting in the way of any sort of actual relationship, and then, when she broke through, a couple of years of really dangerous and disgusting slatternly behavior in which she picked men off the great smorgasbord of sex that was LA and discarded them. 'Relationships' that made (more often than not) the tabloids, like a high school freshman's worst nightmares of a *reputation*. Which in the bizarre high school of Hollywood was almost a good thing, even if it must've been painful for her parents to read about.

The whole Rise to Fame thing was a bit like bouncing on a trampoline and getting higher and higher and then suddenly never coming down. You were in the clouds and there were a few other people up there in the clouds with you, and there were issues with dating anyone who wasn't up there. And the pickings were slim. No True Love for America's Favorite Girl Next Door.

Except, of course, she wasn't the girl next door. No one could be. If someone could, the weight of it (she knew this from experience) would crush you.

What she was was the very carefully constructed illusion of it. She was a uniquely American thing, a part of the alleged American Dream that anyone subject to such illusions was certain that they could one day attain. Except she was even less attainable, more rare, simply because there was only one of her, and the her that was 'there' was an illusion. And but so the pressure, boys and girls, the pressure was inconceivable, as unreal as a man coming to your house intent on beating you to death with a baseball bat.

And so she left.

LAWRENCE OF ILLINOIS

The plane out of LAX was a like a limo with wings. Leather interior, a really good wet bar, an unlimited jukebox, movies, surround sound—the only thing it seemed to lack was a sunroof, but that shortcoming was made up for by the fact that you could actually stand up and dance, if you wanted.

By the time it landed at LaGuardia—warm, a glorious spring Manhattan day—she was drunk on some really good scotch. How pathetic was it to be drinking alone like this?

It wasn't until she got up to get off the plane that she realized just how profoundly hammered she was. She was giggling, calling the pilot Glen, roaring, Glen. Glen Fiddich or is it Morangie. I'd know ye anywhere, ye auld sod, ye!!, doing Robin Williams doing a Scot.

Glen!

How hammered she was was that she almost forgot to wait for her bag. And she knew that this was going to end badly because every time Ellen Gregory got hammered it ended badly.

It wasn't that she was a teetotaler. She drank. She enjoyed a glass of wine with dinner, sometimes before. Sometimes a little more. But serious, concentrated amounts of ethanol did not go well with Ellen's tightly controlled personality. Anything stronger than sherry and she behaved like a teenager after her first beer. Her normally controlled exterior came unbuckled from her brain, and that ever-useful tool, that calculating, scheming, razor sharp, exquisitely well-timed brain became something of a time bomb. But not in the usual, comic, I-can't-believe-the-shit-this-chick-is-saying Ellen Gregory sense. But in the way more usual, What-is-wrong-with-that-bitch? sense. The tight-lidded jar of loneliness she kept sealed away in her head got smashed when she got smashed. The kind of stupid, where-is-my-underwear monkeyshines that landed you on the front page of tabloids—*Ellen Gregory Out of Control!*

The pilot helped her into the terminal, and found the limo driver instantly. He, the limo driver, greeted her warmly—he was a big fan. Ellen was so lonely and drunk and spiritually empty right at that moment—after everything, everything, and then with a nice tumbler or two of scotch in her otherwise empty belly, she might just have jumped the driver had he been even the slightest bit attractive. But he was not, not even in the slightest bit. She waved at the pilot. Bye, Glen. Glued gnawin' ye.

She should have jumped him, Glen, the pilot.

For one thing, the limo driver was old—which she pointed out to him with an outstretched finger, Hey, you're *old*,—and he had a nose that looked like it was made from little bits of partly dried and poorly packed clay, and she started to point that out, too, except somehow the subject got changed and she was nearly knuckle-walking to the limo, following her bag as it swung from the driver's arm.

Driving through Queens and into Manhattan she was glad she was drunk. Oh, God, she sighed, her breath sucking, as they came over the bridge, and she started to cry, and then they were in mid-town traffic and now she was sobbing as the car bounced through teeming intersections and horns honked and it was all the miracle of time travel—hopping into someone's timeshare jet and zinging across the planet from the palm trees of the coast to the damp deciduous East—and she almost got out except she was completely aware that she could not really walk.

She could see herself 10 years ago standing on some lonely corner, winter, people thronging past her, her dressed in her tutu, a fake rabbit fur jacket that made her look like a psycho hooker, her butt freezing as she handed out fliers, did jokes, Come see me at The X. Guys saying, Want to see my funny bone? And Ellen saying—too many rehearsals on this one—So you're guaranteeing me it'll make me laugh. In advance? And cackling.

So much of life was about loss. So much of hurtling forward in time was what you left behind, without even knowing. Where was that kid? Who was that kid? How could anyone be so crazy and naïve and young to decide to dress in a black thong tutu with fishnet stockings with garters and shitkicker Timberlands? (*My mommy makes me wear army boots.*)

The only place she did not feel that sense of loss was on the never-ending present moment of the stage, her life's single little sanctuary. It had nothing and everything to do with the audience. It was something about lights. About heat. About that tight little contract between comic and audience—Come listen to me re-create a world that never existed but will always exist. A world that will hurt you with laughter.

The apartment building—the building in which the borrowed or to-be-borrowed apartment was located—was between Broadway and West End, in the low eighties, brass and dark-wood lobby. A doorman with epaulets—brass and blue serge. A gorgeous building that loomed and hunkered.

Hello, Doorman, she almost whooped, as if she knew him.

Hello, Miss Gregory, he said, as if he knew her.

I have keys for you.

How did you know my name?

I know you.

No you don't, but you think you do. See, that's a problem that I have. That you has. Have. People always say that but they don't.

No. I saw you on TV.

See, that's a big difference, she said, and wiped some drool from her mouth as she did.

Yes, Miss Gregory.

You're not really a doorman, are you? You're really a lobby man. The door thing is just a front.

This seemed hysterically funny at the moment and she laughed.

Miss Gregory is tired from her flight.

Yes, Miss Gregory is really tired, profoundly tired. She is so fucking tired. And she's going to go upstairs and find the bar and get way more tired.

Later, she would not remember what transpired in the lobby. The only thing she would remember—and this she would not be certain of—was a compact man with beautiful eyes and beautiful teeth and a completely shaved, bald sparkling head. A smile like 12,000 watts. In the memory, which gets buried beneath the alcohol haze, it's hard to tell how old he is—30, 40, 50? He simply is. Crossing from the elevator bank through the lobby hush and out the door. Who said 12,000 watts? That smile is at least 50,000. Maybe even a megawatt.

And then she was alone. The apartment was one of those great pre-war jobs with high ceilings and spacious rooms and a fanfuckingtastic bar. Every kind of liquor you could possibly imagine. Gallons of it. Crystal decanters, glasses. A gorgeous sterling martini kit. The actor-client of Marty's was either the kind of guy who didn't drink and threw lots of parties, or drank and collected various flavors of ethanol with fetishistic fervor.

It was of course not just a bad idea, but a compounded bad idea, but she laid into the bar almost immediately. A pear eau de vie, which had the most amazing fruity yumminess. The first glass jumped right out of her hand and broke on the granite countertop before it even hit the floor.

The glasses in this place jump. The scent of pears was everywhere. Have to tell the doorman about that.

She struggled to find a broom, talking to herself and giggling. The apartment faced the street and had those great big windows that threw light into the whole room, and you could see the edge of a newer building, and just a little bit of Broadway, looking downtown. The place had clearly been interior-designed, because everything looked like a magazine spread, each room its own little world. The kitchen was a restaurant—but like most New York refrigerators, there was little more than champagne and butter and some odd condiments in the refrigerator. The living room was a cigar bar, with luscious leather couch and arm chairs, and pelts of large, late feline-type creatures. She had no idea if these were real.

She sang to herself the song 'I'm Just a Girl Who Can't Say No' from *Oklahoma!*, but with bawdy lyrics.

She giggled, and went back to the bar, and, after breaking another glass found another, and poured some more eau de vie. The pears. In one glass, you could smell bushels of pears. Fucking orchards.

She found the remote control from the TV and turned it on. Bass fishing.

She sang some more: I feel pretty, oh so pretty….

And there she was on the screen. She sank down into one of the cigar chairs with her glass, and watched. It was a rerun from the first season of *Girlfriends*, and she watched herself interact with Masters. They were arguing, and he was stroking his waxed chest, beneath his shirt.

It might have been now that all the humor drained out of the day. The lark that today had been now seemed like something deeply pathetic. Canned laughter canned the faux wackiness of the show perfectly.

It was only three years ago that it was shot—she was not yet 30, at the top of her game!!—and now here she was, crying, suddenly, half a life, a world away.

She sipped the orchard and felt the heat of it burn through her lungs and belly, and wondered if, as the *M*A*S*H* song went, suicide was painless. She thought of the pistol, the *nine*, and how much easier it would have been to put the thing to her temple and pull the trigger. I feel shitty, oh so shitty. I feel shitty and shitty and gray.

By the time she found the broom, she had forgotten what she was looking for, broken two more glasses and the bottle of eau de vie. She had also managed to down a glass of scotch, which, once it was done, seemed like another really bad idea. And now there was broken glass, lots of it, a blossom of blood on her finger, which she watched with great fascination as it bloomed.

She thought of the man she had shot with the 9. She thought of how he had looked, the failure of blood. Just holes in his jacket. The whole notion of stalking, of breaking into someone's home—her own in this case—someone you didn't know, with the intent of killing them.

It was the thing she had been trying to wrap her head around for the last several days. Not just since he kidnapped her, but even before, when she'd just gotten weird letters. But she had killed a man. There was grief over that. But it was one of the weird things about grief that it was not profound. The first thing that came to mind was a Johnny Cash song. Which made you want to laugh even while you wanted to sob.

There was blood and liquor on her shirt, so she took it off and put it on the counter, and then, in her bra and slacks, tried to get all the glass into the trash.

The broom and dustpan were designer reproductions of the old tin and wood and cornstalk originals. The trash bag was a plastic bag from D'Agostino's, filling with little translucent razors, the fragrance of some long ago pear orchard. It, too, made her want to weep.

When it seemed to be mostly done, she staggered into the hallway, heading for the garbage chute, and there, in her state of near alcohol-poisoning, was that Kojak fellow, lighting up the corridor like the explosion of a strobe, himself carrying a bag of garbage.

Oh, hello, he said, as though the world were not fraught with grief.

She tried—valiantly, but, it might be said, vainly—to straighten up. But knuckle-walking was really the only thing she was capable of—unless, of course, she wanted the prickly carpet to leap up and attack.

Hello, gorgeous, she said, meaning it to sound equally facetious and horny. It was hard, though, to tell if it sounded either, as the words were slurred. He was kind enough to ignore it.

She held up her bag of garbage briefly, as if to say, Hey, whaddaya know, I'm throwing out garbage, too.

He held up his bag and said, Cheers.

He opened the door, and there was a little room with fluorescent light with a door in the wall. She followed him. Pressed a hand against his back and leaned into the room, but the leaning was more like swinging. She sang: I'm just a girl who can't say no.

He said: Let me help you with that. You're drunk.

Sir, she said, straightening as much as she could and trying to look at him sternly. My good man, she said. I am not drunk.

No?

Hammered. Hammered like a fucking 10-penny nail.

You're hammered, then.

Indeed. One must…, she started, but then began to feel the building sway. She put her hand to her head. You gotta keep these things straight.

Can I help you?

He was leaning toward her, his eyes wide. He wasn't that much taller than she was, but he was bigger, way more solid than he looked from a distance. There was the tinkling of glass as it fell floor after floor. She swayed with the building right against the man.

Oh, dear, he said.

She had her arm around him now, her face pressed sideways into one carved pectoral muscle like it was her pillow and she'd been sleeping 12 hours.

She could see in rough focus the waistband of his khakis (no belt; no pleats; the fold and bulge of the zipper, and to the left of that, the other not-quite-bulge bulge), and, in the distance, white socks and loafers. Her hand came up without her volition and fluttered a moment, and, as she watched, detached, it fluttered, moth-like, to the flame of his fly.

This was the weird part, or at least the first weird part: There was some business-like, purposeful, and instant flight of his own hands, and suddenly she was standing up straight and feeling way more sober than she had a fraction of a second before; her errant hand was at her side. He now had (this all happened with such instant speed that it left her wondering, What the fuck just happened?) one hand on her head, his hand covering her right ear, his thumb against her temple, his fingers wrapped around her head (he had long fingers) and his fingertips were on the back of her neck; his other hand clamped her shoulder.

You need some sleep, he said. His words were not stern or admonishing. They were neutral: merely the detached field observation of a scientist.

He was still holding her in that peculiar way and she looked at him, his gleaming skull, his flashbulb-bright eyes and smile. This was a moment that seemed to extend, her gazing at him, and she felt some shimmer of recognition. Not recognition in the sense that she knew him, but recognition that—unlike most people she met—he had no motive whatsoever. He was here, this was happening, he was doing what he felt, from his perspective, needed to be done. And this was another weird part, the second weird part. Right at this moment, as he held her, she felt safer than she had felt in a long time. And it wasn't the liquor, either.

Who are you? she said, the way a child might say the same thing if a genie popped up in her bedroom.

My name is Larry. (It didn't really answer the question, because who he was was a lot more than his name, it seemed to some dimly lit part of her mind. But it would have to do.)

She giggled. She couldn't help it. Larry, she said. Larry. What kind of name is Larry?

Diminutive for Lawrence, he said.

111

Of Arabia? she said.

Illinois, he said.

This made her laugh. Lawrence of Illinois. Well, hello, Lawrence of Illinois.

And you are?

You don't know?

He raised his eyebrows, widened his gleaming eyes, shook his head. Sorry. Haven't had the pleasure.

The word pleasure did ugly things to her thoughts. He was just shy of six feet, if he wasn't six feet, and quicker than a cat. He wore a loose, white T-shirt with James Dean style plain front khakis. Beneath the T-shirt, which had blood on it now, you could see exquisitely cut pectoral muscles. (Did we mention the pecs?) He was not an ostentatious body builder type, with ballooning, hypertrophic muscles. He was fit. His arms were solid.

Ellen, she said. She could see no trace of recognition in his eyes.

It was when he released his right arm from her shoulder and extended his hand to shake, saying, Hello, Ellen, that she realized that she had come into the hallway wearing only her bra, which was the kind of bra you could pretty much see through. That is, if you were looking. Which he was not. Or not that she could tell.

He smiled when he noticed her noticing. And then he noticed her hand, which had started to bleed again.

You shouldn't play with broken glass, he said, smiling, and took up her hand in his—the other was still on her head and felt wonderfully warm and confident-making there—and flicked away blood and ran his thumb over the wound, evidently to check for the presence of broken glass. Then he pressed down on it.

Let's get you back to your apartment, he said, steering her into the hallway, still holding her head. He did not seem to move so much as flow—his feet moved, yes, his body moved, yes, but the way he moved was completely unified and liquid, cat-like and inevitable.

It's not my apartment, she said.

So you're breaking and entering?

She giggled as she did a sort of wobbly goose step toward the door.

My agent got it for me from one of his other clients.

Your agent, he said. What do you do?

She couldn't decide what to say in response. They were inside the apartment now and he surveyed the place. The television was still on, but muted now.

Nothing, lately, she said at last, suddenly confused and nauseated. I just take up space.

He smiled a completely neutral, gleaming smile. Let's get you bandaged. He left her on one of the chairs, the flat screen TV rehearsing images of soap and food and legal assistance. Without his hand on her head, the feeling of nausea built.

When he returned, he had found a first aid kit, and expertly bandaged her hand. She watched in admiration, hoping she wouldn't vomit on him. She looked up and her image had come back on the TV. For whatever reason, she didn't much want him to see it, but there was no sign of the remote control.

He brought her her blouse. She did not put it on, but pulled herself to her feet and put both of her arms over his shoulders and draped herself against him. God, he felt good. Solid and real and really male. He took her arms in his hands and held them gently, one in each hand, below the elbows.

You're very sweet, he said.

And you're very sexy.

You're wobbling, he said.

I am. Do that thing you did with your hand.

Have you eaten anything recently?

Why?

I believe if I lit a match and had you breathe on it, your breath might catch fire. It was the longest thing he had yet said to her, and it was humiliating.

No. I didn't, I haven't. Eaten. Lately. When she looked up at him, everything was swimming.

I think I'm going to be sick, she said. Maybe she was crying now. She wasn't sure. And I can't remember where the bathroom is. Yes, she was crying. She was wailing like an 8-year-old.

Larry guided her, but they didn't make it far before she buckled and erupted.

She'd never understood how people could be bulimic. Vomiting was about the worst sensation that she could imagine. A total loss of control. There was puke on her, all over her, but it felt a little better.

He lifted her over the wretched puddle and swooped her into the bathroom, lifted the lid of the toilet, and expertly held her hair for her. He was crouched, one hand in her hair, one on her back.

Outside in the hallway, she had thought that seducing him was a fabulous idea. Now, though, she was scared. Scared of vomiting. Scared of him. It was hard not to be scared of everyone and everything, after Townsend.

Go ahead, he said, and as if on cue, she did.

BATHED IN HUMILIATION

When at last she took her elbows off the toilet seat and pulled herself out of her crouch, he was gone. She wondered for a moment if she had just imagined him. She staggered to the sink and ran water from the tap and splashed it on her face, rinsed her mouth. Only after she had dried her face, the water still running, did she look at herself in the mirror. There was always the chasm-like disconnect between the drunk and the drunkenness. The drunk floated along on a feeling of gorgeous and blissful invincibility, oblivious of the appearance of his/her own drunkenness, while the drunkenness itself manifested on the face and bearing of the drunk the ugly visage of a truly ugly and demented evil twin.

There was vomit on her chin, despite the splashing. There was vomit on her bra and on her belly and on her pants. How the fuck did she get vomit in her hair?

Ellen turned off the water and closed her eyes and held the corners of the sink and the world spun. Where did he go? And then she heard the sound of the television in the next room. Her own voice. The cackle of canned laughter.

Oh, God. She had the sensation of standing on top of some precipitously high pile of events, emotional trauma, and it was all now crumbling, and she began to cry again. Even without Townsend, she would likely have hit this personal trough, though it may have been slower in coming. People looked at your 'success' and couldn't figure how being rich and beautiful and famous might make you want to jump off a very high place—if not literally, then at least figuratively. These were the same people who stood in the grocery line (like her mother) and picked up *Us* or *People* and shook their heads at just how fat your ass had gotten—and who on earth let you out of the house in that gawdawful bathing suit?

When she opened her eyes, the 12,000-watt man was standing at the doorway. Filling the doorway, and for a moment she looked at him, then at her bandaged hand, and wondered if this was how it was going to end, Psycho-style, in a beautiful black and white New York bathroom.

Feeling any better? he said. Okay, not exactly a Norman Bates line.

She laughed, but the air moving through her nostrils smelled of bile; tears shook from her cheeks.

You muss thing I'm…, she started, but let it trail off. Her words were still slurred, but not so bad.

We need to get you cleaned up, he said. He said it as though he'd said it a thousand times. As though he was a professional at getting people cleaned up.

That's an understatement, she slurred.

Can you stand okay?

He was next to her now, holding her head the way he had before. When he did that, that thing with his hand on her head, it felt like some sort of Vulcan power grip: she almost instantly felt better.

How do you do that? she said. That head thing?

Ancient Chinese wisdom, he said. She had no idea what he was talking about.

She let go of the counter. As long as you do that, she said, I can stand.

Then the tub. We don't want any injuries.

K, she said.

Why don't you get undressed? he said, and said it not like a lover but like a doctor. She would remember that, she thought. Why don't you get undressed? Let me know if you need help.

It was weird how he could say this, do this, utterly absent any erotic overtones. None.

She unhooked her bra while he kept his hand on her head, then let it drop. She watched him: His eyes were averted. She unbuttoned her pants and pushed them off, panties and everything.

Socks, he said. Then, No, let me help.

There was vomit on her footie socks, and he knelt, his arm around her legs, her butt cheek sort of on his shoulder. He took her right foot and lifted it, peeled off the sock. When that foot was securely on the ground, he lifted the left and did the same thing. You're lucky you didn't cut your foot, he said.

I'm generally a lucky person, she said.

When she was completely and totally naked, he helped her into the tub. It was an old classic claw foot job with brass fixtures, including a handheld shower attachment that looked kind of like a massive, ancient telephone receiver. The tub was cold. She said so, and shivered. But he had already begun fiddling with the water, and in a moment, he was holding the shower head and rinsing her own retch from her.

She wished she'd shaved.

She watched him in something like awe. He was a bath artist. He painted her with water. He started at her feet, worked his way up her legs, then across her belly

115

and breasts, and up to her shoulders, rinsing, still no apparent erotic reaction from him. He made every contour of her emerge from the tub. For her part, however, she could not remember being more completely aroused. But she was also sort of ashamed for it.

Lift up a little, he said, and as she did, he rinsed the tub beneath her to clean it. When he was satisfied, he motioned that she should sit back down, and plugged the stopper into the tub and turned up the heat.

No one's ever given me a bath before, she said. I mean not since I was a baby, I think.

He just raised his eyebrows a little and maintained his businesslike approach. Do you have shampoo, soap? he said. There was a cake of soap by the sink, but none around the tub.

In my bag, she said. I don't know where it is.

I'll find it, he said and got up to leave the room.

Hey, she said when he was almost through the door, and he turned. She wanted to see what his reaction would be if he just saw her like that, the water running, her naked body spread out in the tub, knees up, legs open.

He cocked his head as if to say, Yes?

What kind of guy are you? she said after gazing at him for a few beats.

He shook his head quizzically as though not getting the question. What she wanted to say was, Aren't you turned on in the least? and say it emphatically. But she couldn't.

When he left the room, she couldn't help herself and rammed a hand between her legs and pressed her palm hard against her pubic bone and curled her fingers downward and squirmed.

When he came back, she had removed her hand from her privates and he had her makeup/toiletries/etc. bag. The tub was steaming, and she felt completely strange. Completely strange because she was naked and drunk, in a completely unfamiliar apartment, with a beautiful man who seemed not uninterested, but disinterested. Possibly even robotic. And not only was he disinterested, he was a complete stranger whom she had just met in the hallway, if you could even call it a 'meeting.' She wanted to say something (like, The tub is big enough for two, or, Please fuck me, for example), but she had no idea at all what she could say. She had embarrassed herself enough in front of this man.

He turned on the shower head again and told her to sit up. She obeyed. He wet her hair, spraying and combing his fingers through it. She closed her eyes as he turned the water off and started to shampoo her. In even the most expensive salon, she had never had a shampoo that was this completely perfect—and this had nothing to do with being drunk. It was as though he knew secret things about her skull, where each of the nerves in her scalp were, and it hit her that maybe he was a hairdresser, that he was gay.

Are you gay? she said.

No, he said.

A hairdresser?

He laughed.

Celibate?

No.

In a committed and caring relationship?

Not except that with my daughter.

Not...

She giggled when he splashed her in the face with soapy water. Hey, she said. I didn't say....

Don't get ugly.

Now she was baffled. Sure, people were always different. There were few things about human nature that were as predictable as its unpredictability.

Did you have some sort of injury? Like that guy in the Hemingway book? Shrapnel in Nam?

If you mean something that would make me impotent, no.

Do you have AIDS or something?

No.

I don't get it.

He was rinsing her hair right now, and her head was hung forward, her hair covering her face, water racing.

Don't get what?

Her eyes were closed and a towel was wrapping her head. She reached up and grabbed it, wiped her eyes. She felt immeasurably better than she had but still pretty woozy. She looked at his eyes and wondered.

Do you, um..., she started, but had to make herself stop.

When he held still, he held still. You could have balanced a plate on his head. Do I what?

Find me attractive. She hid her face with her hands when she said it, more as an act, really. She peered at him through a crack in her fingers. I am so embarrassed, she said.

He was at last at a loss for words. No, he said, which was not at all the right or predetermined answer.

What's that supposed to mean? she said, humiliated again.

No, he said. I mean, yes. Yes, I do. But just because I find you physically attractive doesn't mean that I want to have sex with you.

She lay back in the tub. Well, she said. That's different.

This made him smile. Nor that you're acting particularly attractive at the moment.

She glowered at him.

I meet you in the hallway, he said. You're so drunk you can barely walk. You're bleeding and you've forgotten to put a shirt on. I assist you back to your apartment, and you start to get sick. You've still probably got a blood alcohol level above the legal limit for decision-making.

Do you always talk like that?

Like what?

I don't know. A cop.

Too much time hanging around them, I guess.

You're a cop?

No. And besides, I have a ten o'clock flight home in the morning. Listen, he said, Your offer is very generous—he smiled—very generous, but it's one I can't accept.

You can really kill a girl.

I mean no insult.

You're a funny man, Lawrence of Illinois.

You're clearly a very funny lady, Ellen Gregory.

You saw that. The TV?

He nodded.

Not my best work.

She looked down at the soapy water, at her feet and knees and boobs sticking out of it. Okay, she said, But isn't it weird that I feel like a slut because you turned me down but I wouldn't have if you hadn't?

Do you really feel like a slut?

Yeah.

Not just a lonely human being?

She studied his face.

Does that mean if I sobered up you'd fuck me?

He laughed and shook his head.

Will you at least stay with me for a while?

LITTLE MISSIVES

When she awoke, Ellen Gregory had a singularly fascistic headache, a misery that pounded in her head but wasn't satisfied with just her skull, but insisted on a blitzkrieg aimed at the absolute abjection of the body, the subjugation of the limbs, too, pounding on its lectern and shouting down that nothing would escape its wrath. And that limb or organ or follicle which attempted to escape would be greeted with the most savage and vicious brutality known to human kind—rape, pillage, burning of the villages and salting of the earth.

It was a fuckmonster of a headache. That was the first thing.

The other thing was she had no idea where she was, or how she had got there. It was almost like waking without a past, except she had enough of a past to notice that the bedroom was gorgeous, though way more masculine than anything she would ever think of doing for herself. And it couldn't be amnesia because at least she knew her name.

She started to sit up, but the dictatorial little fuckmonster garroted her head and gut simultaneously—Submission! Abjection!—and she went down as fast as she had come up. And speaking of coming up, there was the taste of bile in her throat.

Well, there's always the dry heaves, her interior, stage monologue said.

And then she saw the note. There was a quart bottle of water, and taped to it was a small piece of paper. In tiny, precise male handwriting, it said, Drink plenty of liquids. Start with this. Stay in bed. After you finish this, go into the kitchen.

She did as instructed, trying, as she sipped, then chugged, the water, to remember what had happened last night, and whose mysterious penmanship this was.

She wasn't sure if the water actually made her feel better, but at least it made her need to pee, and she got up, went to the bathroom, then went into the kitchen. There was another note, and another bottle of water, and two tablets of ibuprofen. Take these, the note said, and drink more water. Don't take these unless you've drunk the first bottle of water. Then, new paragraph, Possible liver damage. Eat something if you can. I made blueberry pancakes. Fridge. Maple syrup next to the microwave.

She turned and looked, and there was one of those little jugs of syrup on the counter, gleaming in a spotlight on the granite counter.

Coffee, said the last line of the note, Is ready to go. Bye. L. of I.

L. of I. What was that supposed to mean?

She went to the coffee maker and turned it on, then went to the window and pulled up the blinds. New York. Good lord. Fucking blessed lord. She was in New York. She craned and thought she could see Broadway.

Despite the fascist bastard headache, she felt a little flicker of wonder and glee in her soul, and went back into the kitchen and heated the pancakes, doused them in maple syrup, and tucked in. She had nearly finished them by the time she remembered: 10 o'clock. She looked at the clock, but it was already afternoon. She had no idea what 10 o'clock meant, but it seemed important.

She sank back into her chair and looked at the apartment, looked at the baggy pajamas she was wearing, and started to wonder. Just for safety—or something's—sake, she got up and went to the bathroom to see if there was any sign that she'd had sex. There was not, and she went back to her breakfast, her head throbbing, her body resisting gravity.

The wondering went on a long time, but nothing came.

She had some vague notion of a man, but he was nothing more than a blur. She had some vague notion of undressing herself at his command, but it made no sense. She thought she should feel some sense of dread—the whole Wayne Townsend thing, all the ugly experiences with paparazzi, but she didn't.

When she finished the pancakes, she went back to bed. When she woke again, it was dark, the little dictator had been vanquished, and she felt better than she could remember feeling for years.

DAILY

Okay, so the coffee in the pot was at least a half day old, one cup will get you through the brewing of a new pot.

The notes were still here, in that fascinatingly precise handwriting. The empty bottle of water in the kitchen. The D'Agostino's bag. The maple syrup. When she called Marty, he laughed into the phone. I heard you got way plastered on the plane.

Where the fuck am I?

He laughed again. In New York.

I know that. Whose place is this.

Will Simon's. You've never met him.

Will Simon. Who is he? Where is he?

He's a director. Or a budding director. He had a short film that won a prize at Cannes. He's very good.

But where is he?

Here. LA. He's shooting a music video.

Ellen sat down.

You know you don't handle alcohol well, Ellen darling.

Shut up, Marty.

He laughed again. So, he said, How are you?

Aside from the hangover, which is gone now, thank you, I'm fabulous.

Feel like doing some media?

What are you thinking?

The Daily Show.

Can you do that? I'd love to see Jon.

Well, the interview you did with *Entertainment Now* is coming out tomorrow, but it will be online in no time, so it'd be good. I'll make some calls. Call you back. I love you.

You, too, she said.

Sitting in the green room with a bag of *Daily Show* swag, she had no idea what she was going to say. She'd done okay in rehearsal. But she hated—loathed, despised—doing anything without way more than doing some kind of dry run. Jon was his usual iconoclastic self. For all of his professional swagger, Jon Stewart was one of the sweetest guys she knew in show business. How did you talk about it, something like shooting a man in your own home? You made it funny. They would play Johnny Cash. I shot a man just to watch him die.

She drank bottled water and waited, her head empty.

When she came on stage and the applause drowned everything else out, Jon leaned to her and said, I am so glad you are okay, and so happy to see you.

She said: Thank you. I feel so…, but the countdown had stopped and they had to sit down.

Ellen Gregory!

Jon Stewart.

He giggled his famous giggle. She said, There have been so many famous butts in this chair. Wow.

But yours is the best. [Giggle]

Jon, I really think you need to work on the giggle. See, girls giggle, boys chuckle.

[More giggles.] It's so great to see you. You have been through, how do I put this, oh, yeah, *hell* and back since you were last on the show. And you KILLED a guy, what is up with *that*?

There was almost nothing you could not laugh at when Jon framed it. And she laughed.

Yeah, she said, drawing the word out and letting the moment hang for a few beats.

I don't really like to think about it that way. Killing, as you know, is only for comedy. [Lame.]

But no, a guy breaks into your house, a guy who has already been stalking you, who kidnapped you, for God's sake.

Let that be a warning to you. She said it first to Jon, then to the audience, pointing her finger, gun-like, and then the camera. I am not a woman to be fucked with.

You're not packing tonight, are you? [Giggles.]

Not tonight, Jon.

Can we be serious for a moment?

I don't know why we should start now.

No, really. You had a stalker.

I did. In a twisted sort of way, it was kind of flattering. There's someone out there who makes you the center of their universe. It's a shame to have to kill, like, your total top fan.

[Jon giggles.]

See, she said, you have to make that into a hearty chuckle. Think Ed McMahon.

Chuckle heartily. I'll take that note. [Turns to his papers, pretends to make a note.] Chuckle heartily. So, tell me about your stalker.

My stalker? That possessive pronoun does things I don't really want the language to do. My. My stalker. Jeez. Because when you put it that way, and I don't know too many other ways to put it, actually, but it sounds like I'm responsible for him. Or was.

That's an interesting point, because, seriously, how else do you frame it? So tell me about the psycho who was hunting you like an animal?

[Ellen laughs.]

You're so good. That's so much better.

[Jon nods.] Thank you. [Now he leans in.] You'd been receiving letters from this individual for, like, months, a year. Your people were aware of him, but couldn't do anything.

Nobody could do anything until a crime was committed. So, no. That's the way it should be, but it does make it hard.

Do you have any idea at all what was going on in his mind?

He came after me with a baseball bat. I shot him. If he had any feelings, we didn't get the chance to discuss them.

[Jon giggles. Good applause from the audience.]

We've known each other for, I don't know, six or seven years at least, and in all of that time, I've never known you to have even the slightest violent tendency. Are you…, how are you coping with this?

I feel terrible. In so many ways I can't even begin to tell you. [Jon gets a very sober look. The audience is quiet.]

I do get some consolation, you know, because I have a family of bonobo apes and half a case of KY in the basement.

[Jon snorts, presses his face against his desk, laughing.] You know, I'm wetting my pants, but I can hide behind this desk.

Now Ellen laughed.

He wrote you letters. A lot of them.

Jon, do you read your mail?

[Giggles.] I don't know that I can answer that.

I don't read mine either. Like you, I have highly paid assistants who risk the letter bombs. No. Just kidding. No. I didn't read any of the letters. Any time I get letters that look like they were addressed in crayon by a kindergarten student, I do not read them.

My kids will be so disappointed.

A psychologist who examined them said they were kind of psychotically poetic, but it was like this guy, right, had created a secret society in his head to, like, *displace* whatever normal feelings he might have had. Like, you know, I'm in the army, it's my job to kill people for the society. So he could turn me into an object. An object about which he had no feelings.

That is chilling.

It is.

[Pause. One beat, two, Jon staring.] But you handled it so well. [Applause. Laughter.]

That's what people keep telling me. I can't even think about it. I'm very good at that, you know. I just don't think.

It's the American way.

Jon.

Ladies and gentlemen, Ellen Gregory.

There was a moment after, when the applause was going (really great and uplifting applause) when Jon leaned to her and said, Thank you so much. It's great to see you. If you're going to be in town for a few days, we should do dinner or something.

And when she left the studio she felt a good kind of dazed, the way she hadn't felt in years. It was good to be on her own, without handlers, with out 'her people.' This—leaving LA—was a good thing. LA was some kind of weird intoxication, a lie on a foundation and infrastructure of lies. New York you could trust because it never even pretended to give a shit about you. New York loomed, indifferent, and said, If I'm gone, baby, what do you think becomes of you? and somehow that was more than comforting.

She walked, unmolested, and thought. This was a signal. Life could be different. She could get out and walk, live.

There was water in her mind. She thought of the mystery man with the little missives written in beautiful architect's handwriting, and there was something about it that was like water. The sun in the water of Marty's pool. She knew she'd probably made a fool of herself. But she was alive, and the street was alive, and if anyone knew who she was, no one let on.

THE MIDAS OF DREAMS

The decision, such as it was, came to her on the plane back to LA.

Or later, when she tried to figure out when the moment came that she knew she had to escape, it seemed that it was then.

New York had been good. She had almost felt herself, but still there was a kind of loneliness, the sense of being divorced from herself. At a party in SoHo the night before she went back, she saw people she hadn't seen in years, but as delighted as she was to be there and see them, part of her felt as though she was just going through the motions, a simulacrum of herself.

On the plane—the same time-share deal but a different pilot—she ignored the bar and just looked out the window. Dental surgery would have been a more appealing thought.

She tried to think of where she had come from and how she had got to this point, and there was no real way of rationalizing it. This happened, that happened. Chance, coincidence, life. How did the song go? Life is what happens when you're making other plans.

How often did it happen, the whole fact of having nearly all of your lifelong dreams come true? Dreams you didn't even know were possible came true. And it sort of made you freak, dreams—that ethereal fabric—suddenly turning to gold, which was heavy as hell and hurt like hell when it hit. The Midas of dreams.

She had no real recollection of what she had been like when she left home, unvarnishedly angry at her mother, full of certainty that there was no future whatsoever in her small Iowa town. And then there was the ambition, that *I'm-gonna-show-you-motherfuckers* kind of truly truly truly insane ambition of the alienated, ignored, desperate -to-not-be-perennially-second-third-lower tier in high school. Oh, yeah, she had friends in the old days, the others on gymnastics team and in marching band, and even a boyfriend named Lars who was heartbroken at her leaving (about which she did not inform him) because he really had featured her cutting his corn off the cob into eternity.

She had no brothers or sisters, but it wasn't until roughly the time she hit puberty that she began to feel the crushing sensation of parental scrutiny, which came mostly from her mother. It had, of course, the effect of making her want to be secretive, and, eventually, to do things that would require greater and greater secrecy.

Puberty, for Ellen, was less than an overnight event—yes, she got her period in a more or less timely fashion, but what her doctor referred to coolly as secondary sexual characteristics—namely, boobs—took their damned sweet time in coming. Sometime during her sophomore year in high school, she was bestowed the moniker of Runt, which may well have been the thing that started her comedy. Where all these other girls looked like young women, she still looked like a girl, and so she deflected insults directed at her and made jokes—*Where are my boobs? I had them on this morning*—but it was no less painful.

And so the hijinks began, and of course began with the usual high school shenanigans—sneaking out late at night and drinking—which she soon discovered she was not particularly fond of—the drinking part, not the sneaking out part. But so since she was funny, sometimes scurrilously so, people invited her to parties, and while they got wasted, she got funny. She—literally—made girls pee in their pants. This was a particular delight.

But of course the parties got dull, and too easy, and so she started looking for edgier thrills. Did she really, actively, look? Or did it all just sort of evolve? These were to be found a few miles down the road in Iowa City, where the parties were bigger, more raucous, and entirely more intellectual and wholly more animal. She went with her friend Emily, who was six inches taller, looked like she was twenty, read constantly, looked like a movie star (to Ellen, anyway) and attracted 'college men' (in addition to men in general), as she put it, like shit attracts flies. And since Ellen didn't like to drink, she made a great designated driver.

It was in Iowa City that she met Joshua.

Later, if she'd had the kind of mind that tackled its unconscious like a philosopher, she might have wondered if the fling-thing with Joshua was really love, or some other, more sort of self-destructive behavior. It was Joshua on whom she based the character of the minister in her act. He played the guitar, wrote earnest songs, wore his hair long, and was distinctly retro when everyone else was listening to late punk and jumping up and down, which he referred to as pogo-stick dancing.

She had started to make a name for herself—at least at the parties where she went with Emily, because after studying them in silence for what seemed ages, she started making people laugh again. She was just 16, could have passed for 12 at the movies, and told jokes that were as sharp as nails.

She couldn't remember the name of the girl—a sorority type—now, but at the time, she was Ellen's imaginary nemesis, with brown hair, a perfectly proportioned body, and that entire air of wholesome Iowa goodness. (Exactly whom Ellen modeled her persona on later. Shame she couldn't remember her name.) The night she met Joshua was the night she made Sorority Girl pee her pants. And it wasn't even that good of a joke—about how syphilis got started in Iowa, and she told it like it was true, and, for authenticity, she did it with a kind of earnest, know-it-all schoolgirl air that was just a little shy. It had to do with a particular sheep, a farmer, the farmer's wife, a businessman, and a cast of thousands. It was a sort of a shaggy dog story that accumulated wily and sometimes irrelevant details like a Bob Dylan song, and she was gasping and yapping and really just getting into it, and finally she came back around and smashed the punch line, just knocked it out of the park. And for a moment there was silence, because it had started out with just a few people listening, and others gathering, frowning, wondering, Is this girl serious? and ended with a crowd, Sorority Girl at the center, in short shorts, her hair tied in ribbons (seriously), and the silence was like the moment between lightning and thunder, when Ellen wasn't sure if the joke was going to work, and just stood there tapping her foot, waiting, and then beer started coming out of people's noses, Sorority Girl looked like she was having an epileptic fit, and it was the first time being funny actually scared Ellen. She got a sly look and went, He, he, he, and people laughed even harder, and Sorority Girl peed her pants, and screamed it, *You made me pee my pants*, and Ellen thought, *Damn straight I did*. And the thing was that Sorority Girl wasn't pissed. She was thrilled. Which was the weirdest part. *Nobody has ever made me laugh that hard*, she gasped, still laughing, a dark spot of wet spreading at her crotch.

And then, later, sitting around waiting for Emily to get her fill of older male attention, not to mention beer, and people coming over and giving her, like, high fives and pats on the back, this slim, blondish man with longish hair and John Lennon glasses sat down next to her and said, You ought to do stand-up. You are a very, very funny young woman.

She didn't very often get hit on, had actually and frankly *never* been hit on—if that was what was happening—by an older man (mostly she was ignored because of Emily, and because, after all, she was Runt) and had next to no idea what to do. By that time, she and Lars were dating, but it amounted to not much more than holding hands in the hallways, some low-key petting, movies. Dinner at his parents.

And she had never been called a woman by *anyone*.

He introduced himself as Josh. She asked what his major was, which is what one tended to do, and he laughed jovially. Turned out that he was a teacher. Something called an adjunct lecturer of English. He had graduated from the writing program (which she had never heard of but he assured her was probably number one) and he was teaching a couple of sections of composition and lit in order to make enough time to finish his novel. It was the first time she'd met someone with some kind of ambition that extended beyond graduating from high school, much less beyond state lines, and by the end of the night—which was very very late—she had her head on his shoulder. No one, not even Emily, was sober enough to notice. He was from New York, and determinedly old school, he said. She had no idea what he was talking about. He asked for her phone number. She said, I've got some really uptight room-mates. Maybe you ought to give me yours.

Joshua wasn't that far away, and in a matter of (probably) days, she fell in love with him—though she kept Lars as a cover. She fell in love with his bones, his knees and elbows, and the mercury that ran through his soul (like hers).

He was the alien being, astonishingly and thoroughly dim at times, and at others, slashingly incisive and with (what seemed to her then) incredibly penetrating wisdom. He knew everything there was to know about storytelling, or so she imagined, and she read his manuscript (excitingly opaque—she had no way of knowing; she didn't read the sorts of things he aspired to).

Perhaps a week into the affair, she drove over to his house—an upstairs apartment on Fairchild, and stripped. He was (bizarrely, it seemed to her) stunned that she was a virgin—or had been until that afternoon—and dismayed at the blood. Don't pull a Sylvia Plath on me, he said and, after assuring him that she wouldn't, she had to look it up later, that Plath almost bled to death when she lost her virginity.

She gave up the shaggy dog stories when she read a piece that he was working on, and he had stolen her own shaggy dog story—but rewritten it—and she was shocked at how ruthlessly he had stolen it from her. When she protested, he just said, Anyone who is around a writer should expect his or her life to be mined completely.

That was weirdly attractive, even if it made her shut down a little. The maleness of it, the alien notion that you could steal like that. Why she had never thought of it. And there was his ambition, his secret identity.

It was, in actual fact, upon Josh's own ambition, fired and annealed in the shadow of an older, practically-perfect-in-every-way brother, that her own had been modeled. Which was, of course, what she was really in love with. He was himself almost irrelevant. His ambition gave her a framework, an armature for her own. She fed on it—because her own ambition had heretofore been just some kind of weird inchoate mental illness.

She stole hours from school, from gymnastics practice, from anything she could steal time from to spend with him to listen to how he was going to conquer the world. She learned from him. The world is big. Iowa is small. Iowa is not your oyster.

He had a personal ferocity and foolishness about being a writer—always carrying a paperback that just fit in the back pocket of his jeans—Kerouac or Hemingway or Faulkner or something Russian. That and a narrow reporter's notebook that he was jotting in all the time. The way that some men's jeans pockets have the scars of a wallet or a can of snuff, his bore the scars of books.

The sex part was just a thing to get to his soul, and so she plotted and plotted to have sex with him. She was smart enough to use birth control, but when he found out that she was only 16, he stopped everything cold.

Cold.

Line's gone dead.

You didn't *guess*? I look like I'm *13*!, she screamed in her head. *How could you not know?!?!*

She had told no one, though Emily and some of her other friends had guessed about Ellen's secret boyfriend. But guessed wrong. And there was no one to share it with. You can't keep that big of a secret and then let it out. A professor. Not just an older boy, but a full-grown, actual man. It would have been like admitting to fucking your father's friends.

Not possible.

He was a nice guy, the minister, really sweet and sincere. An ex-hippie who had found God, and I do mean this literally, when he was on LSD. He had those John Lennon glasses. The wispy little beard. And oh, man, was he great in bed. Do you know that you can get closer to God by fucking a minister? It's true. He told me.

The grief of it—the loss of Joshua, not only the contact but the mental detachment that came in the pure fucking unalloyed hope of seeing him, Josh who represented possibility in life, Josh who gave her a vision of the outside of this very small little world that increasingly was defined by her mother's sometimes idiotic ideas—in which every noun seemed to be preceded by the pathetically weak and old-womanly adjective *nice*. *Nice* cup of tea. *Nice* boy. *Nice* time. *Nice* girl. The kind of thing that made you want to run screaming in the opposite direction.

Josh had gone on to publish a couple or three books. She read the first while in New York, and was appalled to see way more than just a hijacked shaggy dog story, but the 16-year-old joke-telling kid who fools the hero into having a baby with her, forcing him into a marriage he does not want. It made her jaw drop and her fists clench.

It was the kind of thing that made you want to spit. Made you want to call the guy up and tell him what an asshole he was for stealing your jokes and your life.

But.

Once she got over the initial shock of it, she found that it was instructive, the merciless theft. This was news she could use. She had not seen him since he found out how young she was and kicked her out.

I thought about it, being a minister's wife. But there were a couple of problems with that. I just felt like I was too young to take on those kinds of responsibilities. I mean, a minister's wife has to be strong and solid and constant, and I considered it, but it was a lot of responsibility for a 13-year-old. I am kidding. Really. No, stop. Really. I was 14.

And I really didn't get along with his wife.

And then one night, her last in New York after her *Daily Show* appearance, on her way to a party, there he was. It had been so long and so much had changed, she had no way of being sure. But when she turned and saw him, the considered dishevelment of his hair, the John Lennon glasses rejected for expensive designer frames, a weird electric thrill of recognition went through her.

She did not pay him the gratuity of acknowledging him. But still the idea that it might have been him—if indeed it was—made her feel the gap in time. The distance. The self-reinvention. A weird thrill of accomplishment.

And so when she had been cut loose, she got a little looser, went looking for the same kind of thrill, but found nothing similar. And then, to compound matters, one dawn she came home, walking up the street after a party (where there was no Josh) and finding her mother sitting on the front step. Her mother in her housecoat who had not slept and had been on the step who-the-fuck-knew-how-long, probably cold.

There ensued a battle, or escalation of the battle that had gone one between them, that lasted until she left, months later, under cover of darkness.

Her mother shook her head in disgust and dismay, and shame. Shame. Her beloved one and only daughter sneaking out in the middle of the night. Walking up the street like a hooker. Which of course meant she entirely misunderstood. And oh, boy, did Ellen in the pre-dawn light of this late spring morning lay into her.

How *dare* you, Mother?

Then the accusatory confessional. (A thing, later in life, she would relive in a kind of post-traumatic stress flashback of horror.)

You want the truth. You can't handle the truth.

Ellen hissed details. (Many of them made up and embellished—which, bizarrely, seemed like a good idea at the time.) Each one hit her mother like a purely physical blow. Ellen, later, much later, regretted this, but at the time, it felt like a kind of freedom, even though she was grounded until she went to college.

In the perverse way of teenagers, she enjoyed the odd freedom of the scarlet S (for slut, slattern, skank) she got to wear around the house for the last eight or 10 months that she was there. So she'd say things to her mother like, I cunt find it, muhtherf, or, Ma? Did you ever go to Las Vegas? Play the one-armed babies—I mean bandits?—just for the gag factor.

Her father took it harder, but more distantly, and she took him on less directly, and even—empowered by her own effervescently foolish reading of *Our Bodies Ourselves*—tried to sit him down and explain to him sexual desire from a female point of view, the Santa Claus-in-reverse explanation of women's sexual desire—*Like, I mean, just because you can't necessarily see it doesn't mean it's not there, you know?*—which, truth be told, went over about as well and about as humiliating as though she were inadvertently suggesting incest. But she couldn't joke her way around his sorrow. She was a sexual being and she had chosen to express it. Evidence of his sorrow lasted. All he said was, I just wish you and your mother could find a way to get along.

Which was at that point asking the impossible.

And then there was the unbearable teenaged itch to leave. Worse than cutting a tooth. The worst kind of directionless craving. Yes, she had put in applications to college; yes, she had been accepted. But even as she went through the motions of getting excited about acceptance letters, she also knew that she was not going. That even if she did go, it would be a waste of her time and their money.

And so on the plane, this came back, likely jogged from her memory by the vision of Joshua, real or not. And with it came her loathing of herself. Or the self that had come to occupy the territory that her own self had once owned.

It was later that day that she bought the hair dye. The compact scissors.

THE DEPREDATIONS OF LOVE

Ellen sat in the cab, staring at her parents' house for a long time. The driver had started to get out, but she stopped him, said, No, no, wait, I just want to think a minute. He turned and put his arm over the black, plastic-upholstered seat and looked at her—maybe wondering if he recognized her—and then turned around again and stared ahead. She was terrified.

Right now, here in front of the house she grew up in, which by the way looked exactly the same as it had on the dewy, fragrant morning when she had fled, it all seemed horrendously complicated—and yet somehow the passage of time simplified it all. She had a sensation behind her solar plexus as if a fist were grabbing her lungs and heart and squeezing them tight.

There was a weird aspect to it all, as though time did not exist, as though the last seventeen years were more like seventeen minutes, and she, a sheepish seventeen-year-old, were skulking back after an abortive runaway attempt.

She had the sensation that she had done something monstrous, cataclysmic, the reverberations of which would be felt for longer than she could imagine. But of course, it felt like she had done the only thing she could have done.

There had always been rumblings about Ellen Gregory that she was not entirely—what's the word?—Oh, right. *Stable.* Not that she wouldn't show up for work. Not that she wasn't funny. Just that there was a certain sort of fissile quality to her— she would say whatever came off the top of her head. But spontaneity was not a commodity that anyone in LA particularly treasured. Despite all of its supposed quote unquote creativity, Hollywood was a very conservative town, and spontaneity, honesty—that was like herpes. After her kidnapping, there was mostly sympathy. But she sensed other kinds of rumblings also. Distant, very low-frequency rumblings that maybe only a dog could hear. A blame-the-victim-ish culpability that a psycho was attracted to her. Of course no one ever said this. No one ever would've suggested that it might have been a better narrative had she been killed by Townsend instead of killing him. But those rumblings were drowned out by the much higher frequency outpourings of sympathy and concern.

For the most part it was true that there was no such thing as bad publicity, and while her smarmy publicist had created a most excellent über-narrative to envelop what was perhaps the most horrific moment in her life; while he had turned it into some kind of fairytale for girls of all ages, she got the sense—and again no one said this—that this just added to some sub-narrative of Ellen Gregory to which Ellen Gregory herself wasn't exactly privy.

Which of course might have been some ugly paranoia.

It was late, but not excruciatingly late, and there was still a light on in the house. The house.

It was not time travel. And yet it was, exactly, time travel. She had stepped out of one world in LA and, at the Cedar Rapids Airport, stepped into an entirely different one.

The house.

The house had not changed a bit in most of two decades. It did, as they always say, look smaller. But pristine as always, her father's German heritage hard at work. Parts of the flower beds looked different, and the maple in the front yard had gone from not much more than a sapling to enormous. But other than that, she could see little different.

My parents are nice, Midwestern Lutherans. I send them money—usually a million a month, you know, small, unmarked bills. It's kind of like a joke, I send them a briefcase full of unmarked twenties, and the IRS investigates my dad. It's just a little family tradition.

So when I called my father and asked if they were doing anything special with it, like getting the house remodeled, buying a penthouse on Park Avenue, you know what he said? I love this. He said he was just putting it away for me in case this comedy thing didn't work out for me. And I'm like, Daa-aad, do you read the papers?

And so I say to him, What I have here, Pops, is a pretty much nonstop orgasm of wealth. A sybaritic sewer of cash.

And he says, You never know about rainy days.

And I'm like, I'm set, Dad. Really. I am so set that I could start a shoe company, and exploit children in third world countries. I am so set. This money is for you. Have fun. Fun. Travel. Meet new and interesting people—and hell, kill them if you want. I've got the best legal counsel on either coast.

Ellen was surprised that her hands were trembling, sweating and cold. She was surprised that she was really really scared, and in her head she went over a million different scenarios, like, *Hey, I know I'm late, but I have a really good excuse.*

She had kept in touch. Called regularly if not terribly often. Received and sent (or sometimes had her assistant send) cards and gifts. The car she had sent to her father for his 65ᵗʰ birthday, a sleek little Honda 2000 convertible, sat in the driveway, a cover over it.

For a moment, she wanted to weep, and then she did. It felt like she had come a long, long way, the flight from LAX to O'Hare, then O'Hare to Cedar Rapids, and then the hour-long cab ride to Fairview Park. It was two thousand miles or more, but it was also way more than that. And it had been a little like riding a wave—the excitement of escape. Which had crested and now she was entering a trough, or re-entering the trough in which she had been becalmed, moored, fucking stuck for the last several months.

This was not a withdrawal thing because she had stopped doing any sort of chemicals, except coffee and the odd glass of wine, when the ephedra made her heart feel like it was fibrillating. But now it took something like two pots of coffee intravenously in the morning just to get out of bed, but she had been, up until a couple of days ago, able to work up the necessary emotional charge to work, but it felt like each time she did, it ate a piece of her soul.

The driver said, You okay, ma'am?

Yeah, she said. Dandy. Just *dandy*. She wiped at her eyes with the back of her hand.

And then she got out and he followed her, except she had no luggage. Just the Hobo bag and an overnight bag she had bought in the airport with a few things she had also bought in the airport. She paid him and tipped him a hundred dollars and then stood on the sidewalk as he drove away and the sky opened up in all its still silence, its throbbing stars, and she felt chilly, indecisive. Her parents' house was typical of those in the small town—three bedrooms, white clapboard siding, crisp lawn. She could smell the indescribable scent of her childhood, the air so different from California air. She shivered, and then, as she did before appearances, she took a deep breath, counted to ten, let it out, and headed for the door.

Somewhere down the street a dog barked when she knocked, and inside there was no sound, and the idea went through her that they were not there, that they had died and she had not been here. Been there.

She was knocking again when the door came open and there was her mother in pink slippers. Lord, forgive her, but her mother looked for all the world as plump and pink and cute as a cartoon piglet, a look that was only spoiled by a fresh-from-Wal-Mart housecoat and blue hair. Her mother—once almost black-haired, had been graying when Ellen last saw her, but she had not expected the blue hair thing, despite having done a bit on it: *You know those old ladies with blue hair? What I realized is that this is not just some snarky joke perpetrated by sadistic hair dressers on half-blind old ladies. This is a personal lifestyle choice… like being gay. He he. No, like, I'm trying* to imagine getting to a certain age and one day going to the hair dresser and saying, *Pauline, dear, I think I'd like the blue. I can't wait to get to that stage in life, when my hair can look all whipped up like blue cotton candy.*

She opened the door incautiously, as though people happened by at 11 or so every night of the week, and then she just stopped, stood there and stared, open-mouthed. Ellen's black hair threw her off, and when recognition went over her face, it was like she'd been hit with a hammer and gone senseless. Her father called out from inside the house, Who is it, honey? the timber of his voice so familiar and yet so completely strange.

Her mother crossed herself. This was a detail about her mother that Ellen had forgotten—she was not a Catholic but a faithful Lutheran, but she liked to cross herself and tended to do it several times a day.

And then her father emerged from the dining room doorway and into the entranceway and stopped himself. She looked between her parents, and she could no longer remember what combination of anger and fear it was that had caused her to leave. Her father broke into a huge grin but—in, like, the most incredibly clichéd display of Midwestern Lutheran restraint—ambled toward her and said, Honey, why don't you invite your daughter in?

Her mother staggered back, blinking and crying and her father came and threw his arms around her, pushed the door shut. Welcome home, he said. Welcome home, meat loaf (this was one of his old jokes—'my love' = meat loaf).

Oh, Daddy, she said, burying her face in the nape of his neck and smelling his drug store aftershave. He said, Say hello to your mother, and released her and she drifted toward her mother and hugged her, and her mother—who had gotten smaller, shorter—showered her with kisses and tears, and then they all just stood there, looking at one another. Ellen ran her hand through her newly shorn and dyed hair, and her father said, after a long silence, New 'do?

Ellen sucked in her tears and stood there pretty much incapable of speaking and just nodded. It amazed her that she could so easily be accepted back, that her parents could so easily forgive.

Then suddenly her mother clapped her hands together and cackled and lunged for the telephone. Ellen shouted, No! and almost knocked the telephone out of her mother's hand. The look on the older woman's face almost broke her heart.

Mom, Ellen said, I'm AWOL. Please. You can't tell anyone I'm here. No one.

Her mother looked at her father with a look of despair that made Ellen cringe. Ellen turned to her father and for the first time in the last few moments, she felt like she actually saw him, the watery look of his eyes, the deepened creases of his face. It was from him she got her fair hair, from her mother that she got her spectacular skin.

Her father interrupted the silence and said, El, you want a drink?

That'd be great, she said.

Good, her father said, as though this was the wisest possible decision under the circumstances. What can I get for you?

Do you have any white wine?

Her father shook his head.

Red?

Again with the head shaking. Booze, he said. I got booze. I got good Kentucky sour mash. I've got good British gin. I've got single malt scotch.

I'll go with the bourbon, Ellen said. Half water, with ice.

While her father went to make drinks, her mother stood looking at her, a simultaneous look of worry and pride in her eyes. At last, she said, Is everything okay?

Mom, Ellen said, looking for the right words, I kind of just snuck out. I was—kind of—freaking out. I am not one for spur of the moment crap but this was that. I felt…. I don't know how I felt. I had to get out. I didn't even pack. I just bought this overnight bag at the airport. Ellen realized that she'd been clutching the thing like a baby holds onto a favorite doll the entire time she'd been standing here, even through the hugs. She was exhausted, she wanted to cry and scream and hide, and it was everything she could do to hold it together. There was also an element of shock, of realizing that home was no longer home, that she was a stranger in so many respects to the people and the place she had come from.

Her father returned with a highball glass with whiskey and water on ice. When he handed it to her, he ushered her into the living room and the three of them sat down, her dad with a glass identical to hers, her mother knitting her fingers.

When she sat down, she scanned the room. It was mostly as she remembered it, but the paint had perhaps changed shades. The only evidence of her work—at least here—was framed cover art from her first comedy CD, *Paint the World Pink*. Maybe the furniture was new. If it was, and it probably was, it was no different from the older furniture she remembered. She sat on the loveseat while her mother sat on the couch, her legs up and her arms curled around them, and her father sat in his favorite armchair (which had not changed). He sipped his drink, and she gulped hers. It occurred to her that she had never had a drink with her parents.

There was still something in the room between them, the proverbial 800-pound gorilla, but she had no idea what it was. She had devoted precious little time to thinking about the past, her mistakes. She scanned her memory and thought of all the reasons that parents might have visited, the invitations she had made spurned, and she wondered which one of them she had hurt the more. Which one of them—they had always presented a united front—she had more deeply wronged.

Are you in any kind of trouble? her father said.

She took another hard pull on the whiskey and waited for it to hit her empty stomach. She said, No. Or at least I wasn't until I left.

The accumulated weight of things began to become vaguely apparent to her—she had traded one untenable situation for another, and now she felt like a cartoon train wreck—she had come to an abrupt and foolish halt, and all the other cars were crashing into her.

She drained her drink and stared at the ice in the glass as she shook it—it was ice cube tray ice, not ice-maker ice—and in a moment her father was up, taking the glass from her and leaving the room. In a moment, she could hear the drizzle of Elijah Craig in her glass. More water, cracking ice. She looked at her mother and gave a rueful smile, a smile that was intended to conceal her weariness and confusion and (really) abject terror but instead telegraphed all of those things more perfectly than telepathy. Her mother pulled her housecoat around her as if the weight of it all made her cold, and she looked down at the coffee table—one that, like the Adirondack chairs in her backyard, her father had made. (*I took a little bit of the money you sent, bought some teak and made these chairs for you.*)

There was nowhere to begin. Or there were too many places to begin, which it made it nearly impossible to find a place.

Do you want to tell…, her mother started, then stopped herself. Do you want to talk about what kind of trouble you're in? Is it that man?

She said this so haltingly it felt like the saying of it might never be said.

Ellen's father came back into the room and handed her the glass and sat down.

Well, I just signed a multimillion dollar contract and I walked out. Breach of contract would be a start.

But why?

Ellen laughed. She almost wanted to mock her mother's question, But why? There was a chilly self-righteousness to her mother that she should have expected, except she had not thought about any of this. Some reptilian part of her brain was scheming in her subconscious and, savagely, dragging her along with its whims.

Mother, she said, but there was heat in her face that kept her from talking, the heat was worst behind her eyes and tears started coming but the heat was worse and it just made for more tears. She wasn't crying exactly, nothing like heaving sobs or even any sort of boohooing she had ever done, there was just this flood of water from her eyes.

Her father gave her a tissue, and she dried her eyes.

I left, she said at last, after another long pull of her drink, I left because it really didn't seem that it would matter.

137

I don't understand, her father said. He was leaning toward her, his eyes beseeching.

I don't really understand it myself, she said, normal tears starting to come now. I know this is not going to make much sense to you, but I feel like there was a point where I sort of subdivided, that there's this other me, this clone of me, that exists out there, and she took everything that I liked about myself. Ellen pointed at a magazine that lay on the end table between the couch and the loveseat. There was, of course, a photograph of her on the cover. It was an older issue, one with an inset photo of Wayne Townsend on it, too. That's her, she said. The other me.

Is it about that man? her mother said.

It is and it isn't and it is and it isn't and certainly he is part of it but it's *everything*. She put her drink down on the coaster her father slid to her and she sat back on the loveseat, put her hands over her face.

Now she reached over and picked up the magazine, then held it up. Do you know how many of these things are sold? she said. She didn't wait for an answer: Millions. Millions. And there are millions of people, who if they are not scheming to kill you or sleep with you or do ugly and very unwholesome things to you, then transfer to you, to your image, a lot of baggage and emotion and concern and it makes your head buzz that everyone knows who you are, that people seem to want some *thing* for you that's....

She stopped because that really wasn't it. She stopped because she was exhausted and depressed, and now, just a little bit drunk.

At last, she said, The reality is, mother, I'm alone. I'm alone.

Big News: America's Favorite Girl Next Door, the Sweetheart of the Airwaves, is an irredeemable shit, she thought. The very sort of diva she most desperately hated. Not only did she have enough money to buy a big house to roll around in like Norma Desmond, but she did roll around in her big house like Norma Desmond. Alone.

Maybe we should all just sleep on it, her father said.

That's a fine idea, her mother said, There are clean sheets on your bed and towels in your bathroom.

Ellen looked up, a weird sense of horror going through her, but she said nothing. They kept it ready. They had kept it ready for all these years. Or her mother had.

I'll make you breakfast, her father said. Just like in the old days. You can sleep in.

Okay, but please, tell no one, absolutely no one, and I mean the police or the FBI or the CIA or Mrs. Schoenblum or anyone, anyone, that I'm here. Or Marty. Especially Marty.

Both of her parents nodded their assent.

She collected herself and stood, picked up her glass, drained it, spilling some down her front, then started toward the kitchen to put it in the sink, and then she turned and looked at her parents, feeling a bit as though she had been punched in the gut, as though she might fall over from the pain. Thanks, she said.

Upstairs, her room was almost exactly as she left it, right down to the ancient *Elle* and *Vogue* and gossip magazines on her nightstand. It was a time capsule. She closed the door and closed her eyes and sank to her knees and sobbed. She woke later, cold, on the carpet, and dragged herself into the cool sheets of her own bed.

HOME AT LAST

Ellen came downstairs, late morning, while her mother was on the telephone. When she came into the kitchen, her mother was speaking in hushed tones, emphatic, but incomprehensible. When she noticed Ellen, she gave a little whoop, as though someone had run an ice pick through her foot, and leapt in the air. Then, trying to erase the look of surprise, she slapped a hand to her bosom and rolled her eyes, and said, Just a minute, into the phone, then, to Ellen: Darling, you startled me half to *death*.

Her mother said: I am so not used to people other than your father being in the house.

Ellen sat at the table and stared at it, then looked at her mother, who had gone remarkably quiet. Where had she learned to talk like that? *I am so not used to...* There was a thin-screen TV under one of the cabinets, one of those disk-combo jobs you could get at Wal-Mart for a couple hundred, and it was on, but the sound was off.

Right at this moment, her head still fogged with sleep, home was a strange concept. Being with her parents felt more like home than being in her own house, which she did not miss. There was nothing about it—except maybe the coffee—that called out to her. She focused on the television. She could not tell what show it was, some daytime crap. She watched this stuff all the time, just for material, to keep up with the cultural zeitgeist, but right this minute she was afraid she was going to see her own picture.

Her mother went on with her conversation—she often reminded Ellen of a litter of piglets, a constant churning of squeals—but not now. Now she was all discretion. Ellen got the definite sense that her mother would have left the room except they did not have a cordless phone in the house and she was tethered there. Finally, she said to whomever she was talking—clearly not finishing whatever it was she was saying, I'll have to let you go. Okay. You, too. Bye now.

You sure did sleep, Ellen, her mother said, suddenly all a-bustle, opening and closing cabinets, scrubbing and wiping. She remembered the TV and turned up the volume, then stopped herself—Does this bother you? I can turn it off.

No, mom, TV is my life.

It was meant as a joke, but it could also be taken literally.

Okay, okay, okay, Ellen's mother said, bustling but not apparently accomplishing anything.

Who was on the phone? Ellen said breezily, trying to pry without seeming she was prying.

Her mother gave her head a shake, which ever so slightly jiggled her jowls, then made eyes like, Oh, you know.

You were not talking about me, she said tentatively.

No, Ellen.

At first, her sleep last night, even after the whiskey, had been an epileptic fit of blankets and shadows and horrid dreams that flung her upright, sobbing, trying to figure out where she was, which shit hammer was going to drop. But her unalloyed exhaustion, physical but especially mental exhaustion, kicked in, and and she slept. Dead.

I would love a cup of coffee, Ellen said. It was astounding how difficult it was to ask for such a simple thing. It seemed to take every last bit of energy. I hope you weren't talking about me.

Ellen, dear, not every conversation I have has to do with you. I have my own life.

Mother, please. The news must be out, Ellen said. The disappearance of America's Favorite Girl Next Door is going to be big news, and people are going to call, and most emphatically not friends.

I'm sure we can handle it.

Just let Daddy answer the phone.

For heaven's sake, Ellen, I can certainly handle a phone call.

Ellen looked at her mother and tried to remember what the last conversation she'd had with her had been about before she left, but she could not. They had not exactly been on warm terms. And while they'd had conversations over the years, they were updates, not time-to-kill, shoot-the-breeze sorts of cozy mother-daughter chats. She and her mother had never been exactly close. Anything in depth, she said to her father. With her mother, mostly, it was hellos and goodbyes. Being here made all that different, although exactly how she did not know right now. She said: Mother, just tell me you weren't talking about me. You weren't, were you?

No. I was not talking about you, her mother said, almost visibly angry, and poured Ellen a cup of coffee and brought it to her. You want creamer or sugar or anything?

Black is fine, Ellen said. She had stopped using cream in her coffee years ago, and sugar years before that. Her mother handed her a mug, spilling some coffee on the table, then wiping it up like the fastest waitress in creation. Then she made herself one, heaping powdered creamer and sugar in before she sat down across the table.

Promise me you haven't told anyone I'm here.

Oh, for God's sake, Ellen, get over yourself.

Ellen could see her mother's mouth, as if in extreme close-up, the vague radial wrinkles around her lips where the collagen had deserted her, the lipstick put on for no one but the house, her telephone conversations. There was a quiver of anger in her mouth, and Ellen did not want to see it. At least not yet. Yesterday had been peaceful, largely because she had spent most of the day in bed.

Believe me, mother, I'm over myself. It's the rest of the world that needs to get a life.

You just have no idea of the awfulness and the ugliness that people knowing I'm here could visit upon us—not just me but you and daddy, too.

It's that Townsend fellow, isn't it? She didn't give Ellen a chance to respond. Ellen, you're talking as though…, her mother started, but stopped. She tried not to allow her exasperation to surface.

Mom, I'm just saying. You have no fucking idea.

Don't get angry. Her mother looked hurt. And you don't have to use that sort of language.

Ellen sipped the scalding coffee and took a deep breath. She was not angry. She was not.

The coffee was thin and tasteless, cheap coffee made frugally. It would take her a whole pot to get the buzz she got from a normal cup. The Des Moines *Register* sat on a chair, its pieces stacked neatly, and she stared at it, wondering if she should even bother to look. But then she heard her name and looked up at the television and saw her picture inset in the upper third, and the talent, a dark-haired woman she didn't recognize, said something she did not care if she heard.

Her mother got up and offered to turn the sound up.

Ellen took a sip of coffee and shook her head. Fuck, no, Ellen said.

Her mother sank back down in her chair, saying, Do you have to talk like that?

Yes, mother. I have to talk like that. I disagree vehemently with you that saying things like shit and fuck signal some sort of poverty of vocabulary. So, yeah, fuck.

Ellen.

Mother.

You're just determined to set me off, aren't you? You've been carrying this thing around with you for half your life, well. I won't rise to it. I won't.

Then don't.

For a moment, Ellen was sure her mother wanted to laugh, but then her face turned dark again, and Ellen had the sinking feeling that not only had she fucked up her own life, but was now fucking up the only thing—this must be true, or why was she here?—that mattered to her.

And now, suddenly, inexplicably, her mother had started to cry. Ellen wanted to scream. Just to let something out.

Mother, *please*. This was a plea.

I just... I just don't know where we.... Dear Lord, listen to me.

She rose up from her chair and patted at her dress, as if looking for a pocket with Kleenex, and then picked a napkin out of the tray on the table and rubbed at her nose, blew it. But now she cried even more, sucking at air and covering her eyes.

Mom, Ellen ventured. Let's try to keep in mind that it's my life that's falling apart, here.

Her mother managed a laugh through her tears.

Do you want to know something? Is Daddy out?

Her mother nodded her head. Through her tears, she said: He went to town to pick up some groceries.

You know what I do sometimes? I leave my fabulous mansion and the gated community in which it sits—which, a lot of fucking good that does me because it's a revolving door for psychopaths, but all that aside—I wait until dark and drive out to the suburbs. Like way out to Tarzana or something, and then I just park and walk up and down the streets and look in the windows, and see people living ordinary lives.

Her mother turned slowly, carefully placed her wadded napkin into the trash, then sat and picked another napkin up and pressed it to her nose, which, like her eyes, was red.

You know, you work and you work and you work and you think that there's something that you're working toward. You put everything else aside and some people—I mean I know of at least 10 people, if not a hundred, people I've been in acting classes with, people I've seen in plays, in small roles in movies, people I've seen on the fucking street, mother, who could play my character Gina as well if not better than I can. But they chose me. I guess there was some skill involved, but I know also that a lot of it was luck. And so there they are, and they have their lives. Life forces them to get a life. And I have my success and my house and my stalker. Or I did. And just because my picture is out there, just because you can see my image a million times a day if you really want to, somehow I'm more important. Except then I go back to my house and I'm alone except on the days when the gardener or the housekeeper comes, and I drive out to the endless suburbs where all the people are living and dreaming and wanting to be just like me, and what am I? I wonder if in another life, if I had just done one thing different, just one thing, I could have been like you.

Oh, Ellen, you're joking.

No. I just want you to know that if there is one person I envy in this world, it is you.

You have everything, Ellen.

No, mom, you have everything. You have a man who loves you, you have a place to come to at the end of the day, and okay, so Daddy isn't Harrison Ford or something, but…. Now Ellen started to cry.

Inelegantly, clumsily, her mother scooched her chair over next to Ellen's. She put her arm around her daughter and hugged herself close.

PAPARAZZINOIA

She had not been gone seventy-two hours when Marty showed up at her parents' door, disheveled and badly in need of sleep and a cup of coffee and probably a really good flossing. A rental car was parked on the street. She saw him from her bedroom window coming up the walk, his hair messed up, and she felt for him, but she was now in the protected bosom of her family.

Last night, after sitting with her mother on the couch and talking, and watching TV and cracking her mother up with cheap old jokes that weren't fit for a comic routine—last night had been the best night's sleep she had had in a while. But she was still in no mood to confront Marty, whom she knew would charm and cajole and persuade and wheedle and entice and speed-talk her into submission, then drag her by the ear back West.

Her mother answered the door. Marty turned on the charm. She could not hear what he said but she could hear the tone of it, and she lay in bed, the covers over her head, but nonetheless a wire of tension running through her, snapping, making every neuron crackle. She could get up and see him, or she could follow through with leaving and be a ghost.

Now she could hear her mother's voice, and, suddenly, her father's. Marty—honed from dealing with the most difficult people in the world—ratcheted up the charm, the heat. Now she could make out a few words. Contract. Lawsuit. I know Ellen better than you do. Here. I would just like to have a few words with her. A few words.

Her parents shut him out. Her mother was fucking spectacular, giving him the verbal equivalent of patting a child on the back and saying, There, there, sonny, run along before we have your ass for breakfast. And for a long time after they (quite conclusively) shut the door in his face, he stood in the street, staring at the house, probably hoping his star student, his anchor, his main client, his main meal ticket for all these years, would appear. Perhaps he thought he could will her appearance as he had done so many times before. But she did not. It was heartbreaking in a way, but it was also liberating in the same way. He knew she would come to the window, come to the door, and she thought of texting him, calling him, just to say, I'm okay and I hope you're okay with that, but she did not. Because she knew he would not be. She let the bed clothing envelop her and fell back asleep.

Later, over watery coffee, her mother said that he had flown into O'Hare, and (so she gathered) deep in paparazzinoia (Ellen's word), rented a car, then drove here. He seemed like a nice fellow, her mother offered.

He is, she said. He's *sui generis*.

Soo-eee what?

One of a kind. I love him but I don't want to talk to him right now.

Her parents more or less nodded in unison.

And when she went to bed, she had the sense of having traveled in time, which, in at least one sense, she had. But in another sense, one of rediscovery, she felt that when she had crossed the threshold into their house, some old self had been shed, a self that was almost entirely carapace, and in this new state—staring drowsily at the ceiling, listening to the distant sound of traffic—she was entirely more aware. All of this, of course, was about her parents, who were far more complex and interesting than she had ever imagined. And, this struck her as particularly weird, who loved her more deeply than she had ever thought was possible.

BROCCOLI, PART 1

Soraya and Hanna conferred a moment (there were unsettling giggles), then Hanna gave Michael a shopping list and pushed him out the door. He once had a thought that women changed the warp of the universe, and right now it seemed a bit as though they changed more than that. He was happy. He had met with Sprague and told his advisor that he had run into a patch of unanticipated bugginess. The thing was *working*, but it was not working as expected. He had backed everything up, put it aside, and was now in the debugging. It would take some time, but he foresaw having something to show soon, very soon. Sprague—who was a multiple award-winning professor popular most especially among his post-docs because he was easygoing, smart, and had an effective sort of Socratic method of asking questions, an effortless-seeming way of getting you to think about things from different angles—had been customarily copasetic about everything, had just offered the one caveat, which Michael wished that he had not, and it was that if he, Michael, wanted to defend before the summer, then he had to have a working prototype very soon or he'd have to wait until the fall.

I don't want to pressure you, Michael, he had said, as Michael was leaving his office. It's just that most of my colleagues, well, have better things to do with their summers.

Michael could have read the comment ('my' colleagues) as a smug, we're-doctors-and-you're-not comment, but chose not to.

And now he found himself the lynchpin of a dinner party whose genesis and particulars he did not feel himself entirely privy to. It was sort of a celebration, the five of them, Soraya and Adam, Jakè (who had done the design on the physical machine) and Hanna, with Michael being the fifth wheel. And maybe this was part of some covert plan on the part of the Soraya-Hanna conspiracy to make him feel that he needed to get a putative life.

He had no idea, really, he was just on his way to Hy-Vee to pick up some essentials. Hanna would cook. Hanna banana was a brilliant, sometimes diabolical cook, creating things you couldn't possibly recognize but that were so fabulously delicious a guy like Michael almost wanted to give up pizza. The thing was, sometimes you really didn't want to know what it was you just ate. Because, she, like, would take strange previously inedible body parts from animals and serve them fried up crispy with tangy sauce that made your diaphragm do strange things; or vegetables unfit for human consumption would appear in strange and gorgeous colors, pickled, and when you ate them things would happen in the depths of your tongue that you had never known your tongue to be capable of. None of which Jake, who shared Michael's fixation with pizza and caffeine, seemed to care about in the least. But Michael felt like he could see through Hanna, or at least into Hanna, enough to know her ache to please others. And food could be a fabulous way to do it.

Adam was the most broadly educated of the lot. A Ph.D. in English literature, he was a maven of culture, a ridiculously well-read (and sometimes insufferable) autodidact, but it was not hard, really, to see how it was that Soraya had fallen for him. Michael never had much to say to him. As Adam liked to say, he didn't speak engineer, and engineers tended not to speak English.

He, Michael, was not exactly the most experienced shopper of the group. He did okay in the frozen section, where things were orderly, boxed or bagged and labeled, but when it came to more nebulous things like *ingredients*, he was at something of a loss. At his house, which, until they had moved out, he had shared with Jake and another grad student who mostly spent his time in rain forest canopies. He had contributed money to groceries, but rarely actually did any of the shopping or cooking. Since then, it had been almost exclusively carry-out or cellophane-wrapped garbage, almost exclusively in the lab.

And so suddenly he found himself in the produce section of the Hy-Vee and looked at his list, and was about to start to make his way methodically around the place, going from green thing to green thing, looking for garlic and broccoli and other things that Hanna and Soraya had listed. Except there was a part of him that said he ought to drop the basket he was carrying and flee back to the lab, order in pizza or Chinese and just call and say he couldn't make it.

But that was before he saw the girl. Girl. Check that thought—she was thirty-ish, obviously a grad student or the significant other of a grad student (or even a professor), so *woman* was clearly the better word. Except she had a girlish quality, an athletic, tomboy-grown-up sort of gestalt. She had short, jet black hair, which had a casual, spiky insouciance that looked like she cut it with hedge clippers, except they were no doubt really, really good hedge clippers. And she had big eyes, really big eyes, even without makeup, and her shoulders had that sort of turned back angling that some women's shoulders had, and she had a shape, a classic, devastating, spectacular, time-space-warping female shape, a narrow waist with that fabulous sort of suspended-teardrop shapely swelling at the waist, into a beautiful, astonishing.... It occurred to him that he was having a really weird conversation with himself, which was probably due to having spent so much time, in the lab, talking to himself—and hoped he was not narrating his adventure aloud.

It was not that she was excessively or extravagantly gorgeous, though she was. But she had a thing. She reminded him—with the big eyes and the black spiky hair and the athletic build—of a manga cartoon superhero. You could build a virtual world around a girl like that. Woman. But weirdly—it seemed to him—his was the only head that was turned. While she was not looking—so long as his act of observation (or, really, drop-jawed spectation) went unobserved, he couldn't stop himself from gorging himself on the sight of her.

The irony of this—what Soraya and Hanna would think—did not escape him.

He was amazed to find himself approaching her (he was, after all, completely stumped by the act of grocery shopping)—and she turned and looked at him—at first it was a scowl and instantly he wanted to shrink and shrivel and disappear, but then her look softened—and he thought he could see that not long ago she'd been crying—and just as fast it hit him that he had seen her before but already he was saying, Excuse me, I know I must sound like an idiot, but can you tell me which one is the broccoli? Which was honestly not a come-on. He had never bought broccoli except as a menu item in Chinese food—a menu item, ridiculously, that he could not identify except in print.

He had seen her before. Where? In one of his classes, perhaps, or running. He knew that look: the combination of the spiky black hair, the clear eyes (which were just the slightest bit puffy right now). And then she smiled, laughed. She said: *Broccoli*? And then laughed like she had heard a lot of pickup lines in her life but that was by far the most incredibly lame.

BROCCOLI, PART 2

When she was a kid, going to Iowa City had been a great delight, the small university town seeming an enormous metropolis compared to the dim lights of Fairview Park, whose lights went out at eight o'clock sharp and whose citizens numbered fewer than 2,500. But her town seemed big enough to a 10-year-old girl. In those days, places like New York and Los Angeles and Houston and even Chicago, which was only a few hours away, seemed incomprehensible and unreachable, things a normal person experienced, if at all, through the television or radio from the comfort of your living room sofa.

The Hy-Vee, when she was a child, had a somnambulant charm—with its sweet unnameable shopping music, its open freezer bins, its seeming cornucopia of foods, at least compared to the local market, with its sawdust floors, its endless aisle of multi-colored cereal boxes, its crypt of ice creams and frozen foods, its gleaming fridges of red and pink meat.

And so—maybe it was nostalgia—a few days after she landed at her parents', she decided that no matter what happened, no matter who happened to see her, she was going to go totally fucking bananas if she did not have a decent cup of coffee. Depression was bad enough, but depression (if that's what this was) without a cup of hi-test coffee was about as throat-slitting a proposition as she could think of. And so—damn the consequences—she was going to get a decent pound of coffee. Somehow it seemed safer to risk the anonymity of a grocery store than risk the faux hip, close-quartered environs of a Starbucks (which in her book made great caffeine but lousy coffee) or some other small, purpose-built shop. And so for several hours (it seemed) she mulled over having her father drive her into town, or to a rental car place, or some other such subterfuge-ish nonsense, and finally she just decided to take the car that she bought him (a red Honda S2000 that had essentially no miles on it because he was a Ford sedan man and even the subdued flashiness of the Honda convertible was too flashy for him).

It took only a few minutes to get out of town and that was when landscape hit her. So accustomed after all these years of being in the city, of being in a place where

150

the streets and buildings seemed to go on forever, it was stunning to be again in a place where the land and the sky went on forever, where it was the city, the town, that was ephemeral. She had come into Iowa and into town in the dark and had been mostly holed up in her parents' house for the last few days. But now, in the open, she was confronted with the landscape of her youth and she was startled at the deep sense of heartsickness and yearning it spurred in her. She had joked a million times about how you could go two minutes in any direction and hit cornfields, but you forgot the vastness of it. Flyover Country.

Between town and I-80, there was a two-lane highway that went for two, maybe three, miles, then crested a hill, then descended to the interstate. And from here you felt like you could see forever. Endless cornfields, rolling, neat and vibrant green. And there was the sky, as endless as the cornfields. The vivid black soil between the rows and rows of corn.

On I-80, out of the relative safety of her parents' house—she was on her way to the grocery! Yeah!, folks. How about that! Iowa City—Mecca of her youth. Bright lights big city here I come!

She wound the Honda up to a hundred in fourth gear for a couple of exits and let the air speed past her, then eased off. She hoped maybe she could breathe a little there. Iowa City at least had the university, some snobs, and some air of cosmopolitan self-importance.

And it all seemed to go as planned. The knot of anxiety that had dogged her all morning as she contemplated this tiny escape, that chewed on her all the way here in the car—the almost naked fear that someone might recognize her—had suddenly eased inside the grocery store. It was the shopping music, the weird hypnosis of all grocery store chains.

Except now that she was here, there were a million things she wanted, and so she wandered, thinking that maybe she'd get something and make her parents a meal that didn't involve potatoes and gravy, but though the grocery had improved since she was there last—by orders of magnitude, really—it was still always a shock to go into a grocery outside an urban area. There was oriental food now, but it was mostly canned. And then there was the nearly overwhelming pathos of the produce section. This was a farm state, so where was the devotion to vegetables? When she was in school during the Reagan Recession, she remembered the indignation of farmers and how they belittled suggestions that they grow something people actually *wanted*, and how they spat out the words 'Belgian endive,' purposely pronouncing it *N*-dive, just so there would be no doubt they were yahoos.

She had been in the store for just a few minutes when, from behind, a young, cracking male voice said, You finding everything okay, ma'am? And she turned around—at that point, she had only an empty basket in her hand—and looked at the young, earnest boy-man with his white teeth and pimply but clean-shaven face (A Smile in Every Aisle), his green store apron over pressed jeans, a white polyester shirt that didn't fit and a skewed necktie. She was too accustomed to the urban attitude of distended disregard to greet his casual politeness with anything but the certainty that it was a come-on. But it wasn't. He didn't recognize her. There was no, Hey, aren't you—? which was how it often began. Or, Hey, I know you. People would say this with such utter certainty. *I know you.*

I was looking for the coffee? she said.

A little later, as she was wandering through the aisles, she saw a man—perhaps thirty, although he could as easily have been twenty or forty, reluctantly pushing a shopping cart, totally hangdog and downtrodden, his elbows on the handle, moving very slowly, lost but no less hypnotized. She ignored him.

(*Michael.* Later, much later, when she thought about this, she would remember seeing him, remember the moments before contact, as though a hypnotist had magically drawn it up out of her subconscious—she would remember his black jeans, she would remember his windbreaker, the periodic table T-shirt, the wiry coil of him.)

But now she had been in produce once already, aimless, trying to decide what miracle of culinary art she could reproduce without a Betty Crocker cookbook, when she saw him again, an angular, sort of anguished looking figure of slender, medium height and pale-looking skin, dark, curly hair. She took him for one of the hundreds of writers who passed through Iowa City in any given year, vain and earnest and needy and pretty likely broke. And it was while she was formulating this profile of prejudice against him—when she came around to the produce aisle again, hypnotized by the refrigerated-Muzak-suspended-animation of the shopping experience (her hands were now full of things like a plastic bag with a free-range chicken in it, a bag of medium-roast coffee)—that she saw him again, still anguishing amongst the fruits and vegetables, and he sort of gave her a little wave and hurried over—the anguished, hesitant scuttle of an athlete unsurely portraying a crab—and said, I'm sorry, but, but could you tell me which one is the broccoli?

There was a feral aura that both your garden variety fan and your sociopath-type nutcase personality gave off when they recognized you, but he displayed none of that. She decided to work under the assumption that he was not a sociopath, but merely clueless.

Broccoli, she said.

This is actually pretty embarrassing. I'm supposed to be helping with a dinner party that some of my friends are giving, well, actually that technically *I'm* giving, but they gave me a list and sent me out and I'm not the one who usually does the shopping—

Leave that to the missus, do you? she said.

He laughed, No, no. Not married. Not dating, even. Just—well I have some friends—

But you're the one giving the dinner party.

Yeah, actually. Or I think so. Yeah. And broccoli, it's on the list they gave me but I was actually thinking of just lying that I forgot it. Sorry.

Don't actually come from this planet, eh? she said, wishing she had her sunglasses. Wishing she did not have to make eye contact.

There was something about him that was doggedly appealing. He was almost like Marty in the way that he talked, except without the sort of oy vay quality.

Follow me, she said—now she saw the grocery cart he had parked near the oranges and it was full, so this was not a come-on, or not entirely a come-on—and walked him over to where stalks of broccoli were attached with fat white rubberbands.

You know it actually says broccoli up here, she said, pointing to the price tag above.

I saw that, but all those tags are close together and here we have…, he said and pointed at the other apparently unidentifiable vegetables.

So what do you actually eat on your planet? she said, and he gave a sort of guffawing laugh that stopped short when she looked at him. She saw in his gaze two things she had not seen in a long time: he absolutely did not recognize her, and he was absurdly, even bizarrely, attractive.

What planet did you say you're from? she said, not entirely kindly. Haven't you ever ordered out Chinese or anything?

Yeah, but—. He stopped, and then said, Sorry to bother you.

He started to move away, but she instantly regretted being snarky. No, she said. No bother. I just meant—

I'm sorry. I didn't mean… I'm sorry. I just, you know, figured everyone knew what broccoli was.

There are certain people—from this planet, I'm sure—who think everyone knows what cat tastes like.

You think?

I sure as hell hope so.

She laughed out loud.

He apparently could hear the apology in her voice and seemed to forgive, and for a nice moment there was a pleasant if embarrassed romantic silence of the type she had not experienced in a long time. Most of the people she hung around always knew what to say, when to say it, and how to say it, even if it was just an act. And she was no different, but right now, in a stupid grocery store in Iowa, she totally forgot her lines.

My name's Michael, he said, and looked at her, then his feet. You in grad school here?

She laughed, not Gina's trademarked snorting horse-laugh, not her *he he he* stage laugh, but Ellen's own real laugh, which was as indescribable as any other truly lovely laugh.

No. I'm not in school. Just visiting. My parents live up in Fairview Park. I'm Ellen Gregory.

You want to have coffee or something, Ellen Gregory?

The way he said it gave her name a new music. She had heard it so many times with her ears programmed to hear her name a certain way, *And starring Ellen Gregory as Gina Perri!*, or, *Now, ladies and gentlemen, a warm welcome for Ellen Gregory,* but this was that mix of excitement and dread that you got when you heard your name for the first time at roll call on the first day of school and you hadn't met anyone and last night you'd dreamed you'd walked naked into the classroom.

He had brightened again and she could see that her profiling of him was way off. For a moment she was afraid that he was only 20 or something, but, oh well. More likely some sort of science grad student.

His eyes were lagoon-green irises set in rounded whites with a pearly sheen, surrounded by long lashes with almost no curl. His hair was thick and curly and he was not conspicuously handsome, but handsome nonetheless. He had brilliant teeth that a lot of her actor friends would envy, straight and uniform and bleached-white looking.

You want to get a cup of coffee or something? he said almost surreptitiously, not looking at her.

Sure, okay. What are you going to do with your groceries?

He bit his lip and looked vacant for a moment, his eyes rolling up sideways. What're you going to do with yours?

She looked at the chicken, which at the moment looked a little too fetus-like for comfort. Ditch, I suppose, she said. Except the coffee. I have to get the coffee....

He laughed, I could swing it by the house and then....

Sure, she said, Okay.

Sweet, he said, all boyish enthusiasm.

What about the dinner party?

He stopped for a moment, a blank look on his face. Then, suddenly: Oh, um, it's not tonight.

I'll follow you.

She went outside with him. It was warm now, not the oppressive heat of summer, but the pleasant heat of a warm Iowa spring day that had started out chilly and damp and but now the sky was clear. The light in the new growth of leaves on the trees that surrounded the parking lot was white and clear and made his hair shine. She helped him load the groceries into the trunk of his (rather messy) Camry, watched his wiry movements—slender, strong, but apparently unconscious of his (sexy beyond belief, suddenly, in her opinion) appearance. Then she followed him to his house. It was one of those formerly splendid old houses that had been student housing for so many years, it had likely reached a threshold of dilapidation from which there was little hope of return without serious renovation. It was white with black and gold trim (school colors, but absolutely hideous on a house) and had a pair of recycling bins outside overloaded with empty beer cans and pop bottles. Mainly pop bottles, blue bottles of some drink she'd never seen before.

THE BEACH IN IOWA

She had the top down still and shouted, You want help? when she pulled up behind his car.

He said, I can do this.

I'll help.

No, no. I'm good.

She looked at him and raised an eyebrow. I don't mind.

No, he said. Really. It'll just take a minute, and he hustled into the house with a ridiculous number of plastic bags. She was glad no one but Michael came out.

She got out of the car and sat on the fender of the Honda, leaning back on the hood on the heels of her hands. Because she was a professional and well-paid to keep an exhaustive mental catalog of her looks (this acquired from hours of sometimes actually grueling and mentally-wearying looking in the mirror, at video), she knew precisely what she looked like. In a way it wasn't fair. He apparently had no clue that right now she might be intentionally deploying her girl-next-door-sex-goddess look.

And then a woman emerged from the house, a gorgeous, buxom woman with a low-cut top and wild, reddish wheat-colored hair. She didn't say anything, but just stood there, looking. Ellen didn't mind. It was actually more fun this way.

Michael hurried out of the house again, and under the watchful eye of the woman, he went to the trunk, got more bags, then hurried them inside. Ellen mulled the situation.

The woman on the porch folded her arms beneath her considerable bosom and leaned against the wall. Another woman, this one wearing jeans and a T-shirt, came out and stood with the first woman, and Michael bustled past them. The more slight woman, who had short, sandy hair and a trim figure, wore an expression of mild amusement. When he emerged again, the buxom one said something to him that Ellen could not hear. The other one laughed. Michael waved her off as he said something that Ellen, again, could not hear. He hurried down the walk, and then, halfway, like a marionette, jerked a little and slowed down and seemed to try to assume a more casual sort of gait.

Part of your harem? she said as he came toward her.

He laughed. More like a coven, he said. Soraya, the one with the hair, she's sort of an ex, but she's also a business partner and a friend. Hanna is just a friend. She's getting her doctorate in psychology.

And Soraya?

She's an MD. She does brain research.

Looks like you've got all the bases covered.

Outside of complete theatric fakery, she had not engaged in this level of coyness in ages, which of course was a kind of theatric fakery, but one with consequences.

I'd never let either of them treat me clinically. Unless of course they're treating me now and I don't know it.

Why don't you introduce us?

No, it'd be, like, weird, he said, and he rubbed his hands against the pockets of his jeans without actually putting them in the pockets. Do you want to go?

Let's, she said. Do you drive a stick?

She did not give him time to answer before she threw him the key. She watched the key on its fob as she watched the women.

He caught it as though this was a bit of stage business they'd rehearsed a million times.

Yeah, he said, holding the key in one hand and marveling at it as though it had simply materialized. With his free hand, he pushed his hair up off his forehead, and then he looked at her.

Then be a gentleman and drive, she said.

She got in the passenger seat and offered him one of the CAT ball caps her father kept in the glove compartment to keep his comb-over from blowing out with the top down. He put on the plasticky blockhead-making hat and modeled it for her, grinning, stressing his Midwestern accent and saying, Oh, you bet, as he rested his elbow over the back of the seat.

The women watched and knew she was watching them.

Very nice, she said as he put the key in and started the car, then took off down the street.

It is. Very nice.

She sat back against the seat and looked at the sky, felt the wind move across her face and through her hair, and felt good. She sat up, and for no reason whatsoever, picked up the bag of coffee she had bought and pressed it to her nose and breathed deeply.

Cool car, he said.

I got it for my dad, but he never drives it. I thought it'd be a cool surprise. I even had them put a bow on it. Look at the mileage.

It was still in the triple digits. Wow, he said.

It was a present for his 65th birthday. I wanted to get him something totally superfluous.

He took his eyes off the road to look at her, said, I should have a daughter like you.

He had taken off the jacket he was wearing at the grocery—and she watched his arms (his skin was just too perfect) and his knees as he shifted, cornered, got the feel of the car.

This is a *way* cool car, he said.

I'll get you one, she said.

Yeah, cool, thanks.

She was joking, but he had no way of knowing that she could have written a check.

Where do you want to go? he said.

You pick, I'm the new kid in town.

You ever been to the Cottage?

Years ago. I used to love their cinnamon rolls.

Then it's the Cottage.

The Cottage had moved—or at least she thought it had—since she was last there a lifetime ago and there were people who were artsy student types, bookish types with a ceramic mug and a newspaper or some serious tome folded open on the table. But also town teenagers, stoking up on caffeine, like at Starbucks. A mom with a stroller.

The looks started shortly after they got in the door. Glances, murmurs, furtive gestures in their general direction. The demographic was overwhelmingly hers. When Michael noticed it, she liked the look of bafflement on his face. Her show was vastly popular in this set, but it actually had a pretty substantial draw across the vista of demographics—magically drawing everyone from 10-year-olds to her father, who thought it was a clever, if weird hoot (read: citified [gay] men as [relatively] normal [and likable] people!). But it, the show's magical draw, was most definitely one of those be-careful-what-you-pray-for kinds of things where Ellen was concerned, and there were days she understood utterly how desolate Midas must have felt, everything real turning useless, if cosmetically beautiful, in his grasp.

Michael turned to her when they got to the counter and said, What do you want?

Just coffee, black.

Then Michael said to the slender, pretty blonde behind the counter, Are you okay? because of the way she gawked, her mouth open, her freckles almost winking.

The girl, probably a student, blushed a little (for the gawking?), then did a little sort of facial wind up and gave a pretty good imitation of Ellen's character Gina's snorting laugh. Her anonymity had been pleasant while it lasted, but she had expected this, and now Ellen felt her stomach turn. She looked at Michael and his puzzlement was almost complete. The girl, startled at Ellen's apparent lack of enthusiasm, hastened to add the obligatory, I guess I'd better pick myself up, now. Michael looked at them both, darted his eyes around the rest of the room.

Oh, lovely man, she thought: Weird scenes to follow after this important commercial break. Her life was a series of weird scenes, and she had been nurturing the delusion that she could go for, like, one day without one. Foolish.

Imitating her character was not difficult; as a matter of fact it was stupefyingly easy, which was one of the things that made it such a popular sign of recognition, but it was also one of the reasons she took flak for it. TV critics seemed to think that a trademark ought somehow to be extraordinarily complicated or otherwise inimitable to be worthy of respect. But it was its simplicity, its I-could've-thought-of-that (but you didn't) simplicity that made it popular.

Michael didn't show any sign of appreciating the significance of the laugh, a lack of registry that, in itself, was charming. He just leaned forward slightly and peered hard at the girl.

I'm a mental health professional, Michael said quietly, reasonably. If you'd like to speak to someone, I could give you a number.

Ellen laughed. *This guy could be good for me*, she thought, but kept her mouth shut and watched from behind her sunglasses.

The girl began to turn red. The guy behind the counter—similar age, similar complexion, similar corn-fed look (not so different from Ellen's own)—turned on the steamer and frothed milk while the girl's face heated up and she turned away.

I just…, she stammered, but thankfully didn't go on.

Two coffees, black, please, Michael said.

Large for me, Ellen said. Really, *really* large. Like if you have a bucket or something that's reasonably clean, that would be good. And a funnel and tongue depressor?

Michael laughed. Ellen made a show of gazing at the pastries in the glass case beneath the counter.

People were still looking, evidently not satisfied. She looked at the cinnamon rolls, which she remembered from long ago as being sybaritically, hedonistically, *voluptuously* yummy. They had a way of making them where they baked them in a

159

muffin pan, which the dough overran in metastatic ecstasy, and then they popped them out and turned them over and put this amazing frosting on them. She had lived nearly a week (a really bad, PMS-inspired week) on them right before she left Iowa for good.

Thing about celebrity was, at least outside New York, it was not enough for people to have seen you, they had a need to make contact, to reach through the mirror. They had to know if you were or weren't her, even if there was a reasonable certainty or even no doubt at all that you were. But if you *were* her then they tended to expect something. Some kind of performance to reward them for the incredibly difficult process of recognizing you. While the snorting laugh of the girl may have been truly strange to Michael, Ellen herself had heard it so many times it got a little scary. That and people imitating the pratfalls she had added to her character, and which the writers had picked up.

I like it here because you don't have to use fake Italian, he said. Nor anthropomorphize the cups.

Ellen said: I am so glad you said that. What do you think? Wouldn't it be good to do coffee in, like, bra sizes? Like, I don't know, I'll have a D-cup latte. That'd be so fun.

Michael laughed and said, utterly genuinely, You're funny.

Thank you, she said.

Michael laughed, but other people had heard the D-cup thing and were repeating it around the room. There seemed to be whispers as to who he was. Why didn't anyone recognize *him*?

The girl had finished pouring now and put the paper cups on the counter. Michael paid and then they stood side by side at the opposite counter where the napkins and cream and milk were stationed. He leaned to her ear as she stirred her coffee—she had broken one of her strictest rules and put two packets of sugar in her coffee—and said, Are people staring at us? It seems like people are looking at us.

She looked at him. Michael, you, um, have blue ink all over your mouth.

His hand instantly flew to his chin and his look was utterly chagrinned.

Kidding. Kidding. She looked around the room and then back at him, folded her arms and leaned against the counter. She looked at him frankly. You really don't know, she said. (This was marginally astounding.)

His eyebrows came together and the space between them went to wrinkles. Know what? he said, still furtively wiping at his mouth. What am I supposed to know?

This was a look she would have preserved in perpetuity, it was such a genuine, lovely expression, like, *Did I screw up the surprise party?* It was a more-than-photographic moment that she wanted to have reside in her head, reside commingled with the scent of coffee, tagged with joy and folded into the warble of conversation and the gleam of midday sunshine, bookmarked at the junction of giddy and love.

She said nothing, but handed him her coffee cup, took off her sunglasses and put them in their case, then handed it to him too, then made as if she was leaving, heading for the door. He looked at her in something approximating alarm, but she looked away. She had a clear shot to the door. There was only a small crowd and a fair amount of open floor space. Everyone in the place seemed to be looking now, and she was looking over her shoulder at Michael and she hit the doorframe at the moment she'd timed, and did a whooping, I'm-wearing-high-heels-for-the-first-time backward fall, catching most of her weight on her hands but flopping when she went down. Had she not hacked off all of her hair, it would have ended up all in her face.

I think I'm going to pick myself up now, she said in a stage voice, and tried, but collided with the doorframe and fell again.

Michael looked on, frozen, not sure whether to go to her aid—except she had handed the coffee to him so she must have known she was going to do this.

Now, she said, I really am going to get up, and she was doing the snort horse-laugh that the girl had imitated. Again she made as if to get up. Again she fell. (David Letterman had said she was the most gifted physical woman actor-comic he'd ever seen. And actually, when she'd taken movement classes, her teachers had always said she'd had the most remarkable phrasing of movement, that she had some sort of innate, almost mathematical awareness of her physicality, her body in motion.)

If you were not from this planet (or, evidently, like Michael, and had very little connection with pop culture) and saw the whole spectacle, it would, she knew, seem desperately weird and out of place—an adult having some sort of global brain spasm—but everyone in the place but Michael understood the context of the thing without thinking, and they were in that special state of awe reserved for those seeing something in the flesh for the first time, but which they have seen on television countless times.

Except Michael. Who really was seeing it for the first time. And when she finally did stand back up, take a bow, then move back toward him, she could see that he was way more than baffled; he was aghast. The girl he'd picked up in the Hy-Vee was a total spaz-ass lunatic. And but everyone was laughing and applauding and he just stood there, his beautiful black eyebrows jammed together.

You go girl, someone shouted.

Bravo, Gina, said someone else.

She took her glasses from his hand and opened the case and put them back on, then took her coffee, too, and said, I may have really fucked up. We need to leave. Now. We should drink these in the car.

161

Maybe we should just drink, he said and stumbled outside.

He followed her to her father's car, the anguished look she'd seen in the supermarket having returned to his face.

She got in, the passenger side again, and cracked open the lid of her coffee. For a moment, she gazed into the cup, the steam coming off it, the fragrance hitting her. He started the car and he did not look particularly happy or comfortable. Suddenly, she felt as though she'd used him. She'd gotten a tremendous rush from that little performance and the attention it brought, the kind she hadn't got in ages, but it was only (or mostly) because she was performing for him. For the first and perhaps only time. For that moment, in the coffee shop, her depression had magically disappeared, but now she could feel the ebb of it. Now she looked at him, figuring she'd blown the tenuous bit of mystery that had obtained between then for the last hour or so.

She said, shaking her head, You really don't know. Do you? God, you must be the only human in America.

Who's Gina?

Are you really a mental health professional?

No. No. I was just kidding. I'm sort of a hacker.

A cab driver or a guy who does bad things on the Internet?

That's a cracker. I'm a developer. A maker. I write code.

What do you do with it? I mean what kind of code?

Morse code. Mostly SOS. At least in this kind of situation.

No, really.

Actually, he said, I'm still trying to figure that part out. I do some, like, stuff that sometimes seems close to mental health, in a way.

How?

Like most of the time I feel like I'm going crazy. He laughed.

The way he hesitated, his eyes flashing, his face reddening a bit, was almost heartbreakingly sweet.

What happened in there? he said, glancing at her, driving aimlessly. She looked to see if they were being followed.

I think those people must have..., she started, and bit her lip. She took a long drink of her scalding coffee before she continued. They probably saw me on TV.

All of them?

I guess so.

Wow, he said. I don't have a TV.

Probably just as well. (She thought of the sex-tape ads, the horrid exploitation of the death of Wayne Townsend. He was spared seeing that, and she was spared his seeing it.)

162

She was glad that, here, they were out of sight of the coffee shop.

He shrugged. He sipped at his own coffee. So is that what you do? TV?

Right now I'm not doing anything. I'm trying to decide what to do.

He nodded, seeming to take it at face value.

But I want to know about you and your code. Let's go somewhere with, like, a destination. Take me away.

Sure, he said, brightening.

They drove out to the Coralville Reservoir. Back when she was fifteen or seventeen, she would have thought that this as a destination the crudest sort of suggestion to make out, to get laid. Not that very many people were asking in those days. But where else did you go? Now she found it charming.

The beach, such as it was, was empty, and they sat next to the water, on grass that needed mowing. The water was greenish brown and scarcely showed any tracing of wind across its surface.

They hadn't said much in the car, and a lot of times she felt uncomfortable with too much silence (read: always), but not talking with Michael didn't feel so much like silence as it did simply a caesura, a place to breathe. She had started to make jokes, started, as she often did, trying to make him laugh. But suddenly, she didn't feel the need—as she often did—to slay him with humor. It was nice just being with him. So much had changed about Iowa and so much had not, and sometimes it was hard to tell what she remembered and what she thought she remembered.

So you said, Michael said, lying back on the grass, propping himself up on his elbows, That you used to live here. Or something like that.

He had this way of moving his hands when he was unsure of something, as though fingering the texture of the air, trying to jumble and recast it.

I grew up here. Or a bit west of here, in Fairview Park. Left when I was about a month shy of my 18th birthday.

Where do you live now?

Not sure, exactly. Sometimes I think I live largely in a fictional world.

He laughed, then sat up. He looked at her, picked up his coffee and drank from it. Are you being evasive? he said.

She shook her head. No. No—I mean *literally* I live in LA.

But figuratively.

Depending on how you look at it, LA is figuratively. I mean, I don't know. I'm just here, now, visiting my folks. She could tell that her spaz attack at the Cottage was still reverberating in him, waiting for explanation.

Sounds nice.

Nice. I don't know if that's the right word for it. She thought of the events of the last week, of her conversation with her mother, and there was none of it that seemed especially nice.

Good, yes. Necessary. But nice was not part of that picture. It had been, frankly, painful.

So, like, who's Gina?

It was funny how this hit her—or later, when she thought of it, she would think of it and feel a hot rush of embarrassment.

She's the character I play on TV.

So is this, like, a show you're in? A TV show?

Ellen nodded. It was embarrassing, suddenly. Most of the time it was a point of pride, having come up in the comedy circuit and grabbed the brass ring of a network TV sitcom, but right now it seemed like something she wanted to forget. Or at least not talk about. Like having done a porn movie.

Interesting, he said.

She'd never heard that reaction before. She'd heard a lot of others, and a lot of them over and over, but never, *Interesting*, the word drawn out in perhaps more syllables than it actually had.

So is it fun?

She laughed, shook her head. I guess it used to be. These days—I don't know. How about you? Is writing code fun?

It has its days.

What are you working on?

I—you don't want to hear about this.

I do.

Well, I—how much do you know about computers?

I have one. I use it.

He said: Email, surfing the web? That kind of stuff?

She nodded.

Do you know what an operating system is?

She shook her head.

You know how when you start it up, boot it, you get a desktop and then you can navigate through your files?

Sure.

Okay, well that's what I'm trying to create.

Hasn't that already been, like, *done*?

He smiled broadly. Yeah. The operating system I'm working on is one that's kind of— He hesitated. It works like the computer is part of your brain.

She furrowed her brow and cocked her head to one side. I don't get it.

It's more like think and click than point and click.

That'd be cool.

If it worked. I mean it's the next logical step, but there are lots of things that have to be overcome. There's a lot of stuff that has to go into it. There's some virtual reality stuff, some artificial intelligence stuff.

So, if I wanted to open a file, I'd just think about it?

Pretty much.

She widened her eyes. It sounds like it's pretty complicated.

And it's all screwed up. I mean, I had it and then I lost it. Sort of. That's why I'm—I'm on an enforced hiatus.

What do you mean?

It means that Soraya, my business partner, has kind of laid down the law. I have to get a life.

Ellen started laughing.

What's so funny?

That's kind of my assignment. To myself. To do list: get a life.

He didn't seem to think it was all that funny. He shook his head.

So who's the woman on the porch? The gorgeous one?

That's Soraya.

You said she was an ex?

You know how you love someone and the romance isn't a romantic romance? Does that make sense?

Ellen nodded. Only too much. My manager, Marty—he and I were kind of like that once.

Except I'm working on my Ph.D., and I am this close.

He winced as he said this, held up a hand and showed the thumb and forefinger millimeters apart.

She looked at him, studied the way he spoke. There was an intensity, a passion that she recognized.

I've been working on this thing it seems like for the last 10 years or so, and about a week ago, I had it. I mean I was there.

He sat up and did that thing with his hands again, fingers fluttering, and the anguished look.

And?

And it crashed.

That's not good.

165

No, it most certainly is not good. And so when I rebooted it, it was doing something else entirely. I mean, I have no idea what it was doing. I saw it, I was there, but it wasn't what I designed.

What happened?

I went to the beach.

Ellen looked at him, puzzled. Come again?

I guess I should just suck it up, admit that it doesn't quite work. Or that it doesn't work.

I hate that. When you work on something and just can't get it to come out right.

Ellen could not believe how much like a schoolgirl she sounded. How solicitous and facile and idiotic. Except it felt good.

The thing is, it does *some*thing.

What does it do?

It simulates reality, almost good enough—no—it does it well enough that you wouldn't believe that it's not reality.

Is that a problem?

He stood up and walked away from her, then turned around.

Yes, he said, a pleading tone in his voice. Yes, it's a problem. Yes, it's a problem when the thing you've been working on all your more or less adult life suddenly becomes something you don't recognize. I mean it's doing something—. Michael was pacing now, talking as much to God and the water as to her. It's doing *some*thing that's kind of like, I don't know. Like the intelligence is no longer artificial. Like it has its own intelligence.

That happened with my toaster? I mean I like my toast just a little teensy bit brown and crispy? But now the fucking thing is browning it. I mean really browning it, like the s'mores setting. It tried to set my house on fire. It told me, I will burn you. I think it meant it.

He laughed. She loved the look of his eyes—it was so idiotic to think of twinkling eyes, but his eyes had this glassy, glittery quality when he laughed, and it was hard not to think of twinkling. And the way he laughed was contagious, and she started laughing. She laughed so hard—not at her own joke but at the situation—that she started to cough.

God, someone get me a glass of milk so I can clean my sinuses, she said, and now he collapsed back down onto the grass, laughing. It was one of those situations where you start laughing at something that really isn't that funny and cannot stop. Somehow, the moment makes it funny, and Ellen couldn't remember having laughed like this for years.

And then, after a bit, it all stopped, and both of them were on their backs, looking up at the cloudless sky.

I'm sorry, she said. It's just you could be talking about my own life. I mean minus the intelligence. So I guess the key is, we both get lives, then go back to work and see what happens.

He laughed again.

So what does it do? Your code.

She propped her head up on an elbow and looked at him. His hair had grass in it—and so, likely, did hers.

I have no idea. I mean in the strictest sense of the word, I have no…. He started giggling again, and then laughing, and while he was laughing he rolled toward her, and suddenly—perhaps he had no idea how close they had ended up during the last paroxysm of laughter, but his face was only two or three inches from hers, hers above his. She could smell the coffee on his breath, make out every whisker on his face. In the time they were silent, staring at each other, she could have counted the rays in his irises. For a moment, she thought he would kiss her—and the sheer improbability of it was head-spinning.

He did not. Kiss her, that is.

He turned away, sat up, said: Truth is, I have no fucking idea. He shook his head.

What?

I have no idea what it's doing.

None at all?

I know that it shouldn't—in fact can't—do what it's doing. It jumped the tracks. I mean, the physics of it are too good. He stood up again, brushed himself off, but he was still covered with bits of dead grass. He turned and looked at her, got a look of near-complete defeat, and said, And what's worse, half the time I don't think I know what *I'm* doing. I had this beautiful idea and I have no idea what happened to all the work that I put into it.

She could not have put her own situation into better words. She stood up, and for a moment she thought she might black out. She wobbled, put her hands out. Instantly he was next to her, taking her arm. She put her hands to her face.

Are you okay?

It was like awakening, to find herself in his arms. Later, she would think, *How fucking 19th century is that? The lady swoons.* But there she was, next to the glassy green-brown water, his hands on her shoulders, his face close to hers.

You okay? he said.

Yeah, she said, blinking. Blood all rushed out of my head.

And now they were just standing there, and he slowly released her.

She grabbed his hands in mid-descent. Thanks, she said. I think I should have eaten something with all that coffee.

He looked away, looked at his hands, her hands. He started to speak but then stopped himself.

She released his arms and he scratched his head, puzzled. She thought it was strange how you could have no idea what the right thing to do was, no idea what was charming and perfect until you saw it. And how it was not so much any single gesture but a host of the tiniest things, accumulated, a gesture of gestures.

So when's your dinner party? she said.

He smiled, closed his eyes. Tomorrow, he said. What day is tomorrow?

Not sure. Friday, I think.

Then it's tomorrow. You want to come?

Are you cooking?

He shook his head. Hanna, he said. Hanna's pretty good. No. Hanna banana, if she weren't a psychologist, could open a restaurant, and, like, kill people. That's how good of a cook she is.

Hanna banana?

Sorry. She hates that.

If you're not cooking, then I'll consider it. But only if you come to my house for dinner.

In LA?

She laughed. No, here. My parents' house.

And then she thought of it, the stunt at the coffee shop. She hadn't been back to her parents' in hours and who knew how news traveled? Who knew what ugliness might already have been visited already upon her parents. Involuntarily, she glanced around. You never knew where people would put cameras, and now there was no doubt some kind of price on her head—*Where is Ellen Gregory?*

What is it? he said.

No, nothing. It's nothing. What were you saying?

I wasn't. You were.

Well, what was I saying?

He said: You invited me to dinner.

Oh, yeah. She could feel the warmth rise into her face as it reddened. Sorry. Did you answer?

Sure, he said. I'd like that.

I have to ask if it's okay. But I'll cook. My mother still cooks like it's 1962 and the casserole is haute cuisine.

What's the matter with casseroles? he said, and laughed.

She punched him in the shoulder, then stood looking at him. I think I'd better get back. I'm kind of AWOL from being AWOL.

What does that mean?

She examined him for a moment, considered how much she should or could tell him. I ran away from home, she said.

LA?

Yeah. It's way complicated. There were issues. I did one of those disappearing white girl things, and before long, I'm going to have to do something about it, I mean there are people who are depending on me and I've let everyone down.

He nodded politely.

I came to see my parents. And I haven't been home in hours. First it was years, now it's been hours, and still they're probably worried.

He nodded. Well, he said. Let's get you back.

He drove again, and again there were long silences. She had to learn that: the art of the caesura. And again there was a quality of being with him that made silence okay. There was a quality to this moment, riding along, when she could simply empty her head of herself, the accumulation of memory, the accumulation of garbage and violence. The wind that blew past also blew through.

When he pulled up at his house, they both got out and stood in front of the car. It seemed to her a propitious sign that there were not camera crews or paparazzi.

So are you going to come to my dinner party?

Sure, she said. I'd love to.

Will you be, like, my date?

She grinned. Sure. I'd like that. No casseroles, though.

He seemed scarcely able to contain his glee and did some footwork that was a little like dancing.

Can I—? he started, curling one arm over his head and fingering the opposite ear, Can I—no, never mind. Now both arms flew into the air and he started to turn away.

She thought he was going to ask if he could kiss her and she would have liked nothing better. But she didn't want to blow the moment by forcing it. It was also okay not to kiss him.

You want to drive the car again, she said.

Actually, no, he said, Well, not—

And now he was doing a sort of loopy sideways goose step, weirdly swinging his whole lanky form side to side.

She laughed. Oh, I get it.

169

He laughed. No, he said, a safe distance from her, I was just going to ask if I could kiss you, but it seemed like, I don't know. Not like you didn't want to.

No.

But....

Too much like having a life?

He started to laugh, then didn't. Yeah, he said, Maybe.

Look, she said, nodding toward the porch and moving in his general direction. Soraya could still be here, watching us through the window—oh, I think I saw the blinds move.

I wouldn't be surprised if she was, he said, though in fact he would.

Then I guess we'd better kiss, she said. She was looking at him, and it was like in the car, nothing in her head but the moment.

I'm not sure I remember how.

I hear it's like riding a bicycle.

I have to tell you, he said, that if it's anything at all like riding a bicycle, I am going to be really disappointed. Except maybe sweaty.

Shut up, she said.

Now he was close enough to kiss, and she leaned a bit toward him, and he toward her, but stopped.

He said: I'm going to start giggling if we don't do this.

"GIRL" SIGHTED

Vanished Actress Reportedly Reappears Near Hometown
Associated Press
Monday, May 20, 2001; Page A04

Iowa City, Iowa, April 30 – Actress and comedian Ellen Gregory has reportedly been seen by a number of University of Iowa students in and around the college town. Those reports have not been confirmed by local authorities or by Gregory's publicist, Patti Gelfman.

Cheryl Strohmeyer, a sophomore at the university, said that she and some friends were having coffee at a local café when Gregory came in with a man Strohmeyer said she did not recognize. "Oh, it was definitely her," she said. "She had dyed her hair and cut it short, but no way that was anyone but Ellen. I don't know who the guy was, but he was kind of cute."

While much of the speculation on Gregory's whereabouts has centered on overseas rehab centers, the media have been unable to confirm precisely where she is. Gregory grew up in Iowa.

"It was, like, kind of weird, because he didn't seem to know who she was," Strohmeyer said. "She came in and people all over the shop recognized her, and when she got her coffee she did one of those falls she does on the show. The guy," Strohmeyer continued, "seemed surprised by the attention. He was, like, clueless."

Gregory's parents still reside in the nearby town of Fairview Park. They have refused comment about their prodigal daughter's disappearance, as they have long refused any comment about her or her work. Her manager, Marty Klein, said he thought it highly unlikely. "It's pretty well known that she left home in the middle of the night when she was 17 and never went back."

Klein indicated that the unexplained rift between Gregory and her parents remained unresolved

and said that Gregory "is fine" but would not say if
he had been in contact with the actress.

Gregory's parents have referred all press inqui-
ries to their lawyer, who has refused all comment.

WHO'S THAT GIRL?

When he got to the front step, Michael turned and watched Ellen drive away. He shoved his hands into his pockets and leaned against the post and stared at the spot in the street where her car—her father's car—had last been. Right now, standing here, he had a sense of particular acuity, every sensation especially intense, the mid-afternoon sky bright and deep, the April air crisp and scented with the fragrance of—perhaps—lilac. He had no idea, really, but trees and flowers were coming into bloom, and this space he had walked through a million times seemed to become visible for the first time—the paint on the wood of the step beneath him worn thin with foot traffic, the grain showing deep ridges, the slats of wood on the porch, painted a perfectly neutral gray enamel. Involuntarily, he withdrew a hand from his pocket and lifted it to his mouth, touched his lips. He wondered.

The last several hours had a sense of unreality to them—there was a part of him that was as naïve as a baby—that she, the beautiful woman with the spiky black hair and the killer bod, could be into him at all left him in disbelief. Given that he had not held a woman since Soraya had broken things off with him, and given that that romance, such as it was, had always taken a back seat to his work, the recent string of moments, which had begun in the supermarket and ended here, had an extra element of disbelief, and now a quality of waking from a dream, but the dream still very much consuming him. He wondered if anything she had said was true. He wondered if he Googled her, he would find that she was, indeed, a TV star on the lam from her show. But he knew as soon as he thought it that he would not do it. He did not want to know what he didn't find himself. And he didn't Google her.

Deep in thought, deep in his renascence of sensation, he turned and climbed the step and took out his keys, but Soraya opened the door before he could, and her sudden appearance startled him and he visibly jumped.

What—? he started to say but he didn't get it out because he noticed that suddenly she looked different. Yes, she was the same outsized character with *in flagrante delicto* hair, but suddenly she was different.

Ellen was gone now. He was in another place. A moment ago, he had thought he would just flop down on his bed and think about her, alone.

Soraya just looked at him, backing away as he came through the door, scanning him. In the hallway, below the stairs, he turned around and looked at her, What? he said, and it was an entirely different 'what' than the one he had uttered when she surprised him.

She was smiling, Cheshire cat style. So, she said. Who's that girl?

You wouldn't believe it if I told you, he said, leaning against the wall, but stumbling as he did so and nearly falling over.

ABSENCE

When she hit Fairview Park, she slowed to below the speed limit and crept along back roads that were sleepy and mostly empty. It was too early for people to be home from work, too late for—what? What did people do between lunch and dinner in Fairview? She remembered, as a kid, riding bikes, wandering endlessly, but now there was no one outside. Maybe all of the younger people were gone, maybe when her parents' generation went, the town would close down like an old theater no one came to anymore. The roads were black and all the cracks had diligently been tarred in with Teutonic precision (not to mention obsession), and some streets looked like a child's scrawling on a wall with a pencil.

She had trusted Michael for no other reason than he seemed trustworthy, and now—or if not now, soon—she was going to find out if her trust had been misplaced. It was entirely possible that the last few hours had not been what they seemed. He could easily have been a creep, a more sophisticated Wayne Townsend—or, even weirder, an actor, someone hired by a tabloid to flush her out, which seemed unlikely (but perhaps no less unlikely than Townsend himself).

She thought about the conversation she'd had with Michael. She could not recall having asked him not to say anything about her. He was a man who seemed—in his non-pregnant silences—to get it that she didn't want to be talked about.

Thinking about it now—not that she hadn't already cringed a thousand times in the last few hours thinking about it—she deeply regretted the display in the Cottage. It was pure showing off, for him, and he was the one person it didn't impress. And it could be the thing that made all hell break loose. People did not keep these kinds of things secret.

She turned the corner on her parents' street and took it wide so that if there were unfamiliar cars or, God forbid, TV trucks and vans in front of the house, she could pull a U-turn and get the hell out as fast as she could. But there was nothing. Just the empty road. It was almost a movie dreamscape, the street. Everything as orderly as a horror movie. No one was out.

She pulled into the drive, grabbed the plastic grocery bag with her coffee and got out quickly, her head down, and went for the side door.

SOMEONE, AS IN A MAN

Ellen's mother, Arlene, sat at the kitchen table in her June Cleaver dress and apron and nursed a drink. It was after five, and there was no scent of dinner in the air. When she came in, Ellen held aloft the bag from Hy-Vee and said, Coffee!, as though her mother had secretly shared her distaste for her own coffee all these years and was just waiting for Ellen to set her free.

She said nothing, didn't even look at Ellen.

Ellen said, What're you drinking?

Arlene said, Gin and tonic.

Can I have one?

Her mother started to get up but Ellen stopped her. I'll get it. Just tell me where to find the booze.

There's gin in the pantry and tonic and lime in the fridge.

Ellen made herself a drink—there was nothing but silence as she did so, ice clinking in the glass, the vaguely incriminating sound of booze glugging out of a bottle. She would have guessed—had someone asked—that the glass contained about equal ratios of gin to tonic. It wasn't so much that she wanted to get drunk, it was that she wanted to get plastered. It would take that much to understand—assuming that a day like today could be understood—what had happened. She squeezed the lime into the glass and thought of Michael, how unutterably weird the whole thing of meeting him was, then rubbed lime pulp around the rim. When the drink was perfect, she put everything away before sitting down.

Her mother said, I wish I could remember more about when you were born.

It was as though they were continuing a conversation that Ellen didn't remember beginning. In those days, her mother said, they doped you up a lot—they had this drug cocktail called 'twilight sleep'—and it had an amnesia effect. I remember you the next day. I remember getting a shot that was supposed to help dry up my breasts, which ached. But I don't remember when you made your appearance. Isn't that funny? I don't mean funny in the ha-ha sense, of course. And of course in those days, men didn't come into the delivery room, so your father has little recollection of it either. He remembers a box of cigars. Did you know we wanted more? Did you know we wanted more?

Cigars?

Arlene laughed. No, children, silly. We couldn't though. I have no idea if I wasn't a good brood mare, but I never even had so much as a miscarriage or a late period.

TMI, mom, Ellen said.

What does that mean?

Ellen just shook her head, but did not say the words, Too Much Information. What she said was: Nothing. Then: I'm sorry I didn't call. Ellen meant today, I'm sorry I didn't call today, but as soon as it was out of her mouth, she realized that it could have applied to virtually her entire history.

Mom, she said, leaning close, holding her glass tight.

Ellen looked at Arlene for the first time, and for the first time, the first time in her life, she could see that her mother was not some caricature of a mother, but a truly beautiful woman. It was from her mother, clearly, that she herself got her looks. The blond hair came from her father, but the rest of her looks came entirely from her mother.

The weirdest thing happened today.

Weirder than a stalker?

Yeah, Ellen said. Weirder for me, anyway. She pressed her lips together and looked at her mother.

Well?

I met someone.

Someone as in *someone*? A man? Her mother was practically squealing.

Ellen nodded.

It was the last thing that I expected to happen, to meet someone. And I mean I have no idea, you know, I mean it's all, like, I don't know.

Her mother gave a smile that radiated astonishing warmth.

But he's like totally awkward, and totally charming, and I am looking back at this afternoon with a sort of disbelief, because I'm supposed to be depressed…. But this guy.

What does he do?

He's some kind of computer geek. Like a really super geek. He's working on some kind of Ph.D.

Arlene took a sip from her glass, then took a long pull and drained it.

If I had your luck, Ellen, her mother said, I'd spend my life in Las Vegas.

Ellen laughed. He's slender and he's beautiful and he can't seem to say anything without doing some sort of dance.

Arlene laughed. A dance?

Yeah, sort of. He just has this wiry way of moving that's…. Ellen had to get out of her chair to try to communicate the eccentric nature of Michael's movements. She said: He's, I don't know, she said, doing a remarkably good impression of him. It's as though the things that he thinks electrify him and he has to dance.

Her mother smiled and covered her eyes. You don't have to describe it entirely.

Ellen laughed and stopped. Right now her father emerged from the basement.

I'm sorry I didn't call. I'm sorry I was late.

Your mother was worried sick, he said. We wondered if you hadn't taken off again. Or who knows.

Eddy, honey, stop, Arlene said.

I'm sorry. I'm really, really sorry, Ellen said. I was just so amazed that something like this…. Ellen sank back down in her chair.

She met someone.

What kind of someone? Ed Gregory cocked his head.

A gentleman someone.

Her father widened his eyes, then thought about it for a moment and turned, made himself his own gin and tonic. There was something oddly enjoyable about them talking about her this way, in her presence, in a kind of parental third person that was quite lovely, now, in her thirty-second year.

He sat down at the table. What does this someone do?

He's working on his doctorate.

In?

He's a computer scientist, Arlene offered.

Ellen liked this, that her mother had transmuted geek into 'computer scientist,' giving it more professional heft.

Arlene gave Ellen a sort of knowing, Let-me-handle-this look.

Well, her father said, Maybe he can come over and help me with my Internet hook-up.

Ellen laughed. There was, at this moment, a familial connection, a thing she could almost see in the air around her, that had a shape like magnetism, the power of electricity. She had missed them. She missed them now, and for a moment, it was everything she could do to keep herself from bursting into tears of joy and grief. Here was a reflection of herself that she had never seen before.

Her father turned to her. It's nice to see you looking happy, he said.

Yes, Arlene said. Not pretend-happy, which you are very good at, but *happy-happy*.

DARKROOM

The first time Michael took her to his lab, she had known him less than three weeks, had been in Iowa for only slightly longer than that, and despite desperately wanting to jump his bones, had not slept with him.

She had grown more comfortable—but also more circumspect—in getting out and about. And she had grown more comfortable with Michael, seeing him almost every day, after that first day, except for one day when her mother wanted to go out to the Amanas and look at quilts. And even then she had talked to him on the phone. He still hadn't had his dinner party yet—or at least if he had, he had not mentioned it.

He had done, in the last few days, amazing, utterly endearing things, like showing up at her parents' house with cups of good coffee and—after she had mentioned missing email and instant messaging—he had shown up with an oldish but serviceable laptop configured so she could establish the appearance of being in a small African nation, in a supportive, rehabilitative sort of environment. And while he was there, he had fixed her father's Internet connection, cleaned his hard drive and made it run about twenty times faster than it had before, all the while chatting amiably with Ed about who knew what and getting along famously. Big Ed Gregory, her daunting father, was utterly charmed. Arlene was atwitter.

Michael also took her cell phone, which had been off since she walked out of the Avid room, saying he could similarly mess with it and while it would not be a bulletproof fix, he could re-route the calls to provide some element of plausible deniability.

This laptop and renewed connection enabled her to get in touch with Marty and Patti—Ellen on her bed, in her old room, Michael watching as she typed—from the distant African nation (i.e. Iowa, through some geek voodoo-type magic), to provide a statement to confirm that she had left the show and the country not for any sort of creative reasons, or for any conflictual reasons, and not because of the Wayne Townsend issue, but because of personal issues that needed working out in a supportive, agreeable sort of rehabilitative scenario. Marty and Patti had, almost instantaneously, and with a sigh of relief that could be heard two-thirds of the way across the continent, put out a statement to that effect, which was picked up by every major news outlet (and zillions of minor ones) and reported on all of the morning news shows.

But there was of course the question: Someone who looks like you has been spotted around her home town...?

She typed back as Michael watched: If you'd ever been to my hometown, you'd know that people who look like me are a dime a dozen.

LOL. Yeah, well. She's got people thinking she's you.

Well, that's good. At least they'll leave me alone if they think I'm at home.

Later, Michael drove them to Iowa City. She turned on the radio in the car and tuned to a talk station—sure enough, the story about her being in rehab in a small African country had already hit the wires. She turned the radio off and stared out the window. Michael said, Wow, and for the moment left it at that.

He parked at his house and they walked—she needed to walk, needed to think. She was silent for a long time. After a while, Michael said, It's fascinating. You can just *say* something, he said, and it changes everything. I don't just mean you, I mean one, one can just say something.

She said to him, Ask any lawyer. It's all about narrative, my love (she used the words 'my love' intentionally and advisedly), it's all about the telling detail. (She had done a quick bit of research and mentioned a particular sort of bird, native there, and the lovely way it looked out the window.) Whoever has the best narrative wins. Narrative is the gold standard. With human beings, narrative is the key.

I think narrative is hard-wired in the human brain, Michael said. Research shows that memory doesn't really begin in children until they acquire language, which I think is the human format for narrative. And memory consolidation is all about establishing an acceptable narrative. When people talk about trying to make sense of events, it's all about establishing a narrative, giving shape and making comprehensible what is really fucking nuts. He laughed.

She took his hand and held it tightly.

Don't you think it's weird how words can have such moment? he said. You say something and saying it changes the thing—I mean, what if language has a kind of dimensionality? If language is something more than.... It's that whole thing of, like, to 'put the mouth to,' as a poet said. Judith Hall.

Putting the mouth to, she said, stopping and looking at him. I like that. And she kissed him, clung to his arm.

Adam gave it to me, he said. The book. He thought I needed something to broaden my horizons.

As in, Get a Life?

Yeah. He's given me others.

You have no idea, she said, how words can change things. Try walking out on a stage, just you and your microphone, and someone shouts something ugly or just something that totally derails you, and there you are, the only thing to keep you company, silence with nasty snickers, and no matter what kind of material you have, you can start your bit dead with no hope for resurrection.

Has that happened to you?

More than once. But I've consolidated those memories.

He grinned at the joke.

She came very close to his face, his mouth. She said: It's not just words, Michael. That putting-the-mouth-to thing.

Oh, you mean like kissing?

You catch on quick, boy genius.

Hey, he said when they were walking again, You think maybe you'd want to see my lab?

She had visions of white coats, test tubes, white rats running in wheels, Erlenmeyer flasks. She knew that he had more or less been keeping himself away from the lab, but she also knew that he had been there, done a little work, and that he and Soraya had been talking often, trying to figure his project out. But it was an intellectual thing, a thing of collaborating on research and trying to get to the bottom of what was becoming a really interesting thought puzzle. (According to Michael.) She, Ellen, was—in her mother's new vernacular—*so over* jealousy.

Is that like, Wanna come into my darkroom and see what develops?

Depends on whether you want it to.

I'd be honored to come to your darkroom and see what develops, she said. And she did feel honored to be admitted into the inner sanctum of his dreams, however inaccessible or incomprehensible they might have been to her.

They were by the student union when he said it. She was impressed that he seemed pretty much unimpressed with the whole celebrity thing. It was as though she had told him she had a crazy uncle and he had shrugged and said, Whatever. Somehow, for him, it didn't define her and she was thankful for that.

They walked to his lab in the balmy warm gorgeous spring afternoon, starting in town, moving unnoticed over a footbridge across the river and then vaguely west. All the way they talked the kind of excited and animated small talk new lovers talk, talk that seemed it would never cease. She told him how in New York at eighteen—well, not exactly eighteen—she had worked at a comedy club handing out flyers. Barking, it was called, and what you had to do, she said, was convince people to come to the club and if you got a certain number of people to come, you'd get a certain number of minutes on stage to try out your stuff at the end of the night. And if people laughed, you'd move up. It was a kind of apprenticeship. Or it was a hazing. You had to be nuts, and then she told him she remembered what it had been like on the bark. How raw and real and naked you felt. You had to want it. No, it wasn't that you just had to want it—because there were a million people who wanted it—you had to be stupid enough, you had to be foolish enough, to go get it, to settle for nothing less. In other words, you had to be nuts.

And of course you had to be prepared to make people laugh, people who might otherwise have been indisposed toward anything but cutting your throat; and you had to be prepared to hand out millions of the things and have to pee so bad you thought you'd, like, explode a kidney or something. You had to be willing to get stomped on like a cigarette butt and stuck to the summer pavement like old chewing gum. But there was something about being young that made it okay, that made it better than sitting around watching TV and, like, going nowhere. That was where she met Patti. There were others, a whole gaggle—these days they'd be a posse—who were dedicated, you know what I mean? We were all going to make it. And they dropped off one by one.

But the payoff, after all that, was dying, because then you got—after handing out reams of paper—a few thankless moments at the end of the show when people were drunk and ready to knuckle-walk home—you know, like a gorilla? You get so drunk it takes four limbs to keep the pavement from rising up and whapping you? Your stuff had to be sharp as a fucking razor. Which it never was, at first. And it could have been brilliant, but you still could have died if you didn't get people's attention. That was when she had come up with the tutu thing, the G-string tutu. In those days it was still a G-string, she said, stripper clothes, a Rio bikini. Now it's a thong, which is cool because it does kind of fit between your cheeks like flip-flops fit between your big toe and second toe. She was going to come on like a psycho, rabid, utterly fearless. And it worked. Having it made, the G-string tutu, had cost her a month's rent—which actually was a month's rent, after which she would have been homeless had it not worked. But it worked. Maybe this isn't true for guys, she said, but the right outfit can completely change your outlook.

He laughed.

She tried to remember who she had been, what kind of girl it was who thought up an assless tutu, who dreamt up black fishnet stockings and Timberland boots to go with it. And then, with a handful of jokes she'd honed over a year or so, put on the tutu in those fishnets and those boots and clomped onto the stage and started talking and slew audiences at will. Took no prisoners. Showed off her shapely ass and made them laugh.

So let me get this straight, Michael said. You made up this obscene tutu. He shook his head. It's hard to imagine.

It wasn't obscene. It was more, like, the suggestion of obscenity. In all kinds of theater you have to let people fill in the blanks. A story never creates a world, just the suggestion of it.

There was silence for a moment and she was wondering if she should have told him. But she was who she was. Or she was who she had been. And she went on:

It's weird. In the tutu I was a different person. On stage. I wore it on the street when I was on the bark. People thought I was a hooker.

Can't imagine why.

She nearly danced along aside Michael as she talked (perhaps unconsciously mimicking him, a thing she had a bad habit of doing without thinking), happy to be happy, remembering, making him laugh, and as she did she had the sensation of what it had been once to be young and burning and on. She had glimmers—could smell the air in Midtown in the fall, car exhaust and incinerators and excitement. Fall in New York. She told him about that. There's nothing like it. The smell of charcoal smoke on every street corner, roasting chestnuts—or who the fuck knows what they were roasting. The smell of charcoal smoke in the air. The lights on the buildings.

Some people, she told him, liked to work in groups, hang out with their friends and they'd all be near the club, but I'd go anywhere, I mean it's not just people who work or live near the club who might come, right? And I wanted to do it on my own terms because there's this thing about a chick standing up on stage trying to be funny. I mean, I bet you could name half a dozen male comics but only about one or two women, at most.

He looked at her. The look wasn't blank, exactly. Just a reminder, perhaps.

Okay, she said. Maybe not you. But *normal* people could. She grinned, and was grateful that he grinned back.

I like not being normal, he said. I think.

There's actually a lot of women comics, she said, barreling along, saying for the first time, really, things she had been thinking about.

It's different for a chick.

Define 'chick,' he said.

A woman who would be considered sexually attractive. There is, in my world view, a delineation between chick and broad. I am not a broad.

And a broad is?

An older woman who can say what she pleases because she's past the point of worrying about saying something that would make her sexually unattractive. Ellen made air quotes when she said 'sexually unattractive.'

He wasn't entirely sure what she was talking about, but went along with it.

I'm still a chick. I'm not a broad. A lot of people just don't like chicks to be funny, if that makes sense. A guy can be a slob and say nasty, raunchy things and it doesn't really affect whether he can be sexually attractive, because 'that's just guys,' you know? People, like, decision-making kinds of people, suits with briefcases full of money, do not want chicks making dirty jokes. In their eyes the world sees things as they do, and in their eyes, they don't want a chick that they don't want to fuck in their movie—I overheard a director say that once—and dirty jokes interfere with that.

Okay, he said, watching her, wondering how on earth all of this had happened, how he was having this conversation at all.

So like, people like Phyllis Diller. She is a hero to me. She's a broad, and I hated her when I was a kid because I didn't get the broad thing. But now I've really come to appreciate the cleverness of her act, the way she packaged herself.

You have very nice packaging yourself, he said.

You're nice.

What year was that?

What? When I went to New York?

He nodded.

I hit the Big Apple in 1988. Summer. New York was in a panic about AIDS, then.

He nodded. That was about the time I got rid of my Apple II and stepped up to a Mac.

Computers, right?

When I was, like, ten or twelve, the TRS-80 was like the first of its kind, a totally hot computer. It had this brick of a keyboard and a monochrome screen, and at the time, anyway, I was in total heaven. It was used. My dad helped me buy it for some ridiculous sum—which was still cheap—from a friend of his. My dad was the ultimate do-it-yourselfer, and wanted to build one from a kit, but I wanted the real thing, which looking back on it, making one would have been better. I can't believe how much it cost, even used. Compared to what you can get now. Well, but then, then. Man, it was like this whole new world of number crunching power.

You like that. Number crunching.

There's nothing like it. Then I got the Apple IIc. It was so sexy. But then I saw the Mac, though, and I had been doing all this command line shit and I saw this magical graphical user interface, and I saw that things could move not just in steps, but leaps.

The building where Michael had sequestered himself for most of the last several years was on the outskirts of the campus, a rather drab and ordinary looking brick, low-rise industrial sort of building. As one of the senior doc students, he had a private office, but it was hardly anything to brag about. It was filled to the rafters with electronics of one sort or another, and not a whole lot else, except a small refrigerator he said his mother had got him, but which was hardly needed—the air conditioning was almost crushingly cold. He said it was for the benefit of the electronics.

She stood outside the open door, leaning beneath a red sign that almost comically read, Restricted Area.

What happens if I intrude on the restricted area?

I have to kill you.

No, really.

Nothing. We pitched in and bought the sign off eBay. Looks cool, though, doesn't it?

Very impressive. Is that geek humor?

He raised his beautiful eyebrows.

She moved into door, close to him, and leaned to him and kissed him on the cheek, then slid inside.

He was thinking: *Sensory information moves through the body in two ways. The amygdala—this weird little section of the brain that's totally reptilian—receives things in a totally different way. While the rest of the brain is processing things for thought (which is itself really amazingly complex), the amygdala is processing things for feeling. You have two nervous systems. You have the autonomous nervous system and the sympathetic nervous system. The autonomous nervous system is pretty much as it sounds. Automatic: it takes care of things like respiration, breathing, heartbeat, and so on. But it also takes care of a lot of other things that are way more subtle. It also takes care of this thing called proprioception, or your sense of the location of yourself. Where are my arms, my leg? that sort of thing. It's also a place where a lot of physical memory resides.*

He closed the door behind them. She put her arms around him and kissed him. He was warm and vaguely damp from the walk. She liked his smell, the salty taste of his neck. She held his head in her hands. It was a kind of astonishment she felt, a thing that went through her—the unreasonableness of life, a chilly predictability that could mask its savage unpredictability.

One of the things that the research shows us is that we are corporeal. So much of how we think relates to how we feel. Literally. It's hard to separate the two. Did you know that quadriplegics experience a diminishing of feeling—emotional feeling—after they lose the sense in their limbs?

So this is the place? she said. This is where all this heavy breathing—I mean *coding* happens.

He grinned. Yep, he said, and moved away from her.

Have you ever had the sense of knowing something viscerally before you knew it literally, intellectually? Well, it turns out that this is a real thing. William James the philosopher first posited it and people thought he was nuts. But it seems to me that it's pretty much essential to survival. To know before you know. I mean survival in the evolutionary sense.

He sat now in a beat up metal and plastic and fabric desk chair and punched a few keys on his keyboard. The larger of the two screens on his desk threw a purple glow at his face that made him look alien. The other was dark and she noticed that there was what appeared to be a very large pile of laundry under his desk.

But the thing that so interesting about the brain, and the thing that's confounding to the researcher, is that there are so many layers to knowledge and to feeling. What you get to study to get insight into them is the anomalies. When things go wrong.

She had no idea what he was doing, but it was a strange turn-on to see him in his world, to see him in the thing that he loved. It was about as alien as she could imagine. The darkness and solitude were about as opposite to her world as possible. The only thing she could compare it to was the Avid room. As though he were cutting a movie that only he could see.

He stood up from the chair, threw out his arms, and said, Well, that's it.

What?

I just had to check something.

Oh, she said, disappointed.

No. I was just thinking. You know how you think, Well, if I left that stone unturned, then maybe....

Yeah.

But I didn't. Leave that stone unturned.

Sorry to hear that, geek boy.

He smiled. Do you want to get some coffee or something? he said.

You think I'm that much of a slut for coffee?

Experience says, Yes.

She put out a hand, but let it float in the air, then drop instead of grabbing him and yanking him toward her.

Coffee, she said. Hmmm. I was thinking of something a little more substantial.

Substantial?

You know. Sumptuous.

Ah, he said, wrapping his arms around her, lifting her. You mean like....

RIVER WALKING

O utside, Michael and Ellen walked to the student union, along the river.
A woman with a little boy walked past them. The boy seemed to want to
look into the water, jump in, even. The woman turned just in time to catch Ellen's
face, and she looked at her for a moment in recognition. Evidently she could not figure out how she 'knew' Ellen before she had to scurry over to her son and keep him
from falling into the water. Fortunately she could not stammer out anything before
Ellen and Michael had passed.

How does that make you feel? he said.

Being always recognized?

She breathed and listened to the air and his own breathing and wanted to say
something true, something that was not a stock, glib answer. I don't know, she said
finally. I guess the ugly but honest answer is that I hate it when it's happening and
dread that it will end.

How does it feel to know that long after you're gone, you will be part of the culture? That even when all this is done—he gestured toward the world around him—
your image will continue to travel into space.

Canned laughter and all, she said. She had not thought of this before, not in this
way.

She said: You know the story about those natives somewhere who think you're
stealing their souls if you take their picture? I sometimes wonder if they're right.
Maybe all those little particles of me traveling out in space, maybe they *are* me. Pieces
of me. Seriously.

He stopped and blocked her path. No. You're you. There's a real you-ness to you.
He was grinning, and his face was alight. I'd like to have a piece of you.

Which one? she said, and then there was a long, delicious silence, a silence that
endured while their eyes locked. Now and again someone walked by. She could feel
him undressing her with his eyes. She was most certainly undressing him.

At last, she said, What are you going to do when this ends?

He looked suddenly and completely crestfallen. She had been talking before about desire. The evanescent moments together, the daydreaming about him, the want that was like dread in reverse. But perhaps it was a Freudian slip. He just looked at her and it felt like she had slapped him.

When is this going to happen? he said.

She tried to keep the conversation where it had been and said, Desire—this kind of desire, the way I feel like I *have* to be with you, that I want to touch you or I'll explode. Don't you think that will go away?

He looked at her, then away. He shoved his hands into his pockets and she looked at his hair, the way the breeze took strands of it and made it whorl around his ear.

I have a theory, she said.

Michael said nothing, but turned back to her, looking vaguely impatient.

My theory is that love is something that is as much mental as physical, a want and a desire. Desire is a constant. People always desire. But want is something, at least in my theory, that's like a decision. You don't make a decision about a desire, but you do make a decision to want.

He cocked his head a little, watched her. Even on stage she did not feel this naked.

Michael, she said, All I know is that I have never experienced it. Want. I mean not with a person. A lover. Want as opposed to desire.

The naked feeling she had made her look at his chest, the buttons of his shirt.

I think my parents have it, want. They get up in the morning and maybe the night before they were sick of each other, but they get up and then want to be together. And I won't say I don't think a certain part of it is luck, blind luck, landing with the right, right, *right* person. But so also, according to my theory, they want to want each other.

I don't get what you're saying, he said. His voice was flat and calm, like a pilot waiting for his disabled plane to crash.

She had not intended this. She had intended to say that she was wondering if she was feeling this for him. Want. Or if she could.

Somehow they were walking again.

She thought: the murderous onslaught of time. The way that time kills everything you love. The way things change imperceptibly, then completely and irrevocably.

They crossed the footbridge, then went up the hill next to the student union, and he was lost in thought. She wondered if perhaps she had said THE wrong thing. She wondered if she had—after knowing him for how many days shy of two weeks?—blown the whole thing. A number of times she started to say something, but no matter how she framed it in her mind, she could not turn it into words. Was she purposely destroying this without even knowing it?

Finally, he said: I'm sorry.

And as the words came out of his mouth she feared it was a kind of rejection, a—

I'm sorry, he said again, Because I, I don't know. We both know. He hesitated again. Then he went silent and they were walking again.

They walked another 10 yards or so in silence before she said, We both know what?

Our lives. Our vast accumulation of—

You-ness.

He smiled.

I was just saying that I kind of want to find out if I really want you, she said.

What would that take? At last, he seemed relieved.

Probably so much sex that we were sick of each other. And dentures. And really ugly stuff.

How much sex do you think it would take us?

She looked at him as they walked, and he had a smiling, this-is-just-small-talk look on his face. And indeed, she felt at this moment that the flighty, skimming feeling she had, of this all being just superficial talk from two people who scarcely knew one another, was the right feeling. To go deeper would be idiotic at this point.

Michael, she said. We'd just have to see.

THE SHAPE OF THE WORLD HAS CHANGED

It all seemed changed now, the campus, the river, even his office, and there was a part of him that wanted to leave the moment and measure all of the physiologic changes that had occurred in the moments leading up to and after lovemaking. A part of him wanted to hook himself up to a machine and measure his brain activity, compare it with some earlier (non-existent) baseline measurement so that he would have some objective correlation of what he felt. Which was buoyant, breathless yet full of breath, superhuman.

He could not remember having felt quite as he did now—it was almost a dream state, a déjà vu sense that he had been here before, with her. Everything seemed—suddenly—to have been foreordained, but it was a feeling more like a dream memory, like trying to pull a memory up from the deepest mists of his subconscious mind.

Her appearance had set off in him something he wasn't quite aware of. His body seemed to know her even if in his mind she was still largely a stranger. His whole autonomic nervous system reacted to her. And if it wasn't too presumptuous, she seemed to have a similar reaction to him.

He lay next to her in his bed—the sheets of which he had washed for the first time in he didn't know how long (it wasn't *that* bad; most times he slept in his office chair)—and propped himself up on one elbow and looked at her. She was naked and it was mid-afternoon and he was naked too and it felt like thieving, like having stolen something from the day. Not doing any work, but meeting up with her for lunch, then coming back to his empty house. He wanted time to stop. He wanted somehow to capture this sensation and preserve it, but maybe that was part of what she meant when she told him her theory of love and sex. That you could keep things like this, but (he knew from his research) that memory consolidation would move this moment from one part of his brain to another, and that where and how it finally resided would depend a lot on what was still to come.

He said, So what's it like, your work? Hollywood and all that.

He sat up.

Hollywood and all that?

191

She turned her head and looked at him for the longest time before continuing. Then she laughed: It's like a really dysfunctional high school, where the administration has no leader and all the kids have money and power and guns. Everyone runs in cliques and there is a prevalent air of surreality in the sense that the whole point of the money is to insulate you from reality.

He had not quite expected this and all he could do was hum.

I've been thinking about it. Money. It's a measure of so many things, so many different kinds of status. (She had been thinking about it because the whole departure thing was the launching pad to the REALLY BIG IDEA: chucking it all. It was like leaving New York and your rent-controlled apartment—not a decision to be taken lightly. But he wouldn't understand it.)

Do you have a lot of money? he said. He wasn't exactly sure why he said it but it seemed like she wanted him to ask.

She took it in stride. She said: More than some—a lot more—and less than others—a lot less. She sat up in his bed but did not bother to pull the sheet around her. Her face got a sharp, angled look that he had not seen before. It was both a little frightening (she was a formidable woman, after all) and incredibly erotic (he liked the idea that she was simultaneously girlish and a hard-nosed businesswoman).

Do you want to know specifics? she said. Do you want figures?

No, he said, and searched his mind for the why of the question. I just— I mean I was wondering where—or how—or why I fit in.

She gave a rueful smile. That, she said, is the most interesting question I've heard in a long time. She shook her head a little and tilted it back.

He watched her intently.

I see it as a very complicated question, she said, her hand going up his leg.

Really?

There's a geographical aspect to it, but there's also a sort of philosophical aspect, which has a longer range. There are probably other aspects, or aspects to the aspects.

He laughed. Her fingers were now on his penis, her fingertips, and it, his penis, was already erect.

The first aspect, she said, and breezes of pleasure went through him each time she touched him.

The first aspect is unanswerable because I just have no idea—at least in the larger sense. At this, she leaned over and kissed his neck.

He was leaning back now with both arms extended, the heels of his hands on the bed. And the philosophical aspect? he said.

She was on her knees now and knee-walking over his legs to straddle him as she spoke: The philosophical aspect is just one that's going to have to take a longer view.

Her hand had closed around his penis and his chest tightened at the sensation.

I'd say, she said, as she positioned herself over him, that where you belong right now is right here. Her hand came away and he watched as her body enveloped his penis. She pushed him down and leaned over him. And by right here, I mean here and now, in the moment.

What about you?

Yeah. Oh, yeah, she said. Me, too.

SOFTWARE IS LIKE LIFE

One morning she met him on a bench on the river side of Hancher, the glass gleaming in the spring light. She sat down on a bench where he sat. He looked tired, and as skinny as Mick Jagger in 1964.

You were working, she said.

Sort of, he said. I thought I had something. After you left last night, I thought I had something. I needed to find out. Soraya and I were talking about it and it struck me. That there was an algorithm that had gone—

An algorithm.

Do you know what an algorithm is?

It's a, um, an if-this-then-that kind of thing?

Yeah, basically.

Oh, yes, goody, you go girl, she said.

He laughed. It's a way of talking about cause and effect. True-false, false-true, 1-0, 0-1. It's a way of talking about the million gazillion little unpredictable particles of cause and effect floating around us that we understand. Assemble them correctly, you have software. I spent a few years working on this thing. It's a kind of extreme programming environment. It's called the EvoCoder. For evolutionary code. And it works off a grid, so you have essentially supercomputing power. Okay, you're glazing. It's kind of like a search engine for code. It goes out looking on open source sites and finds the kinds of code it needs. It's more than that, but let's just—. You start with a heuristic—okay, you're glazing—what you do is instead of reinventing the wheel…. Never mind. Suffice it to say that the Black Box is still weird and I still am not sure what I did, how I got—

He stopped, sighed.

You know what you look like? she said. You look like a junkie. You were on the wagon and you just got off.

Thanks, he said. You sound like Soraya.

It's nice to see you. She touched his face. Pressed her fingers into his stubble.

It's nice to see you, he said.

Did you spend the night in your chair?

He nodded. Then he suddenly brightened. He said, Do you want to go to the beach?

You mean like the dam or the real beach?

The Outer Banks.

She furrowed her brow. Um. Sure, when?

Right before, you know. Summer. Before summer school starts. I have two sections this summer. We all go, Soraya and Hanna and Jake and Adam and me—I mean it didn't used to be Adam. But it'd be fun.

Okay, she said.

Soraya and Adam are going to rent a house with Hanna and Jake. I think they already have it booked.

She nodded, giving him the sexiest look she could. Baby, I can't wait. Let's do it.

We can sleep on their floor or something.

I think not, darling. We can get our own house.

Like Michael, Jake, an industrial designer, was skinny and wiry and smart. He was Keith to Michael's Mick. The two were often mistaken for brothers, and Jake actually did look like Michael, albeit slightly less vivid and less charismatic.

Hanna had dated Jake for something like two years, but Ellen never got the sense that there was tremendous electricity between them. Hanna clearly adored Michael, but she slept with Jake. It often seemed to Ellen that Hanna had settled for Jake rather than fallen head-over-heels.

Clearly, Hanna admired, protected, and pushed Jake. Clearly, she wanted him to succeed. She—with obvious pride—had shown Ellen his web site, which displayed an astonishing array of both the actual products he had designed and theoretical products that he had dreamt he could build. He had any number of major companies that occasionally dangled before him massively attractive offers to come to work for them—on his own terms—and inevitably, he turned them down. Which, for Hanna, was hugely frustrating. Where Michael wore his passion on his sleeve, she said, you were never sure if Jake ever actually had passion. Like Michael, he was driven by some particularized vision that only he could really see. But unlike Michael, it was private. His designs were gorgeous, but they were also like porn, the kind of thing he hid whenever anyone else was around.

Jake's industrial designs drew substantial commissions even as he was working on an electrical engineering degree. As far as Hanna was concerned, the degree was useless. It was a contest, perhaps, just to show that he could do what Michael could do. Or it was a self-inflicted holding pattern. He was going to circle around the airport of adulthood until Michael landed and then, and only then, would he land. But even though he probably could've bought his own house in Iowa City (or, actually, a whole block), he had continued to rent a relatively crappy place after moving out of Michael's.

The two of them had been best friends since Michael's freshman year, Jake's sophomore, when they'd met at an engineering party (at which, according to Michael, there was a predominance of guys), and had become fast friends, although their relationship sometimes seemed more osmotic than verbal. Even though Jake was older, he seemed to look up to Michael and this, too, was frustrating to Hanna. Once she said to Ellen that she wondered if he wasn't in love with Michael in some weird way.

Sometimes Jake—like Michael—didn't talk for hours. And where Michael disappeared into his lab for days, sometimes weeks on end, Jake's lab, such as it was, was a room in his house, and he spent hours in front of his computer with Adobe Illustrator and a CAD software package open, 3-D images appearing to him. He either sketched and stared off into space or stared hypnotically into the dense pixels of space of his Macintosh's screen.

It was Jake who introduced Adam to Soraya. Adam was a recently-tenured professor of English literature, but he looked a bit more like an exotic surfer-dude truck driver. Totally chiseled and buff, but with a perpetual look of perplexion. He was three or four inches taller than Michael or Jake, and probably had fifty pounds more muscle and bone than either of them. He had short sandy blond hair and three, sort of Mondrian-looking tattoos on his right shoulder, beginning at the bottom of his shoulder blade and extending up and over. As if to apologize for his size, he tended to stoop. He had a short thin goatee, but his beard never seemed to grow in, and never seemed to get any longer.

And then of course there was his voice. While you expected something chipper and gnarly and, like, totally cool, what he actually sounded like—but exactly—was a character from Winnie the Pooh, the perpetually doleful Eeyore. It was a lovely baritone, and it lent a sort of weird gravitas to everything he said. He also had a very active but very dry Midwestern sense of humor, and his mournful baritone amplified that. At the same time, however, he spent most of his time listening, and where at first he had seemed to Ellen completely out of place among the others with his comparatively hulking size and standard Midwestern blond hair, after a while he blended in perfectly. It was part of the package that Soraya called the Adam Conundrum.

At some point he had stumbled across Jake's work. He had finished the book that would get him his tenure and with the modest advance money, he had decided to build furniture for the Spartan house he owned near Coralville. According to him, he had looked forever for furniture that he actually liked, but everything seemed to him almost desperately ugly. He had bought somewhere an enormous Persian carpet that covered most of the hardwood floors of his living room, and had decided at some point that if he could not find the furniture he envisioned then he would create it.

He was surprised to find that Jake lived nearby. He had walked over to Michael and Jake's place and knocked on the door. After a cup or two of coffee and some intense discussions about formal and functional anesthetics, he and Jake went back over to his place, Jake almost running to keep up with his long athletic stride, and then the two of them had stood at the edge of the room staring at the carpet. Jake had known just by looking the tribe and the location within Iran from which the carpet had originated. The color, he told Adam, demanded wooden furniture. A few days later he came back and knocked on the door and showed Adam some computer sketches he'd done, conceptual drawings of sleek, Shaker-inspired pieces. He had recreated, from memory, Adam's whole house in 3-D. And then he had left.

A few hours later, Adam knocked on Michael and Jake's door. Soraya answered.

Despite talking on the phone, it was most of a week before Ellen saw Michael again—he had again thought he was nearing something, but it slipped through his fingers. He told her on the phone that he had decided to see what would happen if he just looked at what he had and stopped trying to make it be something it wasn't, and tried to understand what it was doing. Which actually proved harder than he had expected. It was almost as though the code didn't want him to know. It was the kind of thing that made you think that you were losing your mind.

When he called that night, she was watching TV with her father, and almost instantly got up and kissed him and said she was going to see Michael, not to wait up.

When she got to his house, Jake was there, as he sometimes was, and let her in. He was sketching in the kitchen. (Sometimes it seemed that he had forgotten that he didn't live there anymore.) Sit down, he'd said, and gone back into the kitchen, back into his head, his work.

When at last Michael showed up, Jake let him in. She was sitting in the living room, waiting for him, reading one of his magazines. She was so hungry for him she surprised herself. She had gone instantly wet at the sound of his voice on the phone—as he might have put it, a completely autonomic thing. The wait had not cooled her ardor and she was surprised that she was not angry.

They walked down the street in the darkness, no cars. Jake stayed, oblivious, and so they left.

197

Michael liked, for some reason that she did not feel like asking about, to walk in the middle of the street. Not, of course, in traffic, but when there was none. He joked that it gave him more bandwidth, but she did not get the joke. She walked beside him, in the middle of the street, and the air was wildly fragrant. She could smell lilac. There were lilac trees everywhere, and in bloom.

His favorite time in the lab was at night, he said. You get lost. It's less like a job, and the radio tends to be better at night.

She said, hand grazing his backside, Did you clear off your desk?

He turned to her and smiled. He said, I cleared off my desk.

Oh, she said, drawing out the word, You are, I hope, planning to seduce me.

No, he said, Not at all. Not I, and she could see him blush in the headlights of an oncoming car—a car, to her surprise, that sidled up next to them. A police car.

You folks understand that there's a sidewalk here? the officer said more than asked when he rolled down the window.

Yes sir, Michael said.

Then why don't you please be safe and make use of it.

You bet, Ellen said, and, Thank you for the sage advice, Officer Krupke.

Before the cop had a chance to react in any way, she moved close to the car and folded her arms across the frame of the open window. She was feeling good, exhilarated, and wanted to show off. She waited a couple of beats so that he was sure to see who she was; she waited for the reaction.

You're— he started. He missed the *West Side Story* joke. She did not give him a chance to finish but gave him a quick peck on the mouth.

She said: Now you go on back down to the station, she said, and tell everyone else you just kissed Gina Perri. Then she broke away from the side of the car and danced in the headlights as they crossed to the sidewalk.

You have a good evening, officer, she called. It was the first such outburst since the idiotic thing at the coffee shop, which was only weeks ago, but seemed like forever. She had got used to being safe, anonymous. She would be an idiot to think, however, that this could go on forever.

Michael was a good sport. He laughed as they walked between parked cars to the sidewalk. The cop car just sat there, and they started walking faster—she was a little nervous now that he might not like the joke, that he might arrest her, just to be able to say he had. She was missing, after all. By the time they turned the corner, heading toward his building, the cop car had not moved.

Shit, she thought. She said, Was that really stupid?

I probably would have recommended against it.

She felt better when it was out of sight and nothing had happened.

Michael unlocked the side door to the lab building—the silence and darkness that surrounded everything at this very moment seemed monumental. He opened the door and let her through, then followed her down the empty, worn corridor.

She wore a short cotton dress with a light jacket and her legs bristled with goose bumps from the AC. He didn't turn on the lights, but hit something on his desktop and the monitors lit up. He had cleaned. There was space—just a bit—on the desk, and there was no longer a pile of laundry beneath.

There was a pair of weird, rack-looking things against the walls that looked like computers stripped of their cases and piled one on top of the other. There were lights inside them, small green and yellow and red glows that made them look something like insane, miniature Frank Gehry high-rises with the skins torn away. The room was a battle between heat and cold.

He put his arms around her. She took his hands and moved them around to her ass; he lifted her skirt.

This for me? She indicated the open space on the desk.

He nodded. She loved his eyebrows, the look in his eyes.

You're not supposed to keep the great Ellen Gregory waiting, she said.

I hope I can make it up to you, he said. He had pushed off her panties and now she sat on the cold, empty spot on desk, her legs around him, wanting him more than she ever wanted anything.

Later, when it was over, there were footsteps in the hallway that stopped in front of his door. Someone trying the knob.

The look on his face went to curiosity. She thought of the cop.

But there was no key in the lock, nothing else except the person on the other side of the door. She would have sworn she could hear someone breathing. And she could not help herself but thought of Wayne Townsend, the baseball bat coming through the wall, and part of her wanted just to scream. Her heart hammered in her ribs. She nearly strangled Michael, holding onto him.

And then things were silent again, aside from the ventilation system.

What the hell was that?

I don't know, he said. Probably security, he said, which made a lot more sense than a revivified Townsend.

She had told him about Wayne Townsend, but she knew it was something he wouldn't exactly understand: the way it stayed with you. The way she was nearly certain he either was not dead or would come back to life, as he did, now and then, in her dreams.

I didn't only bring you here to make love, he said.

No? She did not know what else to say. She had wanted him desperately and now the air felt disjointed, ill fitting. She wanted desperately to get back to the place they had been just a few moments ago. She felt, right now, that she could have made the funniest joke in the history of mankind and it would not have been funny. She was certain there was a tremor in her voice. The air conditioner had her cold. Cold.

So besides getting to play with high-tech toys, what do you do in here?

A lot of the actual work the machines do, he said. I wrote the scripts for them and they chug along, compiling algorithms.

It's a flashy business compiling algorithms, she joked. It's noisy as hell in here.

I like it. The white noise. It's fans, mostly—it's like a wind tunnel in that rack. The drives and processors make a lot of noise, but it's mostly the fans. And the building's ventilation system.

It's ventilated, all right.

Are you cold? You want my shirt?

No, she said. Tell me what you do.

I'm compiling.

She shivered, thought about making a joke, but didn't.

The rack is really just a single computer running a distribution of Unix that I rewrote to be my great dissertation project. He gave one of his rueful laughs. All the processors are cooking in parallel, so I have super-computing power. There are two things happening here—Do you want to know? Do you really want to know?

Yeah, she said. But—. Yeah. Sure.

The compiler is program I was talking about, the EvoCoder. You start out with an endpoint in mind and it sifts through all sorts of code—things we already know how to do—and finds the most efficient way of doing the thing you want to do. You know all about the Internet, but what you mostly know is the web, probably. That's like, well, only a tiny percentage of the Internet. That other percentage is where my bots are going—

Bots?

Yeah, they're little programs that go out searching for algorithms. They find them, compare them with ones that are already on my storage system, and keep those that aren't already there. It does this really fast. We have like totally amazing bandwidth here. You're glazing again.

Yeah. I'm sorry.

What I'm doing is creating what I call 'informed' code. It searches everywhere. It goes into every account that the university has, it goes into every server, every piece of software, and it looks for the best code. If there are say a hundred ways of doing something, I've put together some algorithms that look for the most elegant way. So if one way takes three steps and another takes a hundred—.

She moved toward him, put her hand on his crotch.

He did not say it, but as he was articulating this, he realized for the first time that he might have really fucked up. That the EvoCoder might be looking in places and adopting code from systems that could be in the realm of you-really-don't-want-to-go-there. Like NSA or DARPA. It was not likely, since secret and top secret were entirely different networks. But you never knew what someone had left hanging out there in freespace. He made a mental note to go back and look.

He took her hand and held it against his chest tightly, closed his eyes. I want to show you this, he said, his mouth scarcely opening. He pushed her hand away. You're distracting me.

I am.

But I want—

Want?

I want you, too. But I want to show you this.

She took her hand away, sat in his chair and folded her hands on her lap, an ironic inversion of prim.

He looked at her appraisingly and this look made her uneasy. It made her want to perform.

He unlocked a drawer and took out a weird looking combination of headphones and glasses and other wiry electronic looking stuff. Put this on, he said.

She laughed. What's this?

That's the portal to the Black Box. Are you wearing contacts or anything?

She shook her head.

Didn't think so. Sit down. Put it on.

He helped her with it, helped her place the flat plastic sensors—she thought they were plastic—against her temples, the little knobby things against her skull. It had a warmth to it, and a darkness. It felt like good to be in his hands, in his world, the rest of the world receding.

Later, when she had a chance to think about it, she was glad she was sitting when it came up because it came so hard and fast and completely kilter-jolting that it would have slapped her off her feet. Literally.

There was jagged, pixellated light, and in the distance—a distance that increased rapidly—she could hear the keyboard going like a herd of tiny plastic horses. Then the light went to blue and her eyeballs were scraping and there was the sound of wind and she was at the head of a massive waterfall. It wasn't wind and it was getting louder. There was the spray of water and now the thunder of the water going over.

She hung onto the chair, because she was fucking hang-gliding and it was *real*. She tried to speak but could not. She had been strapped in, thrown off a cliff, and oh, by the way, there was no fucking *blindfold*. She was a participant, no matter what. This, the moment she had been thrown into, was as astounding for how unprepared she was as it was for what was happening. She had no idea how to get out, or if you could. It did not test, not speak.

The moment was as astonished as if the face saw its own brain.

Perhaps she yelled. She could smell water. She could feel herself being lifted out over the spume of the water, then turning, facing back to it. This thing—a hang glider—had a motor, and the pilot was a pilot, a mad, long-haired-but-balding Anglo dude, and he was winging the contraption out over this enormous gaping maw of a canyon, its lush and variegated green blotched with spectacular shimmers of color—stands of flowers she was too far away to make out. She could feel the shudder of the improbably birdlike sinews of the machine in every part of her body. There was the mineral scent of the water, the roar of air and plunging falls, the bouncing of the wings in the air currents. Now they would rise and then fall, and it was enough to make you vomit. She was hundreds of feet up, floating in the rainbow of the spume. She was sitting but could feel her legs dangling beneath her. She put out her arms, could feel the air over every hair follicle.

Now they flew downward, taking wide, slow spirals so she could take in the whole panorama, hear it, the vision luminous and then the blue sky the shimmering droplets knifed by sunshine and go ahead give the day to the wind. The pilot shouted something that she could not make out. The motor had the high nasty pitch of a monstrous wasp.

Hawaii. I am here, falling.

She had been there, seen these falls. She had taken this ride.

When he stopped it and took the headset off her, she felt like she had punched through another world.

God, she said. What was *that*?

TOO REAL

That, Michael said, is a question I can't quite answer.

This is too weird. This is way too weird. That is so real. What was that?

I don't know. I mean, I know.

For someone who had created—even if it was a *mistake*—the most completely astounding thing she could remember experiencing, he looked remarkably glum.

It's so *real*, Michael. All she could do was shake her head. It's realer than real. The vertigo hung on, the way it had after the actual event.

That's because it is real. But you're experiencing it for the second time, like watching a movie more than once. You see things you didn't the first time.

Can you go into the future?

It doesn't seem so, but I don't know. The present seems to be stochastic. Anything can happen. The past is deterministic. Only what has happened can happen. But I've never been to the present.

How many times have you done it?

Tripped it? I don't know. A lot.

She stood up from the chair and circled the small room, shaking her head.

She said: I was in Hawaii and it was a vacation I once took. I did this insane ultralight plane ride over this waterfall—it's a famous waterfall.

She was breathless. The images were magnificent, vivid.

She tried to remember: This was when, '97? '98? It was right after they had signed on for the show and she and Marty and some others had gone to Hawaii, a sort of semi-working vacation that she'd nearly forgotten. Now it was still in her head. The whole visual thing—no, the whole goddamned thing was just hovering in her head, a memory that had been pulled at random from her head and then revivified. It was mind-blowing.

He rubbed his head with both hands and looked at her. His eyes were bleary and he had a look of both excitement and frustration. He had stumbled onto something incredible, but he had no idea what.

The thing I don't get, she said, pressing her forefinger to her temple and doing one of her signature poses, Is why is this a bad thing?

He rolled his eyes back and shook his head in a sort of you-just-wouldn't-get-it expression that just mostly pissed her off. Michael—, she started, but he cut her off.

Let me ask you this, he said. What if you had what you were sure was the funniest routine you ever did—and you had all the pieces in all the right places, the lines or whatever and, what if, not only that, getting to the next level of your career, or even your career itself, abso-*fucking*-lutely *depended* on it, no question, and then—

He was out of his chair and waving his arms a little—

And then, what you, what you got, what you got was, I don't know, a fucking *poodle*. A real, honest to god, shitting and pissing and yapping and manicured and bow-tied poodle? Something so completely far away from what you originally planned that it just blew your mind? I mean, what if you went on stage and found yourself doing 'Oklahoma' instead?

She shook her head. I guess I don't get it.

He started to sputter in frustration.

She said, No, what I mean is that I've always been totally about mind-blowing. I mean some of my best stuff has been mistakes.

I am trying to get my doctorate here. I have my whole life invested here and I've got a poodle. I can't make mistakes.

There was a long silence. She wanted to make love. She wanted to go for a walk. She wanted a place in the world where she felt as at home as he did here.

Can I ask you a question? she said.

Sure, he said. He was across the room from her, fiddling with something, just to keep his hands busy.

I know you said you have no idea how it works. But have you tried to figure that out?

No, he said. I mean, Yes. I don't know. I've been going through my backups, trying to get it back to where it was before this thing happened.

Don't you think it would make some kind of sense? To take a look?

Yeah, it would make sense, he said, and by the way, that's what Soraya said. Except it kind of goes against everything I know. I don't mean trying to look at what it's doing—I mean actually *what it does*. It makes no sense. There is no way, given the computing power that's in the box, given the video card it has—there is no way it should be able to do that. And believe me, I've taken the thing apart and looked at it. I've run it on both boxes. I've checked the video cards. I checked my disks and my motherboards and my processors just to see if somehow—for motivations that would be completely mystifying to me—someone might have swapped something on me.

He came back to the desk chair and sat down. Ellen sat on the desk. He put his hand on her leg and she closed her eyes. He said: So what do you think?

What do I think?

Yeah.

Bathtub. You need a bathtub.

What's that supposed to mean?

Isn't the bathtub where Archimedes had his eureka moment?

He gave an unenthusiastic laugh. I mean, he said, it seems obvious that the computer isn't doing it. At least it's not rendering all that video—assuming we can call it video—so that has to mean that it's all in your head.

Isn't that what you wanted? I mean didn't you say it was all about think and click?

Yeah, but flit across the quantum?

Which would you rather do? I know my answer.

She stood up, wandered around. She put her hands up near the server racks to warm them. She could still see the waterfall, could still hear the little ultralight's engine—even smell its exhaust. That day, back in Hawaii, she had been terrified, but totally exhilarated to try it. No one else would do it. She remembered telling Marty she had more balls than he did—to which he said, I freely admit this. There was more to it, though, the memory had a significance that she had forgotten. At that time, of course, she was rising, things were happening for her—and there was a part of her that had wanted to prove that she was making them happen. That it wasn't all just dumb luck. She started to say something to Michael. She started, but then couldn't figure out what to say. That she was trying to outman the boys? That she had determined that there was no risk worth taking that was too much to take?

Seeing it all again brought this back, and it made her remember why she left LA, it made her remember what she no longer was. When she had left, it had seemed that there were no risks left to take. Or none that were worth taking. But at 32, was she really an old lady who could sit back in her rocking chair and marvel at how reckless she had once been?

Except she wasn't sure what reckless meant anymore. Certainly ditching the show was reckless—and probably more calculated than she understood, at least consciously—but there was little that had that high-flying sensation anymore. Of course, if you excepted Michael. Getting to know him, getting into bed with him— that was the first thing she'd felt in years that had given her that sensation. And not that it was all about sensation. It was about having some innate feel for what was right, like leaving home when she did, like working with Marty. All of these things had felt incontrovertibly right when she'd done them.

She shook her head and looked at Michael sitting at his machine and smiled. No, the man had something that went way beyond sensation. The man totally confounded her. He was never predictable. Never said what she wished he would say. Instead, like his mistake of a machine, whatever he said was better than what she wanted.

And whatever there was in her head about herself, there was no doubt in her mind that what Michael had done here—mistake or no—was totally fucking brilliant, and literally so. There was nothing to which she could compare the experience that she'd just had. Not even in dreams. It wasn't at all the random stuff that a mind asleep generates, the odd confabulations of dreams—moments pressed together in a simulacrum of sense. Even she could see that if he could do something with this, if he could figure out what it was it was all doing, then he had truly stumbled across a wonder.

Here, he said, and motioned to her with the headset. Put it back on, he said.

She came back to the chair and sat. He helped her fix the thing to her head, and then all was dark. Again the sound of typing. Again there was the pixellated light. But she was no longer in Hawaii. There was a cornfield and it was fall, the corn had been combined and now there was nothing but broken brown stalks. She was there with her father. Both held shotguns. Her father showed her how to break the shotgun and slide in shells—the *now* part of Ellen, the part tripping this trip, was heartbroken at how young her father was, the Saturday stubble on his face not yet grayed, his face unlined—and she broke her own gun (surprised again, after all these years at how heavy it was) and took the shells (cold from the cold air) one by one and put them in. Hers were smaller than his—she had a .410, he had a 12-gauge—and he showed her how to sweep it along the flight path of the pheasant as it leapt up out of the gleanings, how to lead it. He told her how (God, the sound of his voice, the music) you had to keep your entire body relaxed, how you had not to think about shooting, not get tense, just take a shot if you had it.

And suddenly there was a noise, a flash, and then bright light so hard she wanted to close her eyes and she had done it and her father put his hand on her shoulder as the both of them, guns broken, knelt next to the dead bird. She picked it up and was astonished at how warm it was, feverish almost. She tried to hold her tears.

It's tough, he said. But this is what it's like to be alive.

She turned to him, eyes smashed with tears, and looked at the vague smile on his thin mouth, the combination of love and cruelty.

Michael helped her off with the headset. He must have seen the look on her face, because immediately, wordlessly, he started putting everything away. And when he was through, when the box he kept the headset in was closed, he said, You want to walk?

She blinked. I don't know what I want, she said.

AGAIN THE RIVER

They were by the river now—again—this seemed to be the place for them where all was laid bare, all was worked out. There had been silence between them since she had taken off the headset and he wasn't sure what to say. Clearly something had happened, but clearly it was something that she could not talk about right away.

It occurred to him suddenly—glancing at her now and again furtively, worrying that he had hurt her, desperate to glimpse her, smell her, see her face—that he was in love with her. The thing that puzzled him about the thought was not the thought itself, but why it had taken so long to come.

The river was black in the darkness—the lights along the path only made it more so. The night had changed so remarkably since she had pulled the stunt with the policeman. Lately things seemed to be like this, violent jogs between competing realities. There was a part of her that was ready for none of this. There was a part of her that was ready to tell him that they should stop seeing one another for a while. She thought of the image she'd had of standing some twenty years ago with her father, hunting pheasant in a cornfield. What, if anything, did it mean?

There was so much here that was unresolved to take on a relationship with Michael now.

They walked and did not talk.

For a long time she said nothing. It wasn't that she wanted to give him the silent treatment, it was that all of this was very difficult to take in, to assimilate. It had suddenly occurred how real this was. Her falling for him.

After a while, she said, I've been in about four different realities tonight, maybe five. I thought before all of this stuff started that I had no idea what *real* was. But now.

He laughed—it was an impish laugh, a thing that was hard to pin. That's what you get for thinking there's a such thing as real.

What does that mean?

From just a Philosophy 101 perspective, he said, It means that reality is pretty much what you say it is. I don't think that it corresponds in any way with the objective world outside us.

She shook her head and gave a growl and clenched her fists.

He was in front of her now, walking backwards, being silly, but silly in a charming way.

Michael, she said. When I left LA, I *must* have had a reason. I mean I *had* a reason, I was just never exactly clear on anything but that I had to leave. I didn't intend to be *here* right now. I didn't *intend* anything. I just knew if I didn't leave I was going to shoot myself.

There was a part of her that wanted to crush him. She had crushed men before more easily than she could crush an ant. She suddenly wanted to be done with him— be done with everything, to crawl out of her skin like a snake—and what?

But you changed your mind.

What? No. I never really thought of shooting myself. At least not literally. I left. And maybe that was a kind of suicide. I don't know. What I left—that *other* reality, such as it is—still exists. At some point, I have to figure out why I left and how to go back.

You don't have to.

And you could give up your Ph.D. Michael, it's my life.

He slowed and let her pass him, then caught up. Or not quite caught up. He straggled behind just a little. A long time passed when they just walked before he said: Do you want to go back?

Go back where?

LA, he said.

It's really not a question of *want*. I have a multimillion dollar contract and there is no show if I don't go back, so there are lots of other people's livings depending on my being a good girl and doing what I'm supposed—contractually, anyway—to do.

I didn't realize it was quite like that, he said.

She stopped and looked at him, and she wanted to slap him, he looked so fucking clueless. She said: Quite like what?

Multimillion dollar stuff.

Yes, Michael, she said, perhaps too patronizingly. I *am* a *million* dollar baby. I am a *multimillion*—Jesus, you're the computer nerd, haven't you Googled me? I mean you haven't ever watched the show? Jesus, I'd at least think you'd be curious to know who you're dating. Or seeing. Or whatever the fuck it is we're doing here. Don't you think it would be nice to know what kind of psycho you're getting messed up with?

And where would I find that out, but being with you? he said. It'd be great if you'd give me a little bit of, like, I don't know. I don't know very much right at the moment, but two things. One is that you gave me a great idea back there in my lab, and you don't even know what it was. And two, that I *do* know who you are, he said, nodding deliberately as if to punctuate it as he said it. I don't need Google to tell me.

Aren't you even curious?

He came close to her and touched her face with the back of his right forefinger, as though wiping a nonexistent tear from her cheek. I *am* curious, he said. But about *you*. I don't need to know what anyone else thinks about you. I don't need to, to have my experience of you mediated.

She closed her eyes and took a deep breath. Michael, she said, sighing.

So what is this? So what is happening here?

I don't know, Michael. What do you think is happening here?

I think, he said, I think that I'm—no. Wait.

He put his hands on her shoulders, stopped her, held her shoulders as though to fix her to this spot.

I actually just realized this a moment ago, he said. This is not just some bullshit, and I do care what you think when I say this, but I realized that even though we've only known each other for, like, three weeks or something, I realized that I really like to see your face.

A moment ago he had been talking rapid-fire, but as soon as he said, *your face*, he slowed down. Now he spoke with a soft, slow cadence.

I really like to hear your voice, and when I don't, I get lonely. But not lonely for people, for anyone else, only for you. And I really care about what you think, and what you say. And it just hit me, a few minutes ago—we could go back to the actual spot where this hitting occurred, where on this road to Samara the scales fell from my eyes—hell, we could probably even find the scales—it just hit me that—. He stopped. They stopped and just stood in this pool of darkness next to the Iowa River and looked at one another. He started to say something, but then stopped. She could see where this was going, and it was almost like a rollercoaster ride—she wanted to stay on to see the next insane plunge, but she also just wanted to get off. He started again but stopped and she turned.

Ellen Gregory, he said. Ellen Gregory. He just said her name.

He held her shoulders and looked at her for the longest time.

Then: I don't know what I wanted to say, he said. Except that somehow you changed the warp of space around me. You altered the chemistry of my brain. You, being with you has warped my space time. But I want you to know. I'm—. I'm a big enough boy, he said, faltering now, seeing the look on her face. I've, you know, I've never been to Hollywood, but—

She wanted to joke, she wanted to say, No one's ever said I warped their space time before (which was true), but the abject terror was that this discussion, this perilous proximity to the word 'love,' made her break out in a cold sweat, made it impossible to do anything but lift her arms and put her hands over her face. She shook her head. No, Michael. No. This is not. This cannot.

He said: And this was even before I heard the words multimillion dollar.

Michael, this is a problem. This is really a problem.

A PERSON DISCOVERS
THE STRANGEST THINGS

It was long after midnight by the time she got to Fairview Park, and everything had a ghostly, post-apocalyptic feel to it—the dark, empty streets, the looming, quiet clapboard houses, white paint glowing phosphorescently in the sudden bath of headlights. As she crept along, hyper-alert, she could feel the darkness fold back. She could have been entering—or re-entering—another different reality.

When she came inside the house, her father was in the living room, his feet up on the coffee table, watching a do-it-yourself show on the TV.

Were you waiting up for me? she said but even as she said it she realized he was snoring softly. She watched him for a moment, his chin glistening vaguely with white stubble, and it was suddenly too easy to imagine him dead. His skin was slack against his jaw and she could see the outline of his skull. The thought was horrific, and she said, Hey, and pushed his shoulder.

He sat up, looking around. Startled, hazy. His eyes settled on her and seemed to review her for a moment. Oh, he said. Hi, I guess I fell asleep. He stretched and rubbed his eyes, the top of his head. Wow, it's late.

I know. I figured you'd be in bed.

Yeah. Did you have a nice time?

She sank down into a chair, gave a sighing laugh and shook her head in something like bewilderment.

Come here, he said. Sit next to me.

Almost without thinking, she rose and moved to the couch and slumped against him. He put his arm around her and hugged her close. This is a treat, holding my lovely daughter.

In a way, it amazed her that this was even possible. That she could come back after so long and still be loved. And yet, simultaneously, nothing could have seemed more natural. She pressed in close to him, her head a mass of confusion. There had been too much to consider, to figure before she ever got here, and now she had mucked it all up by getting involved with Michael, and now there was even more to consider. All the way home she had had several different realities going on in her head: the ever-present possibility that word of her presence might have slipped out to the media. The things Michael had said about being fond of the sound of her voice, being lonely for her when she wasn't around (she couldn't bring herself to think of the L-word). She could not figure out how the evening had changed so drastically—when she had left the house to meet Michael, she had been in the lightest, the most buoyant of moods, but the bliss of lovemaking with Michael followed by those images of Hawaii, of her father—it had all slapped her into another frame of mind. She felt like her emotions were completely out of control. On the TV, animations of woodworking tools scooted across the screen.

After a long time, she said, Did I ever do anything that made mom happy?

What she wanted to say was that it had—out of nowhere—dawned on her that her parents had been at war over her most of her life. She had been as solipsistic as any other kid, and she had never dreamed before she came back that there was anything other than some kind of Ozzie and Harriet perfect parental omniscience between them. There was, even now, vague as it was, a palpable tension between them, where she was concerned, a wire that coiled through everything. She had gained enough perspective from watching her friends and their children interact that she could see that what had once seemed a monolith—*my parents*—was anything but monolithic. It was two people with different ideas of how to deal with this lump of flesh that had showed up at their house.

Why would you ever think that your mother wasn't happy with you?

Um, like, because she always seemed unhappy with me?

He laughed. Like me, you mother has always wanted the best for you.

Ellen said: She just never seemed—okay, I know you're not supposed to use absolute words like never and always, but she never seemed to like me very much. She always seemed angry at me.

You scare her, Ellen. You're the person she always wanted to be.

Ellen pulled away from him enough to look him full in the face. What?

You know your mother studied music. You know she used to sing. Do you think she just wanted to be some old fart's housewife?

Ellen sank back.

You know, the one thing that is really—really—killing your mother is that she can't brag about you right now. She's followed everything you've done like a stalker—okay, bad choice of words. She's got a chest full of clippings and photocopies of clippings. Oh, sweetie. You have no idea how your mother adores you. Admires you.

Ellen started to cry. There was no reason for it and yet every reason. Her father held her close, pressed a hand against her head.

Is everything okay with your friend Michael? he said.

Yeah, well, except I think I dumped him.

Oh, goodness, he said. He had a way of saying it, it had a kind of wisdom to it. He went on: Maybe you should just sleep on it. Pull up the covers and pull down the shades and just sleep on it, he said.

SHE IS ELLEN

This better be good, Soraya said. Michael was embarrassed when she'd opened the door in an outlandish bathrobe that had what appeared to be suds of foofy pink nightgown spilling out all around it.

You look like you were attacked by a cotton candy machine.

You've been hanging around your friend the comic.

Yeah, but maybe not so much anymore, he said and looked down at his feet. He was squirming against the front step.

What happened?, she said.

I don't really know.

He was half numb with the notion that Ellen had said goodbye to him (maybe), but electrified with the idea that the whole Black Box project might be in some small way salvageable. Which was why he had called Soraya and invited himself over.

Ellen was trying to get me to look at it differently, and I just poked around in the code a little and I think I found something.

She let him in and went immediately to her living room. She had a great sense for decorating—although he was never sure where she got the time. So many of the people he knew had houses or apartments that seemed like temporary quarters, a place to flop. Hers felt more like an actual home. He sat down on the couch. She said, You want a drink?

He nodded. It was somewhere between midnight and six, though he thought it likely far closer to six. She brought him a bourbon, and he grimaced when he sipped from it. So, he said, I was going through all the things I knew the machine itself couldn't do. I checked everything, and it's simply not powerful enough to render graphics like that. It doesn't have the processing power… So, he sipped again, so therefore it can't be.

I don't know that I follow you.

What if, just for the sake of argument, it's doing something to the brain that stimulates the brain to create that stuff?

I don't see how, given the parameters of the equipment, that would be possible, she said.

Then let's talk about memories. We both know that they're not like videotape or something, discreet entities that you can pull out of your head and replay moment for moment, right?

Correct. There are several places in the brain that mediate cognition and memory. I assume we're talking long term.

Correct.

You would only keep snippets, and they'd be rationalized to some extent, wrapped in your own understanding or interpretation.

So how would it be possible to relive a particular moment, as though it were video?

Not possible.

Let's just create some sort of thought puzzle wherein it is. Ellen tripped on the thing twice tonight, and each time, she said, it was real stuff, past stuff, what I gather were kind of emotional things. Far more than she could actually have remembered. But so the way perception works, he said, at least if I understood you correctly, in highly emotional situations, your brain records more data.

Soraya hummed a low note, and rubbed her chin and thought about it. Michael gulped whiskey.

At last, she said: Interesting, and then paused a long while. If we can conclusively rule out the machine itself in terms of creating these scenes, she said, picking up, and if we had to make an argument for the brain, then we'd have to assume that, hmm. No. We can't assume that the brain has some kind of untapped resources that we don't really understand.

But I don't think you can rule out the machine.

Now she was really lost in thought.

Let me lay something out just for argument's sake, he said.

Fire away, she said, sinking into the plush loveseat, I have nothing else to do but sleep.

What if, he said hesitatingly. What if it has nothing to do with the brain? What if it's all the machine?

I think I know where you're going with this and I think it's bullshit. It *has* to be bullshit. I think it's just late night, my-girl-dumped-me-and-my-dissertation-is-in-the-toilet kind of speculation.

Maybe it is, but just hear me out.

Soraya sighed deeply.

Michael said: Remember when, after the Black Box started doing the strange stuff, we did the fMRIs and you said that none of the areas of the brain you expected to react did, and areas where you would expect to see activity were dark while other areas lit up?

Sure.

Well, what if?

What if what?

What if it—and right this second I'm a little drunk, but what if there were some way of tapping into something else. Like—

Like what?

Oh, fuck, he said, I don't know. Like seeing into another dimension.

Bullshit.

You're right. No, you're right.

Go home, my dear boy. Sleep.

Yeah, he said, but did not move.

What happened with Ellen?

I don't really know. After she took the second trip, or whatever you want to call it, she, like, got upset. She looked like, I don't know.

He squirmed a bit.

She was in one scene in the first one, flying over a volcano or waterfall or something in Hawaii, and in the second, she didn't say. All she said was that it was here, in Iowa. In her past. She said that they were not very pleasant.

Soraya rolled her eyes and gave a little frown and shook her head. I think it would be helpful to remember, my dear friend, that if what she says about herself is true then she's in the midst of a major life crisis. Pressure from you or your machine might not help.

Did you Google her?

What if I did? Did you?

No. But you did.

Sure. I have no doubt that what she tells you, tells us, is true.

So what does that mean?

It means she's a really big fucking TV star, Michael, and how you ended up with her is anybody's guess.

Broccoli, he said.

HANNA

It was early afternoon when Ellen awoke. The phone had rung and she had sat up like a shot, and then waited, the room silent, the house silent. And then at last there was the sound on the stairs, the soft knock on the door and her mother's voice, Honey? Can I come in?

Sure, she said, and climbed out of bed. After having gone to sleep so completely confused, Ellen was amazed to find herself clear-headed when she expected something more like a hangover.

Her mother came in carrying the phone a bit as though it were a dead pet a dog had killed. She made enormous mouthing motions as she whispered, It's someone named Hanna.

When Ellen took the phone, said, Hello? sleepily.

Hanna said, Want to run?

Ellen hesitated. It was the first time in years she had gone for more than a few days without running.

Sure. I'd love it.

Ellen had only met Hanna a few times, and she had never seen her wear makeup, which gave her a directness, an elegant simplicity. For Ellen, this was raw courage.

Ellen had developed a fondness for her almost immediately at the infamous broccoli dinner, which, when it finally happened had turned out to be a sort of Thai green curry and coconut chicken stew. The broccoli, Hanna and Soraya had made into a centerpiece, in a vase, a bouquet.

SPEED

Ellen took her father's Honda and met Hanna near her place. Hanna wore white shoes, blue trunks, and a tank top over a jog bra. She wore a ball cap and she looked tiny and impossibly sweet.

Ellen had brought along a stack of towels so she wouldn't sweat all over her father's car. Normally, she didn't like running with other people—that is, anyone who had a different pace than she did, and she wondered if she was going to regret running with Hanna.

They stretched in Hanna's front yard, and Ellen had the sensation that she was being watched, but it was always difficult to tell whether she was being watched because she was a woman or being watched because she was Ellen Gregory!™—or even if she was being watched at all.

They went down toward the student union and then across the river, and then alongside it, by Hancher and toward the park. Hanna was mostly quiet, with a stride like a gazelle, and now Ellen was thinking that she was holding Hanna back. She said: Have you talked to Michael today?

No, Hanna said. You?

Ellen shook her head and let it go.

After a few more minutes, when she was warm and she could feel sweat pricking up all over her, Ellen said, I'm not in as bad shape as I thought.

Hanna just grinned, and then, after two or three more strides, took off. It was an amazing burst of speed, a catch-me-if-you-can burst of speed that caught Ellen by surprise. And then she, too, took off.

Hanna was three or four yards ahead of her, her legs going in long, picture-perfect strides, sleek and pale and flashing, her butt knotted beneath her shorts, the bottoms of her shoes flashing up. And Ellen was angry and happy, and she dug in, counting Hanna's strides, lengthening her own, determined to catch her.

As soon as she came shoulder to shoulder with her, they both slowed down and started laughing. Hanna said: That was great. Yeah, Ellen said, Want to do it again? And then she took off.

Her lungs and her legs were burning by the time she slowed up with Hanna right next to her. Hanna took off her hat and wiped her forehead. Ellen said, I'm glad to see somebody else sweats as much as I do, because she was soaking. Ellen had never seen Hanna grin so broadly. She, Hanna, said: We should do a marathon together.

Ellen laughed. It was a wonderful invitation, and she thought of it, the impossibility of it, being anonymous in the crowd of other runners.

They took an easy pace back to Hanna's, chatting, joking, and Ellen said, at last, I think I broke up with Michael last night.

Hanna stopped. Ellen stopped, too. Hanna looked at her and Ellen expected that she would scold her or something but Hanna just laughed. Ellen liked it that Hanna was so relaxed around her now. She was a kind of person, Ellen guessed, who took a long time to get to know, but when you did, she was your friend for life.

That was stupid, Hanna said.

Actually, Ellen said, It was.

There were jogging again now, slowly, So what happened? Hanna said.

I don't know. Everything is just, I mean I, I mean how could I just, like, fall in love with some guy that I met a few weeks ago?

You think you're in love with him? Hanna's expression turned serious.

Well, sort of, yeah.

Wow, Hanna laughed again. Ellen laughed, too.

I didn't even expect to have a fling. I didn't want to.

So what happened?

So he's amazing and charming and wonderful and all that stuff—

Hanna cut her off. I know *that*, she laughed. I mean what happened last night?

I think he tried to tell me that I, that he, you know.

They were at the edge of Hanna's yard now and Hanna stood for a moment and put her hands on her hips, idly stuck one thumb in the waistband of her shorts and snapped the elastic. She said: Of course he's in love with you, stupid. Anybody can see that.

No way.

You have to be blind. And for that matter, anybody could see that you're in love with him.

But it's not possible.

You mean it's impossible? Or that you don't want it to be possible.

Either. Both. I didn't come here to fall in love.

Hanna grinned. Everyone falls in love in Iowa. What're all these haystacks for, anyway?

Ellen laughed.

220

Are you coming to the beach?

Ellen hesitated. This was all out of control. Except that there was something about this particular out-of-control feeling she liked.

Yeah, she said at last. Yeah. Sure.

SLEEPOVER

It had not exactly been a hard thing—explaining to her parents that Michael was going to spend the night with her and sleep with her—but it had not exactly been an easy thing for her to do, either. Here, in her parents' house, she was still seventeen. At least in her own mind. She knew before he even got there for dinner that she was going to sleep with him, that she was going to crawl all over his bones.

She wanted to say, Listen, I'm a grown woman. She wanted to say, Listen, Daddy, in some circles I am considered A-List pussy. Do you have any idea what that means? Neither do I.

But even as a joke, it would have been too hard. And so she just said, Michael is staying over. I hope you don't mind.

Her father shrugged, a knowing smile lighting up his face.

Her mother said, I'll get some sheets, but then stopped and turned away, trying to keep the embarrassment from showing on her face.

She said: I mean I'll get some towels.

Michael said, Thanks. That's great.

Ellen took his hand and led him upstairs. She stopped him on the steps and put her finger to his lips, then kissed him. She said: I've been trying to break rules forever, and then she hesitated. For the first time in my life—in my adult life, I mean—I feel like I really *am* breaking rules. I feel so silly.

He took her head in his hands and said, God, you're beautiful.

I'm sorry, she said. I haven't... I don't.

He said, You don't have to say anything. Then he kissed her.

Now she led him up the stairs, walking like a drunk trying not to wake anyone. At the top of the stairs, she said: My room's a little weird. I mean it's....

You don't have to say anything.

I know. I just feel—, well, fuck, I don't know what I mean. She laughed and looked away. There was something about this man that made her feel naked all the time. Made her feel as though there was nothing she could do that he could not see through—and furthermore would not be okay with in at least some way.

I just feel like a girl, she said.

That's a good thing, he said.

He ran his hands across her bottom then drew them around to her front and up over her breasts and then down between her legs. She shivered a little. Actually, he said. You feel like a woman.

Don't stop, she said.

Of that I have no intention, he said and kissed her again.

When she got him into her room, she stripped off her pants and unfastened his, took hold of his penis and pulled him toward the bed and down onto her and she took the heat of him and he mashed into her. He held her face, then kissed her, lifted her shirt and pushed aside her bra, and then she was sobbing quietly into his shoulder as he shuddered.

It was all quiet, desperate.

When he said something about her tears, he looked scared. No, she said, These are good tears.

They got dressed. They put away his things and they had dinner. Ellen felt completely dazed and she came into the kitchen, back to the duck that she had been preparing when he arrived. Her mother gave her a look. It was a woman-to-woman look that Ellen had never seen cast in her direction.

And then later, when both of them were on their backs, staring at the ceiling, when she was certain he was asleep, she said, I had forgotten.

But he was not asleep. He said: Forgotten what?

Not forgotten, exactly, but not remembered. Why I left. How I left.

Like leaving the show?

She put herself up on one elbow and looked at him. There was something about Michael that made her feel like a girl standing at a window, breeze going, the tissuey curtains billowing against her.

I never thought of it that way. But maybe. But what I was going to say. She hesitated for a long time. I never said it. I mean I made up this whole narrative that I used to do in shows about how I left his tiny little town, and I made up all sorts of Garrison-Keillor-on-crack stories, and, after a while I sort of started to believe it. The stupid farmer jokes. My mother as a piglet.

Narrative is life, Michael said. Narrative is the thing that humans have that no other animal has, that enables us to envision the future, to create and use complicated things. It's the thing that enables us to create happiness.

So what I keep wondering, she said, Is where my narrative is going now. I mean, like, we all have these little visions that almost never accommodate chance. And in that regard—chance—your deal with broccoli really screwed me up.

What did you envision? he laughed. I mean before the broccoli.

Something ugly, probably, she said. I have no idea, now. I guess I had some notion that I would reinvent myself, post-Townsend. Post-*Girlfriends*. Given that the terms of my life, my narrative, were no longer in my control.

But control is just an illusion, he said. I know that as well as anyone.

Well, she said. If that's the case, then it's the most important illusion we have.

I guess it is, he mused. It's actually the root of all happiness, or so the studies show.

Ellen propped herself up on one elbow, and looked at him. This may sound sort of dumb, she said. But thanks.

For what?

Just being you. How you've helped me to see myself as myself again.

What then? he said. His voice was suddenly guarded, as though he sensed himself being disposed of.

More sex, she said, and grabbed him.

She put her hand on his chest and started to say something else, but did not. She could feel his heartbeat. She could feel his breath and his ribs and the life in him, and she wanted to absorb it all in her hand and make a ball of it and keep it like a stone a child finds, a smooth pebble, and always have it with her to touch, to keep.

THE OTHER ELLEN

One night, at Michael's house surfing the web—he sat with her, his own laptop open—she came across a totally nutcase blog that posited a theory that the whole Wayne Townsend affair (as she had come to think of it) was an elaborate piece of stagecraft, from the kidnapping to the shooting, was an elaborate, if twisted, publicity stunt. The Townsend Hoax.

She showed it to him. He laughed, and then his face got serious. That must be so strange, he said. To see yourself everywhere.

You have no idea, she said. It's strange because it's not me. It's her, the other Ellen. Or it's even another Ellen.

You're right. I have no idea.

The sex tape ads for the new season were out now, and they were in heavy rotation on her network. People just seemed to eat up this seamy crap. There had been controversy over them, and her network (read: Jayson Grainge), in its infinite wisdom, had decided to ramp up rotation in direct proportion to the controversy. Which was a PR stance she would not have disagreed with. But it also fed the weirdness.

There was a part of every conspiracy theory that made for a better narrative than the reality. And so this was true of the so-called Townsend Hoax. It went like this:

Townsend was an actor—how else could he get on the lot without being seen?

Townsend slipped through police custody because he was in fact never in police custody.

Townsend was not dead at all. The gun had been given to her, loaded with blanks, and it was all a Hollywood-style moon landing.

As good as the sex-tapes were—and they were really, really good—and as much creative control as she'd had over them, they now shook her, watching in her mother's kitchen in Iowa. They felt humiliating, debasing, and left her feeling heartsick. The Ellen in those pictures was another Ellen, one she was certain that Michael would not like very much, largely because she, herself, did not like that Ellen very much. It was the first time, actually, that she had seen herself this way: A relentless publicity hound. And she could see how someone might think that she was the kind of person who would do anything for attention. Which was hard to argue with. And then of course, there was the way the publicist Jayson Grange had manipulated it to profit the network. She had been, at the time, so close to hysteria that she had not really thought, and she cursed herself for that.

When she read the hoax narrative, it chilled her. It was so easy for it to have been true. She thought about the conversation she'd had with Michael about narrative. In many ways, the hoax narrative was far more believable than the reality.

PART THREE:
THE LONG WAY HOME

OH, THE WATER

Hanna fumbled with the automatic door opener of the rental car and climbed in. Jake climbed into the passenger seat. She was still in her bikini, in bare feet. She had run all the way to the car once they'd loaded Ellen into the ambulance and now her feet were raw.

She could see the helicopter with Michael onboard and it was just a speck now. She drove in circles, trying to find the road that would lead to the road so that she could follow the huge boxy ambulance that held Ellen, and it was like a cartoon, running into barricades, walls, obstacles, and then, suddenly, she was behind it, slamming down the gas and trying to keep up. Everything was so real. There was a part of her head that was picking up every detail, soaking it all in—the oversized dormer windows on an enormous white house, its spindly looking telephone pole legs, the way the sand crept up on the roadway, the scruffy grasses on the dunes—but the biggest part of her was ignoring everything but the lights, the gold lettering on the back of the truck.

In her head she could see the two of them on the beach, the blood on the sand—and in her head she knew that in a matter of hours—if that—the sea would take it all back.

She jumped on the gas, the car sandblasting along, and Jake, who had seemed to be holding his breath all this time now said, *Jesus fucking Christ*. And then said it again. It was just muttering. His face was blank, pale. She paid as little attention to it as she did to the speedometer and the ragged-looking dunes. It occurred to her now, in some weird parenthetical way, that he was silent too much. That she wanted him to talk. To talk more. And suddenly, she could see the mortality of their relationship, perhaps because right this minute, she could see the mortality of everything.

Can you tell, she wondered, about the condition of the patient by the driving of the ambulance? She could not get the picture of Michael out of her head—that first Polaris-like ejection from the water (she had just happened to turn at the moment it happened), that amygdala cognition-before-cognition that something was way, way fucking wrong, coming long before the intellectual knowledge: the way he rose up out of the water, the acrobatic but contorted look of it. Her feet had begun to move without thought as she sprinted toward the water. And how long did the whole thing take? Three minutes? Thirty seconds? Thirty minutes? She had no idea. Sometimes time was meaningless.

The passenger side window was smeary and the light hit it and Jake's head leaned against it. He had blood on him, on his chest, his hands, from where he'd dragged Michael out of the water. She couldn't look at him, but had the sensation of being alone, a solitary soul, flying forward through time, profoundly human and lonely, a human missile with only one possible target. She could have reached out to touch Jake at that moment but did not.

When at last they hit the parking lot of the hospital, she slowed the car, and everything seemed to swim in the sudden stillness. The ambulance had suddenly stopped, and now it was backing—an electronic bell or tone was dinging, like a garbage truck backing up—but it seemed impossibly slow.

She knew Michael had to be dead, but he didn't have to be. It was what Ellen had once called 'one of those rewind moments,' where you're sure you could just hit the rewind button and make it all back up.

She had seen him. The damage that could be done in a few moments. He was almost cut off at the waist, and there had been so much blood where his legs were, or should have been, that she had no way of knowing if they were still there.

But Ellen. It was just her leg. Her foot. Hanna had no idea. She could be dead—shock, blood loss—because that's what the ethereal slowness of the ambulance seemed to say. She stopped in the middle of the parking lot and stared.

It was a small hospital, hardly a hospital at all. More like a large clinic, even by Iowa City standards.

Jake said, Sweetheart, park the car. But she just sat there, staring. The lights were hypnotic. It was how long ago—an hour at the most?—that she had sat with Ellen on the sand, talking. She was trying—for the sake of record keeping, for the sake of memory—to remember the last thing Michael said to her.

Jake got out of the car, banged on the hood. Park, he shouted. She sat still, terrified of moving from this moment, this fragment of a moment, terrified of what she would find. Jake, exasperated, turned and headed toward the door. She mouthed the word, No, several times, but never gave breath to it.

When she got out of the car, suddenly Soraya was there, and took her arm. Hanna could have collapsed at that moment, just fallen into Soraya's arms and let go of consciousness, but she was still walking.

Soraya said: This is not going to be easy.

Hanna wanted to vomit.

I don't mean seeing them. What they look like. I mean seeing them. Being *allowed* to see them.

Hanna looked at her, bewildered.

Just let me talk. This could end up being a media circus.

She turned abruptly to Jake: You stay outside. We can't have too many people.

Hanna didn't turn around but plunged through the door, the air conditioning freezing her in her bathing suit.

MARTY KLEIN

When Marty Klein opened the door of the rented limousine and stood in the parking lot of the tiny hospital in North Carolina, he was overcome with the most ridiculous anguish, a monstrous cascade of guilt and horror, a complete and disastrous failure of the dam that generally kept his compassion compartment sealed off from the rest of his brain. It was an ugly thing, a middle-aged man, a Hollywood scammer, ready to fall on his knees and weep for something other than money. This was suddenly real.

When Hanna had called him in LA, he had felt a weird kind of relief, one of those final-exam-cancelled moments. It was purely selfish, because while it was clear that all of the morning shows, afternoon shows, and evening shows wanted Ellen on her mysterious disappearance and her reappearance—everyone from *This Morning* to *Late Nite*—and wanted her big, it was not warm and fuzzies he was getting from the bookers. There was an undercurrent of joyful hostility, hammers and sickles, donning of black robes, a gleeful, evil *schadenfreude*. His whole mental state had been storm clouds, black hoods, snarling dogs. He had had no idea until now where she was (he had suspicions, of course).

There were narratives circulating: the Kidnapping Narrative, the Emotional Breakdown Narrative, the Scheming Bitch Who Just Wants Attention Narrative, and weirder ones. Such was the human mind that a well-crafted fiction was way more satisfying emotionally than the shoddy, ugly, unbelievable truth.

And on the telephone night before last, when she told him she was returning, reappearing, it was clear that the truth was frankly just so banal—exhaustion and depression from the pressure, thoughts of suicide—that it was stale crackers compared to the juicy red meat of the complex and ludicrously believable yarns.

And so he had been relieved—pornographically elated, actually (about which he was completely disgusted now, as the reality of *hospital* settled in) that, again, somehow, some way, he had managed to pull a rabbit out of the hat. There was no way that she was not, now, the *single* most purely sympathetic creature on the planet. He had no idea what would've happened had the media found out that she was not, after all, in South Africa, at a private clinic, nursing some understandable and ultimately forgivable sort of chemical dependency or emotional breakdown or whatever without this, this *blessing* of a shark attack. Having her foot chewed off by a monster. (He cringed to think that he had sunk so low.) He had, in fact, no idea what on earth she'd been doing for the last six or seven or eight or 10 or however many fucking weeks she'd been gone. But there could have been no more golden rescue than to have had her foot gnawed off by a fucking tiger shark.

At least that was the way his LA thinking (or calculating) had gone until he walked across the parking lot and set foot in the hospital and the whole thing was no longer a story but a chilling reality. *What is the deal with the AC in this building?*

And so this sweet feeling of relief at having been rescued from a truly ghastly LA-style buttfucking that had gripped him from the moment Hanna had called his office, all through the chartered plane ride east, suddenly began to melt, shrivel with his first glimpse of the Atlantic. The thing, the shark, the animal, was out there.

Now, he was looking out onto a small parking lot—at least by hospital standards that he was accustomed to—that was so full of media vans, trucks, cars, reporters, cameras and satellite gear that it had taken his limo a good 10 minutes to navigate up to the door.

It was morning—he had gotten on the plane in the middle of the night, LA time, and flown against time, and here he was, so close to the Atlantic that you could hear the waves, if not see them. There were reporters doing stand-up spots in pure white light even as he walked to the parking lot. He had counted at least six languages that he did not recognize.

When Patti alerted the media, she sure as hell alerted the media. But it was already The Summer Of The Sharks, at as least Fox was presenting it, with two boys already dead, one in Florida, and one up the coast in Virginia.

He had smelled disinfectant as soon as he'd walked through the doors, and though the place had a workaday mood of controlled bustle, he was feeling bristly—like he really should have been to a hotel, shaved and had a power nap before trying anything this stressful—and a little bit naked, his Hollywood varnish having peeled off during the flight. His crepe-souled shoes squeaked against the polished floors, and he began to feel woozy, not because he had a particular dislike for hospitals, but because with each step it became less a story and more a reality—an experience he had almost completely left behind when he left New York for LA.

It was impossible to imagine, really, what it must be like—*Damn, you read about this shit in the newspapers, but you never think that it'll happen to somebody you know. Or yourself.*

Maybe it was nerves, sleeplessness or just dread, but his knees kept doing this thing where they turned to rubber. Maybe it was being a little bit of a hypochondriac and being in a place where they could rescue you and diagnose that occult cancer lurking in your spleen.

He went to the desk and put on his most uncompromising I-am-the-single-person-on-Earth-that-you-don't-want-to-fuck-with face that he could muster and glared at the nurse at the station. Hi, he said, charisma machine grinding away, I'm Marty Klein. Ellen Gregory's manager. What the fuck is the meaning of all the media in the parking lot?

From lawyers he worked with, he'd adapted a tactic of always entering a room with a hostile question when he was dealing with nonprofessionals. It tended to have the effect of disarming, of immediately making the subject feel small and insignificant. Unless of course they knew the tactic.

I..., the nurse said, sputtering a little as she did so. She was youngish, but plump in that overfed American sort of way. (*Stay away from spandex*, he wanted to say, just to have the chance to be cruel to someone in return for all the cruelty that had been recently heaped on him.)

Um, I'm sorry, what did you say her name was? Clearly, she was stalling for time.

My *client*, Marty said, is somewhere in this building. She had her fucking foot gnawed off by a fucking shark, and your response is to fill the parking lot with media from all over the planet. I personally counted twenty-seven foreign languages as I walked through the parking lot.

As he spoke he reached for his wallet, and took out a business card. The card was sharp and bright, and he put it between the first and second finger of his right hand and banged it against the counter. It made a satisfying clack that was almost like a yogic chant for him, centering himself.

It was intended to declare that he was not to be fucked with. *Clack.* He flipped the card over in his fingers and thrust it at the nurse like a dagger.

It was going through him now, the reality of the situation and his knees were doing that thing again and felt as though someone had taken the bone out of them. He leaned against the counter to keep from wobbling.

Let me see, the nurse said, regaining a little bit of her composure.

Fuck, Marty said, drawing out the word, stalling for time, not actually wanting her to say anything even remotely sensible that he would have to act upon.

He had flown all this way, and now he had no idea what he was doing here. In more than a decade of working with Ellen—or, for that matter, with other clients—he had never come upon a situation in which he had been confronted with a golden opportunity that was at once so perfect, and so fraught with abject horror.

233

Hanna had said that she, Ellen, was in love with the guy who had got killed, and he, Marty, had said, (asshole), What makes him so special? and the woman had just been silent for a long time before working up enough of a polite—and she was really polite—way of saying goodbye.

He said: let me start over again. Your hospital—somewhere in your hospital is my client, Ellen Gregory. You know who Ellen Gregory is?

The nurse had a sweet, pliant, innocent face, not unlike a kindergartner on the first day of school.

My husband and I, we watch her every night, she stammered. Well, not every night. You know. Every night she's on.

Then you have some idea of just how important my client is.

She shrugged, nodded, gulped, as though searching for some gesture that was not part of her repertoire. By now she was probably believing that she herself had caused Ellen Gregory irreparable harm.

Where is she?

Room 322.

Marty slapped his hand against the counter and turned, then turned back again, confused. Which did not entirely fit into the story he was trying to weave here.

Where is the elevator?

In truth, Marty wasn't that much of an asshole. Not even close. He had learned, however, that sometimes you had to be.

Soraya brushed her hand across Hanna's scalp and stood. She herself was stiff and sore, and her friend looked small and drawn. She knew that Hanna had been in love with Michael, that Michael had always been unaware of it, had always treated her like a much loved younger sister. And that Jake was something of a consolation prize. But she also knew that Hanna bore no ill will or jealousy toward Ellen. In fact, if anything, she was as clear-eyed as any of them with respect to the magic of Ellen's personal charisma—it was of the same order as Michael's—and she was no different from any of them in falling head over heels for her. It was completely possible to have a total crush on someone you should have wanted to hate.

Soraya leaned down and hugged Hanna, said, I love you, darling.

Hanna looked up, her eyes rimmed with red, tears welling again.

This totally sucks, she said, something she had said already. But it did. The unalloyed sense of helplessness and impotence.

Soraya said: I'm going to go see if I can find Adam and Jake, she said. It didn't matter that Hanna likely didn't want to see Jake.

They were sitting on hard, institutional chairs in the hallway just down from Ellen's room. Hanna let her head rise to her friend's hand. Her skin was sunburned and there was still sand, blood-spatters on her suit. Any other time, a tan would be a hallmark of a good day, but this was a day—and a night—she would as soon have erased, rewound out of existence. There was Michael on the beach, broken like a toy. The word dismembered went over in her head. It went over in her head, what she could have done differently—a common, she knew, but unwanted, symptom of grief. A solipsism, a centralization of the event in the self.

When Soraya had gone down the hall, Hanna was alone and leaned forward and pressed her head into her hands for the millionth time. She tried to remember the last thing Michael had said to her and could not. She could still hear him yelling at Ellen to swim. Swim. The way he had gurgled, I love you, to her on the bleeding sand.

When they had brought them in, Soraya rode in the helicopter with Michael, or what was left of him. Hanna admired her friend's steel. Then, in the hospital corridor, Hanna standing next to Ellen, Soraya had appeared suddenly at her side, no longer wearing the bathing suit and shift she had been wearing when she climbed into the hatch of the helicopter but now in hospital scrubs. She had been completely emotionless, her face composed, her hair knotted severely behind her head in her Total Doctor persona when she laid a hand on Hanna's shoulder and said that he didn't make it.

Hanna had shaken her head, No, she said, because she had already known what the truth was. And that truth was one that wanted her to wail. Except, and she knew all of the emotional and physiological reasons for this, she was totally numb.

On the way down the hall to the morgue, Soraya passed a frumpy little man with graying hair lunging purposefully through the corridor. He wore a very expensive suit that looked very rumpled, and—perhaps because of the scrubs she had borrowed to wear instead of her bloody clothing—grabbed her by the arm as she passed.

I'm looking for Ellen Gregory, he said. Soraya knew without asking that this must be Marty, the famous manager.

Soraya looked at him emptily, shrugged, waited a moment, then shook her head and pulled away.

When Hanna lifted her head, there was the man sitting next to her. She smelled him before she saw him—it was not an unpleasant smell, cologne, travail, some other thing that fell below conscious perception. He had taken Soraya's chair.

Do you know, he said, where room 322 is?

She lifted her head and looked at him wearily. The fabric of his suit had a buttery quality even though it was gray. It just had a quality that made you want to reach out and stroke it, like a cuddly animal. He was himself exhausted-looking, and she was guessing (she hoped not) that this was Marty, the manager she had telephoned, who had sounded at first pissed off that she was bothering him, then weirdly jovial once she had established her bona fides with him. Now, sitting near him, the lizardy way he had talked to her, the sort of buddy-boy, can-you-do-that-for-me-sugar tone of voice made her skin crawl. So there was still a lot to Ellen that she did not know. How she could be associated with such an unguent creature.

She gave her head a little jerk to indicate down the hall. She said, Over there, but it came out as a hoarse whisper.

He looked at her without looking at her. He seemed to be struggling with some sort of inner conflict. As she watched him—Ellen had liked to say that she, Hanna, would be a great poker player, because she had a deceptively girlish look that concealed one of the most cagey faces Ellen had ever seen—he seemed to talk to himself although he vocalized nothing. Maybe it was a prayer. Maybe it was something else.

The man stood, looked around the hallway like someone who'd forgotten where he'd left his really expensive suitcase. He muttered softly—it was as though she abruptly had ceased to exist, or had only existed in a bit role to tell him where Ellen's room was, and now the camera was on him as he squared his shoulders and went to face the inevitable.

How was it, Marty wondered, that you could know someone so well, be so close with a person, and then, over a period of time, increment by increment, drift farther and farther away from them in the personal, Intimate Conversations Over Too Many Glasses of Wine into the Wee Hours sense to the point where you ceased to know them at all? How was it that she had fooled him so completely? How was it that he had underestimated or failed to read the last person on earth he ever would have expected to underestimate or fail to read?

All this time—as a tectonic layer of studio lawyers rumbled, as a huddles of studio honchos were muttering, This Psycho Chick (or another, somewhat shorter and entirely less pleasant C-word) Is Costing Us Money—she had been right under their collective nose. It was as galling as it was funny. But of course they, the humorless legal drones, would not find any humor in it. And it was an axiom of Hollywood that you could do whatever you wanted as long as you did not Cost Us Money. CUM, Marty thought.

Now, suddenly—almost as if he had floated here like Jeff Bridges in *The Big Lebowski*—he was in her room. She was asleep, or at least sported the customary gestalt of slumber, and he was silent. Seeing her was as shocking as it could have been: her hair was black and hacked short, she was as gorgeous as ever but it was clear that she was missing her left foot (the failure of the hospital sheet to tent where it should have). He looked at her, then looked for a chair, then, even after seeing one, stayed frozen where he was, looking at her dumbly.

The two of them had been through considerable weirdness over the years, Townsend being pretty much the nadir of that, but this was of a higher order than even that. He had the sensation—at this moment—of having fallen out of his own, real (so he thought) life and into someone else's skin. He had an almost psychotic sensation of being himself and yet not. He was sure he could go to his hotel and take off his clothes and look in the mirror and know that he was looking at the same form he had seen this morning, down to the last wrinkle, the last follicle of hair, and yet he knew if he did so that he would have the creeping suspicion that he was looking at an imposter. He rubbed his hands together and then rubbed his face and nothing felt real. He tried to think what his acupuncturist would say, but nothing would come. (His acupuncturist was a better therapist than the more than a dozen therapists he had seen over the years, and so he subjected himself to twice-weekly sessions of lying nearly nude, needles thrust into various areas of his Qi, little bonfires of some brushy, alchemy of special plants being set and snuffed all over his body—just to talk.)

There were sounds in the hallway, the normal sounds of hospital, and he moved into a pool of dirty light and laid both hands on the bedrail. Ellen, he said, but was not sure that he had even given breath to the word. Somewhere down the hall, the TV or radio buzzed with the news. He heard the words, Ellen Gregory, Timothy McVeigh, and nothing more.

She stirred, as if sensing someone near. She looked up at him groggily, and sounding (and looking) drunk, she said, Marty, drawing the word out in a simpering, cooing voice.

Hey, girl, he said, wanting to say a million things but uncharacteristically settling for nothing.

Marty, Hi. Where's Marty? she said.

I'm right here, he said.

She giggled strangely. Michael, she said, Where is he? Her hand came up and touched his sleeve, grabbed onto it. He saw now that it was bandaged, too. I love Michael.

He shook his head. I don't know. I just got here.

Thanks for coming, she said, and closed her eyes.

I'll be here, Marty said, doing his Mighty Mouse—*Marty Mouse*—impersonation. I'll find out what's going on.

When he turned, the girl he had seen in the hallway was standing there, looking at him. You must be Marty, she said.

He nodded, winked (which was probably invisible in the dim light), said, And you are?

Hanna. I talked to you on the phone.

He sized her up. When he had seen her in the hallway, he'd mostly ignored her—small, slight, insignificant—but in this mottled light he could see that she had a slight, athletic build, with plain-running-to-pretty features that were at this moment rather haggard looking. He started to scratch his head, but stopped himself.

Apologies, he said, and put out his hand, Marty Klein.

Suddenly, as she shook his hand, there were weird atmospheric oscillations. Again, there was this volition-less-type movement and they were in the hallway, nearer to her former chair than to Ellen's room. Marty felt his skin crawl. He had a concussive sense that he had seen her before like this, that he had been at this place, in this moment before. Every bit of it was familiar.

Marty searched for where to start and chose the banal. So, when did this all happen?

After lunch, I think. I mean, after lunch. Maybe two or so? They were in the water and I just happened to be watching—they were fun to watch together, the two of them. They were a kind of kinetic wonder.

Marty had learned to read people well enough to know that she was concealing something—or if not concealing something, there was something she did not want to say. He could see it in her gray eyes. That flicker you sometimes saw. A shadow.

And Michael was doing the weirdest thing, I mean, at first, I thought, like, how is he swimming like that? But he wasn't. The thing had got him. He was yelling at Ellen to get out of the water.

She hung her head, as if seeing it all again. At the same time, her aspect was the blank aspect of emotional shock.

Normally he would have just asked her to cut to the chase—what did the doctors say, what was the plan? After all, he had heard this all on the phone. But he found something beguiling about the woman. Watching her, he had a not-entirely-unwanted stirring in his loins, and as it occurred, he had an image—this took place over a matter of two or three seconds, no more—he saw the two of them wordlessly walking away from here, finding a closet, stripping enough to make sex possible, and banging away like dogs. He said, What about you? How are you doing?

He had no idea if he (a married man) was hitting on her (well, yeah, he was). There was something about her that felt familiar, almost Ellen-like.

Me? She said, surprised apparently to be forced to acknowledge such a concept as her own self. She gave a rueful laugh. Me? I have no idea, actually. All I know is that all is changed.

Changed utterly, he said, finishing the quote.
She nodded in recognition, then turned away from him.

A FAVOR

In the doctors' lounge, Soraya looked at the cup of coffee that the attending physician, a Dr. Gravely, had bought from the lounge coffee machine for her—it smelled like coffee more than it in fact tasted like coffee—and said, I appreciate your candor.

Well, yes, certainly, Dr. Gravely said. He was an avuncular sort, balding, a bit paunchy. A perfectly competent physician who understood the limitations of his facility. He went on: I do want to apologize regarding the sudden appearance of all of these, the trucks and reporters and such. We've never quite had anything like this. And while we do have a policy in place for—, for crises, it does not contemplate—

I'm sure your people had little if anything to do with the media circus.

She sipped the coffee, leaned back in the chair and looked at Dr. Gravely seriously. I would like to ask a favor, she said.

He raised his eyebrows obligingly but noncommittally.

I'd like to have a moment with Michael.

Doctor, I'm sure you know the extent of his—

She cut him off: Doctor, I helped pull him out of the water, and I rode in the helicopter with him here. I am fully aware of the extent of his trauma.

Yes, I'm sorry, Dr. Ouellette. I'm sure you are. Let me make a call.

He rose from his chair and she crushed the paper cup the way she wanted to crush the world and everything in it.

THE WATER IS NOT FINE

When she awoke, the first word she said was 'broccoli.' She was drunk from the pain, from the heavy Dilaudid drip, drunk from the memory of it her body still held while the drugs fucked her brain.

She mouthed the word and heard her mother's voice from a great distance and then sank down into the warmth, the shark pulling her beneath the water. Hey, mom, the water's fine. No, it's fine. Look how long I can hold my breath.

I didn't know this was going to happen.

What.

This.

This what.

Stop it, Michael.

I will reiterate: This what?

She was driving now, purposely not looking at him. She had said I love you to him in a freakishly unguarded moment (either all of her moments were unguarded or they were all guarded, she wasn't sure which), but that moment, outside a Starbucks, a cup of coffee in her hand, it just came out because he said, as he was going back inside, Do you want some something? And at that moment there was a gleam on his eyes, in his hair, his teeth; her panties were still damp with his semen, and it just came out. I love you, because at that moment nothing could have been truer.

He just smiled, not condescendingly or knowingly or anything, but genuinely. I know, his eyes said, I love you, too.

(One night, in bed, staring at the ceiling, she said to him, Why is it with you I don't feel like I have to perform? I mean I've been, I don't know. Everything has been about making people look at me, even those who don't want to. With you I have not yet felt like I need to. Why is it that I just feel like I can *be*?)

Listen, he said, now, in the rental SUV. Before you say anything, I want you to know something. I think this kind of thing is not the kind of thing you want to talk about so much. It's pretty much, as far as I'm concerned, like someone knocking on the door and an asteroid falling through the roof where you were just standing. You know?

No. Oh, wait a minute! I'm the person in the house, you knock, and love is the asteroid?

Stop it. I'm trying to be serious.

Me, too, you putz.

I mean, Ellen Gregory, I love you. What is this? In a very short time we go back— you go to LA and I go back to Iowa City. I can't talk about much more than how wonderful the sky is after the rain, how much I look forward to fucking you again before we hit the beach.

Say that again, she said, and wriggled a little in her seat.

It was then that the two dogs charged into the road out of the dunes and head-first into the truck—big dogs, mastiffs, maybe, that ugly mottled color that reminded her of hyenas. One of them cleared the car, but the other caught on the right-hand of the bumper, and the thud came as the dog flew sideways off the road, whirling, legs in the air. Michael slammed on the brakes. They both sat and stared in the stopped vehicle. In a moment, the dog got up, wobbled a little, and then ran off into the dunes.

Say again?

Keep an eye on the drip and call me if she starts to rouse.

Will do.

She had come through one thing and now she was in another. The ocean was gone and there was nothing but the nightless glow of fluorescent lamps. Michael, she said.

I'm here.

It was her mother's voice and seemed to come from very deep inside her head.

Where's Michael?

You got pretty beat up, young lady. Scared us all.

Where's Michael?

We saw it on television before we even got the call. Your father was watching CNN and there was the story, people getting attacked—

I'm not sure this is a good time.

They didn't even know it was you, but when they found out, boy oh boy. Your picture was everywhere. I mean they were talking about the McVeigh execution and quicker than you can say jackrabbit they forgot about him and it was you, the shark—

Dear.

Her eyes would not focus but she could see that her mother was scrubbed, pink, and neither she nor her father wanted to answer the Michael question, and perhaps she did not want to have the question answered.

We're here. The doctors will be back around.

It hurts so fucking much.

Dear, her mother said to her father, pulling the word out long, polysyllabic.

Where am I?

You're in the hospital.

Even drunk with Dilaudid, she could be sarcastic: And here I had this wild idea I was in Disney World, because Mickey and Minnie and Donald—

It's okay, Ellen, her mother said.

It was most certainly not okay. Nothing was okay. *Who the fuck invited these people?* she wanted to say. And where the hell is the man I love? But she said nothing. Nothing could be said.

We're in Virginia, in Norfolk. You flew here, in a helicopter.

This she could vaguely remember, the board that held her tight, the faces looking drawn and ashen, the clatter of the folding metal gurney, the whoop whoop whoop of rotor blades of Michael's helicopter, slowing the motion of pain so that you could think between the whoops.

The doctors had been in with their entourage of residents and interns, a group she suspected was artificially inflated because of who she was. She had not seen herself in a mirror since before the attack and she had no desire to. Her mother had gone back to Iowa for a few days and would close up the house for a bit while the two of them took an apartment nearby. Marty was here but he was out looking for a *Times*.

She had been awake for two days now, out of intensive care for three. Yesterday, when she came around, the doctor explained about her foot, how her ankle was essentially amputated from her leg. They had performed surgery to clean the wound. More surgery would have to be done in LA, perhaps, and then there would be rehab, a prosthetic. All of this came at her in a weird cloud, a story about someone else.

Oh, great, I can star in the Broadway production of *Where the Fuck Is My Left Foot*. I'll have them all weeping.

Good. I'm glad you've got a positive mental attitude. Humor will help.

Positive schmozitive. Clouds of depression were creeping up her horizon, glowering over her personal landscape. The shark had taken her life away. Sarcasm was a genetically-programmed response, nothing more.

She should consider herself a very lucky woman.

Indeed.

243

She had asked about Michael ten times or more since she regained consciousness, but there had been elisions, circumlocutions. And so the lack of an answer was
itself answer, and she stopped asking because if the answer was no, then this was
knowledge she did not want. Except it was knowledge she had, and it built up in her
head, a dam of ice stilling a river. If the answer was yes, then it would break and rage.

Her father worked the crossword in the local newspaper, now and then asking
for a word. She felt drunk. There was a drip and she could push a button and have
painkillers, and she pushed.

It was Ed, her father, who told her.

The left side was the chewed side and she lay either on her back or her right side.
She hadn't eaten solid foods since her last meal with Michael and she never wanted
to eat again, and although the doctors told her she could start slowly, she refused.
She stared into the wall, which had some sort of plastic wallpaper with a vague beige
veining and the television was on a swing arm that came down so you could pull it
up close. The screen was probably four inches, diagonally, and it hurt her head to
watch, not because of the size of the screen, but just because of what it was. It hurt
more not to watch, though, so she kept it on, the sound down, not talking, dazed
from the Dilaudid, reading the forgotten language of the wallpaper veins. It came to
her that it was plastic so it could be wiped off easily.

The bed breathed. The doctor had been there and now he was gone.

You're front page news, he said. What are the odds? I actually hate crossword
puzzles, but AARP says they will keep your brain from atrophying.

The silence was not a silence. Toilets flushed with a sound like a far-off F-16
slamming down a runway.

Are you awake?

I think so. I'm having a hard time telling.

You sound drunk.

Close.

—

You never were good with silence.

I can't tell you how hard this is, seeing you like this. I can't imagine it.

I can't remember much. I re—

Someone came in to empty the trash. This older gentleman in green scrubs apparently did not speak English, but smiled a lot as if to compensate. He left the room,
quiet as a cat.

I remember being in the water. I remember the day, the moment being so beautiful I could taste it. Then I remember Michael. For a minute he looked like a bad
special effect. Then I remember the sand, the sand in my mouth.

This was all very hard to say, very hard to make her lips move and form the words without slurring, so she slurred.

He saved your life. I don't know the whole story, but the others, your friends—

His friends.

Your friends said that you would not have made it to shore if it hadn't been for him. He was in love with you.

Was.

I'm afraid so, kiddo. He lost too much blood. The last thing he said was, I love you. Or so your friend Hanna said.

He had beautiful legs.

The dam broke now, tears beginning to flood. She wanted nothing more than to hide.

He was a very nice young man.

First one I've ever met. Did I tell, tell, tell, she said, but it wasn't the grief that kept her from speaking, it was the Dilaudid. Her mouth was as dry as Utah. Broccoli, she said, and pulled her good knee up toward her chin and closed her eyes.

When she roused briefly, Marty was there, crooning. Oh my God, everyone has called. I talked to Patti, and Dave's people have called, and Jay's and, like, everybody, *Good Morning America*, *Today*, Fox. *People*, *Time*.

I'll do Dave, and I want to do it soon. He's pissed that I did *The Daily Show*.

Sure sure sure, he said. But of course he had no intention of letting her go on national TV looking like this. They'd wait till she got back to LA.

You okay? All right, dumb question. You want me to get anything? I could use a cup of coffee.

MR. & MRS. WEBSTER

She was still in the hospital in North Carolina, before they moved her to Norfolk, out of her mind on the Dilaudid drip, when Michael's parents came to visit. She would not remember the visit, but they were there to bring his body home. They just seemed to drift into the room, a man and woman she did not recognize but who nonetheless seemed familiar.

There she is, said the man, by way of saying hello. Is she awake? the woman said.

She roused herself, blinked, pushed her eyes open.

Hello, the woman said softly, sweetly. He didn't want us to meet you, yet. We wanted to, but he wasn't ready yet, and he wasn't sure how you'd react. I'm so sorry.

Her eyes welled with tears and she stopped herself, turned away. Michael's mother was a handsome woman, the source of his eyes, his hair, though her own hair was now the color of steel. If it was possible, this was how she wanted her own hair to look in twenty, twenty-five years.

His father was slender, professorial, and had the same sort of sweetness of aspect that Michael had had. His parents had a dignity to them that she admired. They admitted to having never seen her show until he told them about her. She could tell that they hadn't liked it very much, and if one of them had said it, she would've said neither did she. They thought that she was very talented.

I'm sorry I can't get up.

Please. You needn't worry.

I was so curious about you. About how he came to be like he was.

For what it's worth, his father said, a soft, carefully drawn, Midwestern flavor to his voice, He said that you... You two. That if things worked out he—

He gasped in a way that perhaps was only possible for a man who has lost his son.

For what it's worth, Ellen said, numb, I never felt about anyone, you know. I know you've seen my character, my TV performance, but I'm—

We know.

No, what I want to say, that's not me. Her.

I think Michael knew who you were, his father said.

If there's anything we can do, they said, almost in unison as they hovered at the door. You can call us any time.

Ellen struggled. Her mouth felt as though it was full of glue. I would have given it up in a minute. I wanted to. I was going to tell him, but I was afraid that he—I was afraid. I was afraid of myself. My ambition has been—*had* been my best friend until I met Michael.

That's sweet of you to say.

She sank back into the bed. She could not keep her eyes from tearing. In a moment there would be rain everywhere.

They had turned and his mother was out the door by the time she said, There is one thing. She was choking on tears and their affect approached pity.

Yes, dear? his father said. (How would she live without this man as her father in law.?)

I don't know if you know this, but I first met him at the grocery. He said he was looking for broccoli. He said he didn't know what it looked like.

His mother frowned, stopped, and she could see that they were both remembering him.

I'm sorry to say that he probably didn't.

I—I thought so, she said, and started to laugh. I just thought it was sweet.

PRIVATE ROOM

When the helicopter took off for Norfolk, she was on her back, an intravenous line in a vein on the back of her hand, her left leg elevated, making it impossible not to see. She saw ocean. She saw sky. She saw news crews in the parking lot covering both the arrival and departure of the helicopter. Her mother rode with her, a look of terror on her face, while her father drove the rental car from North Carolina to Virginia. Ellen fell asleep even as her mother was chattering the kind of chatter people do when they're trying to distract themselves from gut-wrenching anxiety.

Ellen awoke when the helicopter set down at the hospital. Michael had been dead for days—actual time was a bit sketchy—and what did that *mean*? Ditto her foot. It was morning—they had moved her at the crack of dawn—and she could still feel Michael on her skin, the shape of him in her head. His whiskers. Mornings so far were the hardest parts of the day. Mornings and evenings. The middle parts of the day were okay, and being asleep was tolerable, but to wake afresh was to be forced to remember.

Her room at Sentara Hospital in Norfolk was private, but nearly every staffer on the floor came in and introduced themselves, even the guy who mopped the floors. Ellen asked Arlene to tell them to knock it off, and it was while Arlene was at the nurse's station that a man came in and said, Ellen Gregory.

She looked up from the way-too-easy *USAToday* crossword, which she was working while watching a re-run of *Bonanza* on the TV.

The man was bald as a cue ball, with a gleaming, million-watt smile, but she hadn't really looked at him when she said, exasperated. Jesus *Fucking* Christ. Do you knock?

You don't need to call me Jesus. Just call me Larry, he said, grinning, bouncing on the balls of his feet, thousands of watts of energy setting her room aglow.

And, no, I don't knock.

She stared.

I KNOW YOU

L arry McGuinn was dressed in hospital scrubs, and one of those white, sort of utility blazer-type jackets that the nurses wore, but he didn't carry a stethoscope. Only a clipboard.

She knew him. She had no idea *how* she knew him, but his cue-ball, Kojak-bald head and 12,000-watt smile were unforgettable.

She said: I *know* you.

He was watching her. He had a way of looking at you that seemed to use all of his senses, not just his eyes. He grinned. I'm surprised you remember anything.

Where do I know you *from*?

I once bandaged your hand after a nasty little encounter with a broken bottle of some sort of really strong liquor.

Her eyes went wide. You were in New York.

Arlene came back into the room and stopped.

Suddenly remembering, Ellen said: I got hammered on the plane, and you were in the apartment. Mom, this is Lawrence of Illinois.

Larry turned to Arlene and extended a hand to shake. Call me Larry, he said. I'm Ellen's PT. Arlene shook his hand and fluttered a little bit, and gushed, too, in a way that entirely bugged Ellen. We met in New York when we were both borrowing apartments in the same building.

PT. As in Barnum? Because I am not entirely feeling up to my usual circus-style antics.

What a small world, Arlene said.

PT as in physical therapist. But you can think of me as your Personal Trainer, if you prefer. That's PT, too.

She started to remember that morning, the vicious hangover, the notes placed around the apartment—notes which, by the way, she still had, somewhere. And then she started to turn red.

You make really good blueberry pancakes, she said. She looked at the TV. Hoss and Little Joe were saddling up. Is it true Hoss was gay?

I have no idea, Larry said.

Mom? Ellen said, Would you leave me alone with my physical therapy—therapist?

I'll just go get a cup of coffee, Arlene said, and exited in a flurry of movement that looked like an entire Japanese tea ceremony compacted into a few seconds.

When she was gone, Ellen said, I have to ask. Did we fuck?

You certainly have a way of coming to the point. Larry came to her bedside and pulled the chair over, reached up and turned off the TV, and sat down, clipboard on his lap.

Well, did we?

No, we did not have sex.

Did you see me naked?

You seemed to have a lot of trouble keeping your clothes on.

You didn't take pictures or anything, did you?

He smiled: he had a way of smiling so it that was utterly impossible to attach any kind of emotion to it, except happy, totally and completely content and centered in his personal body and space. He didn't seem to do wry smiles or snarky smiles. He just smiled his neutral, 12,000-watt smile. He said: I didn't think of that.

Why didn't we fuck? she said.

You were plastered, if you want to use the clinical term for it.

That wouldn't stop most guys. Ellen shook her head, put a finger to her lip. The guy was gorgeous. He was average height, with the whitest, straightest teeth she had ever seen, even in LA. His eyes were an almond brown, and the whites of them were almost like they'd been bleached. Through the loose fabric of his scrubs and blazer, she could see a very solid chest. No wonder she'd tried to fuck him. She said: But, wait a minute, what are you doing *here*?

That's what I'm here to talk about. Physical therapy.

Uh-uh. But so you're a therapist? I mean a physical therapist? Here? You live here?

He nodded brightly. You're really catching on.

So, I still don't get why we didn't fuck. You're gay? He shook his head. You didn't think I was attractive or something—no, no, you're part of some weird celibate religion.

We can talk about your physical therapy, if you'd like.

No, she said, a little angry and hurt. A girl throws herself at you and you turn her down, I think the least you could do is offer her some kind of explanation.

You're quite beautiful, Ellen, Larry said, crossing his legs and leaning toward her, his gaze into her eyes quite pure and unbroken. But you know how attractive you are. Let's just say I didn't find your particular condition attractive. And call me old-fashioned, but I tend to like romance.

He examined her leg, unbandaged her stump.

She hadn't seen it yet and couldn't watch. He said gently: You need to look.

I can't. I will, just not— I'm not ready.

It is what it is. Ignoring it will accomplish nothing.

She snarled at him, Nothing is *exactly* what I want to accomplish. Then something horrible broke inside of her and it was almost an out of body experience, the way she screamed at him. It seemed to go on forever, her face exploding. She couldn't remember anything so horrible ever coming out of her. Anger and betrayal and grief, and horror and shock and hatred, and when she couldn't scream any more, she started sobbing. She expected people to come running, but no one did.

It was, of course, not directed at him (except that in the literal sense he happened to be there and her face happened to be pointed in his general direction).

He put his hand out and placed it on her shoulder, and it felt familiar and warm and good. His fingers were strong and she looked at him while she was sobbing, and he seemed to be massaging her neck. Whatever it was he was doing gave her a kind of peace. He was smiling his infuriating smile, and she started to laugh, spitting tears and slobber into the air. She said: I didn't actually know that I felt that way.

It's a lot to assimilate, he said. And if you'll excuse the expression, you might want to consider taking things a step at a time.

He moved his hand farther up her neck and she remembered this.

She cried and giggled simultaneously: How do you do that? She wiped her suddenly-quite-copiously-running nose on the back of her hand.

Acupuncture, he said. In some countries—not this one—I'm considered a doctor.

When she dried her face and regained most of her normal composure and color, he helped her get out of bed and, first, into another of those wonderful hospital gowns (to help cover up), and then into a wheelchair with a support for her leg, so her stump led the way. He did all of this very deliberately, trying to minimize whatever pain it caused her. He told her if she wanted more pain medication, he could get her an epidural, but he didn't want her falling.

They left the room, and he took her to another floor where there was a sort of gym, and there were old people. The thing about hospital gowns was that they made everyone look like a heap of shit, and seeing this, the old woman whose hair was completely pillow-fucked, who tottered along a railing along the wall, quite suddenly telescoped everything for her—age, infirmity and death—and she started to cry again. Not violently like before, but just quiet, self-pitying sobs.

I want to go back, she said to Larry.

He didn't seem to hear her. He parked her and went away and came back with crutches, which were wrapped with plastic. He opened the package and made some adjustments.

Then he put the crutches down and knelt on the floor in front of her, his smile going, his eyes bright. I want you to stand. I'm going to help you, and it's not going to be easy, but you're going to do great. Okay?

She sniffled back tears and wiped at her eyes. There didn't seem to be any way to say no to him.

He made sure that the wheels were locked, and then slowly lowered her leg.

What I'm going to do, he said, is help steady you. I'm going to put my arms around you and we're going to go on the count of three.

He came close to her and lifted the crutches with his left hand, then put the other arm expertly around her. He counted, and then together they rose. It was the first time she had stood since she walked to the water with Michael, and for a moment, this thought hit her hard. She could see him as she ran toward him.

She thought she was going to throw up and said so. Larry said, Whatever you need to do. He was solid and steady and she felt like a child clinging to the one grownup left in the world.

The floor was soft. There were rails and handles everywhere. Larry's white hospital blazer was starched and had a good smell to it. He had a good smell. Not a cologne scent, but a human scent.

He helped her with the crutches, asked if she was feeling steady enough, and then put them under her arms one at a time, then held her and stood back a little, his hands firmly grasping her. She tottered a little and he steadied her.

Tell me if you get dizzy or light-headed, he said.

She was crying again, but nodded.

Now, he said, what I need you to do is walk toward me.

It feels too weird, she said. When she looked at him, his face exuded nothing but confidence.

It's going to, for a while. You'll feel like you're going to topple over. Do you want to just stand there and get your breath for a moment?

For what seemed like forever, he had her walk around the room with the crutches, explaining only that it was important for her to be up and moving around. Everything hurt. Larry kept up a steady, soft stream of questions about how she was doing, how she was feeling. The way he asked them, and just the way he *was*, his whole gorgeous strange ascetic gestalt, you had to answer honestly.

It was just like that.

She told him how awful she felt. She told him the worst thing, aside from losing Michael, was losing running. He told her she'd be able to do that again with a prosthetic. (She nodded but refused even to listen.) She told him about leaving LA, and for a while how it had come to seem a sort of immaculate suicide. Suicide without dying. She told him how being with Michael and just being herself, that somehow, a Rip Van Winkle version of her own, nonprofessional self, had enabled her to feel again. And all that just got eaten up. I mean, it just sucks.

He nodded, and accepted what she said without judgment.

It all ended in tears and she collapsed against him, and again he did this thing with the hands, but this time it wasn't a sense of peace that went through her, but a really ugly fit of slobbering and sobbing that left half of his jacket and scrubs soaked with tears and mucus and God knew what other sorts of other unladylike excretions.

The thing about Larry was, even though she had only known him for a few hours—not including the lost hours back in New York, she trusted him, *knew* she could trust him, and he was about as hard to ignore as a glue trap.

She held onto him and held and held and held, and when she got herself together, she let go and he helped her into the chair.

He was quiet when he walked her back to the room. She said: I am deeply ashamed of all the snot and tears I got all over your clothes and would be willing to pay in the high six figures to have them completely forgotten.

Later, the surgeon came to visit and examined her leg. The wound had been well cared for but they were going to need to do at least two surgeries, he explained. The first would be to shorten and cap the bone and begin shaping her stump (she hated that word more and more). The second would leave her with a nice stump onto which they could fit a prosthesis. (She wanted to pet the stump, and say, Nice stumpy stump.) He talked about prostheses, how far they had come, how she should be able to do most anything she did before. He was a nice man and she didn't really want to tell him to fuck off.

Later in the evening, Larry came back. He floated in, silent in the ambivalent semi-darkness of the hospital.

You hospital people, Ellen said. You don't let anyone sleep.

You saw the doctor.

I'm going to have surgery. I get the good drugs. Sorry I can't share them.

How do you feel about that?

A wise man said, 'It is what it is.'

Well, he said. I'm on my way out. Just wanted to see how you were.

Today, she said. The therapy. I'm sorry that I slobbered all over you.

I've had worse things happen to me.

Hey, she said, after a long time of the two of them looking at each other in the dark, You're a mensch. I don't know too many. Mensch-types, that is.

He smiled, then slipped away. He seemed to leave a small space in her brain glowing, which was some small offset against her grief. For a long time after he was gone, she thought of him, his gentleness and grace. His spectacular smile. There were so few people who simply cared.

NORMAL IS NOT

She had the first surgery at dawn, the day of Michael's memorial service. By that afternoon, she was up walking, going down the hall on her crutches, her stump swinging, Larry next to her, her mother and father in her room. She talked to Soraya and Hanna in the afternoon and asked them about it. They took turns getting on the phone, and sometimes just put their heads together and talked at the same time. There had been media at the funeral. People wanted to know about Ellen Gregory's mysterious boyfriend. And then there was of course the whole gruesome shark attack angle of it. The both of them, plus Jake (whom Hanna was no longer seeing) and Adam had been besieged with interview requests, but none of them had yet succumbed.

The service was nice, Soraya said. It just felt like Michael should have been there. And you.

Ellen knew, from talking to Michael's mother, that the burial itself had been private.

She walked the halls with Larry, or her mother or father. Marty came again and she walked with him. A week crept by, and almost everyone along the hallways had introduced themselves. Friends came in. People she hadn't heard from in years were calling or sending flowers. It was strange suddenly to have time to talk to people, which, talk or text, was mainly what she did when there was no therapy or her mother was snoring in the chair. In some ways, even if she was holed up in a hospital, it was a pleasure to have time, which wasn't something she'd had in ages. In some ways, it was torture, too, because for as long as she could remember, she'd been on the move, jumping to the next thing and then the next. Some days there was too much time, and thoughts of Michael flooded in, and she prayed for something, anything, to take her mind off her status as a living and breathing human animal. And so she talked and texted, now that she had time, now that she was back in circulation—talk and text. She was, in an odd way, delighted to find out just how many friends she had. Sometimes, in LA, you forgot.

Larry, with his remarkably sunny disposition, was always there, and whenever she felt like she was sinking, she would just look at him, and his presence, his whole aura, was a tonic.

When they were alone, she tried to draw him out. Who he was.

She was surprised to find that he was a decade older than she was because at times, he seemed ageless, as though he had slipped through time for thousands of years just like this. He had the kind of patience and affection that didn't seem it could be learned, that seemed it had to have been earned over millennia.

At others, he seemed to have the boundless energy of a twenty-year-old.

He had been divorced twenty some years ago and had a grown daughter, who was—or at least had been—the reason why he lived in the Virginia Tidewater area. But she had moved to New York two or three years earlier to go to school at Columbia, and now he was essentially by himself. His degree, at least his first degree, was in psychology. Like Ellen, Larry was from the Midwest. Like her, he had lived in a small town and left as a teenager, but his story was way more tantalizing and weirdly American than hers—or at least that's what she thought.

He had worked for years at a jail in a town outside Chicago, doing psychiatric evaluations of incoming inmates. It was then that he had studied acupuncture. He tended to refer to those years and that town as the place in which he had surrendered to life, and thus found it.

He was there because his father, with whom he'd had a rocky relationship, had come to die in a nursing home. He, Larry, came to visit in nearly every night in the months of his father's dying. And that was, tangentially anyway, how he had got another degree in physical therapy.

When, about a week and a half after the surgery, when this particularly ugly June had almost closed its book, the doctors had mentioned discharge, she panicked. Call it abandonment issues. Call it terror at being alone. Call it a strange and profound sense of trust. Or call it typical Ellen decision-making.

She offered Larry a ridiculous sum of money to come back to LA with her and be her personal PT—physical therapist or personal trainer. It didn't matter. Just come with me, she said. If nothing else, you'll like the weather.

When he agreed, which of course she was sure he would not, she was actually surprised and touched.

No one said this, but she got the perhaps delusional feeling that he might have been almost as lost without her as she would have been without him.

PLAY IT AGAIN

They were walking along the path by the river. It was late morning and Michael was laughing at something she said but his laugh was so magical that whatever it was she had said was gone now. She turned to him, put her hand against his face. He hadn't shaved in a couple of days and his whiskers were long and bristly.

Are you planning on growing a beard? she said.

He grinned and brought his fingers to his face and rubbed a moment, then put his face close to hers, kissed her lightly and briefly, then grabbed her face with both hands and rubbed his whiskers against her cheek. She laughed and pushed him away.

The air was sweet and the fragrance of it brought memories of growing up. Nothing specific, just glimmers, moments, but all of it was imbued with a sense of hope, the way the thaw followed the brutal winter, frozen ground suddenly damp with crocuses, implacable, pushing up.

He stood now facing her, both of her hands in his and now he kissed her cheek again, but this time gently. She had that marvelous sense of wholeness, her foot back where it was supposed to be, and walking was almost like floating. Now his face turned a little darker and he studied her. She bit her lip, cocked her head, and returned his gaze, but she couldn't figure what he was thinking.

What? she said.

Who's monitoring you? he said.

She wasn't sure, but it seemed as though this was the first time that he knew, or made it known that he knew, that she was here because of the Black Box.

Is there someone monitoring you? he said.

No, she said. His gaze went a little darker still. It's on the timer, she said. The Black Box.

He sighed, his eyes wet and weary, little crinkles showing up at the edges.

Ellen, he started, but then didn't go on, just gazed at her.

I can't live without you, she said, surprised at herself for this naked show of emotion.

Don't, he said. Do not. You're not living without me, even if you don't come here.

Something strange was happening. Sometimes you had that sense that reality wasn't quite real, that where you were at a given time was yet another surprise, and being in the place where you were was somehow open to scrutiny. If she had never known about the Black Box she would've just thought it was a mind trick, something like déjà vu, something that maybe happened when you'd had too much coffee or too little sleep, but the Black Box made her wonder if this was a kind of normal—the mind, or perhaps the self, hopping through slices of time.

I want to make love, she said.

Right here? he said, grinning.

Again, she felt that exhilarating sense of wholeness. Here, she said. Anywhere. I don't care. I want to make love with you and never stop, she said. I want to be with you.

He was no longer touching her, and she wasn't sure exactly how he had released her. Right now his face seemed unbearably sad. He shook his head, as if to clear it of an unwanted thought. Now he looked away.

What? she said.

I'm not sure it's a good thing for you to keep coming here, he said. He didn't look at her when he said it.

It could kill you, he said. I don't know. I'm still working on it. There's so much to figure out.

What if I just stayed? she said.

What do you think your body is doing right now? he said.

Suddenly she felt weakness, not real weakness, but the threat of weakness, which was somehow worse.

I don't care, she said.

Now there was a long silence, and later, back in her real life, she would wonder how long it lasted.

Finally, she said, Why don't you come to me?

I do, he said. She thought of it, the sensation she'd had now and then that he was watching her, the one time she was dead certain she'd seen him, and she knew that he was telling her the truth, but she was also certain that if he had come to her, they had never had direct contact.

I've been to church with you, he said. I've watched you in rehab. Some of it. I like Larry.

It was oddly buoying to think of him watching over her like some guardian angel from another world. There were tears in her eyes when she leaned toward him and kissed him.

When the timer stopped the machine and she was again back in her media room, the ugly little secret of the Black Box spread out beside her, she felt a not-unfamiliar sense of self-loathing. It was a feeling she got when she fucked Masters, or the time that she'd been at a party and done a couple of lines of coke and suddenly felt it was the most marvelous invention on the planet only to come down later and feel as though the only sensible thing to do was to put a bullet in her head. She felt like trash.

She lifted her footless leg and stared at the stump and began to cry. And now she looked at the Black Box and, eyes blurry, shoved it back into its case and pressed it beneath the chair. She swore she wouldn't go back, but even as she swore it she knew it was a lie, that eventually she would, because she couldn't help it.

THE VALUE OF INSANE CHARISMA

She learned, the more she got to know Larry, that he was the kind of guy that she herself might have been had she been a man whose lifelong spiritual quest had morphed into a passionate fascination with the workings of the human body and mind.

It's a strange thing, human nature, he said. Endlessly fascinating.

And then he gave one of those smiles, his fingers going to his chin and his eyes sparkling. He could be like this. A long possibly aphoristic monologue and then one of those sly smiles. And then hours of concentrated silence as they worked.

Perhaps the thing that Ellen found most attractive about Larry was not his whole buff Buddha thing and his insane charisma, which was totally a plus, but his aura of measureless calm—it was real. There seemed to be essentially nothing in the world that could elicit from him anything more than mild bemusement. It was exaggerating of course but you got the idea that he could get hit by a meteor and he'd just give a cagey little smile and rub his chin and go, Hmmm.

Which is pretty much how he addressed the surgery that she had in Norfolk, with an almost blank calm as she emerged from the operating room under a sedative and local anesthetic, her head echoing with metal, with lights, the sound of power tools, grinders, strange scents and sounds, and he would appear at the foot of her recovery bed in the cloudy haze of her medication, looking at her stump, and rubbing his chin, and the thing she would feel was elation, he was real. It was a fact, undeniably, that in all of this, he was her life preserver. He was the single thing that kept her from going absolutely mad during that time, when otherwise all she would have done was pine for Michael, her foot, and the life that could have been. There were times when it occurred to her to worry that he didn't really work for the hospital at all, that he was a Wayne Townsend type, that he had just walked up out of the crowd and taken control of her screaming and hysterical situation. There were times when she worried that she trusted him too much, that, after Wayne Townsend, she ought to have a complete and exhaustive background check on every human being who came within a nautical mile of her, but she knew—the same way she had known she could trust Michael, that she could trust him. There were things you could not lie about. And in this sense, he was, like Michael, the flip-side of Townsend and the shark, the inexplicable *good* thing.

THE MAD WOMAN

By the time Soraya got to the café, Hanna had been there more than two hours, anxious and worried, on her second medium-sized bucket of coffee, and almost through the *Good Housekeeping* magazine she'd snatched from an empty nearby table. After being in Michael's office for most of the morning with Soraya, helping start to clean it out, it was a good distraction to read about window treatments (balance the valance!), tummy control, getting the row back into your romance with tandem kayak adventures. So much of life, it seemed, was the restlessness not to be alone. There was endless comfort in this kind of chatter, affirmation and reification. Someone else's life made your life possible; someone else's love made your love possible.

They had attended to the business of cleaning out Michael's office ruthless and cold-eyed, and it wasn't until they had filled two garbage bags with old magazines, hundreds of packets of soy sauce and ketchup, and other junk, and several copier paper boxes with notebooks and files that would have to be shredded and disks that had to be destroyed that Soraya showed the slightest bit of emotion. While Hanna'd had training on grief counseling—and done not a little work with others on grief—it seemed to her that it was almost entirely uninstructive. Sometimes you operated with utter detachment; others, you broke down and sobbed. And being with people—letting your subconscious churn away while you stayed in the here and now, getting things done—was the best approach, the least painful. And in thinking this, she could not help but wonder about Ellen, how she was doing.

They had talked little. Hanna knew that her best friend was still in love with Michael (as, to some unexplored extent, was she), and that in the absence of a romance, that Soraya had taken it upon herself to look after him as though he were a boy whose life needed close, feminine oversight. Ellen's arrival had been more than a surprise. Anyone could have seen how Michael had changed, how some previously unknown layer of his being had been revealed. Anyone who knew him could see how she had electrified him, given him something that he had always lacked but never seemed to want. In just a few weeks, you could see that his eyes were brighter, that he looked taller, healthier.

And Soraya, God bless her, had taken to Ellen as much as Ellen had to her. In fact, Ellen had changed them all.

You could see why she would be so madly popular, even though none of them had ever heard of her before she appeared. She had some indefinable something that just made you want to look at her, be with her, listen to her. Maybe that was where the girl-next-door thing had come from. She was electric in some way that likely she didn't even understand. And she was vastly more charismatic in person—funny, charming, sweet—than she was on the videos they'd rented to see what she did in her other life. She, Ellen, credited that to what she called 'the Michael effect.'

More than once, over glasses of wine or cups of coffee, she had said that before Michael, she had been ready to throw everything out the window.

It was not until after the attack, after the stories came out in the papers, that Hanna went back and read the stories about Wayne Townsend, and the details of the hell Ellen had gone through.

The affection that Soraya had for Ellen was genuine. If there were traces of jealousy, Hanna had never seen them. Soraya had a sort of family orientation toward the world (which is to say that she seemed to want to be its mom). Though only a year or two older than Hanna, Soraya had more or less adopted Hanna, and then Ellen, and the two of them were for her somewhere between daughters and sisters, young women to be loved, cared for, mentored, admired, and occasionally dismissed. So with Michael, who was first her lover, then her little brother or her son.

Ellen—clearly—genuinely looked up to her, as did Hanna. There were few smarter people Hanna knew. And fewer still people who cared to be patient enough to share their smarts, along with everything else.

While cleaning his office, they had come across a box of disks that neither of them knew existed. Like everything in his life that was related to the Black Box, they were meticulously (even obsessively) labeled, with dates, details, all in his fine, draftsman's hand.

Soraya was going through these when she gave out a little, involuntary cry. Oh, Jesus, she said, reading the dates and the labels. He recorded them.

What do you mean?

Him and Ellen. These disks, they're sessions, Black Box sessions. Of each of them.

I didn't know you could do that.

Neither did I. I suppose it's possible that he was just trying, to see what happened. She had looked at Hanna then and back at the disks. If he did find a way, then—. But she didn't say any more.

Soraya sank down in his desk chair. His desk was one of those old steel institutional models from the fifties or sixties, and now it was completely clear, Windexed, and she put down the little box and went through each of the disks, reading labels.

You want to go for a walk, Soraya? Hanna said. She was trying to figure the implications of this, and they seemed to be manifold. She suddenly wanted to walk, to be out of here. She said: Let's go for a walk. Let's get out of here for a little bit, get some air.

Soraya said nothing, but stared at the box.

Come on, let's go for a walk.

Soraya shook her head slowly. No, she said. I have to see this.

Hanna did not like this idea. She, in fact, thought it foolish and selfish, and the idea made her inexplicably angry.

Soraya, she started, This is something…, I think we need, you need to think this through.

I don't need to.

Yes, you do, Hanna said, coming to where Soraya sat and putting her hands on her friend's shoulders, brushing aside her hair and kneading the area around her neck. This is too much, right now.

Soraya said. I'm gonna trip them.

Hanna did not like this at all. It was bad enough that the whole Black Box was uncharted territory—this was something entirely new, and something that neither of them had any honest clue about. Neither of them had known before this moment that this was even remotely possible.

I don't think that's such a great idea.

Soraya turned to her, her eyes brimming with tears. I have to, she said. I'll meet you in a couple of hours at the café. Okay?

Listen, I think we should talk about this. I know it's hard to live with, but this is not exactly like flipping through the old family scrapbooks, she said.

Soraya turned to her again and snapped, I have to do it.

Hanna knew her friend well enough to know that there was very little she was going to say that would dissuade her. What if it's dangerous? I don't have any warm and fuzzy feelings about this in any way.

Neither do I, but it doesn't mean that I'm not going to do it.

Now, more than three hours later, Soraya looked a bit like a mad woman, which wasn't entirely unusual for her. Sometimes she could get so involved in what she was doing that she forgot that her hair had twelve pencils holding it together and she was in her housecoat. But this was different. Hanna put her magazine away and said, You want a coffee?

Soraya blinked, Yeah, I think. What are you having?

It was a simple sentence, *What are you having?* but it seemed to take forever to get it out.

Just the light roast. Then: What is it? Hanna said as she got up to get her friend a cup of coffee.

Let me sit a minute. Soraya wound an enormous hank of hair into her fist. Let me—I don't know.

When Hanna came back, she said, So. Then she put Soraya's coffee on the table. What happened?

Soraya folded her hands in her lap and stared at the coffee, which was black, as she liked it.

Soraya was not one to stumble over her words, but she stammered I, I. She squinted, closed her eyes, took a deep breath. Okay, she said, Let's first stipulate that we both know that I'm not crazy. Or at least I don't think so.

What happened?

I *saw* him.

Michael?

Yeah.

Well, wasn't that sort of the point?

This made Hanna uneasy. Beyond simple grief and the frank horror of Michael's death, all of the events of the last several days, especially the last few days, first with the attack and then the media blizzard (seeing yourself on TV, dumbly trying to answer a reporter's rapid fire questions, your answers edited down to tiny, fragile seconds of tear-blistered face), all of it had left her feeling completely exposed and raw. Even if there had been no Ellen, all of their lives would have been changed by losing Michael. Ellen's part in all of it just made it weirder.

Soraya almost snarled, No. Not like that.

Soraya shook her head furiously and blinked rapidly. I saw him. Now, I think—I think we can be pretty certain that he did not record any of this stuff at the beach, but it was at the beach. When they went into the water, right before the attack, I was sitting on the beach, watching. And so I set the trip up, I set the Black Box up for just half an hour. I didn't want to go any further than that, you know, in case something happened.

Soraya was practically panting now, a frantic look in her eyes.

Okay, so I'm Ellen. I mean, I'm not just seeing through her eyes, *I am her.* I—Ellen—come out of the water and sit on the sand next to me. I sit next to me!

Somehow in this thing her DNA has crawled down into mine and utterly replaced it. I'm in the water with him, I'm—or she's—kissing him, holding him, and believe me, he never kissed me like that. I, for that matter, don't kiss like that. I was her to the skin of my lips, to the tongue in my, in her, mouth.

Hanna looked around and people were looking at them. This had happened a lot since the attack, but now people weren't looking at them with that hey-didn't-I-see-you-on-TV look, but that uh-oh-there's-a-wacko-nearby look.

Hanna, whispering, said, Look, sweetie, lower your voice. Please. People recognize us. (This part was truly the weirdest—and certainly it would go away after time, Ellen said it would—but it was, as she had said, like having a piece of yourself taken away.)

Soraya went on, evidently oblivious: So then, I was totally freaked and super curious. I mean, this is something that could be useful if any one of us understood what it was doing. If Michael were still around to tell us what he did. And but so I put in his disk. And again, I set it so that the trip was only half an hour.

Soraya had not lowered her voice and Hanna glanced around and people were still looking.

Come on, Hanna said, and took her coffee and held Soraya's for her. Let's get out of here and walk. Soraya stood.

Murmurs rippled through the room.

They walked down Market Street toward the Union and the river. It was a gorgeous summer day and traffic was heavy for Iowa City. Hanna wanted to pee but she also didn't want to stop Soraya, didn't really want to let her out of her sight at the moment.

And so again, again, I was him. Him. I mean, have you ever, like, tried to imagine how guys think? Have you ever, I don't know, even with a guy like Michael whom you don't think about as a testosterone-addled freak, a guy you know really well. I mean, never in a million years. Never. I mean—*oh, Jesus.*

But so again, it was like his DNA, his everything. Me. Him. It was almost—no— it *was pornographic.* I was fucking her. I was him and I was fucking her. It was in the shower, their shower at the beach house.

Had you ever seen it before? The shower?

Soraya thought about it and shook her head. I probably was in the bathroom there, but not that one.

When they got to the river, they crossed over the bridge and found a bench. Soraya sat with her head in her hands. When she sat up again, Hanna put her arm around her. Her bladder screamed. The coffee had gone cold and she did not want it any more.

The first thing, Soraya started, then hesitated. The thing I really wanted to tell you—you know how each of us carries around, you know, a bundle of memories and sensations and all sorts of crap that makes us us? You know what I mean. You never even think about it. It's just you, it's just, you know, the edge of us. The thing behind the face that makes the face the face. Hanna laughed at the sound of this.

The thing is, when I was tripping Ellen, I was carrying that, her like personal narrative bundle. I mean you know how when we've tripped before it's just like, you know, something like a dream but not as weird. Like a totally interactive 3-D reality. Maybe weird, maybe exciting, maybe boring, but never painful.

Hanna looked at her. It was painful?

No, I don't—. No. Not painful, exactly. But it was like slamming through something. With her it was a surprise, but with him, yeah, maybe it was painful. It was like breaking something. The only thing I can compare it to is running into a wall. But then going through it. And that's not what it was like, either.

Hanna sat and tried to take this in.

So the thing I was going to tell you—about her, about when I was tripping her. Soraya stopped and stared at Hanna, her eyes wide and suddenly full of tears. She sniffled and wiped at them, laughed. God, this sounds so, so, idiotic, I can't believe I'm going to say it. I could *feel* the way she loved him. I could say it the way she would have said it. I could feel how completely confused and scared she was. She wanted to stay with him. She was furiously working out in her head how she could be with him, how she could make it work. But she was also scared that there wasn't a place for her with him.

Soraya gave a weird laugh. I had this idea about her, I mean there was at least some part of me that refused to believe that she was doing anything but playing with him. For some kind of amusement. I mean she never said it, and I will admit a certain level of resentment or something.

Hanna stopped her. First, that's wrong. You loved Michael. We all did. So stop with the would've and could've crap. That's just grief. But beyond that—and frankly I'm not sure we're going very far beyond grief at all here—but....

She stopped. She looked at her friend and saw that there was nothing particularly hysterical about her; she was still who she was, a scientist.

She said: Soraya, you and I both know that this is not possible. We both know that there has to be some kind of rational explanation for this. Hanna said this hesitantly, more trying to make herself believe it. If there was a rational explanation to it, she had no idea what it was, and she could hear what Ellen had said to her on the beach: the Black Box knows things that no machine could possibly know.

267

I have no idea what it does or how it does it, but it's real, Hanna. It's real. Oh, God, it is *so* real.

I'm not questioning you, Hanna said. I'm not questioning what you think you saw. Soraya, you're a scientist.... Maybe, she said. Maybe he didn't intend them to be tripped? Maybe they were just for playback?

No, he intended them for tripping. Maybe not you and me, but he was doing something none of us knew about. I don't know if Ellen did.

How could he have recorded them at the beach and got it back here when he was dead.

I'm not suggesting that he did. I'm suggesting that in all his playing around with the thing, he managed to do something and wanted to experiment further with it.

What?

What what? I mean which what? What was he doing? I have no idea. What did he do? I think he left this as a kind of will.

There was no part of this that Hanna was not resisting. In the first place, it was just plain creepy. How could you record someone's essence? How could you take a person and put them on a shiny little disk? It was preposterous and creepy and really, really scary.

We've got to end this thing, Hanna said. This is not good. We should finish it. Turn it all over to Dr. Sprague and be done with it.

There was a part of Hanna that just wanted to shrug off the last two or three years—to say nothing of the last week—and get back to her life. Except this *was* her life. Michael had given them all a kind of purpose, his obsession had become their obsession in many ways, and it had shaped their lives. It was all about the machine.

Are you kidding me? Sprague is utterly clueless about this. If he isn't, then we may have a huge problem. We don't know enough about it to turn it over to him and his cadre of bland mediocrities. That's exactly what we're *not* going to do.

Hanna bristled a little, but said nothing. Soraya's imperiousness sometimes had this effect on her, too much like bullying. But she knew Soraya was probably right.

Look at you, Hanna said. Look at you. I would think you of all people would want this finished.

Believe me, honey, I haven't finished. And you haven't either.

Soraya sat back on the bench, her limbs splayed, her hair sprawling.

She said: The sunlight hurts. I have a splitting headache.

Drink your coffee.

After a while, Soraya went on: It was like this. I set up the machine. I hit start and sat back in the chair and it was like something picked up the whole room and threw it through a wall, and then I was standing in the bathroom in their house at the beach.

She drank from her coffee and sat forward, then put the cup on the bench and held her head in her hands, pressed them against her head.

God, she said. There are times when it feels like reality has such a thin skin.

She looked at Hanna and Hanna thought she saw something in Soraya's eyes that she had never seen before. It was a strange mixture of fear and desire and determination.

Once I went through the wall, I was no longer me. I was Michael. This is very hard to describe, very hard to....

Soraya..., Hanna started but Soraya cut her off quickly.

I was naked and I could feel my whole body and it was not my body and I'm not sure it was me, she said, speaking rapidly, staccato almost, as if compelled to get this out and get it out accurately.

And she was in the shower, and I was walking toward her, and I could feel everything he felt, the hair on my chest, the distended penis swaying as I walked, the way my feet felt on the floor tiles, crossing onto the bathmat. Oh, Jesus. I could feel the hot essence of her in his desire, which is something I actually never realized before, desire from a man's point of view—the way he—I—took in the room, the predatory way I looked at her skin, the alienness of it, a sensation of promise, payoff, renewal. Not so different from female desire but completely different.

Hanna almost felt like tearing her hair out. She wanted her friend to stop. Michael was dead. Michael was dead—she wanted to say it over and over—let's bury him.

And I was Michael. *I was Michael.*

Hanna wanted to get up and find a place to pee, but she was too morbidly fascinated by the story. If she had never tripped on the Black Box herself, she would've thought her friend was completely insane, overwhelmed by grief. But she'd seen what the machine was capable of and began to understand that what Soraya said was more than possible.

Soraya kept talking. And I was not me anymore. I mean this was not like some sort of role-playing game, Hanna, this was—I was him. I looked at her the way that he looked at her and saw the way that she looked at him and—

The idea left Hanna feeling strange and—oddly—lonely.

And I walked into the shower and I put my arms around her—and remember, I was taller than her, stronger than me, and I picked her up and carried her out of the shower and she had her legs around me and I put her up on the counter and I fucked her, and I felt what it was like for him to fuck her.

Suddenly, she started to cry. It wasn't a massive, sobbing thing, it was just that her eyes welled up and tears dripped down her face.

Hanna felt like her bladder would explode if she did not find a ladies room soon. Soraya hugged herself and closed her eyes and tears streamed. She sucked at the air.

So that's why you looked so, like the Mad Woman of Iowa City when you came into the coffee shop.

No, Soraya said, her face wet, her mouth sucking at the tears, her hair caught on her face. God, my head hurts. This is why you have to trip again before we do anything.

I don't want to trip them.

You don't have to. You just need—please—just trip one more time.

Why?

Because this is the weirdest thing of all. After I did the two of them, I did a conventional trip, like we've all done a dozen times, no disk. And that's when I saw him. I wasn't him. I was me. I saw Michael.

THE GATES

Soraya leaned back in her circa-1976 office chair and stared at her blank computer screen. It was closing in on noon, and she hadn't had any breakfast, but neither did she feel hungry. She hadn't done any work either. She knew, of course, that it was a result of grief, a mild depression. But it wasn't just that. Certainly the loss of someone as important to her as Michael left an enormous hole in your life. There was another thing—the possibility that what she knew to be true wasn't entirely true—that bothered her.

The image of herself as Michael seared in her head, Ellen in the shower, the brilliant halogen lighting of the rented bathroom, picking out every facet of every crystalline water droplet, rainbowing the steam—and she couldn't make it go away. It was as real as it was indelible. And yet, of course, it was impossible. Which she would have said herself, had she not seen it—so there had to be another explanation. But of course, there wasn't.

On a normal day, say, three or four weeks ago, there would have been at least three or four e-mails already from Michael in her inbox, but today there was essentially nothing—department-wide stuff, university-wide stuff, seven or eight unsolicited offers to enlarge her penis (which now might have been funny) or make her rich with penny stocks, and at least one or two that offered her the exclusive chance to see bestiality in full HD color. She stared at the screen, which was a background of wispy clouds and rolling hills of mown wheat, in the foreground some sort of blurry flower.

Without really thinking, she picked up the phone and called Hanna from her office.

When Hanna answered, she said, Can you come over?

Soraya? Is that you? Where are you?

Soraya sighed. Hi, oh, sorry, weird train of thought thing going. I'm in my office. Can you come over?

Soraya, I'm in the middle of grading papers.

Then it's nothing that can't wait.

Soraya, please. I'll come over if you tell me it's not about the Black Box.

What if I said it was?

There was a long silence but Soraya couldn't even hear Hanna breathe.

Soraya, I have thirty-seven papers to grade and a long day's work ahead of me.

In the past, Hanna had always been (at least in her own mind) too compliant with almost anything Soraya had asked—but in the past almost everything that Soraya had asked had been inconsequential. Now that it was something of substance, suddenly Hanna was reluctant. Soraya sighed. It was a long, weary exhalation.

I have an idea, she said. I don't know whether it's a good idea or a bad idea, or what kind of an idea it is, frankly. But I have an idea. Will you come over?

Hanna paused, feeling the energy of her refusal dissipate. I'll be there in half an hour, she said, finally.

Soraya wasn't sure whether the sigh she breathed was a sigh of relief.

Hanna hadn't told Soraya, but she had been IMing Ellen since about ten o'clock that morning—that she had in fact been IMing Ellen for a while now.

Hanna hadn't mentioned anything about the Black Box, about Soraya's weird experience, about her claim that she'd seen Michael. Ellen was talking about her flight back to LA, the way she had broken down on the plane, the way in the twenty-four hours since she arrived, she'd broken down at least two or three more times, which was wholly and unquestionably not Ellen.

Not that it was really any of Soraya's business that she was talking to Ellen without Soraya knowing. Except that Soraya made it her business to know everybody else's business. Soraya seem to have the sort of almost organic sense of herself being involved in everything. This was not something that Hanna begrudged her. Everybody wanted some small way of feeling that they were in control of the world. Knowing everything about everyone was Soraya's way.

It was an odd thing, the IM conversation. In some ways it was even more disembodied and impersonal than a telephone conversation. Yet she felt that she had gotten to know Ellen in a way—through IM—that she had not known her before. It was an oddly sweet feeling, after all the loss of the last several days, the last couple of weeks.

How R U?

Sucky!!!! All sucks. U?

Hard time eating/sleeping

Me 2. Pain. I miss him. I keep doing awful sobbing things. Frog noises.

Frog noises?

Like my throat is making the sound of 1000 tortured frogs.

I dumped Jake.

Did he notice?

LOL.

She had rented and watched videos of Ellen, and there was a certain kind of weird disbelief that had come over her as she was watching—that she knew this woman. Not the kind of starstruck disbelief that people got when they meet somebody famous, but a sense of the depth and multiplicity of a person's—a particular person's—character. Ellen had mentioned something to her—she couldn't remember if it had been at the beach or sometime before—that she felt as though she had lost control of herself, that the Ellen she had once been had somehow slipped away from her, and in watching the videos, she could vaguely understand. Hanna had no idea what it was like to be either an actress or a comedian, what it was like to pretend to be other people for your living. In both occupations, but particularly in her comedy, her ability to mimic people, her facility with language and with accents was startling—how she could go from being the sweet little girl next door to an Indian cab driver, a Chinese restaurant deliveryman, a highfalutin sorority girl, whatever. Watching her was almost a dizzying sensation, the people seemed so real. It was almost as though you could read her mind, as though she could turn her mind inside out and let you see her daydreams, her terrors.

There was something strange and wonderful about opening iChat and finding Ellen's screen name there among available buddies—there was a distilled essence of Ellen in there, the eight characters of her screen name (ELLEN!!G). There was pleasure in firing little bursts of text back and forth.

Hey, girl. Wassup?

Sobbing now. U?

Me 2. Keyboard wet.

Partly it was the anonymous quality, the words stripped of everything. They could as easily have video chatted, but there was a quality to the text chat. It seemed a little bit like little girls staying up late at night—even if it happened to be in broad daylight—doing some forbidden thing.

Walking out of the building and toward her car, she felt weirdly guilty because she was telling herself that she would not tell Soraya.

It had been no more than 24 hours since Hanna had seen Soraya, but even in that short space of time, Soraya looked like she had lost weight—there was a look of something like madness in her eyes. Or if not madness then evangelical conviction and zeal, which was just as impossible to deal with.

Ordinarily, this would have scared Hanna, but today it really didn't seem to carry the same sort of alarm.

There was a point you got to in love or grief where suddenly you felt that you were being carried by something entirely out of your control and either you suffocated yourself in that loss, or you simply accepted it and went forward because there was—acceptance or not—really no alternative.

Soraya had always been the single most solid individual Hanna had ever known, and to see Soraya even vaguely unhinged, despite whatever Hanna felt herself, would—a month ago—have terrified Hanna.

But now, having been through the unspeakable, she had an almost entirely new and different perspective on life. There was nothing guaranteed, there was the evanescent and imminent and insistent possibility that it would all be over in a moment's notice, that *it* was all meaningless, and this, this fact of grief, in its way, perplexed her. At one moment you could be overcome with love and exaltation and at the next you could be being chewed to bits by an animal ten times your size: And so, from a sort of formal, scientific and hypothetical standpoint, where did that leave you? Fearless, ready to plunge headlong into whatever came along, clinging to the moment? Or was it God's way of telling you that you had better watch your pretty little ass and spend your life terrified?

There was a weird euphoric part to grief that no one ever told you about, that in someone else's death you could find the most amazing exaltation. The glorious inhalation after being slugged mercilessly in the solar plexus.

Hanna said, So, what are we doing here?

Soraya seemed vaguely surprised to see her take the initiative like this and gave her one of her Doctor looks (head dipped slightly as though to peer over imaginary glasses, brow furrowed with skepticism). Hanna had hardly come in the door. Looking at porn, what else?

Soraya, please. Soraya ushered her in and closed the door. Sit, sit. Please.

Soraya leaned on the edge of her desk. Her heels anchored her on the floor.

You look like shit, Hanna said. Did you sleep at all last night?

Thanks, darling. I'm going after the heroin chic look. She made as if to poof her hair.

You do a crappy Ellen. Did you sleep?

I don't know, maybe a couple of hours. But that isn't why I called you.

You said you had an idea.

Well, Soraya said, hesitating. She drew the word 'well' out, and rolled her eyes. Last night after, after everything, I came back here, and it was weird. It was almost like it was timed, but the phone rang. And wouldn't you know it. It was Dr. Sprague.

What did he want? This wasn't a question but a place marker in the conversation.

He just wanted me to know that there would be some other post-docs coming by to clean up Michael's office. He said that, of course, they would have to assume possession of all university-owned property. I didn't say anything. I just listened. He said he understood the pain, the grief, the blah blah blah, etc. and so on, but of course university property was university property. I reminded him that I, in fact, have donated more, excuse me invested more, in Michael's research, than had the university. I reminded him that I was Michael's business partner and was, therefore, a co-owner of all business-related property Michael owned, which therefore devolved to me.

Jesus, Hanna said.

Why it was that Dr. Sprague decided that he had to call me and tell me this at 10:30 last night, I have no idea. In any case, I hightailed it over to Michael's office and packed up all the hardware—except, of course, the university-owned servers, and took it all back to my place.

What did you do with the disks?

They're at my place. And I scrubbed—at least as best as I knew how—the servers.

Please don't tell me...

Hanna, I don't see why you don't want to know about this. I'm really surprised that you don't want to face this. I saw him. I saw Michael. I talked to Michael. Yes, I know he's dead, but.... But he's also alive.

Hanna resisted the temptation to put her hands over her ears, stamp her feet and chant some silly stupid children's rhyme.

Soraya, please, I know how much you loved him.... I loved him too.

No. No. No. It's not like that. I know you think this is some kind of, like, weird grief kind of thing, but it's not. Everything about this goes against my training as a doctor. As a scientist. Everything about this, frankly, makes my skin crawl, but you're the only one I can really talk to about it. Adam... Adam, thinks I'm nuts.

Hanna thought: Maybe you are, maybe you're totally out of your fucking mind. But Hanna said nothing; inside her head, however, she was screaming.

Soraya pushed herself away from the desk and started wandering around the room.

Inside, Hanna was boiling. There was so much she wanted to say. Except there was none of it that she actually *wanted* to say. All of it she had tried desperately to avoid saying. She pressed her head down into her hands. In her head she saw Ellen in the hospital room. She saw Marty in the hallway. She saw Michael's ragged body on the beach afterwards. She wanted to tear out her hair. She wanted to jump up and scream. She wanted to take hold of the very fabric of time and pull it backwards. She felt like she was on the verge of exploding. Soraya, she said, You don't get it.

Don't get what?

Soraya leaned in the corner of the room and Hanna looked at her. There were tears in her eyes. Don't you see? Hanna said. Oh, never mind. Never mind. It's always about *you*.

What the fuck are you talking about?

Hanna looked for a way to express what she wanted to say, but everything seemed to be moving so fast. At last she shook her head and said: You just don't seem to give a shit about anyone but yourself. I broke it off with Jake. Before we even got back. Ellen knows. I told her. *She* listens.

What? What are you talking about?

I broke up with Jake. On the plane.

Soraya sank down into the chair behind her desk. She took the tie out of her hair and held it in her fingers. With the other hand, she gathered up her hair, started to tie it up again, but then looked up, looked at the band and let it fall onto her desk. She gave out a long sigh. Things were silent between the two of them for a long time. If there had been an analog clock in the room, you could've heard it tick. At last she said, I'm sorry, sweetie. I'm really sorry. You're right.

For long time the two of them sat in silence, neither one looking at the other.

At last, Hanna said, So you have the Black Box at your place.

Soraya thought of all the things they had planned together, she and Michael, how they were going to change the world with their experiments, the research, the millions of possible applications of a mind-machine interface. Now it came down to last thing she ever would've wanted to admit. She said: It's at my place for now. But I think we have to destroy everything.

Hanna looked her in the eye. You tripped them again, didn't you? she said.

Soraya was surprised at this. She had, but she had had no intention of telling Hanna.

Hanna said, You said you had an idea.

Soraya almost jumped out of her chair. Let me get a few things, she said. And we'll go to my place. Hanna nodded. She felt dead. She watched Soraya got a blood-pressure cuff, her stethoscope, and some other medical equipment. And she followed her dumbly out the door.

THRESHOLD

Being back in LA, coming out of LAX in a wheelchair, the riot scene of photographers and reporters on the sidewalk next to the limousine, shouting questions, the whole awful spectacle was almost an out-of-body experience. Everyone wanted to see the stump. There was nothing of this that she wanted.

Larry and the nurse sat in the back of the limousine with her, and as they headed over the freeway toward her house, she had the sensation again of her lungs and heart being smashed by a giant fist. For a moment she was certain she would vomit, certain she would have a heart attack, or at the very least pee her pants and vomit at the same time.

It seemed to take forever but at the same time it seemed to take only about twenty seconds to get to her house. It looked somehow different than it had when she'd left, like the landscaping had changed, somehow. Maybe Marty had put in a couple of new fully grown palm trees. She watched Larry as he looked at the place. In the few weeks she'd been working with him, she'd discovered that Larry had approximately three public expressions: number one was a pleasant medium-wattage look of mild bemusement; number two was a look of measured interest, but with a low key, minimal-wattage grin attached; and number three was a blinding, full-wattage grin of joy. All of these expressions were accomplished with a minimal movement of facial muscles. It was all Buddha-like in its simplicity. As soon as the limo got to the gate of her community and slid through, it slowed to a crawl. Now that it was at her long driveway, it slowed to an even more crawly sort of crawl and inched along with the determined patience of a very large, very shiny black slug.

And then here they were. Ellen said: Well, here we are. My not-in-the-least humble abode.

The nurse—who had been recommended to Marty by some executive who'd used him during his convalescence from some undisclosed surgical procedure—said, Sweet.

Larry said nothing.

277

Ellen had watched the nurse as they'd been driving and she had been going back and forth on the don't-like-him to hate-him-passionately continuum. As soon as he said *Sweet*, her continuum slider landed on hate-him and pretty much stayed there. When they got out of the limo, he futzed around trying to look busy by directing the limo driver and Larry and essentially doing nothing but getting in the way.

Larry helped the limo driver get the wheelchair out of the trunk. She scooted herself over to the door and Larry did one of the effortless maneuvers they'd done countless times and slipped her into the chair. He was not a tall man, but he was astonishingly powerful. When she was settled, he leaned in close to her and said in a voice that was scarcely audible, It's going to be okay. It isn't going to be wonderful and sometimes it's going to be really hard, but it's going to be okay.

Her head almost jerked toward him when he said this. He was wearing expression number three (maximum wattage), and it was the single thing in the day that made her feel as though the force of gravity still obtained on the planet.

I'll take that note, she said.

When they got to the stone step at the front door Larry lifted the wheelchair while the nurse—whom she would fire before the end of the day—fluttered about like a startled moth. The limo driver carried her bag—that was it. That was all she had to show for her escape. It was, concomitantly, both exhilarating and pathetic—pathetic because after the hugeness of the last six weeks, there was only a bag; exhilarating because it didn't even take that much to disappear.

There was an uncomfortable moment on her stone porch of pocket patting and fumbling (*I have no idea if I even have my keys anymore*), from which they were rescued by her maid, who opened the door and beckoned them inside. Ellen was too exhausted to wonder if her maid had come to her house regularly three times a week since April. She probably had.

Larry lifted her over the threshold and there they were.

SYNESTHESIA

Hanna sat stiffly in the chair while Soraya finished hooking up all the electronics. Soraya had brought home every bit of portable electronic equipment that could be used for monitoring neurological or physiological activity. She wanted pulmonary and cardiac response. She wanted galvanic skin response. She wanted brain waves. Hooking all this up had seemed to take nearly forever. Now she helped Hanna put on the headset. She, Hanna, had dreaded doing this since the moment she told Soraya she would—no way did she want to end up with the wild-eyed look that Soraya had had the day in the café—but now she was just bored and wanted to get on with it.

Soraya said, Just another minute.

You're going to set the timer?

Yeah. No more than half an hour. And don't worry. I'll shut it down if anything starts looking weird.

I'm not worried. Should I be worried? Hanna had insisted, when they were discussing it, that she did not want to do Michael. That was more than she could've taken.

I told you. Don't worry, Soraya said.

It was strange to be using this thing without Michael. And the weirdness of the possibility that she might actually see him was as terrifying as it was tantalizing. Now, Soraya had wrapped the headset around her and her vision was limited to the field of blackness that was the interior. Distantly, Soraya said something that Hanna couldn't make out. There was a hum, and then the familiar, brain-teasing tangle of lights and sound as the thing negotiated with her brain.

It was only when her feet hit the sand and her hair did not fall onto her face as it usually did that Hanna realized she was no longer in her own body. It would have been impossible to put into words how alien it was, how vastly awakening, how completely insane, to actually be inside someone else's skin. It was a combination of things that signaled how different it was: the utter strangeness of the feel of sand on her foot, like no way of feeling she'd ever known. There was an element here of—what was the word? *synesthesia*—feeling colors and seeing sounds, smelling numbers. The sand sparkled against her skin. And there was the changed physical sensation of the location of self in the world—the word for it was prioproception—that was a whole new universe of sensation. The combination was simultaneously thrilling and sickening.

Oh, it was stunning. She steadied herself and looked up. Michael was ahead of her on the sand, wearing the suit he had worn the day he died. *He* was stunning. More completely gorgeous than she had ever seen him through her own eyes. He had a cooler on one shoulder and his arm was wrapped around it. Had it not been that her own self was receding as Ellen more completely took over, she might have been completely stunned to see him alive, intact.

The sensation of seeing him, his gleaming hair, his angular shoulders and knotty legs was now completely different. He was a different Michael than she had ever seen, almost as though he were more vivid, and she were more alive. She walked as though on some invisible thing that held you aloft, and she was borne along on something bright and sweet, as thick as it was buoyant. She noticed the hat on her head, the big, silly sunglasses on her nose. She noticed the green bikini (to complement Michael's eyes). She noted the way that the filmy shift she wore swept against her skin. She noted the sensation of having recently made love. And when she noted that, she also noted the memory of it—clearly not her own—the warm sense of the recent delicious. There were fleeting images, both visual and tactile. His chest, his eyes, the press of his body and his fingers on her skin.

This was simply astounding. Walking into someone else's head. The dwindling part of her that was still Hanna said that this was wrong, that this was an unforgivable intrusion. Except she was not Hanna. She was Ellen.

For several minutes after hooking Hanna up and turning on the machine, Soraya watched the monitors, heart rate, respiration. Everything appeared to be well within normal ranges. The brainwaves were different, though. Not a normal waking state, and nothing at all like sleep. From what she could see of Hanna's face, which was obscured behind the mass of cables and tabs and technology, she seemed placid, and without any sign of distress—or any affect at all. Soraya got up and got herself a fresh cup of overcooked coffee, and when she returned, Hanna appeared no different. The machine was whirring and outside the apartment you could hear the sound of midday traffic.

About ten minutes in Hanna gave an involuntary jerk. Her hands rose from her sides and hung in the air is if touching something—or someone—and one hand dropped away and the other reached down and touched her foot. She seemed to brush away something. Soraya looked back at the monitors and, overall, things were normal except that there was one area in her friend's brain that seemed to be more active than others. She listened to Hanna's breathing, she pressed her fingers to Hanna's wrist, just for the tactile sense of her best friend's pulse beneath the tender damp skin of her arm.

Hanna/Ellen watched as Michael turned around on the sand, cooler still in the air, and she came to him. She could feel Ellen's whole body flushing with warmth. In a moment she stood inches away from him. Michael lifted her sunglasses gently from the ridge of her nose and looked into her eyes and gazed at her. You're beautiful, he said. I love you.

Whenever Hanna had been hooked up to the machine before, she'd always retained the awareness of herself as a separate and distinct person—she was always herself, but she was always (or so she recalled) sort of on her own shoulder. Two places at once. Herself aware she was watching another version of herself, even if through her own eyes. Now she was virtually all Ellen.

It was the first time these words—I love you—had been spoken by either of them, and now they hung in the air between them.

Excuse me? she joked in a British spinster's accent, pursing her lips. What was that? Now, she wanted to wrestle him down and make love again right here in the sand.

Soraya watched the time as she watched the monitors. She had no idea what she was expecting, but this was not it. It seemed to be almost like Hanna had left her own body.

When it was done, Soraya said, Are you okay?

Hanna said nothing. She was gasping but she was also smiling.

Soraya held Hanna's face in her hands. Are you okay? Talk to me.

Hanna wore a vague smile, but her eyes seemed empty. Soraya lifted her hands and pulled off tabs, unhooked wires. She rubbed her thumbs against Hanna's temples. She remembered the weird, out-of-body sensation she had felt. She just took a deep breath and kept massaging the soft skin of her friend's head.

After what seemed unbearably long time, Hanna finally made a sound, and that's all it was, a sound. Soraya slid her hands around Hanna's neck and rubbed her shoulders.

Tell me where you are, sweetie, Soraya said. Tell me where you are.

I.... Here, Hanna said. Her voice was hoarse.

Where's here?

In a more normal voice, Hanna said, Here, right here.

It took a while for Hanna to recover sufficiently to be able to talk about what happened. During this time, she didn't say much except made small exclamations, the most intelligible of which was, Wow.

Finally, she got up and walked around. Looked at the mess of wires and cables, and shook her head. Blinking. At last she said: You were right.

Meaning?

That was the most amazing and weird thing I've ever seen, ever done. I was her. Every time before, I was always still me, but before it ended…, I was completely her.

Soraya sank into her chair, exhausted.

The idea of being able to record your own memories in such a multidimensional way was as totally cool a concept as Hanna could think of—to an extent. But the idea that someone else could live them was truly creepy.

Hanna said: It seems like such a violation.

Soraya hung her head. I know.

Reflexively, Soraya picked up her stale cup of coffee and held it for a moment, sipped from it briefly and hastily put it down. She couldn't help but wonder if the same physiologic and neurologic changes hadn't happened to her when she'd become Michael. Had she almost been comatose? Except it wasn't a coma. She remembered the washed out, rundown feeling she'd had for hours afterward. The way it felt as though her mind had been put through the ringer. And yet there was the electric excitement of it.

For a long time, Soraya questioned Hanna about what had happened. Her recall was excellent. It was the last day at the beach, Hanna said, when Michael had told Ellen he loved her—which Ellen had told her about at the time.

At first, she'd had the sense of being herself being Ellen. But then that sensation of being two people at once—which she began to think of as the on-the-shoulder sensation—had diminished until she was entirely Ellen. Ellen had been waiting for it. This woman of blinding ambition was waiting on *him*, and convinced that it was never going to happen. She said: I could feel the churning of ambivalence. There was this sense of incredible delight, you know? But then there was also this sense of real, profound confusion. I could see all of these ideas, these phrases, these glimmers of people and things, stuff I—I mean myself, Hanna—didn't know anything about, but stuff that I, as Ellen, knew all about. I still can remember faces, ideas, but they're so completely unattached to anything.

Soraya looked at her hands. They seemed like someone else's hands—some old crone.

God, Hanna said, You should've seen—did you see?—how they were in love. She shook her head. There was simply no way to communicate what it was like to have been inside someone else so completely.

Hanna ran her fingers across her chin and her mouth. She said: I can still feel his whiskers. It's so weird. I mean, I can still feel it—Michael's whiskers on my own face.

She could also still feel the passion, the physical arousal, the hormonal flooding, but she didn't say it.

It wasn't much more than that, she said. At least in terms of, like, action. We walked up over the dune. We stood there and looked at the ocean and the waves, the seagulls, and we talked about the last day—you know Michael's wacky last day thing—and there was some kind of disappointment. He was disappointed, and she wasn't getting it. Now, now—this is strange—I can see this as an outside observer. But I wasn't outside it then.

She shook her head. God, I feel exhausted.

It was dark by the time Hanna left Soraya's, and the walk back to her place on this warm, pleasant summer evening had a feeling of unreality to it. She had no sense of time, no sense of how late or early in the evening it was. She had just seen—not just imagined, but seen—a person she had seen die, and die horribly. She thought she should feel lonely, but she didn't. Her head was swimming, but part of her felt clearer than she had ever felt.

Michael is alive.

When she got to the house, she didn't go in but sat on the front step and listened to the evening, the incessant chirring of the insects, occasional traffic in the distance. She now knew that Michael was alive. It wasn't like dreaming that he was alive, only waking to discover the reality. Somehow, unquestionably, Michael was alive. It was just a question of getting there.

She resisted the urge to go inside and call Soraya. There were too many things to think about. Millions of possibilities and contingencies. The implications of what they had done or were doing. Was it just the brain? Was the Black Box a trick of the mind, or something different?

Without really thinking, Hanna went around the back of the house and through the rickety wooden gate and onto the grass. It was damp and black in the darkness. She lay down and looked at the stars. They were too many questions. Too many possibilities. Her head swam. She could see Michael, the way his swim trunks clung to his hips, the way his waist flared to his shoulders, the gorgeous ripple of his ribs.

Inside, she could hear the phone ring. She thought of getting up but did not. The house had four apartments in it and she wasn't even sure it was her phone.

Much later, she was tired but still buzzing at the bone with the experience, she sat in bed with a style magazine, trying to distract herself into sleep. The phone rang again. She looked at the clock, and wasn't sure she believed it was nearly dawn.

She knew instantly who it was, without picking up, even though she didn't have caller ID.

She smiled as she put the hand piece to her ear.

It sounded almost like a prank call, as Ellen's calls often did. What it sounded like was a gaggle of 12-year-old girls at a slumber party tussling over the phone, all talking at once. Hanna had seen her do it, but could still never quite believe the vocal dexterity.

How did you know I was thinking about you? Hanna said.

You mean you're not always thinking about me?

Hanna laughed.

What have you been doing? Tell me everything.

Hanna giggled. I was over at Soraya's for a while. Then I came home, and lay down in the backyard and looked at the stars.

Either it was gorgeous or boring as hell.

It was gorgeous. The stars, I mean.

There was so much Hanna wanted to tell Ellen, but could not. At least not yet. Her head swarmed with images, sensations. It was strange how if something happened to you, if you saw it, it was almost impossible to deny.

They chatted idly for a while, Ellen asking about everyone: Is Adam finished with his book yet? (No.) Are things still off between you and Jake? (Yes.) Hanna delighted at the stories that Ellen told about the famous people who came by to visit. How Robin Williams made even her stoic, Buddhist-monk-of-a-physical-therapist choke with laughter, kept calling her Stumpy, which she thought was hysterical—but only when he said it. She talked about material she was putting together, how surprised she was by what she was discovering about herself.

Hanna asked her what she meant.

Her parents had been out, Ellen said. It was the first time they had seen her place, and she could tell that there was a part of her father that disapproved of what he would inevitably see as waste, but of course he was also totally awed by his daughter's accomplishment. Which meant wealth. And when after a couple of days they acclimatized, it was all background.

But what did you discover?

Oh, Ellen said. I was never really sure where I got, you know, the funny gene. And it had been so long since I saw my parents just being, you know? Being people. I mean my father, he is a truly funny man. I thought I was the, like, black sheep or something. And he was helping me one day, and he said something about, you know if you could learn to laugh about this, then it would all be worthwhile. And I'd heard myself say that a million times, but in different ways. I just then at that moment realized how much of him I carried around with me.

I think that's really great, Hanna said. Then, hesitantly, she said, But how are you? I mean, you know, coping?

Oh, Ellen said. Oh, well, it's kind of like…. People talk about grief as though it's a single emotion, you know? The grief process, a phrase I hate, by the way. It just makes it sound like you could throw your emotional cabbage into the grief processor and make cole slaw. What do you think? You're the pro. I don't think it's a single emotion but pretty much every emotion that you've ever experienced, plus another dozen or so you never even knew possible, all balled into one really ugly little package. Throw *that* in the grief processor.

I tend to agree with you.

But the main one is that I am one pissed off cowgirl. I get so angry sometimes at everything I want to go outside and yell at God. Or sad. Sad. I get worked up by the stupidest things. A fifteen-second commercial can bring me to my knees. A guy looks at a girl and I am like, I'll just start sobbing.

Well, Hanna said, That's pretty standard issue stuff. We're all…, you know. She had no idea what to say.

There was a long silence, and in it you could hear cornfields, wheat fields, mountains, deserts.

It feels like the whole world should come to a stop, Ellen said. I came home and I was back in my house and it was all the same and yet it was all changed. Michael had never been there, but it was weird. Crazy-making. So much gained and lost in such a short time.

Ellen started to cry again. It was a quiet thing at first, but then she was talking and it sounded like the inverse of her comedy, a long stream of consciousness, and I just never got to find out. Never. And it feels like pure horror but you drive down the street and there's a pregnant woman, her husband holding her arm, and they've got this look of hope and…, and you think, Fuck. Fuck. Horror and yet, yes. Well, it's ordinary. Ordinary grief. It shouldn't be ordinary.

No. It shouldn't be, Hanna said.

There was more silence, and Ellen sighed, little sobs still coming.

Hanna said: So Larry seems good.

He's really stellar, Hanna. He's…. Let me ask you a question. Have you ever had a man—a really good looking man, help you undress, bathe you? I mean, as an adult.

Hanna giggled. She didn't want to, but couldn't stop herself.

And this hypothetical guy, he's not gay. He doesn't want to jump you. Or if he does, he has such self-control that it, like, never comes up, so to speak.

So to speak.

Stop that, you silly girl. It's just that that's the kind of guy Larry is.

Do you? Hanna said. Want to jump him?

No. What I want to do is jump Michael again, you know? I want to hear his voice. I want to hear him talking about something and he sounds like he's speaking geek, but also being kind and asking if he's boring me.

Ellen was crying again.

Maybe, I don't know, sometime there might be a chance with that. With him. But it's such a stupid trope, you know? People falling for their doctors or bodyguards. But he's wonderful.

And he's gorgeous—and single, Hanna offered.

And he doesn't seem to mind a one-footed woman.

Ellen. Don't do that.

It's what it is, Ellen said. It's kind of um, like, a, you know, significant cosmetic problem.

So what's the next stage? Hanna was careful not to say 'step.'

Surgery in a couple of days. That should be the last one. And then Larry and I are going to do ballroom dancing.

So are you feeling good about it?

Totally. I'm, um, like. Stoked. I'm stoked.

Do you think Larry—? Hanna started.

Ellen sucked in air. Maybe. I guess. I don't know. Dad went back to Iowa and Mom's still here, and things are busy, you know? I try not to think about it. Larry makes me....

What?

I was going to say happy. The word kind of surprised me.

I'm glad, Hanna said. I'm really glad.

TAI CHI

They had established a routine quickly. It was comfortable living with Larry. Each night he helped her get ready for bed, get in bed, then soundlessly padded out of the room, down the stairs, out of the house and to the pool house.

In the mornings, he woke her early. He brought her coffee and gave her a light shake of the shoulder.

Often, she would be dreaming of Michael. She would be dreaming that she had two feet. They would be talking, Ellen and Michael. She would blink, and he would be gone. She'd try to go find him, but trip and be unable to get up.

I've fallen and I can't reach my foot.

She came downstairs on crutches, and Larry was in the yard, doing tai chi, his balletic movements hypnotic. She would pour another cup of coffee and watch as he crouched and spun and stopped, frozen as granite.

He was good, too, in that if she happened to be crumpled somewhere and sobbing, he always seemed to know if it was a good idea just to leave her alone, or to see if she wanted to talk.

GO TOWARD THE LIGHT

Sometimes it went over and over in her head, the six odd weeks that she knew Michael, that she had lived another life.

And every time this unwanted movie played in her head, part miraculous enchantment, part utter horror, she pushed it away. It was easier to watch TV, to read crappy airport-type novels, to take an extra pain pill and have a couple of glasses of wine. To put herself in a state where nothing at all mattered.

She thought of her newest friends, Hanna and Soraya, chosen not *by* her but *for* her, it seemed, as if they were sisters, by default, and it seemed to her that they were her actual best friends. And after a couple of glasses of wine (which were not recommended), after Larry had retired for the day to do whatever inscrutable things he did in the pool house, she picked up the phone and dialed Soraya or Hanna's number.

It rang twice, three times, then a fourth, and she prepared herself to leave a voice-mail, but Soraya picked up.

Ouellette, she said. Two simple syllables. We. Let.

Wassup, girl? Ellen said, the wine or the pain pills perhaps slightly slurring her fearless voice.

Hey, darling, Soraya said, her voice instantly softening. How are you?

They had talked countless times between her airlift to Virginia and now, but each time it had a sensation that it was both the first and last time they would, or could, speak. I'm hanging in there, Ellen said, then added, Wherever *there* is. How are you?

I'm okay. We're okay. Things are a little strange here.

Soraya didn't offer to elaborate, but she didn't really need to. Losing Michael had no doubt deeply screwed up her research. *Her own grief had blocked any emptiness but her own.* This was not something that had occurred to her before, and suddenly she could see the gap that his death had left.

Adam is finishing up his book.

So if he gets it published, he won't perish?

Soraya laughed ruefully. Something like that. You'll have to ask him, but he said that you had helped him with it somehow. Something about about fictional personae—um, the distance from the real thing that literature or art represents, and the second and third layers or levels of remove that you get in representing the represented.

Oh, I remember that conversation. I told him about how weird it felt when people would think I was my character—not just Gina, but the Ellen Gregory in my act—the character that's in the media. The person who is the character who is the character and the sense of not knowing the real you.

How's your houseboy?

Don't say that. It's bad karma. He's astounding. Who ever thought there would be so many ways to create pain? No, it's just, just, well. I graduated this week. I not only get to go to bed on my own, I have to.

Does he, like, assist...

Yeah, he has to help me in the bath. It was kind of weird at first. I mean I have to keep my leg elevated. I actually got into the bathtub in my underwear the first time. I mean, I was thinking, Do I wrap myself in a towel? Do I just get completely naked in front of him? Mind you, getting undressed is not the easiest thing in the world.

Soraya giggled.

I mean, I was so uptight, and so I'm sitting there, and I'm supposed to be undressing, and I say, OK, I'm ready, and he comes in, and I'm sitting there in a bra and panties, and he comes in, and really patiently, he says, I appreciate your modesty—which I didn't even know I had—but I hope you can trust me. And I'm like, okay, a few months ago some psycho guy breaks into my house and tries to kill me. Now, I'm sort of living with this other completely non-psycho guy, and I no longer have a left foot, and I'm in pain all the time, and suddenly we both just start laughing. I mean I was the one who started first.

Soraya laughed.

And then I started thinking, Maybe I'm not sexy at all anymore. And I started obsessing about that for a while. I mean, who would want a woman without a foot?

There was a silence, and then Soraya said, I really miss you.

I miss you, too.

Ellen felt herself choking up and desperately needed to change the subject.

You should have seen it, she said, when he helped to color my hair.

What have you done with your hair?

It's back to an unnatural natural blond. The roots were beginning to show. And it's growing out. It's all dried out and screwed up. I'm kind of going for the Joan Rivers with her finger in a light socket look. Have you done anything with your hair?

No, Soraya said. Adam would never hear of it. I think he has a hair fetish.

Anyone would have a hair fetish about your hair. *I* have a fetish about your hair.

There was a silence and suddenly Ellen could hear every inch of distance between LA and Iowa. And after a moment that seemed to blow new life into the smoldering embers of pain, she said: Are you still doing your, like, brain stuff? Research?

Yeah. Hanna and I—we're playing around. Trying to get our footing again. Soraya said this slowly, almost achingly so, almost as though trying to convince herself. *Trying to get our footing.*

She went on: We've been…, well, you know, technical stuff.

Technical stuff, Ellen repeated mechanically, her head feeling prismatically split. Mental eyes on more than one prize.

Can you? I mean, is it possible? To go on?

Well, you go on, said Soraya's disembodied voice. Maybe not like you would have, and maybe not very well all the time. But. You go on.

But where to?

I don't know. You walk toward the light, Ellen. She laughed. It's my fundamental belief that life is about hope. You go just because you have to go. You have to believe that there is some better thing, that there is, somewhere, some kind of hope. Else, why not just slit your wrists?

I've been wondering that.

Soraya laughed, hoarse, confiding. We're making some progress. Seeing some things.

I was thinking, Ellen said, What do you think, what would you think, I mean, do you think Michael's mother would mind if I called her?

She's a sweet lady. She's where Michael got his temperament. I don't think she'd mind at all.

Do you miss him, Soraya?

Why wouldn't I? God. Why wouldn't anyone who knew him?

Ellen only smiled, tears coming to her eyes. Sometimes, she started to say, and then, I don't know.

What?

Sometimes I see him. It's weird. Sometimes I wake up and he's sitting in my room. Sometimes I'll be somewhere and I'll see him. It's not like those out-of-the-corner-of-your-eye things, not a trick of the light. One time I saw him, Larry and I were out. And he was there. I know he was. I watched him and then he just disappeared. I was looking straight at him and he just disappeared.

There was a silence. It was like the line was dead, so Ellen said, Soraya? You still there?

Yeah, she said. I'm here.

So is that like, medically, is that grief?

Could be, Soraya said after a long time. It could be.

Later, after she had clicked off, Ellen remembered very little, except that whatever it was that Soraya said—from not only a doctor's but a friend's perspective—seemed to act like a cushion, some great soft thing between her and the tiny emotional room in which she had placed herself. Hope. Go toward the light.

Then later, half asleep, the television going, she heard Soraya's voice again, almost as if it were in the room with her—or in her head—*We're making some progress. Seeing some things.* There was something there that she hadn't heard before, and now it was here. We're making some progress. Seeing some things.

What did that mean? Were they messing with the Black Box? But then she was lost in sleep.

HEN PARTY

It was midsummer when Soraya and Hanna came to visit. Ellen was giddy for days before their arrival, and although she'd seen a million people, and had about seventeen million flowers to show for the visits, she was excruciatingly lonely without her two newest friends. The way that Larry put it—this longing to see them—was that they had been through something unusual together and it gave them an exclusive bond.

Whatever.

Ellen just wanted to see them.

The landscape was brown except for the garden oases that got regular water. There were rattlesnakes, and in the daytime, the air buzzed with insects, the incessant soughing of breezes in dried grass. There were coyotes, and at night you could hear the distant—and not so distant—howling. At night the sprinklers came on.

At the airport, on crutches, oblivious to everything else, Ellen was overcome with emotion when saw the two of them as they emerged through security.

Soraya was as gorgeous as always. And Hanna just seemed to glow.

There were gawkers, people pointing their cell phones at her [Ellen Gregory and her pet stump, on crutches!], cameras whipped from luggage and purses, but she didn't pay any attention. She just dug in her crutches and dashed toward them, the three of them squealing and giggling, then threw herself into the crush of their arms.

She was sobbing, and when she realized it, she buried her face in Soraya's hair and said, I am leaving this airport with my head under your hair.

Soraya laughed. You're a blonde again.

Larry, for his part, responded as he often did, with little more than a raised eyebrow and a vague smile. He stood back near the airport security gate and watched as Ellen charged toward Soraya and Hanna. He had met perhaps dozens of her friends, but this was the first time he had seen her so completely electric about anyone or anything. There were hugs and kisses and squeals and he turned away. It made him think of his daughter, of long ago when her friends were over, and how he felt that he had entered a not entirely disagreeable alien land.

When she introduced them, Hanna shook his hand, the model of politeness and reserve. Soraya extended her hand, but when she did it, it was to place it flat on his sternum and look him in the eye, a stern, serious appraisal. She saw. And then, quite inexplicably, she hugged him, and there was hair in his face, the scent of her, the soft mash of her body. It made him a little weak, the instant sense that she knew something that he had never exactly verbalized to himself. She saw the way he looked at Ellen. She saw the way he guarded her. So at least there was a part of it that was out in the open and he didn't feel so alone any more.

When he drove them home, the three women sat in the back seat, Ellen in the middle, and giggled like seventh graders at a slumber party. Hair—they had never seen Ellen blond in real life. Ellen joked: Is it better to have jumped the shark or get jumped by a shark? A moment of seriousness, then more giggles.

He might have predicted, from Ellen's descriptions, that Soraya would have an unreasonable amount of luggage, but hers was the smaller bag, and with it, she carried only her purse and a largish laptop case. Hanna's suitcase was a big, plastic tortoise shell affair, an heirloom suitcase you might have gotten from your mother, who last traveled in 1974, or a decent thrift shop. And it was impractically heavy.

Soraya was the kind of woman you could easily imagine picking the miniature bride and groom off the top of your very own wedding cake, licking the icing off, and offending absolutely no one.

Hanna was reserved, catlike, almost, with the taut, agile body of a gymnast, and an air of what he could only think of as Midwestern ingenuousness.

It was late afternoon by the time they got to Ellen's house. She offered to make dinner and did her best to make it sound like a spur-of-the-moment thing, though she had planned it since she'd known they'd be coming. She had cooked for Larry, and she'd cooked for herself, but cooking was a pride spot with Ellen, and she'd never had the chance to do a proper dinner for them.

When they agreed, Larry went out for ingredients.

He was glad to be out of the house. At least for an hour or so. It gave him time to meditate a little, clear all the female hormones from his head and to try to think of what it was that had made him feel that Soraya had seen through him. Yes, he was pretty certain that, under different circumstances, he could have found something romantic with Ellen. Yes, he had developed more than a caretaker's affection for her. But she didn't need a boyfriend. She'd just lost one. She didn't need a lover. All she really needed from him was help to stand on her own two feet—so to speak—at least as soon as she got the other one. Except that, for what seemed like the first time in years, the carapace of his solitude had been cracked. And even if he had had plenty of practice displacing his emotions, thoughts of her often invaded mental spaces that had previously been walled off.

Hanna and Soraya had of course known that Ellen had no shortage of money. But being aware of wealth and experiencing it were about as profoundly different as knowing there was such a thing as the ocean and going sailing. Ellen knew they were awed, but she did her best to ignore it. Middle class Midwestern guilt. When she showed them around her house, showed them where to put their things, Hanna looked slack-jawed, the reality of who her friend was setting in. She looked at the photos of Ellen—movie stills, stills from the set of her TV show and other shows she had been in. Her sitting with Letterman and Leno. Awards. The soaring and weirdly heroic Emmy, which made it seem like she had discovered the cure for something. It was suddenly, for Ellen, somehow embarrassing.

Ellen had been around unreasonable wealth enough to know that it was, most of the time, in fact, unreasonable and completely unjustifiable. She had long understood that there was seldom any rational correlation between work and wealth.

Both of them, Hanna and Soraya, lived ordinary lives, the lives they wanted, and here was Ellen, who had about fifteen fewer years of formal education than either of them, and yet was a multimillionaire beyond a scope that they could ever possibly imagine.

Ellen had become pretty good with crutches, and when the three of them were alone in the house together, she made a big show of whipping around, cornering. Showing off. Gliding down the stairs. Soraya, of course, had to examine her stump, and pronounced the job that her doctors had done not just good but masterful. But it was Hanna who asked about her foot, the new one.

After a while, things got a little quiet and uncomfortable. Sooner or later Michael was going to be the topic of conversation. He could not be avoided forever.

There was an uncomfortable silence as Ellen moved around the kitchen, sipping from a glass of wine that never seemed to get empty.

From both Hanna and Soraya's point of view, however, the uncomfortable silence was more the result of the thing that had not been said. Both of them had seen something that they wanted to share, but were not sure how.

What would you say, said Soraya, finally, running her fingers across the gleaming counters, watching the prismatic display of light within the fused fragments of stone. What would you say....

Hanna said, What she's trying to say, Ellen—

Soraya said: What we're trying to say, Ellen, is that we've seen him. Michael.

Ellen was in the midst of turning back toward them and almost fell off her crutches. What does that mean? she said.

In a low voice, Hanna said: Michael. We've seen Michael.

Ellen looked at them. What the fuck are you talking about? Like, in dreams?

No, said Soraya. In the Black Box.

Suddenly, Ellen was on the verge of hyperventilation. She searched her friends' faces for some hint that this was some kind of weird joke, but there was no indication that they were being anything but completely earnest.

It wasn't that Ellen was in any way coming to terms with grief. It wasn't that she was in any way *whatsoever* learning to live with the loss. It was just that by going forward she, by endlessly plodding along, was at least learning (?!!?) to live with what she had no choice but to live with. At least, in her endless plodding, she was going somewhere.

So what the fuck was this? This—hearing this—was like hitting a brick wall.

This was as unreasonable as a big dark fish. As Wayne Townsend. She wanted to crumple.

Sweetie, I know it's nuts, Hanna started.

He's *dead*, Ellen shouted, anger prickling up all over her.

Hanna and Soraya started to talk at the same time. But Hanna glanced at Soraya and Soraya said: Neither of us is contradicting that. Soraya's eyes were wet as she said this. There's also—well, we thought you might want to see.

I might want to see what? Ellen said.

You might want to see, Soraya said, You might want to—

Hanna took over. Even if it actually seems kind of horrible right this minute, she said, We thought it was only fair to offer you the opportunity to see what we've seen, and then you can make the judgment.

But, Ellen sputtered. But what? But what if I *did* see him? What if I did? Would that *change* anything? She was completely ready to scream. Would that bring him back to life?

Soraya said: Honestly Ellen, I don't know. I mean I think the answer is no. Not in any conventional sense.

Half of Ellen felt utterly outraged, furious, but the other half felt like a door had just opened that she thought had been shut forever.

Soraya shook her head and let her hair fall all around her.

I have about a dozen explanations, or rationalizations. And the honest answer is that I don't know. I've seen what I've seen and..., there's a part of me—

Hanna took over: Call it intuition, she said, tears coming into her eyes. He seems....

Alive. Soraya said. But elsewhere. She spoke as though stating a fact that she deeply objected to but could not disprove.

Ellen laughed. Where, exactly, is he alive? Because if he were alive, wouldn't he be in this room? What are you trying to do? she said, pleading. This is hard enough as it is.

She could feel the tears in her eyes, could feel the wetness on her cheeks.

She saw the look on Hanna's face and there was nothing malicious or hurtful in it.

Sometimes it felt like grief was the defining emotion of her irony-clad generation. Everything, it sometimes seemed, was about grief. About preventing it or avoiding it or pretending it couldn't swim up and bite your fucking foot off.

Then suddenly Ellen knew they were right. The memory rose in her like a wave, and almost blacked her out.

SOME COLD KNIFE

It was at the beach house. Something that never made any real sense, and which she had long ago dismissed. Now it came back to her full force.

It was the second, maybe even their first night there. They had gone to bed and made love and Michael had fallen asleep. Being with him, being away with him made her feel alive and excited. The week had still felt pregnant with possibility. That day she and Hanna and Soraya had gone shopping in the little beach town, and it had been one of those riotously funny days, trying on hats and shirts and giggling, and she had felt funny again, her head agile and elastic. Good lines popping out of nowhere. She had got out of bed—she was not a big sleeper anyway—and gone to the dining room, got out a pad and pen and was jotting down some ideas. So that meant that it had to have been the second night.

And so she was sitting there, talking quietly to herself and writing, when the house phone rang and she picked it up.

She had assumed it was a wrong number. There was no one who could have known she was there, and besides, the only calls you ever got when you were traveling were on cell phones anymore. She only answered it to keep it from ringing and waking Michael.

The voice—male—on the other end said, *Ellen.*

She had no idea what she'd expected, but this was not it: a familiar voice, saying her name. Goose flesh zapped through her and instantly every muscle in her body went tense. *Who is this?* she demanded, thinking Wayne Townsend.

Ellen, he said, and the voice was familiar.

Fuck you, she started to say, but then it hit her.

Michael? she said.

How are you? he said. She could hear in his voice that he was grinning.

Relief flooded through her. She sat back in the chair and twisted a strand of hair with her pen. She said: I'm doing rather well, right this moment. But then I would think you should know that as well as anyone.

He gave a warm laugh. Doesn't hurt to hear it, he said.

Hearing it is good. Tell me something good.

He laughed. I love the sound of your voice. You have such a delicious voice.

She hummed. Delicious. That's a good word.

I'm trying to remember. The lovemaking.

So now you've got Alzheimer's? You don't remember the hot fantastic sex we had, like, ten minutes ago?

He gave that warm laugh again and then there was a long silence. He said, Don't you think there's so much of a person's body in their voice? Your voice has the same deliciousness as your body.

She squirmed a little. You're having an effect on me, she said. I'm coming back to bed, she said.

He hummed. Wake me up. I love you.

She could remember how it felt—hearing the words *I love you*—like everything inside her skin was melting into some sweet goo. She said, I'd prefer it coming face-to-face.

It will, he said.

And when she hung up, she went back into the bedroom expecting to see him sitting up in bed, grinning, her cell phone in his hand. She leaned over him and kissed his whiskery cheek, but he was sound asleep, really asleep, and the lights were off, and she could hear him snoring gently—and unless he was a way better actor than she ever could have expected, he was not faking. She whispered Michael, Michael.

Wake me up.

She knew his voice, and there was absolutely no question it was Michael.

He hadn't roused, and she didn't wake him. She thought at the time that it was just a very clever joke. Probably done electronically. Now, thinking of it, it sent chills through her.

There had been other times, when he had simply appeared. Here, in the house. At the beach, going into one room in shorts and a T-shirt and coming out of another in long pants and a button down shirt—then returning in the same shorts.

And now she was remembering a time just after her kidnapping. She was driving home, and had the nagging sensation she was being followed. The sensation of another person being near. But it wasn't that creepy Wayne Townsend feeling. It was a good feeling. Like someone was there, just out of sight, protecting you.

Right now, though, she wasn't sure anything was real. Sleep or dreams or memory. It all felt completely frangible with grief.

WHAT ISN'T WEIRD?

So, Ellen said, What are you saying? That he's alive in some sort of parallel universe?

Soraya said, Maybe.

Ellen sighed. God. With Michael, I don't know if I should be surprised.

Both Soraya and Hanna smiled, and Ellen felt that she could see the relief going through them.

When we were cleaning out his office, Soraya said, We found a pair of disks.

Hanna stepped in: The disks, I mean, it would appear that he had recorded the both of you. *In* the Black Box. We didn't know he could do that.

Ellen shook her head. Once I asked him if, you know, it might be possible. To preserve a moment. It was one of those really, like, marvelous moments. And I said, like, wouldn't it be great if you could preserve it on the Black Box like a photograph? He said that he was trying.

Soraya sat back and pushed hair out of her face.

The disks we found, everything on them is at the beach. Everything that happens on the disks happens at the beach. But it's weird.

What about any of this *isn't* weird? Ellen laughed.

Weirder, then. In a way, it seems like, almost, like—I don't know, Soraya said.

Like he knew it was going to happen? Hanna said.

Ellen was surprised it was a question.

Soraya ran her hands through her hair and shook her head. Maybe.

When Larry came home with the ingredients for dinner, all three women started at the sound of the door opening, and quickly changed the subject. It had not been spoken, but they were all in agreement that the Black Box was a secret not yet to be shared. When he came into the room, they were talking about Ellen's hair. Soraya and Hanna thought Larry had done a pretty good dye job.

Keep your day job, Ellen said, Australian accent on the 'day.'

Huh? he said, but the women laughed.

299

He came into the kitchen and put the grocery bags onto the counter. Ellen watched him. Weirdly, seeing him felt like the first time she'd ever seen him all over again. He was *so* good looking. His megawatt smile and eyes.

Ellen told you about my hair stylist duties, I take it, Larry said.

They all giggled. It's nice to play with something you don't have yourself, he said. Now they all giggled even harder. He had not intended the double meaning and probably turned red. Soraya's eyes burned on him, but not in a bad way.

When he excused himself to go to the pool house, he beamed at Ellen.

This is such an occasion, he said, I'm going to dress for dinner.

When he was gone, she still had that pleasant sensation of his presence. An entirely benevolent presence. Someone there, just out of sight, watching over you.

LARRY GETS DRESSED

Out in the pool house, Larry found himself fretting, in a completely uncharacteristic way, about what he was going to wear. He showered, shaved his face and head, and then came back to look through his clothing again. Ellen had given him a shirt, a clingy black button-down that he had never worn, except to try it on for her (this was back when she was trying to do her best to keep him, before he made it clear that he didn't need koa floors or new window treatments to stay).

He put on his boxers and sat on the bed and looked at the clothing he had spread out. He tried to think of how he had come to be in this place. The ramble of segues his life had taken. He was not one to regret the decisions he made. His relationship with the world was organic: for all of his adult life, he had done what seemed to need doing. And in every way and in everything, he tried to do the best he could. Even the divorce, which even though it had completely blindsided him—when his wife disappeared with their daughter and he was served with papers, which included a temporary restraining order barring him contact with the child—seemed, in the end, as much his fault as anyone's.

He hadn't seen his ex in years, though his daughter gave him occasional updates. She was prosperous. She had a great practice in Chicago, an apartment that looked onto Lake Michigan. Her partner was a lawyer—a corporate litigator—she had lived with for something like 10 years but had somehow forgot to marry. She was working on a self-help book. He had no idea at all what life would have been like if he had—as she had wished—taken the same tack that she had, started a clinical practice and given up the ideal of 'making a difference' (as she put it; always with air quotes), something he had honestly tried but for which his eternal spiritual restlessness could make no room.

He put on the black shirt and stood in front of the mirror (something he usually only did the way you glance at the speedometer), and was surprised by the look of it. He rarely wore black clothing, and never black shirts, but he was impressed with how he looked, how, perhaps, she had envisioned him.

301

DINNER

Ellen seared scallops in olive oil with shallots. The thing with scallops was that you had to have them just right, and her fifteen-thousand-BTU restaurant-grade cook top was the kind of implement you needed to get them right. Browned. Golden. She removed the scallops and deglazed the pan with champagne, added a little chicken broth, a little lemon zest, herbs, cream and more champagne, then cooked it down slowly. It had to have a tang, the sauce.

She steamed *haricots vert* that Larry had got at the market.

When he came in, she stopped and gaped. Oh. My. God. Will you look at this man? Ellen said.

Larry could feel Soraya looking at him. He wondered what, if anything, Ellen had said about him.

I think that's the first time I've seen you blush, Ellen said.

They had met him in the hospital, after the funeral, but neither Hanna nor Soraya had paid very much attention to anything but Ellen. The world, at that point, had been off its axis, and it took everything to focus on the moment.

Larry watched her cook as he sat with Soraya and Hanna. He sipped iced green tea while they drank white wine. He noticed that Hanna had a stern appearance when she wasn't smiling. When she smiled, it did something to her whole mien. Softened her. Gave her an aspect of vulnerability or unguardedness.

It struck him the power of what Ellen did. The comedy, not the cooking. Not that this was something he hadn't ever noticed, but when Ellen turned from the stove and made a comment that cracked Hanna and Soraya up, he saw what kind of insane charisma, what kind of power she had, the way she could light other people up, and it opened a window for him onto how much there was to her that he had never seen.

Ellen cooked and chatted and every time anyone offered to help, she refused, told them to sit, damn it, and he watched her, amused and impressed with how she had assimilated her crutches into her movements. How natural they had become in such a short time.

This—Ellen cooking—was something he had not seen, and it mesmerized him, the shape of her, the concentrated expression, the lithe movement, the way she grabbed a crutch and swung over to the fridge, then back again, made a wisecrack or comment, and kept going. The gorgeous concentration of Ellen at the stove, handling the skillet like a kitchen pro. He was mesmerized. Did it show?

So Ellen tells us you're from the Midwest, too?

Illinois, he said. I grew up in a small town. I left, then I went to the university, met my ex-wife, had a kid, got divorced. Left again. Came back.

Soraya watched him. Hanna watched Soraya.

Ellen also tells me you're a doctor, Soraya said.

Larry looked at her in something like surprise. Acupuncture, he said.

It's a fascinating science, Soraya said. Maybe she was a little drunk.

She wore a light, low-cut sweater that showed ample cleavage. She poured the Viognier that Ellen had instructed him to buy—a little in Hanna's glass, a little in hers, then gestured toward him with a vague wave of the bottle's neck.

He shook his head.

So what are your intentions? She whisper-growled this, leaning toward him so that Ellen couldn't hear.

Larry raised his eyebrows and grinned. He was surprised at this, but didn't show it. She sounded like the mother of a high school girl quizzing her daughter's date.

Hanna jumped in. Don't listen to her. She thinks she's everybody's mother.

They both were clearly a little tipsy: wine on an empty stomach.

Did anyone ever tell you you could be very nosy? he said.

Soraya let out a hoot of a laugh. She had been sipping her wine and rushed a napkin to her mouth to keep from spitting it onto the table.

Hanna laughed, too. Just, like, *every*one, Hanna said.

Ellen turned. What's going on over there?

They all laughed.

When Ellen and Larry brought dinner to the table and sat down, Soraya raised her glass and said, To Michael, who brought us all here, together.

This surprised Ellen a little, but she raised her glass, touched glasses with everyone. Her eyes burned.

HOME MOVIES

Larry put the video in and turned down the lights. It was a tape that Marty had made of Ellen years ago, so long ago it hardly seemed possible that this artifact could still exist. They all settled into their seats. Hanna and Soraya were on either side of Ellen. Larry was next to the video machine.

The lighting was poor, and in the muddy graininess of the video, you could make out a jumble of people, tables, and then a thing that soon became apparent was a stage, although it wasn't much of a stage. Just a riser. And then the blond girl batted her way from behind a curtain. Her hair was shoulder-length, and she wore a tutu, *the* tutu.

For Hanna it was a strange sight. She had of course heard about the tutu, had imagined it, but the reality was so weird. And the weirdness came from the energy. The way that Ellen—this long-ago Ellen—bounded out, moving like a tennis player ready for the first serve. She had watched Ellen's HBO video, and it was much more polished. In the HBO video, people were (it seemed) sober and primed. This had a broad, raw edge. It was a battle. Here they were drunk and wired. In the HBO video, there were no hecklers. Here, everyone seemed a prospective heckler.

And so there she was, the lights on her and the tutu was a combination of pink and black. She introduced herself. There was some clapping, but the audience, such as it was, mostly seemed to ignore her.

She wandered around on the stage a little—a little wandering was all that was possible—and looked up, started talking in a low voice, mimicking the conversation, and doing it really well, doing half a dozen voices at once. The audience was noisy as hell. She brought the volume up slowly. People were chattering, but starting to take notice. The audio picked up bits of conversation—a gaggle of girls talking about a wedding—*she said she was a size ten, but she was a twelve at a minimum, and sixteen was more likely, and so—* And then Ellen said in a male-sounding voice, Shut the fuck up.

There was a bit of quietening, but not much.

No, seriously. *Shut the fuck up.*

Someone shouted—a man—Fuck you.

Hmmm, Ellen said, and found the source of the voice. A light followed her. Lit up the guy. He was pretty wasted, had that drunk look of puffy eyes and a belligerent, pallid expression. Hmmm, she said again, coolly appraising him. Nope. Not much of a chance of that.

This got a couple of laughs and quieted people further.

And then she did a weird, electrifying voice that sounded like a computer talking. In that voice, she said, *You know why I've summoned you here.*

This seemed to stun people. Just the weird incongruity of it.

She did some patter—turned and thrust out her butt, said, Does this tutu make my ass look fat?

Good laughs.

So I went to the theater the other day. It was a low-budget production of this play, The Vagina Monologues. Have you heard of it?

Ellen watched this old version of herself, the pre-ELLEN! version, and the sense of loss that she had felt before, the sense of disconnection, was gone. The thing she felt now was something akin to pride. Affection for the girl up there, battling it out.

It was all downhill, after the rocky opening. She could hear her friends laughing, could feel the movement of Soraya and Hanna next to her, and as it played, she felt as though she were expanding, filling with air. Floating.

MICHAEL, AGAIN

Soraya helped Ellen put on the headset and when it was wrapped around her head, Ellen descended into familiar darkness and waited.

Hanna held her hand. It's going to be okay, sweetie, she said. If you see him, you'll know what to do.

Here we go, Soraya said. And then there was that rhythmic jumble of light and the strange, 3-D humming in her ears as the machine greeted her brain once again. And then she broke through.

Suddenly she was in the Hy-Vee in Iowa City, walking down the cereal aisle, feeling sort of dazed, and she looked down and saw her foot—still attached as it had been months ago. A thrill went through her about what was to come. She had a sense of déjà vu—not about what she knew was going to happen, but about this situation, being hooked up, being back in time—but she couldn't have said why. Of course, she'd been in the Hy-Vee in Iowa City hundreds of times, perhaps thousands. She thought to reach up and touch her hair. Again she had that thrill. Her hair was cut short and spiky and as best she could see from her peripheral vision, it was dyed black. She walked around the corner of the aisle and a young man, pimply faced in a shirt and necktie that didn't fit very well said, Are you finding everything you need?

The thought went through Ellen that he recognized her, then she just dismissed it. She'd been in New York and LA too long.

Her foot was there.

Yes..., actually, can you point me to the coffee?

The young man brightened. Next aisle over, he said, Just a third of the way down on the left.

Thanks, she said.

Later, with a bag of fresh coffee beans in her basket, she turned the corner and headed toward the produce aisle. It was there, standing in a daze, that she saw him, Michael, a man she had never seen before but recognized instantly. He was slender, angular, and she was seeing him with new eyes. He had curly hair that was dark and unruly. He pushed a cart and seemed completely lost. He reached up a hand and ran it through his hair and turned, and he turned with a look of something like frustration on his face. When he saw her he gave no hint of recognition, but approached her. They were near the produce.

There was a sweet thrill to this, in knowing him but not knowing him, but there was also a kind of sickness she felt in her heart, too. What world was this? Was this a dream? Where was everything that happened between them—had that not yet happened here? Except the more she was in this moment, the more the current moment took over. Gradually, but rather more quickly than before, she lost the sensation of being two places at once. She couldn't say later when exactly it was that it happened, but it was like slipping into another version of herself. She had become her own self again.

He said, Hi, I'm sorry, I hope you, oh this is so embarrassing. Do you know which one the broccoli is?

She laughed. She took his arm she took his arm she took his arm and she led him to the part of the refrigerated container where stalks of broccoli were piled up.

He seemed almost unreasonably grateful, but also a little freaked out. Was there recognition in his eyes? Was there something more than gratitude in his eyes?

But she was losing him. The him she knew. She thought she knew him. Whatever it had been in her mind—what was it? For a moment she felt dizzy and confused.

She stood there in the grocery store looking into Michael Webster's eyes—which by the way were the most uncanny color of green she had ever seen—and how did she know his name?

She could feel the weight of the last several days on her shoulders, Marty at her parents' house, but here she was just enjoying a moment, and all of that crap, LA, was just disappearing.

Was that a pickup line? she said.

No. No. He looked aghast. Was what?

Broccoli.

God, no. He laughed. God, that would be, like, the worst—

The worst pickup line in the history of pickup lines. They laughed together.

Hey, he said, Do you want to maybe, I mean, my friends are having a dinner party, and they invited me, you might say, too, um, to do some shopping. Maybe you'd like, you know, to come?

The dinner party? she said. Or shopping?

Yeah, he said.

She laughed. It wasn't a yes or no question.

Oh, the dinner. The dinner. Do you want to come?

These friends of yours, she said, What are they like?

Pretty much your garden-variety, you know, well..., you know, oh well, they're pretty much geeks, like me.

You're a geek? she said.

Yeah. Card-carrying.

She said: I think I'd like that. I think I'd like that a lot.

Are you doing anything now? he said.

Grocery shopping.

She couldn't believe she couldn't have thought of anything more clever to say. She was, after all, a professional.

So after the *grocery shopping*, he said. You think you'd maybe want to go, like, to the Cottage, and get a cup of coffee?

I'd love it, she said.

He had the most joyful expression in his eyes when she said this. His whole being—which was frankly a bit sallow, as though he avoided the sun prodigiously—lit up.

Having her foot seemed so natural—and why wouldn't it?—that she hardly noticed it. It felt as though she were walking on air.

When they went outside, she did nothing except follow what she had already done. She wasn't sure, in fact, that she had done anything else the entire time she'd been inside the trip. But it all felt different, it all felt so much more charged.

Soraya brought Ellen out of the trip, Ellen sat blankly, utterly dazed.

So what happened? Soraya said.

Ellen shook her head. Gasped for air. She was completely disoriented.

Finally, after a long time, after a time in which it seemed that she returned to herself, Ellen said, I met Michael all over again.

Soraya smiled and sighed.

Ellen said: I had my foot back. It was just, like, there. I was walking.

Soraya sipped from her wine glass silently.

I want to do it again, Ellen said.

ESPERANTO

Careful, Ellen said, you'll get peanut butter on your head.

Almond butter, Larry said. It's good. You should try it. Shave your head and rub it with almond butter—it has to crunchy—and organic cherry jam. It will blow you away.

Hey, I'm the funny one. You're the dour Germanic woman in white who orders me to put on my prosthetic foot and keeps detailed notes of my bowel habits.

Speaking of which.

Very funny. I wanted to tell you about Michael.

Hanna and Soraya had gone and the house felt empty without them. But she could feel the presence of Michael from the Black Box.

Tell me about Michael, then.

She looked at him appraisingly, biting her lip. Even though she found these Thos. Moser barstools to be incredibly comfortable, she could never be comfortable on any stool without her left foot. She grabbed her crutches and pulled one close for balance.

What do you want to know?

Whatever you want to tell.

She shook her head. It was so short. There was so much compacted into a small space of time. I don't know.

You said you were in love with him. Why?

She laughed. Why? That is the weirdest question I've ever heard.

She shook her head, brushed hair out of her face.

When I met him it was like I was the only one in the world who spoke Esperanto, and everyone else spoke some different language, and suddenly there was this other person who spoke Esperanto. Bang.

Bang.

Bang, she said softly. She had tears in her eyes.

So picture this. I'm at my parents' house, she said, and I haven't been there in years and I still feel completely like a seventeen-year-old, and they are being incredibly sweet and kind and so Michael comes over to dinner. Mind you, I have never done this. I had one psychotic fling with a guy I thought was a college student when I was in high school, and he turned out to be a professor. So he was not exactly the kind of guy I could bring home. I had been in movies. I had been on television for years, and I had never brought a guy home to my parents' house. Which is really weird and sad if you think about it.

Larry wagged his head a little and chewed. Ellen, in the time she had known him, had watched Larry do this—mincing little bites that he chewed for like for*ever* and then was indefatigably silent, which sometimes made conversation incredibly one-sided and painstaking.

Well, I met him, and suddenly I went from being a nervous wreck to being someone who might actually have a life.

Larry nodded.

The phone rang and Ellen looked at it, but did not touch it.

And my dad, bless him, had missed so much of my life, and suddenly I'm middle-aged. And here I've fucked half of Hollywood—

Which half? he said. He rubbed his eyes, as if trying to come awake.

So anyway, my dad, like, he didn't get to screen anyone. He didn't get to have those awkward conversations in the living room, you know, about plans and how are you going to take care of my daughter should the day come to pass over my dead body and perhaps the dead body of God as well that you even get to extend a hand much less your penis in the direction of my daughter. And so Michael comes over and my mother goes all out. I mean, it's Sunday dinner on a Tuesday or something. I almost want to cry for watching her try to make something that will impress him, impress me, and that daddy will actually eat. It was a superhuman effort. Michael would have been good with ordering out pizza. I didn't need to eat.

Seriously, the only thing on God's green earth I want to do is jump his bones. And so I take him up to my room and jump him. Not that it wasn't mutual, of course.

And so I tell them he's spending the night—like over my dead body am I not going to make love to him tonight, and I had thought about this over and over and there was not a small amount of anxiety about it, but they're totally cool. My mom says something about getting sheets, then corrects herself—towels, and then goes red in embarrassment. But the funny thing was, they were happy. Happy.

Actually, then I jumped him. But whatever. Before dinner, drinking wine, we talk for a bit, have a glass of wine or two, and then sit down to dinner, and Larry, I do not know how I would have made it through that dinner without him. I mean, even though it was kind of all about him.

She stopped. Picked up a crutch from where it leaned and grasped it, stared at the cuff. That was when, talking with him, with them, that it started to come out. Which sort of blew me away.

What came out?

It. They would never have told *me* this stuff. Shared. How much it hurt them, my leaving the way I did. It came out in these little snippets of information.

Her voice quavered here.

There was so much I didn't know. It was at this sweet and peaceful dinner and in the conversation I learned how that when I left, how that when I started up the diabolical $500 car, that my father said, *laughing*, mind you, said he had come out and stood on the lawn as I went down the road.

Larry rubbed his head. He told Michael—and me, but sort of in the abstract— how he had waited a minute or two and got in his own car and followed me, lights out, until I got out of town, then with the lights on until I got safely to the Illinois state line—not this side of the Mississippi but the other side, and then let me go.

How did that make you feel, hearing that?

I was just glad that Michael was there. That we could all sit there and chuckle about what a wacky and zany past we had. I *never* suspected. It hit me in the gut, hearing that. Like I was punched. That hurt, Larry. But at the same time, it was the most wonderful thing.

She wasn't crying, but there were tears in her eyes. My dad, Big Ed Gregory, laughed about it, like, weren't we such *nutty* folks back then. He wasn't going to stop me. He knew there wasn't enough in our little town for me. But he also wanted to make sure I was safe.

She wiped at her eyes. She hated her own sentimentality.

Larry, she said, are you *listening* to me? This is totally for real. Do you know what he did? When I was in New York, he secretly came to see me. I never saw him. I don't remember even possibly thinking, 'That guy looks like my dad,' but he told us how he'd seen me at the Laugh Lounge and Gotham Central and these clubs where I was wondering how the fuck he did it, you know, those clubs were so small, and there got to be a point where I just choked up so bad and went into the living room and sat down and cried. My dad came to see me perform, came and never showed his face, but saw mine. He just wanted to make sure that I was okay. He even talked to Marty now and then. They wanted to give me space.

Marty never told you?

No. I wouldn't've wanted to hear it. I wasn't there yet.

All throughout this last part, her voice had been halting, and now she stopped and sobbed.

And Michael, she started. And Michael, she started again, trying to get her composure.

And Michael, he just watched him, watched me. And chuckled when it was appropriate. And when I got up and left the room, I was just in the living room, sobbing like a fool, and when I got control of myself, I could hear Michael telling them how when he met me, he had no idea who I was, when he thought I was just some interesting looking grad student, well, my father started laughing. I think he endeared himself to my father forever.

And it was my dad that came in the living room and got me, because of course after all of this stuff, my mother was crying, too, but she hid in the kitchen.

And Michael, he didn't just sit there in the dining room. He came in, and after my father had hugged me and said, I love you, my dad got up and said, I'm going to help your mother. And Michael and I were sitting there and he came over and I started apologizing like crazy, because it was like the most amazingly functional dysfunctional thing you could imagine.

Larry looked at her with his megawatt eyes and smile and gave her a moment, then said, You're soaking your crutch. Which she was.

She laughed.

Well, my father fell in love with him. It didn't hurt that he was brilliant as an engineer, and he did a few things around the house—things which I could not even begin to name—that made him the real celebrity in my father's eyes.

She couldn't help the gasping sigh that came, thinking of him.

TIME ANNEALS

L arry woke her. A gentle shake to her shoulder. Hey, Stumpy, time to get up.

Where's my coffee? she said. He usually woke her with coffee. And stop calling me that. Just because Robin does…, she started, but rolled her face into her pillow.

No coffee today. You're NPO. *Nil per os.* Time to wake and shake, he said. Got to get to the church on time.

Do I have to have surgery today?

Never as good a time as the present.

God, she said.

This one is going to be easy, he said, his ultra-wattage smile going. Piece of cake.

I hate this, she protested. Why do I have to go through this?

It is what it is.

Oh, shut up.

This surgery—this was the one that would at last, when it healed, make her leg ready for a prosthesis, a word that made her angry just hearing it.

In the evenings, after dinner, when Larry had gone to the pool house and she was alone, she talked on the phone. She talked to local people, LA people (who mostly wanted to know things she didn't want to say but didn't want to hear what she actually did want to say), but so mainly she talked to Hanna and Soraya, even though she wasn't sure that this was the best thing for getting on with life.

She asked Larry what he thought about it, if talking with Hanna and Soraya was wallowing in the past.

Only, he said, if it actually is.

What do you mean? she said.

I mean, he said, they're friends, correct? To which she nodded, They and you went through a singular moment in your lives together, correct? Why shouldn't you be close? You told me that they were the first people you met after you became famous that didn't know you were famous that you liked—and they liked you—and so, are you wallowing in the past? Or are you making plans, thinking of the future?

313

Future, she said.

Good, he said.

When she came downstairs—on her own, on crutches—her mother was sitting and reading the paper, drinking a cup of coffee. Are you ready, El? she said.

They rode to the hospital together, Ellen and Arlene, with Larry driving. It was early and the traffic was light.

The media had not been alerted to her surgery—this was, after all, a private, Beverly Hills sort of hospital with high level hush-hush protocols—and they went in unescorted and unmolested.

When she woke from the anesthesia, she was still in the operating room. It was a weird, dreamy sleep, and she had dreamt that Michael had been in the room with her. They had been having a conversation, but he disappeared. When she finally found him again, he disappeared. It was almost a relief to wake.

A nurse, a sweet-faced woman, asked her how she was doing.

Sleepy, she said, and went back to sleep soon thereafter.

When she woke again, eons could have passed. Larry's cue-ball head had replaced the sweet-faced nurse's. He wore expression No. 3, 12,000 watts. She thought she remembered kissing him, the way he had kissed her back. That wasn't a dream. Or was it? So much that she had been through recently was like that. Things, people, places—they were here, and then they were gone.

She reached up and touched his face. I love you, she said. It was true, in its way. But the anesthesia would wear off and she would forget it. He would forgive her.

And perhaps knowing that this was the case, he said, I love you, Ellen.

She laughed sleepily. Did you ever think about calling yourself Mr. Melon? she said. Because you are as bald as a melon.

And then she was asleep again. She dreamt she lay in a bathtub, warm water soaking her, both feet on the rim of an old, claw-footed tub. One of those gorgeous, old style Manhattan bathrooms. There were her boobs, her nipples doing nip-ups in the water. There were her feet, feet, feet, and she was waiting.

314

MAJOR THIRD

Can I ask you a question? she said to Larry. She was still in recovery, groggy from the anesthesia. The doctor had told her that she would remember nothing, and she was still having a hard time filing anything away.

He smiled, fully electric. That's a curious question, he said gently, because you *are* asking a question.

Stop it, melon-head. I'm on drugs.

(More wattage.)

Remember that night we first met?

Sure, he said. Do *you*? He was sitting next to her bed. Somehow she had found his hand and she was clutching it in her own, and pressing it against her belly. She noticed this because it seemed to be outside of her volition, but it made her happy just the same. If he noticed, he didn't seem much to mind.

What did you think of me?

He gave a laugh. You were very drunk. You were in a hallway wearing only khaki slacks, if I recall, and a brassiere. And your hand was bleeding.

Brassiere. My mother is the only person who says that.

It's a perfectly good word.

But what did you think of me.

I thought you needed help.

That's all?

I thought you needed a bandage.

Larry.

He gave a sigh that was not quite exasperation.

If you want me to say, Ellen, I thought you were beautiful, then fine. I did, actually.

Why can't you say things like that without me asking?

Interesting, he said, exactly like Mr. Spock.

Was I really awful?

I guess I don't know exactly what you mean. You were awfully drunk.

315

God, I wish I could get into your head and know what you're really thinking.

Later, in her room—a really nice room that didn't look at all like a hospital room, with maple floors and cabinets—she did not remember the conversation.

She slept for a bit. The doctor came by and asked how she was doing, and checked her bandages, studied her chart. Larry sat in a comfy armchair and read a magazine. The doctor ignored Larry, mostly, and Ellen thought of what he had said, that in some countries he was considered a doctor.

The doctor said they were going to keep her for about two days, just to make sure everything was on the right track, and then she could expect a few weeks of recovery before she could start with a prosthesis.

When he was gone, she cried. This part of it was over. The only thing that stood (so to speak) between her and her *new life!* was a little bit of healing and a fake foot.

Larry sat on the side of the bed and wiped the tears off her face with a hank of sheet.

She sniffled back tears. I know, she said, You don't have to say it. It is what it is.

She took his face in her hands and pulled him close to her.

When I heal up, will you, I mean, would you want, like, to make love?

With you? he said.

Yes. With me.

He didn't say anything. He just looked at her. His skin was warm against her fingers, his cheeks were vaguely whiskery. His eyes were clear and he just looked at her.

You don't have to love me, she said, hurrying, letting her hands drop. I just need, you know. Some kind of, like, closeness.

Ellen, he said, and ran his hand through her hair. Then, catlike, he crawled into the bed with her—cautious of her leg—and held her.

Does that mean you will? she said.

He looked at her seriously. Are you frightened that you might not be attractive?

What girl would? I mean, it's not like I'm actually *disfigured* or anything, right? Is that it?

You stupid fuck, she said, and pushed at his head. I can't believe you'd say that. So far, in this world, you seem like the only person who *doesn't* want to have sex with me. And I didn't say, have sex. I said make love. There's a difference.

He didn't say anything, but lay on his side, one arm around her shoulders, the other over her middle, where her ribs dropped off toward her belly. He didn't move, but just held her and, after a while, she fell asleep like that.

Back at home, he said nothing about it, just assumed their normal routine. Arlene went back to Iowa, and the stump slowly started to heal.

She said nothing about it, either, wondering if he really didn't find her attractive, if she had wrecked their friendship (which it didn't *seem* she had) by bringing it up. She wondered if he would ever hold her like that again. She wondered how it would be, to be naked like this.

One day he was in her room, changing her bandage, and she said, pretty much out of the blue, When did you decide to shave your head? I mean, what made you do it?

Larry laughed. It was a miraculous grin that he gave, all gleaming with white teeth and his bald pate and bright eyes.

He kept a Cheshire grin for a long time, but then it slowly faded into a kind of sadness. But he said nothing.

No. Really, she said. Why? When?

It was sort of an accident, he said.

An accident?

Odd sounding, I know, but if not an accident, a matter of a kind of fate.

She propped herself up on an elbow and looked at him. So?

I don't know that I'm at liberty to say.

Don't bullshit a bullshitter, she said.

Now he narrowed his gaze on her and examined her (it seemed) for a long time. She could feel his gaze the way she felt his fingers, his hands: she knew his touch but it was such an evanescent thing.

It's the story of how I became a physical therapist, he said. You don't want to know.

But I do.

She sat up and brushed her hand across his pate and was surprised at the very slight stubble of it. She had expected something else, a smoothness that mimicked his own streamlined slippage through the world.

He laughed again, but this time it was a quiet thing, more like musing than a real laugh.

He said: There was a woman.

And then he told her a story about his father, with whom he was not close. How he and the old man ended up in the same town, outside of Chicago. How he worked at that time at a jail, doing psych evals on intake, and then in the evenings after work, would go to see his father, who was dying of lung cancer in a nursing home. The man in the room next door had early-onset Alzheimer's, and he would have bouts of madness that could be very violent. And Larry, because of his studies, his work, had become pretty good at calming people who were out of their minds.

Let's just say I'd seen far worse, he said.

And there came a time, Larry went on, when these outbursts were of a shall we say masturbatory nature. He was a big man, my father's neighbor. Tall and big, probably—when he was at fighting weight—something like 250 or so, and six-three, six-five. He was priapic, if you know what that means, which, if not, means at least in his case something like Viagra forever.

And when he got into these masturbatory fits, it terrified the mostly unflappable nursing staff, who were otherwise wonderful. It was just that he was so big.

I knew enough from working in a jail that I could help bring him down. And I would if things got violent. I would talk him through it. I would go in the room with him, while this massive man was jerking himself off—which was no mean feat for him. And he would say the name Mona over and over again.

This was of course a phase. Early-onset Alzheimer's is a relatively fast moving disease, you know, so I read a bit about it and knew that this was just a part of his brain betraying him. And then one day—this had been a couple of weeks after this part of his disease started—one day, a woman showed up.

She was the pearl of beauty, this woman. Utterly spectacular. Like Jean Harlow in her day. A platinum blonde. She almost looked more like she had been extruded from some previously unknown miracle substance than like she came into the world the customary way. And in that place, with the crowds of withered old flesh sitting around in wheelchairs, in various states of infirmity, the smell of urine and age—in that place, she.... Well, you might as well have put a halo on her and shown a golden light. She was the picture of feminine promise, of radiant sexual health. And in her, you could see something like hope. I could. In the face of death—

He asked if she wanted him to go on.

Ellen had never heard Larry talk this way. He always had a kind of animation, always had the aura of joy if not the actual outward expression of it, but this was different. Where in other musings he was almost entirely philosophical, here he had a wistful dreaminess to him that was just a little unsettling.

In the time she had known him, he had never said anything that she would even vaguely have considered sexually suggestive. In any way.

He said, As an aside, there was—ironically, perhaps—an antiques store on the ground floor of the nursing home. I used to go in there and cruise the antiques before I went to see him, and one day this woman appeared in the store. We talked—I think. I can't exactly recall.

Ellen felt something happening to her as he talked. She wasn't entirely sure what it was, but it was a core sort of thing, something that starts in the most basic parts of the brain and body. Something that made her skin more acutely aware of the fabric against it, the air moving over it. She was rapt.

Later that evening when I was in my father's room, I ducked out for a moment, just for air, and there she was, talking to the head nurse. She was my father's priapic neighbor's daughter. It elides a good deal to say that one night I asked her out to dinner. This antiques shop, one of the curious things about it was that the man who owned it, a sort of very old but also an ageless fellow, had a fascination with old shaving gear. He had this one straight razor that was like a samurai sword. I have no idea where it came from except my guess was that it was a World War II souvenir. It had the most incredible steel, what's often called water steel because of the texture of the grain of the metal. But it was clearly intended to be a razor. In any case, she flirted with me when I was in the shop and sort of bullied me—in that nice way that women sometimes have—into buying it. I bought it and I bought an old shaving brush and cup.

Ellen could not take her eyes off him.

So we went out to dinner, and she made the suggestion that the only reason I bought it was because I secretly wanted to shave my head. As I had never thought of it until she mentioned it, I disagreed, but it was an interesting proposition. I was going bald. She had told me before that I would look better with a shaved head, and so this was sort of full circle.

She was a business widow. She was married, but her husband was mostly gone on business. She was reasonably certain that he had affairs in other towns, or at least prostitutes. And he was older than she was. She had come to town by herself and was staying in the hotel where we had dinner. A good hotel. One of those with people around all the time to be tipped for one service or another.

After dinner, I walked her up to her room. She said, You really should *save* your head. She misspoke, she meant to say 'shave' but it came out wrong.

He sat and looked off into the distance, out toward the garden, and fingering his chin idly, musing. He said—now looking back at Ellen, This was after my divorce. This was when my ex-wife was still living in the Midwest and I saw my daughter on weekends, and she was mostly the only social life I had.

When I was reluctant, she said, I'll do it for you.

What did you do?

I laughed.

Why?

I don't know. I had been alone for a few years and I had never found anyone whom I found particularly attractive.

And you found her attractive.

I should say.

Ellen lay on the floor next to him, looking up at him, marveling.

Am I boring you?

No, Ellen said, no. Not at all.

We went into her room and she left me for a moment to change, and when she returned, she wore one of those hotel bathrobes and carried towels. She wet one of them and then heated it—the room was a suite and had a small kitchen with a microwave—and she wrapped my head in it. I felt like I'd been drugged. And there was always the possibility that she had drugged me. Or that it was just the wine, the meal, the heat of the towel. She lathered up my head, took off my shirt and wrapped the towel around my neck, like a barber. And I will add here, because we are all adults, that her bathrobe was falling open—I imagine purposely—and I was not above looking.

Ellen laughed. I imagine not, she said. Listening to this story was like some sort of erotic bath.

And so she took out this miniature samurai sword, which the antiques shop owner had honed and stropped and polished, and I remember sitting there, with this siren behind me, and I remember thinking that I was offering a lot of trust to someone I knew very little about. She could have as easily slit my throat as she could have shaved my head. Or *saved* it. I closed my eyes, and she drew the thing across my scalp, scraping gently, and when it was through, she washed my head. Then she found a mirror and stood and held it up so I could see myself. I ran my hands over my scalp and it was the strangest feeling. Not just that it was so perfect, but the whole odd way it had come about.

Wow, Ellen said. Who'd'a thunk it?

I imagine you've guessed that the evening had a rather electric erotic charge.

Ellen laughed, and she thought of Michael and how charged being with him was, how different and yet the same it was for each of them.

I can guess what happened next. You were Samson in reverse.

Larry smiled. Something like that.

When I left her hotel room the next morning, I was curious. I wanted to know who this Mona was that her father had moaned about. I had ideas, because if her mother looked anything like her, well, he said and trailed off.

So who was Mona?

An old family dog.

Ellen almost choked with laughter. And then she laughed so hard she did choke, and when she got control of herself, she slapped him, said, You made that whole fucking thing up just for that punch line, didn't you?

Not all of it, he said.

She laughed again. It felt good. She felt like it had been years since she laughed. She slapped him again, and then grabbed his head and held it to her in some sort of weird wrestling pose. And when she had held it long enough she let it go and kissed him. She was surprised at herself, this outward and naked sort of thing. But it was what it was. And he did not resist.

He was a good kisser. He was not just a sort of peck-and-goodbye sort of kisser, but a passionate, thoughtful, even artistic kisser.

She stopped for a moment. You wanted me to do that, she said.

I suppose, he said.

And she kissed him again.

Will you carry me to my bedroom and undress me? she said.

He had carried her up the stairs before, and down, and yet this felt different. Simultaneously stronger and gentler. He put her on the bed and she sat, one foot on the floor, her other leg dangling. She took off her shirt and bra and tossed them on the floor. He stood, watching. His gaze made gooseflesh go up all over her.

He crouched and unfastened her pants. She lay on her back and let him pull them off. He undressed. It was late afternoon and the light was good but on the edge of waning and it was so sweet to be naked with him that her lungs felt shallow and her head felt weak.

He said, Here, and moved her so that he could lie next to her. He pressed his body against her, and said, Here, again, so that she was lying on her side, her stump on a pillow. He slipped behind her, his chest against her back, his face against her neck. Now his hands came around her and caressed her breasts, caressed every inch of her shoulders and belly. She could feel his penis, erect, pressed against her, but just closed her eyes and let the feeling of the warmth of his physical presence soak her.

He reached down and moved her a little, and then she could feel his fingers opening her, the astonishing insistence of his penis pressing against her. Now he slipped inside of her with almost excruciating slowness. She wriggled a little, and he was still slipping into her. And then he stopped, fully erect, fully inside, and did not begin to thrust, but just held her like that.

She did not know what she had expected, but it was not for him to lie so still. She started to say something, but he said, Sshh, just wait, and so she did. It was almost unbearably sweet, just the physical sensation of intimacy, but there was also a strange sense of wonder that descended on her. Minutes went by without his moving except to touch her with his hands, gather her hair away from her neck and kiss her spine. Touch the skin of her shoulders, her neck. Her skin had become exquisitely sensitive. She had no idea how he could resist the simple rhythmic urge, but he did, and as minutes continued to go by, she began to feel strange, the emotional equivalent of a piece of music shifting from a minor scale to major, a sadness displaced by triumph.

The movement of air.

Every pore of her body was becoming increasingly aware of everything around her, even as she was focused inward, acutely aware of the heat and pressure of his penis inside her, her own wetness, her own desperate longing for his touch. The blousey miracle of the sheets. His fingers everywhere but where she wanted them. All of this came with an almost particulate depth and nuance.

Do you feel it? he said.

I feel strange, she said, wishing he would just touch her in the customary way.

It's good, he said.

Yes, she said. In actual fact, she was utterly desperate for the brush of his thumb across her nipple, the plunge of his fingers against her clitoris. But he had another agenda.

Both of them spoke slowly and quietly, deliberately. Even the words had that magical nuance. The way they felt in your throat, in your ears. Almost everything he did made her curious, but she did not want to break the spell by asking questions.

Minutes continued to go by, and she shifted a little to get comfortable, and just that little bit of friction sent such a wash of delight through her that she felt dizzy, the pleasure some delicious weight that could knock you off your feet.

As he held her, she listened to his breathing, to the sounds of the house, to her own breathing, and she found herself concentrating on the rhythm of her breathing—something she had tried to do in a meditation class and could never do. She felt her head emptying of thought. There was a network of nerves that sparkled from her vagina to her ribs, and it was there, in some nearly visible nimbus of joy, that her concentration lay.

One of his hands moved to her nipple, and he touched it, took hold of it with the same gentle purpose as a man picking berries. His lips grazed her neck, and then moved to her nipples. She had never been more awake.

She had no idea how long they had been like this when again the emotional chromatic shift began to happen. She could feel herself beginning to come, a strange, spontaneous, external feeling. When it hit her, it was a convulsive wave, and then it hit her again. She had not moved yet she was in the middle of a storm. She let out a wild groan that was almost a scream. She grabbed a bunch of loose sheet and balled it in her fist and shuddered. She shuddered again and jammed the sheet into her own mouth to muffle the next scream. Again the wave went through her. Another scream, purely involuntary. Now Larry held her, wrapped her in his arms, and said, It's okay. Except okay didn't begin to describe it. It was an exorcism.

When the wave began to abate, she could feel—in an almost prehensile way— Larry's own convulsions, and when he ejaculated, she could feel the spasms and the flood, and she could feel it throughout her body. She could feel a wild, unhinged sort of outburst like the one on the plane, but it was also different. A good thing. A sweetness to the tears.

PROMISE. HOPE.

She remembered running her fingers over his scalp. The raw way that the whiskery hair there felt. She had done this before, in a playful sort of way, but never quite like this. He watched her, watched her eyes, and she wondered about him, if he was always like this. She trusted him more than she trusted any other human being on earth, and yet she felt as though she knew nothing about him. In so many ways, he seemed like a wraith, a spirit, as transparent as glass. Except of course he felt entirely more substantial than that.

She had no idea what she'd expected when he laid down next to her—some ordinary thing, perhaps—but as with the lovemaking (if you could call that exorcism that), her expectations—whatever they were—were confounded.

Afterward, things were strange. It wasn't very much more than a month since Michael had died and it seemed indecent that she should know such pleasure in another man. She had joked, privately as well as in her routines about being an unforgivable slattern, a slut, and it had always been a joke.

And yet the thing she had experienced with Larry was as strange as the Black Box. Or stranger, since it was real. But also the thing she had experienced was something she could talk to no one about. She couldn't bring it up with Soraya or Hanna for fear of what they'd think of her. She couldn't talk about it with anyone in LA because it would get out—and let's face it, there were already rumors, rodent hints of innuendo. And it was hard to talk to Larry about it. She had all but begged him. She had asked him. It felt even worse because it seemed like a kind of servicing—*Can you just do a lube job and make sure the clitoris is working properly?*—like some previously undisclosed part of the therapy.

Afterward, Larry was not strange. He was himself. He did everything the way he had always done it. He woke her with a kind, multi-megawatt smile, a shake of her shoulder, *Ellen*, and then disappeared. She woke and made her way downstairs on her crutches and ate fruit and yogurt for breakfast and, as she drank the coffee he had made for her but didn't himself drink, watched as he worked out his tai chi moves in the yard. He was a beautiful thing to watch, all sinewy concentration, and in those moments she wondered if he had any feelings at all, or if he was some kind of emotional reptile, active only when superheated, then able to crawl in the shade and cool. And she thought of what he had said about the thing that caused him to shave his head. The woman who was the picture of whatever it was. Promise. Hope.

And what did that make her? He had not said if they—he and the woman who looked like Jayne Mansfield or Jean Harlow or whatever—had done this thing, this weird mystical exorcistic sex in which she could almost see the demons flying from her.

He had not said whether he had just spread her legs and fucked her.

And so she worried that she had ruined it. The one person on earth whom she trusted. The one person on earth—at least the one person alive—with whom she knew she could trust anything. Who had proved it again and again.

He did not suddenly become lovey. He had not mentioned it. He seemed to treat it as though it had never happened.

A day went by, then two, three. She thought of it and it became more distant the more that she thought of it. The world swirled with grief, not just for things like losing a lover or a foot, but for the small things, too.

The seventeen-year-old girl who had sneaked out of her parents' house and hightailed it in her $500 car to New York after graduating high school.

That moment in the grocery store when Michael asked her if she knew what broccoli looked like.

Soraya—before she knew her—standing on Michael's porch, appraising her as though she was so much fruit.

Driving over the landscape of her youth, having not seen it in more than a decade, the springtime wonder of it.

Her mother's face when she opened the door. The *Elle* magazines from half her life ago on the nightstand, still.

CALL ME JIM

One fine day the representative from the prosthetic company came. He was like any salesman, smooth as hair gel. They all shook hands. Pleasure to meet you, Ms. Gregory.

The salesman's name was Jim—*Call me Jim*—and he came in with his fat briefcase and two sample cases.

Ellen had resisted this happening. Had fought against it because of subconscious garbage that she wasn't aware of, but also because it was an admission that it was real. Despite having had to look at the damned thing—her shark-foreshortened leg—every day, she still harbored some insane notion that one day she would wake up and it would have come back.

Except.

Except that as much as she despised and hated and loathed and feared having a prosthetic, hope was as much of a product as the prosthetic itself. Not just a thing but a way to move forward. Progress. He showed them a video. Let's watch this and then talk. They sat in her posh media room with the lights out and saw a businesswoman walking briskly and purposefully on her stump with their prosthetic on her right leg—*and in a skirt!!!*, without any sort of camouflage—and *in completely fabulous patent leather stiletto heels!!!*, and a guy rock-climbing with two—*not just one, but TWO!!*— prosthetic legs.

She wanted to hate the thing, but there in the dark, after weeks and weeks of therapy, there it was. The ability to walk again. To run again.

When the slick video ended, she—like a little girl at a carnival—was completely freaked. Except she wasn't. She got up and staggered around on her crutches, stunned with possibility. She had hated it and now it seemed like part of a process. She went all the way around the room and then just leaned against the sliding glass door that Larry always used to go to the pool house. She stopped. She noticed movement outside and there was a hummingbird.

He lifted the right trouser leg of his suit pants and showed the Super Flex Foot™ that he himself wore, and slipped it off his leg and showed his stump, and the nice socket that the leg part of the foot had, and demonstrated the ankle. The flexion of the foot. The pad he wore on his stump.

The idea takes some time to wrap your mind around, he said. Believe me, I know. The way I lost my foot, well. It just isn't as interesting as you. Stupid, really. But the Super Flex Foot has given me back my life. Really. It's a very depressing thing, losing a limb. You have to expect that. And then you have to move on.

Even as he said it, she knew she was. That somehow the thing—things—that Larry had done to her, with her, were helping her to move on, even if some deep, core thing in her didn't want to acknowledge it.

And in her head circled the question, Which is worse? Losing a foot or a lover?

The meeting ended. She ordered up a custom foot. Jim, the salesman, took measurements of her good foot, made a cast of it. The prosthetic itself was just some kind of metal. There was a foot-shaped plastic foot that went over it. Five toes. She didn't give a fuck.

STRING THEORY

The stump was healing. The reality of the prosthetic was becoming more concrete. There had been no more lovemaking. No hint, except the reverberations in her head, that it had ever happened.

Some days she hated Larry for his superseding calm, his ability to deal with anything. One day, just to see, she threw a knife at him. He caught it by the handle, the way you might shag a fly ball.

One day she said: You asked me about Michael, she said. Larry had come in for breakfast from the pool house and he sat on a bar stool at the kitchen counter. He ate almond butter and Rye-Vita crackers with organic whole fruit jam in a very methodical and slow way. (You could not eat intelligently, in Larry's book, without eating slowly.)

One of the things I remember him telling me, she started—the Black Box was at the surface of her mind, a thing wanting to be said but wanting more to be left unsaid. He told me to imagine time— He said, Imagine one of those vertical blinds that you hang by patio doors. Each slice of light is a choice, and, you make a choice, you walk through one and you take that path. But he also said to try to imagine taking more than one. Parallel yous. And each time you come to some sort of decision point in your life, you are confronted with another one of these. And the parallel yous might take different paths. Might take multiple paths. So you are suddenly exponentialized. Could it go on forever? This exponentialization? Could there be a sufficient number of dimensions for this bifurcation to continue, ad infinitum? String theory seems to say yes. Time is not at all like a river. But it does only go in one direction.

There's something called the world plane. The world plane is now. What is in front is infinitely variable. What is behind is as it was. Done. Set. Solid. Gone. Like my foot.

WHAT IS THE REAL WORLD?

When the Black Box started to connect with you, before you dropped in, as it went through its strange little light show, the jumble of sound and light, it gave you a Pavlovian itch, the same sort of thing she imagined a cokehead might feel at the scent of the drug, the clicking of a razor on a mirror. *Anticipation.*

Each time she did this, she set the timer to disconnect her a little bit later than the last time, and each time she dropped out of the trance feeling weaker. Except she couldn't help it. Or she could (perhaps), but chose not to.

And then she dropped in and she was in the shower at the beach house.

This was priceless, the thrum of the rain on the roof, on the skylight of the shower, the clap of thunder, and of course she knew what would happen, what *had* happened, and turned to see his slender, angular form slipping into the shower with her, his penis erect, his eyes holding her eyes.

Hi, he said. Come here often?

She grinned, taking his lead. Come? Come again?

And now he was holding her. She kissed him and held him, on tiptoes, and the water hammered at the back of her head as he slowly descended to his knees. She moved backward, out of the heat of the spray and he was kneeling in front of her, water jetting onto his black hair, and he put his head back, opened his mouth, eyes closed—she could see his open mouth, his hands cupping and scooping in a mouthful of water. Then his hands were between her legs, thumbs mashing open the folds of her vulva, mouth jetting a hot stream of water into the crease of her, followed quickly by the soft jam of his tongue. She had let out a small yelp, steadied herself, leaned against the marble wall (which was cold despite the hot water) and looked up at the skylight, then closed her eyes and it was all water, water everywhere. More. More. Delicious. His tongue and fingers were all over her, and she gasped as he rose, one hand on her butt, one between her legs. He shut off the water, his penis bobbed and prodded at her as he put both hands on her ass, and she put her arms around his neck and jumped, wrapped her legs around him as he lifted her. He fumbled a moment and then was inside her now, the sweet violence of it, and he banged open the

329

shower door, carried her out across the bath mat. She held his slippery neck tightly, not wanting to release any of him. He put her on the bathroom counter, against a mirrored wall.

She said, Where did you learn to do this? That. In the shower.

I'm just making it up as I go. As. I. Come.

She put her heels on the edge of the counter and she could watch him fuck her, and how strange it was, how completely unprotected and dangerous, how vulnerable she was, and how much she wanted to be this way.

She thought of this and wanted to swim back now, relive that moment a million more times before the sun went down.

When she dropped out of the trance she was on the floor of her media room, sore, weak, her stump shoved uncomfortably against the leg of one of the seats. She felt ancient, close to incontinent. It had to stop. He was right. It would kill her.

LET'S CHECK OUT THE WORSHIP

L et's go to church tomorrow, Larry said.

She looked at him and laughed.

For any simply decent moment Ellen had, there were countless that were just plain awful. Pain, regret, grief. (The Black Box was really no help, here. It seemed to have the effect of temporarily bridging grief, but afterward, the bridge sank beneath her.)

It's a thing I like to do, he said. Sundays. Go to different churches. Check out the worship.

While he was talking, his eyes were doing something else, scanning her, making her feel like she did when she was a teenager coming home late and her mother rose from the couch where she had been waiting and appraised her, the unsaid thing being that there was distrust. Mistrust.

Check out the worship? she said, almost disbelieving. It was a Saturday and she was leaning toward him, on her crutches.

Tomorrow. Or this afternoon, he said. It was all jovial, bright, but his eyes were looking at her eyes.

Are you okay? he said.

Sure, she said, lifting a crutch, waving it a little. Why? She didn't want to know. She knew.

You look tired. Were you up all night IMing with Hanna or something?

No. I don't know. Don't feel tired. She looked away.

Anyway, he said. Lots of churches have Saturday night worship. Do you want to go? Tomorrow, I mean.

I…, I don't. Sure, I guess. Seems, I don't know. Sure.

She wanted to get out of his gaze. Slink into the media room and make sure the Black Box was hidden.

You can think it's weird, he continued, perhaps too breezily. I view it as part of my unending spiritual training.

Twelve-thousand-watt grin.

What does *that* mean? She was grinning. There was so much to Larry she had only heard and never experienced.

It seems to me that there are two elements to spirituality, he said. The private and the public, and it seems to me that they are often in conflict.

I'm not following you, she said.

You know in church they always talk about fellowship. In AA people have sponsors to help them through the rough spots. But when it comes right down to it—and you should know this as well as anyone—when you're lying on the table, or you're in the valley of the shadow of death, it's just between you and your higher power.

Like stand-up.

Larry laughed, and it made her brighten. Exactly.

Going to church, he said. It's fun. It's good to be with people. Get some fellowship. Sometimes the music can be really good.

Can I steal from the collection plate?

Not on my watch.

Do I have to donate?

Now he giggled. That's between you and your God. Pray on it.

So what do you do?

Just drive around and find a church and go in.

That's totally weird.

It's in the nature of churches that they tend to encourage this sort of behavior. Visitors.

On Sunday, when he woke her, he was already wearing a suit. He beamed and showed it off for her. He looked absolutely freakishly fabulous. His head sparkled and his eyes sparkled.

He helped her get dressed, and she did her makeup and then they drove around LA, looking for a church that looked like the service was just going to start. It was almost like shopping. She pointed out one and he swung the SUV into the parking lot.

They were the only white people in the place, and yet it was not as she had stereotyped it to be. She had expected a rollicking service, enough amens and hallelujahs to decorate a small office building. But it was not that.

They were some sort of Quaker group, and they said nothing at all unless someone felt like getting up and testifying. And the testaments were deeply personal and, like, you had to be there to get it, except even being there, Ellen wasn't sure she got it. Ordinary moments of grace. God in life. People were thanked for sharing. She and Larry sat politely and looked at one another, hands folded on their laps. No one recognized her, and no one seemed to give a flying fuck that she was an amputee.

When they went back to the car, both of them fell into a laugh fit. She loved him, then. Larry. There was a kind of streetwise innocence to him that was infectious. He was as bulletproof as an angel. She had seen the way he could pacify even the most aggressive panhandler on the street without so much as a dime changing hands. She had seen him handle anything. Except there was nothing jaded about him. Nothing at all.

Later, they found a Lutheran service. Big church, well attended. The flock sang hymns and liturgical songs (or whatever you called them) and she closed her eyes and was back in her own childhood, and then she opened them again, not that far away, standing, singing, was Michael. She stared at him, tears in her eyes, and as she watched, he simply disappeared. He was visiting her.

She did not tell Larry about this.

GIRLFRIENDS ON HIATUS, GREGORY ON THE MEND

Los Angeles, Calif., August 3, 2001, AP— Actress and comedian Ellen Gregory, now recovering at home from a second surgery following the savage shark attack that took her foot and her lover, is "looking forward to getting back to work," said her manager, Marty Klein.

"She's healing well and very anxious to get back to work," Klein said of his top client.

Meanwhile, network brass have not decided whether to air the five episodes of the fourth season of *Girlfriends* or to wait until Gregory is sufficiently recovered to begin shooting again. "We understand that Ellen could be walking again very soon, and the producers are very much committed to going ahead with Gregory in the show," said a network insider familiar with Gregory's status, "but we have to be sensitive to her situation. She's been through a tremendous ordeal, but we understand from her people that she is champing at the bit to get back to work."

Gregory was injured in June after she disappeared from Los Angeles earlier this spring. At the time, Klein said that his star client was exhausted, and, citing undisclosed "personal reasons" said that she had checked into an unnamed rehab facility. It later came to light that Gregory had fled the city of angels to the small town in which she had grown up.

According to other cast members, Gregory had always been restless on the set of *Girlfriends*. One, who requested anonymity, said that the comedian deeply missed her work in stand-up comedy, and found the show "constricting."

Rumors that Gregory might make her reappearance on the *Late Show with David Letterman* have so far proved groundless.

THE MAGICAL FOOT

A week before the Letterman crew were set to arrive, she got the call that her foot had arrived, and now, at half past the crack of dawn, they went to the doctor's office to embark on her brand new life with her brand new high-tech bionic peg leg.

I need a parrot and a really high-tech eye-patch, she said.

It was a Monday and yesterday they had done church again. Yesterday it was a nondenominational mega-church with theater seating for about 2,500, she was guessing. Everything was Hollywood quality. Some of it better than Hollywood, despite it actually being Hollywood. There was a band that was tight and sharp, and even had a spectacular brass section. Forget the bad coffee and dry doughnuts of her parent's Lutheran church—this place had a full bore espresso bar with stupendous pastries. Before the service, they milled around, Larry in front of her, running interference as she made her way along on her crutches. A few people recognized her, greeted her kindly, more like she was a neighbor than someone on the other side of the TV screen.

In the big black SUV afterwards, she said to Larry, There's something I need to tell you. I mean, talk to you about. I don't know.

They were stopped at a light, and the midday Sunday sunshine was almost blinding. Sometimes you could get fooled into believing that LA was heaven.

She hadn't been looking at him, but when she did, she saw that Larry had a look of mild confusion and had perhaps even turned a little pale.

God only knew what he thought of her.

I mean, I was thinking, she said. For some reason, she had her cell phone in her hand and she rubbed her thumb over the little viewscreen as though it was really dirty.

For the first time since she'd known him, he didn't look completely unflappable. He looked like a little boy. The look of surprise that he gave her was almost heartbreakingly beautiful, his eyes glowing and wide. He looked so handsome in his tie, his collar embracing his neck perfectly. There were zigzaggy veins at his temples that always stood out, but now they looked blue. Or bluer.

I just wanted to know, because you're like Mr. Spirituality and everything.

This made him laugh.

Don't laugh, she said, and punched him on the shoulder with her palm. You're, like, the wisest person I've ever met.

Thank you, he said. I think.

How do you say goodbye to a dead person? I mean not in the conventional dead person sense of, like, going to the funeral or scattering their ashes.

She bit her nails as she said this, which was something he was pretty certain he'd never seen her do before.

You're biting your nails.

I know. It's something I used to do as a kid. I mean, I was a totally big time nail biter. You would not believe what it took to stop, but this isn't about nail biting.

It's about how you say goodbye to Michael?

She hesitated for a long time, as though it was painful even to think about it. Yeah.

He did not look at her but looked at traffic.

I don't know, he said. You—. I don't know.

I've been thinking that I have to. I can't have a relationship with someone who's dead.

Certainly not a conventional romantic relationship.

No.

She looked at him, and the way he looked at her before looking back at traffic was a little hard to figure. His eyes were wet and he looked like a kid. He said nothing, and he gave the impression of someone trying to give the impression they were lost in thought. Sometimes she was grateful that he wasn't particularly chatty. Others, she wanted to peel his skull open and discover what on earth he was thinking because she couldn't stand his silence.

Later, at home, they were in the kitchen. She was on one of the marvelous Thos. Moser stools. Her crutches nearby.

Well, she said, looking for a place to start conversation. Thanks for taking me to church.

Sure, he said, and then sort of hovered between here and there.

I don't know why, but it makes me feel good. Church, she said, hoping he would not leave her alone but stay.

It's a sort of mental trick, he said.

What is?

Church. It gives you the chance to imagine yourself as different than you are. Or rather, imagining yourself anew as you really are, but not alone. Reimagining your aloneness, with a loving God to look after you. And a big group of people.

Is that all it is?

Honestly, I have no idea.

She had never seen him look like this. Defeated in a way. Ended. His astonishing wattage dim. It was then that she realized. It was something she had known forever but not known. She loved him. She wasn't sure if she was *in love* with him, but she was certain that she loved him. That the world was a different place when he was in it with her. But that wasn't the realization. The realization was that he was in love with her. She felt like slapping herself, it was so glaringly obvious. And equally obvious was his desire not to show it. Which was at least sort of explicable, given that he was—at the core of it—hired help. The realization hit her harder than she might have expected.

She said: You never told me what I was like when we met.

He looked at her, curious, gazing.

In New York, she said. You never told me.

And she knew, from the look in his eyes, that he was not going to say any more than he already had.

And you won't, she said.

He shook his head.

She had a weird sense of relief. Joy, even.

She hopped down out off the bar stool and hopped on her good foot toward him. When it seemed that she might lose her balance he put one gentle hand on her shoulder to keep her from toppling.

See? she said. That's what you do.

She put her hands on his chest, then pressed her head against his shoulder.

What?

You have this ability to keep me balanced.

A crutch would do the same thing, he said, and she smiled, but didn't let him see, mock-punched him in the chest.

But you're warmer, she said.

He squirmed a little. It was a wonderful thing, him squirming. She had figured, since New York when he so completely turned her down, and even here, after their strange and wonderful little tryst—or whatever you called it, his ability to make it seem that there really wasn't much to it.

The doctor's office was cool and bright and there it was. Ellen Gregory's new foot, brilliant as some kind of sculpture.

Larry sat on a stool and watched Ellen's expression. The doctor checked her stump and pronounced it ready, and soon she was wearing her new foot.

She sat and looked at it. Shook her head. It feels…, she started, but said no more.

Larry stood, reflexively.

The doctor said that he wanted Ellen to stand slowly. Larry moved across the room. Can you do that?

She did it. The pain was amazing. Fire.

It hurts, the doctor said.

That, she said, buckling a little, is a fucking understatement. And it was. Worse than the surgery. Worse than she could have imagined.

It's going to hurt until you get used to it.

Oh, goody. More good news.

No. the good news is that it won't take long to get used to it.

She stood and though she was unsteady, she could feel a completely unexpected burn of desire to get on with it. To be walking, running, again.

I want you to walk to Larry, the doctor said, and he leaned his face down, gave her to understand that this was non-negotiable. He pissed her off. She was, actually, surprised to know that she could be this angry. She had not been this angry in ages, and there was something about it that felt good. She looked at her crutches, which lay where she had left them. They looked like a skin that had been shed.

She took one step, the weight on her good leg, then the weight collapsing on her severed leg. She closed her eyes and concentrated, felt a tear squeeze out.

Now, gasping with the fire, she took another step, and then another, and each time she landed on the bad leg there was an explosion of pain. By the time she reached Larry and collapsed into his arms, her face was wet with tears but she had not cried.

Larry grinned. Full wattage. Instinctively, almost, she kissed him. Leapt at his face and pressed her mouth against his.

Now, the doctor said, I want you to walk back to me.

PART FOUR:
FINAL APPEARANCE

I did well because I didn't care. I just wanted to be a comedian.
—Jerry Seinfeld

NEW YORK CALLING

The *Late Show* location crew packed up a little before seven. They had arrived midday yesterday like a crack special forces squad and after a few minutes of sizing up her house, had found the best lighting and the best space to shoot Ellen's reappearance. They had everything working this morning and they'd done a couple of run-throughs with New York, all of which had been 'funny enough' for everyone else but left Ellen feeling as though bombing was a certainty.

And now the crew was gone, at least for the evening, having trickled out into the wild panoply of sybaritic indulgences that LA had to offer the mostly Manhattan-bound 30-something hipster. (Not that Manhattan had any shortage of sybaritic delights. It was that the New York work ethic, that whole if-I-can-make-it-here thing, kept people focused in a way that she had never seen in LA. In Manhattan, everyone was constantly looking over their shoulder, with the full understanding that someone would overtake you if you let your work ethic lapse.)

It had been good to have a house full of people, to have the bustle and hum, to have the sense that the world wasn't completely sneaking past her little compound here, leaving her unnoticed, the kid no one wanted to choose for their team anymore. It was nice to feel that she still mattered.

One of the first things she had sensed about New York, way back when she'd rolled into town in her satanically possessed $500 car, was its indifference. In truth, it wasn't that New York was any more indifferent than the rest of the planet, but somehow in the concrete and glass and steel canyons, in the incredibly rapid, corpuscular human traffic, that indifference seemed way more blatant and insistent.

You had to be a very special person to stand in the middle of a cornfield and feel its indifference. You had to be very special person to sit in a meadow at sunrise and feel the absolute indifference of God.

Granted, there were people who had the sort of existential intellect to do that, but it was way easier for the average Joe to get a clue just by standing in the middle of Times Square and thinking about how much would really change if you stepped in front of a speeding taxi and got turned into so much wet mucilage. No one would weep for you—more likely people would be pissed off how you'd fucked up their commute.

New York was highly instructional that way, showing you how little you mattered, did matter, in the ultimate scheme of things.

But it also became quite clear that celebrity really didn't make much of a dent in the monumental indifference of the universe. Wayne Townsend was a really good example of this. In fact, Wayne Townsend seemed almost like the universe's cosmic confidence hit man, the guy come to tell you that despite 'mattering' to some slice of humanity, you really just didn't matter. And that was to say nothing at all of sharks.

The world relentlessly continued to turn without Michael. She woke up in the morning, and it was true. The world had not put on the brakes.

And memory—according to Soraya—the more you recalled a memory, the more worn out it got. It was like an old newspaper clipping and if you pulled it out too much, the picture would smudge, the paper would disintegrate.

She poured herself a glass of white wine and sat at the counter in the kitchen. Larry came in, stood a minute framed in the doorway that led out into the darkness and the pool house. She looked at him and smiled. I love you, she thought, but did not say it.

So, she said, What did you think? The rehearsal.

You were funny, he said.

Not funny enough, she said. Anyone can be funny. She lifted the wine glass to her mouth and looked at the extruded rim of it, the reflection of her eyelashes in the glass, the yellowy wine and its fragrant notes of wildflowers and citrus. She did not look at Larry.

I've never been so naked, she said, looking into the wine glass, staring hard at a piece of floating cork.

Naked? he said.

Since I was a scrawny little titless Runt, I never did anything that was not absolutely and completely *practiced*. I do not do chuckles, Larry. If you have not at least torn a gut muscle, I have not done my job. Shit.

She put down her wine glass and leaned her forehead against her hand and rubbed. She said, her voice hoarse and subdued: That's exactly the first time I have ever done any of that material in front of people. And I have never gone in front of an audience any bigger than about fifty with material that raw.

Larry stood with his arms folded, his feet parted exactly the width of his shoulders. It was funny, he said.

Comedy is not the material. Comedy is the comedian. You can do the same joke in a million different ways and it takes time to work it out. Find the place where it hurts.

He shook his head. Okay, he said and shrugged. It made me laugh.

Ellen picked up her crutches and rattled them together.

Larry's eyes were gleaming. No matter how many times she saw his face, Ellen was always amazed anew. She often felt that it was impossible that he was here, with her.

Ellen drained her wine glass and refilled it. She was thinking of the Black Box. She was thinking of how easy it would be to see Michael. For her, right this minute, there was an almost knee-wobbling allure to the mere thought of it, the thought of dropping into the Hy-Vee again and meeting Michael, or sliding into bed with him, the gorgeous oblivion of the warmth of his arms. Sometimes it was difficult to tell if what she wanted was to run toward something—Michael—or just away from this life, which was so much different from and yet so much the same as the life she had deserted a few months ago.

Larry said: You have that look.

What look?

That girl-with-the-faraway-eyes look.

She pointed a crutch at him, gun-style. Don't make fun. I'll have to kill you.

You know I don't make fun.

She said: I need… I have something I need you to know about.

He cocked his head.

She needed Larry to know about the Black Box even though she had kept it from him the way a teenager might hide cigarettes or booze from her parents. In not telling him about it, in keeping it hidden, there was a tacit admission that it was Not A Good Thing. But she needed Larry's opinion of it. Of her. And so, perhaps out of guilt, she said: Michael's research was about computers and brains, being able to control the machine with the mind.

Yeah, he said.

Something sort of went wrong, as far as he was concerned, and it started doing *something*.

She hesitated for a long time. She was going to say: something very like a drug, but couldn't bring herself to say the word.

Something, he said, and she couldn't be sure if it was a question.

I don't know exactly how to describe it, she said. It's kind of something you have to experience to understand. She was biting her lip so hard she could taste blood.

And?

342

I think you have to try it. I want you to. I need to know what you think. She realized that she was almost whining as she said this.

What is it? he said.

The machine. The Black Box. A computer. A computer that's doing something a computer can't possibly do.

Ellen snapped her crutches on and pushed herself to her feet. She could not disguise her discomfort or restlessness. Was it about the Black Box or was it because she was so very unsharp in the rehearsal today? Was it because she hadn't been sharp at all since the shark attack and Michael's death? Or because she cared more about the spectral promise of one more moment with Michael in some machine-made alternate reality than she did about her life, her career.

She looked at Larry and here he was, flesh and blood and totally alive, and also evidently loving her pretty much unconditionally.

Ellen sighed. She clicked her crutches together. Do you want to see it? she said at last, very deliberately.

There wasn't much to see, except someone hooked up to a lot of electronic crap. It was about as interesting as watching someone sleep, until Soraya and Hannah had shown her how you could hook it up to the TV and see what the person and the box was seeing, like watching some strange home video. The thing about the video was that it didn't quite convey the sense of *there*-ness that you got when you had dropped in, the sense of pure reality.

He cocked his head curiously, traces of a worried smile. If you insist.

Come on, she said, and led Larry to the media room.

She flicked on the HD monitor with the remote and dug out the machine, which she kept (really lamely) hidden beneath one of the seats. She put it on the seat next to her, cradling the headset in her lap, and booted it. A white band showed on the monitor and cycled down the screen. She plugged the HD monitor cable into the back of the flat, black, modified laptop.

She told him what she understood of how it worked. She explained how the machine seemed to get to know you when you used it. How it seemed to establish some sort of rapport with your thoughts. How the machine seemed to set up some sort of loop between itself and your brain. How a person would drop in and then the spectator would see on the monitor pretty much what the person in the Black Box was seeing.

Ellen helped Larry on with the headset, which immersed him in darkness. He sat and waited while she fiddled with the machine, and then there were lights, and at first he was reasonably certain this wouldn't—couldn't—work, that it was all some kind of overblown silliness.

When it first came up, the thing that struck Larry was, Is this what all this is about? Because this was just a jumble of lights and some weird buzzing. Almost, at first, like a disco light show. Different colored strobe lights. A weird humming sound that seemed to be coming from everywhere at once and nowhere at all.

But then he began to feel the hypnosis of it. He began to see, in the rhythm of the lights, flickers of real images beginning to stabilize. A face connected to a neck to a shoulder. A bridge, a sidewalk. The images were so clear, it surprised you. And then suddenly there was a moment of intense vibration—it felt like the whole room, the whole house, was shuddering, though it probably did not—and suddenly the bits of image that had begun to coalesce around the edges of the monitor snapped together. The buzzing was gone.

Instantaneously he was here again, in her house, but in a completely different room. It was almost dizzying how fast it was, this entrance into another world, not to mention how astonishingly real—realer than real. The front door was open, and upstairs he could hear someone, and he started to call out, but he did not.

Ellen sat watching: Horror. Fascination.

He went toward the stairs, but when he heard the crashing in the hallway, he sprinted. There was an enormous man—something like six-four, 250—wearing coveralls and holding a baseball bat. There was broken wall board on the floor, and dust, and the man swung again. He could see the impact shudder the man's upper body. Debris went everywhere, gypsum dust, chunks of wood and wallboard.

Ellen thought she was going to be sick.

The man was winding up again when Larry said, Hey. Put the bat down. He moved closer to the stairs, right hand raised, palm out.

The man did not hear him. He leaned down and reached inside the wall and grabbed at something, and Larry could hear Ellen let out a cry. He could see the man use enormous force to drag her by her left foot partway through the opening. It was clear that he could have pulled her all the way through the wall, breaking it or her as he did so. And now he let her go and picked up the bat again.

Again, louder, Larry said, Put down the bat. The man was ready to swing again, but this time he heard, and looked at Larry querulously, a lizard whose meal was interrupted. He had a blank look, Wayne Townsend. Small, inset eyes that registered nothing. There was no expression on his face except one of concentration. For a man so large, he registered so little, but Larry had seen men just like this during his days of doing psychiatric evaluations.

What the…, Townsend started, but then there came a series of small, sharp explosions, and he stood up straight and dropped the bat.

And now Larry was gone. Back in Ellen's media room.

Ellen was trembling when she unhooked him—no, the shuddering was more than trembling. It was something like the uncontrollable shaking she remembered from the hospital after losing blood. Shock. The memory that went through her and the implications of what she had just seen were almost too much to bear. He, Larry, had been there that day. He was what she had heard that day. He had distracted Townsend long enough for her to get off the shots that stopped him.

It all went through her like poison, the memory, the hand grasped around her no-longer-extant ankle, the gypsum dust, the thick solid weight of the pistol in her hand.

When at last the headset came off, she was shaking and crying and of course Larry knew.

Free of the electronics, Larry reached out and held her. It took a long time for her breathing to slow, for the shuddering to subside.

That seemed very very real, Larry said slowly and deliberately.

As far as I know, it is, Ellen said, voice quaking, tears spilling into her mouth.

He just shook his head. He rubbed his eyes. If there was sense to be made of this, he was not the one to do it. At least not yet. Although he had heard the story of how Wayne Townsend broke into her house and tried to kill her, what had just happened seemed almost too surreal even to consider the possibility that it might have happened in any real sense. Not what happened to Ellen, but to him, now, with the Black Box. Did he give Ellen the moment she needed to kill Townsend?

He had no idea what to say.

THAT'S NOT ENTERTAINMENT

When he was doing intake psych evals, Larry met a guy who had been a sniper in Vietnam. The man told him about pink mist. He used a .50 caliber rifle, and a scope that made someone a thousand yards away appear close enough to kiss. That was the way the sniper put it. When you fired, you could see through the scope the pink vapor that the round created as it smashed through the enemy's head. For years, the sniper had been thinking about this. The people he had killed from so far away they had never even been aware of him. The former sniper had no idea how many people he'd killed. But he dreamt about them. Some unidentified target, a man in the jungle, then the cloud of vapor. Did you die the moment the .50 caliber round blew your head into mist, or was there some sort of transcendental moment?

The wondering got to be a little more than curiosity. It had become a kind of torment. He quoted a line from Tennessee Williams about being stuck in your own skin. And in his torment, he decided he had to know, and he didn't care what the consequences were, because he had to know. He'd got the idea that if you breathed that pink mist, you could be the guy. You could connect with his thoughts. Not like you could be him forever, but you could be in someone else's skin for that transcendental moment. And so he'd done it one last time, as a civilian—which was why he was in the jail and Larry was doing a psych eval on him. It had taken planning. It had taken the kind of single-minded focus that you develop when you're on your own in the jungle with nothing but your rifle and your ammo and an enemy to kill. This time he couldn't do it at long range. He'd had to be close, and so he'd engineered and built a .50 caliber pistol—a monstrous, ugly thing that Larry had seen briefly. He had tested it, done some pretty interesting things to it—as he told Larry—so that there was almost no kick. So, finally, one day he did it. Right out on the street. He'd breathed the mist, and nothing happened. The man he had killed lay on the sidewalk and people shrieked and the sniper was left with nothing but the horrible existential loneliness of humanity, the awfulness of knowing you could never really, truly connect.

He said: So your friend Michael invented this thing.

She nodded. Soraya did part of it. Half of it, maybe.

Larry nodded. She's a neurologist.

Ellen nodded. There was a long silence as Larry tried to rationalize what he had just seen, done, but he couldn't.

I never dreamed something like this could exist, Larry said.

Ellen smiled ruefully. I don't think Michael did either.

Larry ran his hand over the gorgeous dome of his head. It seems wrong, he said.

I guess, she said. Except, if I get what just happened, Michael—and you—saved my life before I ever met either of you.

This thought made tears come again.

Larry shook his head, and when she glanced at him, she thought she saw something in his eyes that she'd never really seen before, but she wasn't sure what it was.

She sat forward in her chair, her left leg crossed over her right, her stump dangling. Larry slumped against the back of his chair and looked at the ceiling.

So this machine you have, Larry started. How does it work?

Her expression darkened. She looked at him as though it was a stupid question. I have no idea, she said. Some kind of weird geek voodoo.

No, he said. I mean, do you have any idea why it takes you were it does?

Her expression softened a little. It just seems to know, she said. Michael was using some sort of software he called a code scraper—at least I think that's what he called it. It ran on one of those giant computers and it crawled around out there, cyberspace or whatever, and hunted to find the things that the program, the system, needed. He said that he was trying to speed the development, because most of the functions he needed already existed.

So, Larry started, but Ellen cut him off.

I don't think he, really, knew what it found or what was in the program. He never said that, but I don't really know.

Larry hummed. He felt as though his sense of what was true in the world had been profoundly changed. Where he had 'gone' sitting here was a 'place' in the time before Michael and Ellen had met. And, as she had pointed out, he had, arguably, saved her life before he'd ever known her. Even if it was just a coincidence, even if it was just something the Black Box had manufactured, it seemed true and it seemed to matter.

His face got knotted up. She had never seen this look before.

It seems wrong, he said again.

It's not what he intended.

What do you use it for? Larry said.

347

She looked at him, uncomfortable and perhaps embarrassed. Mostly to visit Michael, she said quietly. In whatever place it takes you, if place is what you can even call it, he's still alive. I still have a foot.

Larry nodded, beginning to understand the weight of what she was telling him.

I'm sorry, he said. He gazed at her a moment before saying anything more. That's what you were going to say the other day. In the car.

She said nothing for a long time but stared at her stump. After a bit, she looked at him, tears in her eyes, and said, Now me.

She showed him how to keep an eye on her vital signs, unless he wanted to make a really weird 911 call.

Larry watched, listened, nodded.

He settled back and watched her until the HD screen lit up.

I hope I don't do anything gross or embarrassing, she said. And then, in a way, she was gone.

Larry felt himself gasp.

The thing that struck Larry, aside from the remarkable sense of reality that he got as he watched what was evidently going on inside Ellen's head, was that it was almost painfully intimate. Not intimate in the sense of watching someone have sex, but intimate in the sense of getting way inside someone's personal world, beyond even reading someone's diary.

The experience itself was harder to explain—the video was not like video. Because it was on a video monitor, it was constrained to being a *kind* of video, but even though it was on the screen, and was, therefore, vaguely like TV, it was also clearly nothing of the kind.

To start with, it was far brighter. The colors were spectacularly vivid, and everything—after the initial, almost psychedelic confusion, seemed to have a laser-etched clarity. But there was also a fundamental weirdness to it, something it seemed that—not in a million years—you could never do with any sort of special effects. Which, in a sense, was part of the problem with what he was seeing.

What he was seeing now may have been on a video screen—and, for that matter, one of the highest quality video screens on the planet. But the only thing he had ever seen to rival it in its brilliant weirdness was what he had just seen in his own head. Or his own dreams. This was something from another world. The machine was a leech's mouth that had found some wormhole it could endlessly bleed.

The images he was seeing were quite clearly anything but objective. If she mistook a stick in the grass for a snake, you saw it the way she did, you started the way she did; you had her fear of snakes.

348

When she watched Michael walk away, you could see—no, you could almost feel—the things her mind, her eyes, were doing to his jeans, his butt, his thighs. This was nothing that Larry's own mind could have conjured.

And for that it seemed—despite the invitation—the most unspeakable invasion of privacy.

The images also didn't seem to be memory—they seemed to be absolutely of the moment. The wormhole effect, perhaps.

The situation in question was a party—as he understood it—not long after Michael and Ellen had met. It was the famous broccoli dinner. And it took place in what were clearly grad school environs—a small rented kitchen, cobbled together sets of plates, flatware, glasses. People flushed and ruddy with wine and big ideas.

It made him nauseatingly homesick, in a way, because it was the way it had been for him, way-back-when in his own youth.

It was astounding how clearly he could see the reflection of himself in Ellen's thoughts, her presence in that grad school setting.

Right after he had gotten married, when he and his ex still were in love, still talked in a language specific to the two of them, before his daughter was born, when the world seemed pregnant with possibility and before the grief that had characterized much of his middle age had set in. It made him think of cooking in a crowded kitchen, the nutty smell of brown rice steaming.

Larry looked at Ellen. She did not look asleep, but she also did not look awake. What she looked like was something he had never seen before. At least not in her. Not any state between wakefulness and sleep, but an entirely different state. A state of absence. A state in which none of the things he thought of as characteristically Ellen were at all present. Ellen, as he knew her, was not there. He glanced at her vitals and they were within the normal range.

It was, in the end, the kind of thing that made you want to weep. Not the box and what it did, but Ellen and her love for Michael. He thought of it, the way she looked at Michael. The way you could see in this strange, non-video-video, the way she saw Michael. Only once, during the whole trip, did he actually see Ellen—instead of seeing through her eyes, and that was when she looked in a mirror, and that was the weirdest thing of all—the way she saw herself. Almost entirely unrecognizable to him. Was it possible she actually saw herself that way? The woman he saw in her eyes was small, aggressively plain, nothing like the vivacious person he knew.

And but of course there was Michael. Again, nothing like he expected.

Larry had seen pictures of Michael. He knew what he looked like. The machine images were not photographs. No photographer or videographer had that kind of magic, that kind of voodoo.

349

But now, seeing Michael as she did—and this must have been what he was doing, seeing him through Ellen's eyes—was like seeing him for the first time.

Later, when the machine cycled down and he helped her off with the headset, she said, Well?

He wasn't sure he was ready to talk yet. This was not like anything he had expected when she first told him about it. He had expected some video-game-like toy. He had not expected to see inside her heart.

He tried to brush her off. He understood that she would see this as entirely uncharacteristic of him, but he had not expected to be so completely floored.

What do you want me to say? he said.

Just what you think.

I have no idea what to think, is my honest answer.

What did you see? she said, looking pale and exhausted.

I saw things I never thought it was possible for a human being to see. I saw what you saw. I saw it how you saw it. Him.

At least you understand better, she said.

I don't know if I understand anything.

She raised her eyebrows. Nothing more.

The two of them sat staring at one another for a long time. It was the first time that Ellen ever even remotely felt equal to Larry. And the strange thing was, she saw something in his eyes, the thing she'd seen before, something she'd never seen before. The chink, perhaps, in the armor that was his glistening smile and pate.

Ellen, he said, What do you feel?

What do you mean?

When you're there. When you crawl through this wormhole, what do you feel? Are you there?

Yes. You saw it. You were there.

I was, but I still don't believe it. So you're there completely? Not like lucid dreaming.

Not like lucid dreaming, no. I'm just there.

Then why be anywhere else? Who's to say that this world—here, where we sit—isn't the dream?

She smiled, but he stopped her. He felt that he needed to caution her.

I have no idea what is happening, here, he said, But you have to destroy it. The idea had been slipping around the edges of actual consciousness, and he was surprised that it had come out.

She looked at him, surprised. What?

He said, It's the thing any drug would aspire to be.

It is. Like a drug, she said. Wearily, she said, It has side effects, too.

Of course it does, he said. When she was silent and wouldn't look at him, he said, At least put it away, lock it away.

I'm so fucking confused, she said, tears coming again, her face descending into her hands. What she did not say was this: Michael is dead, and yet he's not. You're here with me, real flesh and blood. And it's not a dream. Of course he had no way of knowing what she was thinking.

He looked at her blankly and she looked back, her eyes begging him to understand. She was close to tears. She understood that he was right. That the machine at the very least needed to be locked away, forgotten. And she understood, at least intellectually, that she needed Larry far more than she needed Michael.

I think I'm a bit confused, too, Larry said.

Larry, she said, you keep levitating my heart right up out of my skin. You carry me upstairs and make love to me like no one or nothing I've ever experienced, and then you're just…, just nothing. I mean you totally blow my little center of equilibrium, and then—

She stopped. She was surprised that any of this had come out. That all of this had come out. She regretted it.

So, he said, looking genuinely confused (or, perhaps, scared himself) and then hesitated. So what are we talking about here?

She laughed, spat tears, shook her head.

He said: Language is such a beautiful and supple tool and yet connection is so much more complex than words can do—, he started, fully aware of the connection that he had just shared with her. But she cut him off.

Language is fucking useless if you don't actually use it, Larry.

He loved the way she spat his name, right then. As if they were an old married couple and she just couldn't get through to him. She wiped at her eyes. She laughed but there were still tears. She took a crutch and lifted it into the air, then pulled it down again and pressed the cool metal against her face.

For such a smart and sympathetic man, you can be amazingly stupid and dense.

He rose out of his chair and backed away from her, as much for poise as anything.

But I think we haven't—or I haven't—established exactly what we are talking about here.

She let her crutch fall on the floor, got up and moved to where he stood and held herself up on her good foot, her only foot, palms flat against his chest. She looked up at him. His perpetually quizzical expression had changed to something like complete confusion.

I love you, you idiot. That's what we're talking about.

Oh, he said. His eyes were as bright as a thousand suns. Again, she saw something in those eyes that she had never seen before. Another 'Oh' escaped his mouth, but he didn't seem to be aware of it.

Nobody in the world has ever cared for me the way you have, she said. And maybe that's because before I never let anyone.

He nodded.

The thing is, she said. At first, I *had* to let you care for me. Now, she said, tears coming, but nothing like the flooding before, Now, I *want* you to care for me.

I'd like that, he said.

What I'd like, she started. She smiled and gazed into his eyes. What I'd like is for you to run me upstairs and do that thing you did to me again. And then, if it's not too much trouble, you could tell me I'm pretty or something.

Larry suddenly felt as though he could hardly stand, much less lift and carry her. His eyes burned.

Well? she said.

I think I can do that.

CHARLIE KAUFMAN

Marty couldn't sit still. He was so excited that he got up off the couch and then sat down again, then got up. Larry sat on the floor and watched. It had been a long time since Ellen had seen Marty this animated.

I really want you to consider this, Ellen. This is just too fantastic. Really.

He rubbed his hands together and paced.

Since she'd been back, she'd had lunch with him half a dozen times, and seen him other times—she'd taken Hanna and Soraya to his office to meet him—and each time, Larry had been with her. She had tried to engage the two of them, but Larry's economy with words and Marty's Hollywood paranoia—or some personal animus—kept the two of them at a distance. And Marty had seemed older. His entire gestalt had aged a decade. But now he seemed mostly like his old self, rabid with enthusiasm.

Things are changing, he said. We're getting into a different world. The sitcom is dead.

Good, Ellen said.

Funny, he said. I don't know that we'll see too many more shows like *Girlfriends*. Everything's in flux. He went to the kitchen, got a glass of water, then only took a sip and poured the rest out.

Okay, he said, This is it: I had a call from Charlie Kaufman. He said he had an idea he wanted to pitch to me. Marty waved the glass as he talked. I'm thinking, why me? I'm not his agent.

For Larry's benefit, Ellen said, Charlie's a screenwriter. A really good one.

Good does not begin to describe Charlie, Marty said. He's really *sui generis*.

Ellen nodded. Larry just sat, watching.

And you know how Charlie is. And, you know. Well. So he came down to the office and it, it was *way* more than an idea. He's got a *vision*. This vision is a thing of beauty.

Marty stood in front of the sink, puffed up and jumpy. He moved with a peculiar élan that reminded her of nothing more than a hedgehog.

He's put together a treatment of your whole story, like, from the letters right up to now. And it's fucking fantastic. The weird thing is, I mean unless you guys have been talking or something, he knows you better than you probably do.

What do you mean?

I mean his insight into your whole narrative, the motivations, the tribulations—if it's all completely nonsense, then it's just incredibly believable. Incredibly. It's got the usual Charlie Kaufman flourishes, but the Ellen Gregory he invents is—I mean from my perspective as your oldest friend and someone who knows you like he knows his own right arm—is just uncanny.

(In her head, a voice was saying, *We do not need more Ellens. There are too many Ellens.*)

She said, Like how? Ellen sat forward. It was already starting to creep her out. But she didn't know if it was creeping her out in a good way.

Marty was now even more animated.

On the one hand, he sees you as a victim of a weird kind of multiple personality disorder, a thing that doesn't have anything to do with you, you know? It's more like multiple narrative disorder. One woman with a lot of out-of-control narratives. And on the other, he sees you as a victim of a sort of identity theft, which is of course integral to and dovetails with the multiple personalities. I mean it's identity theft in the sense of whatever true Ellen there was has gotten sucked up into this vast sort of sub-celestial electronic repository of swirling magnetic particles.

There was spittle coming off his mouth.

Ellen's jaw dropped—or rather, it had been dropping in a sort of a super slow-mo that had begun when he said 'multiple personality' and just kept happening as he talked.

Marty stopped. He gleamed because it sensed he'd hit a chord. Ellen, for her part, felt like she was vibrating.

She took a breath that almost felt like a gasp.

Um, she said at last, Go on.

He sees Townsend as a metaphor. He's like a chance metaphysical intrusion. I'm not saying this very well. He's like a karmic signal. (This made Larry smile.) He sees Michael as kind of the obverse of Townsend, the flipside of the karmic coin. He's sort of the yin to Townsend's yang. The unwarranted good thing and the unwarranted bad thing.

And?

And the ugly karmic twist is, of course, that the shark is sort of karma itself, the mechanism by which your own karmic whatever—

Again, Larry smiled.

—is balanced in the universe.

She could not have explained exactly why there were tears in her eyes, but there they were.

Larry said, Isn't this yet another kind of 'identity theft'? This other, new, narrative about Ellen's 'narratives'?

It was the first time Larry had spoken since Marty had arrived, and Marty had pretty much been talking to Ellen as though Larry didn't exist. But this insight evidently suited his purpose, and his grin exploded.

That's the fucking incredible, *magisterial* beauty of the whole thing. You'd leave the theater with your mind just completely fucking blown.

Ellen took the tissue that Larry offered her and wiped at her eyes, then blew her nose. Do you have a copy? Can I see it?

Marty hedgehogged to his briefcase and snapped it open and grabbed a stack of paper.

Here's the treatment, he said. She took it and flipped through it without actually looking at it.

Ellen turned to Larry. A treatment, she said, Is sort of a description of what a movie would be. No dialog, really. It tells the story as the writer envisions it happening on the screen. This happens, that happens. This is where we are. This is how it looks. He or she is this kind of character.

Larry nodded.

Marty seemed miffed by this, her inclusion of Larry. Like it threw off his timing or something just to have Larry around. He made little movements as though he was throwing shadow punches as he composed himself.

No one would ever make it, Ellen said.

No, no, no, no. We have real, serious interest. No one would ever make it if it were *fiction*. But since it's all happened, it gives it a special cachet. Seriously. He's been showing it around. I've had calls. A-List. Totally A-List. Renee Zellweger, Reese Witherspoon, wanting to play *you*. People are leaning on me to lean on you.

Larry grinned one of his 50,000 watt grins.

The grin threw Marty again. What? he said. What?

Larry seemed surprised that Marty was for the first time talking directly to him, even if he didn't really look at him. Larry didn't say anything. He shook his head, grinned more brightly.

Marty shook his head. So, anyway, yeah. It's fabulous. A fabulous opportunity. To get your own version of the thing out there.

It's Charlie's version.

But he wants to work with you. The idea is, you would produce.

She repeated the word emptily. She was thinking about the Black Box, which of course neither Marty nor Charlie Kaufman knew about. The reality of unreality. The unreality of reality. There were so many parallel universes at work in her own personal universe that there was no need for an actual parallel universe.

This is weird, Ellen said. This is totally weird.

This may be a stupid question, Larry said, But why wouldn't Ellen play Ellen?

Don't be a dickhead, Marty snapped. That would ruin the meta quality of it. To pull off the whole meta idea, you'd have to have someone who looks like Ellen, who could do Ellen, but isn't Ellen.

He was clearly irritated at Larry for having to explain what seemed so obvious. You could almost see the steam come out of Marty's ears. He took a deep breath. Listen, he started again, but then stopped and stared at Larry.

The staring seemed to go on for a long time. There seemed to be something transpiring between the two of them on a bandwidth that she was locked out of.

At last, she said, Marty.

She knew Marty well enough to know that he was worked up. Big time.

I'd like a word with your physical therapist.

Larry raised an eyebrow and gave a beautiful, placid smile. You mean me?

More steam.

His name is Larry, Ellen said.

Fine. Whatever the fuck. Can we have a word?

Watching Larry rise to his feet was like watching something melt in reverse.

Sure, Larry said.

They actually stepped outside. Larry guided him out the door by the pool. Larry was grinning, ever patient. Marty was steaming. She picked up the treatment again. It was a stack of three-hole punch paper with those brass thingies in the holes. The title was 'The Final Appearance of America's Favorite Girl Next Door.' Which, the title, the word 'final,' gave her pause.

So, Marty said. I kind of want to draw more of a bead on the role you're playing here. Because I'm getting the sense that there's a little more going on than physical therapy in the, um, strictest sense. We all need a little physical therapy, he said, and gave a dirty laugh. I've watched Ellen go through a lot of men. She's never been exactly the relationship type, if you know what I mean. So I'm wondering where you fit in. What's the relationship.

Larry folded his arms and nodded. He was not exactly smiling. Marty felt himself being appraised, a deep, personal kind of survey. There was now silence, and that made Marty anxious, made him do little involuntary chorea-like movements. It was hot, and he noticed that he was sweating.

When Larry didn't say anything—or at least not in any normal rhythm of conversation—Marty said, Is it about money? Maybe that's it. You've got a nice thing going here. Are you like the Kato Kaelin character who lives in the pool house? Keeps the master of the house amused? Or is there something else I should know about? Is there some kind of Svengali thing going on?

Finally, Larry nodded and spoke slowly: So this is about control.

His head was cocked a little, sideways, and it was more like one of those question-statements Marty's therapist might ask than one from somebody he was trying to threaten.

Marty sputtered a little. Maybe I'm trying to figure out if you—he jabbed a finger in Larry's direction—are controlling her. Since she's been back, she hasn't been the same. She hasn't been the Ellen Gregory I used to know. We've worked together for more than a decade and this is a woman who has always been about work.

You don't think she's been working? You don't think it takes work to come back from an injury like the one—the ones—she's been through?

Fuck, of course, I know it takes work. It's just I'm not accustomed to being left out of the loop.

Are you angry that she left?

She left… What? You mean the show? LA?

You? You tell me.

Of course I'm fucking angry. I'm so angry that I could fucking spit teeth. But that's not going to do me much good.

So am I some kind of metaphor for you, here, Marty? Larry raised one arm and ran his hand over his bald head.

This was not going at all the way that Marty had thought it would. This was pretty much out of control. Or in Larry's control. Now Marty looked at Larry for what seemed like the first time, really looked at him straight on. All along he had seen why he was attractive to Ellen (and the gaggle of other people who gushed about him, all of which just pissed Marty off), in a purely physical sense, but now he was seeing something else.

So where is this going? This physical therapy?

Whatever innuendo there was or had been, Larry had just let pass. Marty couldn't help but admire this. He'd be good negotiating contracts.

Larry smiled, raised his eyebrows and shook his head. It surprised Marty a little when Larry said, One day at a time, Marty.

The treatment was good. Better than good. Eerie. Was this some kind of thing—the sense of the soul escaping the body, the narrative out of control—was this an LA thing that lots of people felt but few put into words?

She was going to make a decision on this right now. It was so uncanny—Marty was right about that—that she had no idea how to feel about it.

Marty was laughing when the two of them came in the door. Larry was smiling. Larry must have done some kind of Vulcan mind meld on him.

Marty looked up. Did you read it?

Skimmed, Ellen said.

What do you think?

I don't know. You're right. It's so uncanny it's creepy. Seriously creepy. It seems like I'm being crushed by own narrative.

You need to look at this as though you're being relieved of the weight of your narrative, Marty said.

The weirdness is, just too, I don't know. I mean, here's my own, personal narrative: I'm this actress/comedian, right? and I leave my show in a fit of depression because I'm having almost completely out-of-body sensations of losing myself, which is actually like this *actual* diagnosis, the sense of being removed from your self. I'm almost Wayne Townsend. Subconsciously, I've found a way to remove myself from my own narrative. I just refuse to attend. And this is not me talking, but it could be. This is Charlie imagining me.

Ellen.

No. So this thing that I was feeling was real, the sense of losing control of my own personal narrative. I mean—and you *know* this, Marty—so, I, this Ellen, this *other* Ellen in Charlie's idea, but also in my *own* reality, my past, I or she or whatever the pronoun is, we are or I am really having bizarre thoughts, particularly after the incident with Wayne Townsend. I mean I shot the guy. I killed him.

Marty threw up his hands, floated around the room, listening, deeply frustrated.

So I leave the show, sneak out, go back home and reunite with my parents, I stay in bed for days, crying, trying to figure out what's going on. And I happen to meet this guy. And the guy turns out to be, like, *the guy*. The first guy, at least as far as I can really remember, that I've actually been in love with.

We meet. And we have this marvelous little romance. Great stuff. Great stuff. I see the bravura performances. Then the disappearing actress/comedian and her lover get attacked by a shark. He dies a valiant death. And okay, I go back to Hollywood and everything has changed because I no longer have a foot. I make a triumphant return without my foot. But. But. So how does it end? *How does it end*, Marty?

Where does the transformation take place?

Marty was smiling now.

Because we know that in any kind of dramatic narrative—she looked at Larry as though she was saying this for his benefit—in any kind of dramatic narrative you have to have the scales fall from the main character's eyes. So, where does it end? How does it end? Where do the scales fall from my eyes?

Marty was positively beaming now. He said: That's the beauty of it. This is *Charlie Kaufman*, Ellen. This is Charlie. It doesn't. It doesn't end.

What?

Marty laughed.

It doesn't. That's the brilliance of it. It's a kind of recursive loop.

And you want me to say yes to this. You want me to say yes to being stuck in a recursive loop.

It's fucking profound, Ellen. Yes, yes, yes.

Get Meryl Streep to play my mother and you have a deal.

THE LAST GOODBYE

They were walking and it was hard to remember that this was not real, not of this—or her—world. The river flowed brown. It was fall.

She sat next to Michael on a bench near Hancher.

So you know everything that happened, she said.

Soraya told me.

So you know that you…, she started, but hesitated.

You can say it. I died. He laughed, and his eyes sparkled and he looked anything but dead.

You know that you died. That you saved my life.

Yes, he said.

Did you come to see me? Have you?

He looked at her and she wondered if it was all delusional. If maybe she had died along with him and this was all some hellish recursion.

He nodded.

I saw you once in church.

Yeah, he said.

It's hard to accept. That you're dead but you're not dead.

He grinned. Think of how I must feel.

Stop it, she said, hit him lightly on the leg. She missed his grin.

Soraya said you were, um, getting a new foot.

Yeah, she said, and lifted her left leg, crossed it over her right, ran her hand along the contour of her ankle and heel. I really did like this one.

Yeah.

The sun had made the shift it does in the Midwest when the seasons change, and the angle of it made his dark, curly hair shine.

I'm sorry, he said. I'm sorry if I caused you trouble.

Michael, she said and reached out, took his hand in hers. You never caused me trouble. Trouble sleeping sometimes being without you, sure. But. She stopped. She wanted to sob with love or loss or just break down for the hell of it. But she didn't.

So what happened. In this world?

We left. The beach, I mean. You went to California, I came back here.

Did I call you?

All the time.

Did you call me?

Sure.

Have we seen each other?

Twice. I came out and you came out here.

What did I do? Did I go back to work?

Do you really want to know?

She thought about it, being on the sound stage again, all of the lawyers and studio suits and knew that she did not want to know.

No.

So, if I'm here, another me, can I really be here, too?

Apparently. I don't know, exactly.

What is this? Where is this? I mean, she said, Is this real?

I don't know yet. It seems—and I have no idea, really, only hypotheses to be tested, disproved—that there are multiple threads of time. Multiple instances of us. I mean that somewhere, in all of these threads of time, there is probably a you, actually multiple yous that never left home. That got married and had kids or opened a bar or I don't know. Or never got on *Girlfriends*, or who bombed as a comic and wound up bitter and old. According to the math, whatever can happen will happen and continue to happen.

It seemed so easy to be sitting with him, here. You really had to stop and think to know, to understand, that it was not real, or real in any useful sense.

He said, It seems that time is both deterministic and stochastic.

Stow-what-the-fuck?

He laughed. Stochastic. Variable. Things are infinitely variable until they happen. The future is stochastic. But the past is the past. It's deterministic—or in a game you would say that. In life, it's determined. What happens happened and stays that way. So—at least this is my working hypothesis. apparently you can visit the past, but not alter it.

So there are also all of the other threads. In this one, the one that the Black Box has—I don't know—*found* or something, I happen to be alive.

She said: So once something happens, that's it.

He nodded. Yeah.

But Larry *did*.

What do you mean?

The one time he tripped in the Black Box, it was the day that Townsend came to kill me. I heard someone else in the house at the time. Someone distracted Townsend long enough for me to fire. Hanna and Soraya showed me how to hook it up the the monitor. I saw it.

Now Michael looked at her quizzically. No, he said. Not possible.

Apparently, she said. He did.

There was a breeze and it smelled of earth and vegetation and the river and, somehow, promise.

That doesn't fit with the math.

Fuck the math.

He grinned and moved closer to her and put his arm around her shoulder. The touch, the scent of him: this was familiar stuff. The smile faded. That's not good, he said. That raises really bad possibilities. Even if it was a good thing for you.

She looked away from him. She looked at the way the river jagged through the fields. She looked at the sky. She did not want this to end, but understood that that was what she was here for.

I need to say something, she said.

He looked at her, waited.

I can't, I mean.

There were tears in her eyes.

Michael, she said. She took his face in her hands and kissed him hard. It was a gorgeous kiss, raining in her memory with desire.

I can't anymore. This is going to have to be it. I can't make another appearance here. I have to live my own life. Or get my own life.

I know, he said. Because also you're still here, in this world. We're doing okay, you and me, here. I just want to know that you're okay.

I am. I'm okay. She heard herself saying this, and it was actually true. I really want my foot back, but that's not going to happen. And I want you back.

But I'm dead, he said. She moved away from him and put her head in her hands.

What would you say if I said that there was someone else?

Larry? He smiled. Is he good to you?

Very. Better than I deserve.

Then I'm glad. I'm glad.

He *was* glad. Relieved, even. He was blinking, his eyes wet but not exactly teary. I love you, he said.

Yes, she said. I know. I love you, and she could see that he was glad. She grabbed his face and kissed him again, and when she stopped, she looked at him for a long time.

Goodbye, Michael, she said, and then got up, turned, and started walking, and waited for the Black Box to suck her back into her own world again.

TOTALLY READY FOR COMEDY

Evan, the location director, wore a headset and was listening to New York. He also had his cell phone clapped to the other side of his head and was talking (Ellen couldn't hear what he said; her house was buzzing with the crew, the lights) and now the phone was gone.

He said, Okay, people, thirty seconds. Twenty-nine, twenty-eight....

She sat on a barstool, her good foot and her new foot on a stretcher bar between the front legs. The shot was a medium close-up.

Evan was a wolfishly good looking guy, thirty-ish, angular, medium height, with legs that were longer than his torso would seem to warrant, blue eyes and sandy, carefully mussed bed-head hair. He had perfect teeth and he was always smiling, always showing his teeth. He had come and transformed the sunroom at the back of her house, which looked out over her back yard with its adirondack chairs into a mini TV studio. Right now, Ellen was suddenly terrified of going on air, even though it was just a taping. She was almost ready to call her whole appearance off. She felt she could see right through him, Evan.

It was almost like a vision. She could see exactly how he seduced women; she could see his insecurities—later than average puberty, bullied at school in his small town—but now, while the bullies were struggling with early marriages and kids and mortgages in some surreal suburban landscape, he was doing what he pleased, and while he looked like a type—the quarterback and captain of her high school football team, a guy for whom nothing arrived but with ease—she could see, suddenly, that this was all a well-studied exterior. It was weird, because up until this moment, the countdown to 'live' TV, when he had strode across in front of her, checked her mic and then backed off out of the shot, she had been obsessed with this, her first appearance on the *Late Show* since her disappearance, since being mauled by the shark, and Evan had just been part of its backdrop. Now, it was like something in the fabric of reality had come unfolded. A year ago, she might have slept with a guy like Evan just so afterwards she could murder his self-importance (and, if lucky, his self-esteem) in the most ugly and painful manner conceivable. [*Had she really been such an ugly person then?*] And now, here, abruptly, there was a weird empathy thing going on; she could suddenly see the vague and divergent contrails of different realities—she could see that the person she had become before her disappearance wasn't just lonely and depressed, even malignant. America's favorite girl next door was a witch. But at the same time she could see that Evan adored her, her talent, her work, and that he had a deep well of sorrow—not pity—for her and not just the foot, but Michael as well. And it was not pity, it was real genuine sorrow. Her story was just this simple thing: True love dies.

It was, again, that her life had been wrenched from her, but no one seemed to see that but her. Except now she saw it differently. Now, because of what had happened with the Black Box, things were different. She was beginning to see the layers, the places where the folds were.

Dave was on screen now, reeling through his nervous habits, tapping a pencil, tossing note cards, sipping from his mug, bantering with Paul. Marty was here, and Larry. And Charlie Kaufman.

If Evan had been a little brusque, a little abrupt over the last couple of days prepping for her appearance, he had also been admiring and kind. And he made her appear beautiful again—a beauty she could see with her own eyes on the monitors.

Evan counted—twenty-two, twenty-one—and even as he did he had a lean, single-minded mien, alert and aware and alive. Over the last few days—the weekend and yesterday—he had come into her house with the crew and directed everything.

Now he hit six out loud and then went silent but extravagantly mimed the rest of the glorious countdown to live, taped TV.

For the last several minutes she had watched the show on the monitors as Dave did his parcel of stand-up, his pitch for tonight's show, then talked current events with Paul. His frame was lanky and his arms swung and his hands jabbed now and then. Envious of the ability to stand on two feet. She had been on his show, live and in person, half a dozen times, but this was the first time since the very first—the one marking her arrival—that she had felt collapsingly nervous, physically ill. That first time was thanks to serendipitous events. Tom Hanks had told Dave, *You have to see this girl*, and he, Dave, had come to the club she was working to see her act, and she didn't see him (thankfully) until it was over, when he, Dave, came back stage and invited her on his show right there. He was buck toothed and nervous. *He* was nervous.

And tonight, she was as nervous as she'd been a decade ago, the taste of bile was in her throat. (She was, actually, now running. The prosthetic foot was a marvel, if a long way from what it had replaced.)

Back in the old days, it had been one of those explosive things, chains of explosions. First in the green room with Marty, shaking like a leaf, pretty much completely certain that there was no way she could do it, pretty certain she was going to fail at her one really important opportunity. Marty had said, Go on, get it out, because he knew her too well, and she had retched until it was dry heaves—millions of fucking people; millions—and then bang, she was going down the corridor with a woman in a corduroy sweater, her mouth rinsed out but Saharan dry now, and bang, the bright lights sudden, the sound of her name, promising young comic, Ellen Gregory, and the woman released her at the edge of the cliff and invisible hands, the hands of God, pushed her though and she strode, and then the tentative laughter and then bang, she had arrived. As soon as she started in on her act, there was a whoosh of comfort. The material carried her, she was on familiar ground, and then the laughs started coming, and she began to roll in it, the excitement, the electric crest of the wave lighting up her neurons, these carefully wrought lines, these jokes that she had told at least a thousand times before and that a few moments ago had seemed distant, old, now sparkled in her mouth and floated her, and people were rolling, rolling.

In a sense, this almost felt like a bookend to that beginning. By Ellen's count, there were at least two ways this could go—three if you counted 'to hell.' Best-case scenario, it was the smash hit reappearance of America's Favorite Girl Next Door, a gut-bustingly funny twelve minutes of sheer brilliant comedy that left you with absolutely no doubt that Ellen Gregory was back, *Back*, BACK!!! Second possibility, worst-case scenario: a scene like the O.J. car chase, that weird and, as far she was concerned, unequaled piece of television performance art in which a helicopter had followed a white Ford Bronco, on commercial-free TV, for what seemed like hours on end, as said Bronco crept along freeways that had been emptied for this purpose, while supposedly the distraught O.J. Simpson was in the back seriously contemplating a suicide no doubt many millions of Americans would later wish he had committed.

And so, worst-case scenario, Ellen Gregory comes on The Late Show with David Letterman and talks for twelve minutes, but isn't even close to funny. People peer at their television screens, so close they can see the individual colored pixels, but can't figure out, is this really Ellen Gregory? And people watch but it's that kind of watching that people do when they simply can't avert their eyes. And they shake their heads, and they say, do remember when...? Do you remember that commercial, with stuff falling...? How funny she was. Used to be. Sad. So sad.

And somewhere in between those poles, there was possibility. Not just the Irving Thalberg Award for Surviving Shark Attack and being *spunky* enough to come back on TV with a stump.

IN SAVVY CAREER MOVE,

AMERICA'S FAVORITE GIRL NEXT DOOR
GETS FOOT BIT OFF BY SHARK

Arrival. Departure. *Fuck it all this was what I was born for.* The vast sea of self-doubt she had been swimming in even before the attack disappeared, and she was that twenty-something kid again, so naïve, so ambitious, so wet behind the ears, but so fucking funny you would do well to wear your Depends Adult Undergarments, ladies.

Then Evan finished his countdown, mouthing the numbers, and then, *We are live*, and you could see the glow that *LIVE* gave him, and he gave the glow to her, handed it off like a fiery baton, *LIVE!* and she was jacking into that energy again, for the first time in so long. Even at this remove, she could feel the heat of the audience.

There were several monitors, one for each camera, and she could see herself in her own monitor, eyes wide and glassy. Beautiful mouth vaguely open, gorgeous, famous, plump lips utterly still. For the first time since she had been in this business, the face that was on the screen was recognizably her own.

Hi, thank you, she said, falling into a rhythm she had no idea was there. Thank you. That's really really nice.

I'd like to talk about death tonight. Some of you may know that I recently lost someone very special to me. Now, you didn't know him, but he was really very special. We've put together a little tribute film of his life and—*Ellen starts to choke up*—if I can keep it together, I'll do my best to tell what I know about my dear, dear friend.

Do we have that footage? [Ellen gets very teary-eyed here, and the audience is quiet as church.]

Ellen watches the monitor go black, and as it does, she starts to sing very softly:

If I had a hamster, I'd hamster in the morning, I'd hamster in the evening, all over this land.

[As she's singing, a low-quality home video of a white, long-haired hamster shares a split screen with Ellen.]

[A hard explosion of laughter.]

I'd hamster out danger, I'd hamster out a warning, I'd hamster out the love between my brothers and my sisters, all over this land.

[Laughter.]

She lets her singing fade to a sorrowful croak.

[Sniffle.] This, ladies and gentlemen, was my best friend in the whole world. [The video shows the hamster climbing onto his wheel.]

[Laughter.]

His name was MC Hamster, and while he could dance, his great passion was running.

[Now, softly, the theme from *Chariots of Fire* plays. Hamster running on the wheel in slow motion.]

My little MC Hamster would run all night. And his little wheel would squeak and squeak and squeak and squeak, and sometimes all that squeaking through the night, midnight, one o'clock, two o'clock, three o'clock [starting to weep] drove me so bat shit I came close to—it shames me to say this—hammering his little head in.

And then one night, my little Ham just didn't have what it took to make that wheel in the cage go round and round.

I took him to the vet. It was so cute. According to the vet, MC Hamster had far outlived his cute little hamster life expectancy. There was little that could be done.

One day, I found him in his cage, gasping for breath. He had just one word to say to me—no really—and it was [one beat, two] broccoli.

[Puzzled silence.]

Really big segue, here, folks. [Here, Ellen mimed a steering wheel, a sharp turn.] Some of you know that I took a little vacation.

Ellen stared at the camera and felt almost as though her head would explode with grief. *Loss, she thought, what can you do but rip into the beast of grief. Tear its heart out before it can tear out yours?*

So. Broccoli. The single worst pickup line in the history of the world…

She went on, talking about Michael, and there was no laughter, not really. She had veered completely out of control.

The simple act of looking at something changes it. The act of looking at a memory dulls the vision. This was the fate of grief: Michael, dimming. Dimming.

A song you can't quite remember the words to. Fuck. Even this talking about it would be the eraser on the chalkboard.

When it was over, she was exhausted, and Larry was instantly at her side.

Evan said, You, Ellen, were fucking awesome.

He gave her a high five.

That was totally brilliant.

They were all around her, the crew. Marty. Larry. Charlie. They were hugging her, and she was completely bewildered, certain she had bombed.

Ellen and Larry watched the appearance when it aired later, and watching it was like watching a whole new Ellen, some version of herself she had never seen. Or a version of herself she never quite dreamt possible. As if the Black Box had transported her. She had seen herself a million times on beta tape, and she had always seemed to herself unreal, some weird amalgam. The very practiced comedian she knew she was. Yet not quite her. This Ellen was someone else, which was to say that this Ellen was her. This Ellen was real. The one, longer shot that showed her new foot, bouncing on the rail of the stool, the shot in which it all became really real, was the thing that did it.

Her mother called and gushed about how wonderful she was, and then put her father on, who said only, You were wonderful. I love you.

Hanna called, and then Soraya. Michael's parents. A million others. Ellen fell asleep weeping in Larry's arms.

When the appearance was reported on the news, the reviews were stunning. Apparently, her performance, for once, was not entirely about funny. 'Don't Call It a Comeback,' read one headline. Another, simply, 'Phoenix.'

ON HER OWN TWO FEET

It was a gorgeous early September morning, and Larry stood in the kitchen, wearing the black shirt and a pair of silk and linen pants she had bought him. She was standing. She had been waiting all morning for this moment. Dreading it.

I'm ready, he said.

Totally ready for comedy.

Or not, he said. Ten-thousand watt grin.

The doctor had been right. The prosthetic was going to hurt like a mofo until she got used to it. And then it was going to seem second nature, and suddenly, it seemed like that. Its movement was so natural that when she walked toward him, it was like floating.

I am standing on my own two feet, she said.

Literally, he said. The figurative part comes slower.

If she didn't know better, she might have thought he was ready to start to cry.

You don't have to, she said. Move out, I mean.

I do. And you need me to, too.

Do you always have to be so practical?

I don't know if it's practical, he said. It's just the right thing.

To leave me alone to fend for myself? She was half teasing as she said it. But only half teasing. She'd been standing on her own two feet for so long, she didn't want to any more. But she understood his rationale. Whatever came next in her life, it had to be because she was—figuratively—standing on her own two feet.

He grinned. Maybe fifteen or twenty thousand watts.

Just think of me as Mary Poppins, he said. The wind has changed.

She laughed, but there were tears in her eyes.

She walked outside with him. The used Honda Civic he had bought sat in her driveway. God knew he could have bought a Maybach Mercedes with the money she had paid him, but he didn't desire in that way. Nonetheless it was a signifier. He was here, in LA, for the duration.

So this is it, she said.

Larry put his hand on her shoulder, nodded, eyes wet and gleaming.

You don't have to move out, she said.

You said that, but I already have.

But you don't have to.

She had not intended to provoke anguish in him, but this was what appeared on his face. He rubbed his skull, then his face.

Larry, she said. Just the word, the name. He nodded, as if expecting her to say something more. But that was enough.

He opened the door to the car. You want to check out some worship on Sunday? he said.

Let's see, she said. Sunday. I'll have to check my calendar to see if I'm free.

Great, he said. He started to climb in.

Great? I didn't say I was free.

Do you cook? she said. Of course she knew he did, and well.

Some people think I'm pretty good at it, he said.

Then it'll be fun to come over to your place. You can make me dinner.

Can I make broccoli?

If you're man enough, she said, and laughed. Not her stage giggle, but what an interviewer once described as her home laugh. Rich and pealing.

She kissed him before he drove away, and then she stood there for a long time and watched the empty driveway and pondered how, in such a short space of time, a life could change so drastically.

The sunshine was gorgeous, and she went back inside and got ready to go for a run.

www.ingramcontent.com/pod-product-compliance
Lightning Source LLC
Chambersburg PA
CBHW021432240626
47153CB00001B/126